Witching Hour

Leo McNeir

Enigma Publishing

Copyright

Dedication

For Cassandra and Mog

Acknowledgement

I would like to thank Susie Tory for her invaluable assistance with technical aspects of this novel.

Index

About this book

Marnie Walker always looked forward to the spring as a time of optimism and renewal. But that year it brought the return of malevolent forces, threatening violence and destruction. When their tentacles encroached upon Marnie's tranquil corner in the countryside she and her friends had no alternative but to take action.

The situation facing them grew ever more dangerous, with one section of the community singled out for persecution. When a harmless old lady is brutally murdered and her husband badly wounded in their own home, Marnie and co team up with new allies to oppose the common enemy.

The dilemma facing them is that if they succeed in driving out the malefactors they may never succeed in identifying the killer. It seems that justice may never be done.

Witching Hour

"Tis now the very witching time of night,

When churchyards yawn and hell itself breathes out

Contagion to this world ..."

Hamlet: Act III, Scene 2

Prologue 1

The Southern Front
Voroshilovgrad, Ukraine, 1942

Dusk was coming down, a late spring evening with night fast approaching, and the air mild on their faces. The pilot and navigator stood together with the other aviators at the side of the airfield without speaking. They looked on while the ground crew pulled back the camouflage netting from their aircraft. The armourers manhandled the clutches of bombs and attached them under the biplane's lower wings. The tanker lorry was huddling alongside, its hose locked onto the fuelling nozzle like an elephant's trunk. All around, other groups were busy at the same tasks. The regiment was preparing for action.

There was still just enough light to make out the dark green of the fuselage, the bold red stars with their white edging on the side and tailplane, the grey and black of the exposed radial engine and the brown of the single wooden propeller. Soon all these would merge into monochrome shades of grey.

The ground crews began hauling the bombers into place, lining them up at the side of the field, watched by the weapon technicians whose task was done. A dozen or so aircraft were now ready for taxiing onto the grass strip. The lead mechanics gestured, and the aviators began stepping forward.

This was the time of maximum nervousness. Once they were airborne all their attention would be directed to reaching the target area. They would have no room for personal anxieties.

First to mount the wing was the pilot who clambered towards the open front cockpit and climbed into the seat. The navigator followed, raising a leg over the leather-rimmed sill and dropping into place with a bump. Neither was encumbered by a parachute. At their operational altitude such luxuries were in any case impractical and would be nothing more than surplus weight. The plane's only armaments were a single rear-mounted ShKAS machine gun and six bombs, each weighing fifty or a hundred kilos. In holsters on their hips, pilot and navigator carried a Nagant revolver, intended only as a weapon of last resort if shot down. Based on past experience, no one could expect to survive that eventuality.

Now, the technicians withdrew, leaving only one mechanic standing by with the compressed air cylinder attached behind the biplane's lower wing. The pilot turned in the cockpit and made a circular motion in the air. The mechanic raised a hand and seconds later the starter motor whirred. Almost at once the engine clattered into life, its five cylinders popping and stammering on tickover as the oil warmed up, and a blast of air was thrown back from the propeller. Pilot and navigator fastened the straps of their leather helmets and pulled down their goggles. The pilot turned again and waved at the mechanic who replied with a perfunctory salute.

One by one the U-2 night bombers rolled forward onto the flare-path, gathered speed and took off. The last sight of them from the airfield was the occasional flame spitting from the exhausts. Moments later they merged almost silently into the black of the cloudless night

Chapter 1

I t began with a phone call one Saturday morning in early spring. Marnie Walker took it on her mobile, reaching into the back pocket of her jeans to fish it out. With the other hand she was holding the tiller of her narrowboat, *Sally Ann*. She took a deep breath of clean cold country air and pressed the green button. The tiny screen on the mobile showed the name: HEMINGWAY, Angela.

'Angela, hi. If you're phoning to try to convert me in time for Easter, you'll be disappointed.' Marnie hoped her friend could hear the smile in her voice. 'What can I do for you?'

'Where are you, Marnie?' The vicar of Marnie's home village of Knightly St John, sounded worried. 'Do I hear an engine? Are you on the boat?'

'Out for a tootle on *Sally*. Something the matter?'

'When will you be home? Are you far away?'

'We're up near Hanford, just out for the morning, back by lunchtime. Why, what's up?' A pause on the line. 'Angela?'

'I'm probably being hypersensitive, but ...'

'But what?'

'It's about the so-called Easter parade.'

'You're organising an Easter parade? I didn't think we did that in this –'

'Not me, Marnie. It's that far-right organisation ... fascists, you know ... New Force?'

'I'm not with you, Angela. Something's clearly bugging you, but where do I fit in?'

'You were involved the last time they tried to cause trouble, and frankly I couldn't think of anyone else I could turn to.' This time the pause was at Marnie's end of the line. 'Hello? Are you there, Marnie?'

'Listen, Angela. If you want to talk, why not join us for lunch?'

'I suppose ...'

'Good. We'll be back by about twelve-thirty. Meet us at the farmhouse. Okay?'

Marnie checked her watch. She was calculating journey time when she was joined on the stern deck by a thin girl with ultra-short pale blonde hair and sharp urchin-like features. This was Marnie's close friend and work assistant, Anne Price.

'Who was that?' Anne asked. 'Did I hear you talking to someone?'

'Angela, on the phone.'

'Is she hoping to save our immortal souls?'

'I think she gave up years ago, Anne.'

'So just the usual juicy gossip from the fleshpots of downtown Knightly St John, then.' Anne noticed Marnie's expression. 'Have I said the wrong thing?'

'No. it's just that Angela seems troubled. Something's bothering her.'

'Did she say what it was?'

Before Marnie could answer, a third person came up the steps from the cabin. He was tall and slim with dark hair slightly greying at the temples. Professor Ralph Lombard, a distinguished economist from Oxford, was Marnie's lover. They had been living together for the past three years. Until the previous winter they had slept aboard Ralph's boat, *Thyrsis*, and used Marnie's boat, *Sally Ann*, for eating and short trips, known as *tootles*. Ralph suspected that he was the only academic in the country who used a narrowboat as a fully-equipped floating study.

Ralph continued his research and writing on *Thyrsis*, but he and Marnie had recently moved into the house on Marnie's canalside property. Separated from the Grand Union Canal by a spinney some fifty yards deep, the cluster of buildings at Glebe Farm comprised the main house, a terrace of three cottages and various small stone barns. One of the latter had been converted by Marnie to create an office base which she shared with Anne, and from which she ran her interior design business.

'Am I interrupting?' Ralph asked.

'I was just telling Anne I had a call from Angela. She's fretting about something.'

'Really?'

'It's something to do with an Easter parade, she said.'

'What, here?' Ralph said. 'Thought they were just in the States.'

'I've asked her to join us for lunch to tell us about it.'

'She wants us to get involved in a church thing?' Ralph pulled a face. 'Surely she knows we're –'

'Not a church thing, Ralph. It's being organised by New Force.'

4

'The neo-Nazis?' Ralph's expression combined puzzlement with anxiety.

'Why would they have an Easter parade?' Anne asked. 'It seems an odd thing for them to do.'

'Why do they do anything?' Marnie said. 'Their aim is to cause disruption and havoc wherever they can.'

'I wonder what Angela might have in mind,' Ralph mused.

'We'll find out over lunch.' Marnie glanced at her watch. 'Thinking of which, we'd better turn round if we're to be back in time.'

Ralph peered ahead and pointed. 'The canal widens between those clumps of trees. We can wind there.' He pronounced the verb like the wind that blows.

Marnie slowed the boat and threw the tiller hard over to swing the bows towards the gap. She pushed the heavy gear lever into reverse and pressed down on the throttle, straightening the tiller as the water bubbled on either side of the stern. *Sally Ann* eased gradually to a halt with her bows just clear of the bank. Almost imperceptibly the boat began to back away from the shore. Marnie waited until the boat had crossed the canal and the stern button was within a yard of the opposite bank. In one fluid movement she eased the throttle and pulled the lever into forward gear. She pushed the tiller hard over to the right and accelerated. *Sally Ann* swung easily round to face the way they had come and built up smoothly to her impressive cruising speed of some three miles per hour.

'Nicely done, skipper,' said Ralph.

'Thank you, kind sir.'

'Anyone fancy a coffee?' Anne asked.

There was unanimous assent, and Anne went below to the galley leaving Marnie and Ralph on deck. Marnie handed the tiller to Ralph and stepped forward to sit on the wooden lid of the gas bottle container.

She bit her lip. 'Angela sounded really worried on the phone.'

'Hardly surprising,' Ralph said. 'We had riots on the streets last time they were here. Had you heard anything about them?'

'Nothing, but then I don't have Angela's community connections. She picks up a lot from her committee work.'

From inside the cabin they heard the kettle whistling. It was cut off to be replaced by the clinking of crockery. Moments later

Anne came up the steps bearing a tray. Marnie stood up, took it from her and set it down on the container lid.

'Maryland cookies?' she observed.

'Inspired by Ralph's mention of the US of A,' Anne explained. 'The coffee's filtering. Won't be a minute.'

'The filtering no doubt inspired by Donovan?' Marnie suggested.

Anne nodded. 'Not just inspired. It's his *Melitta* filter and his *Jakobs Filterkaffee* in fact.'

Donovan was Anne's boyfriend, a student of media and communications at Brunel University in London. He was of part German, part Anglo-Irish descent, and a regular visitor to Glebe Farm. The rest of the time he lived in the house in west London that he had inherited from his parents. They had been killed in a coach accident while on holiday in South Africa when Donovan was ten years old. He had survived the accident and been brought up by relatives of his mother's family in Germany. It was his custom to bring back a range of goodies from Göttingen when he returned from his frequent visits to his continental home. His German family had suffered greatly at the hands of the Nazis, and he detested all far-right organisations.

'I wonder what Donovan will think of New Force being in the area again,' Ralph said.

Anne paused at the top of the steps. 'No prizes for guessing. I'll fetch the coffee pot.'

When Anne reappeared, she found the boat had slowed almost to a standstill. Marnie had walked along the gunwale towards the bows to check that no traffic was coming their way through a narrow bridge hole. She signalled all clear and stepped nimbly back to the stern deck where Anne was pouring coffee.

'This is good stuff,' Marnie said appreciatively after her first sip.

Ralph murmured agreement, and the three of them stood together in silence while the coffee steamed before their eyes, and the gently rolling Northamptonshire countryside slipped by. As usual, Anne gripped her mug in both hands. Marnie always thought it made her look vulnerable like a waif, a lost child, a refugee. It was strange to think that Anne would soon be twenty. An outstanding student at art school, she had one more term before completing her foundation year. If all went well, she was hoping to transfer to Oxford in the autumn.

Marnie looked at her watch. 'It'll have to be omelettes for lunch, and we've got the first of the new crop of Jersey Royals. I can steam those and serve them with butter and chopped parsley. Should we offer Angela wine, Ralph?'

'Sure. If it's good enough for Elizabeth David ...'

'I don't get that reference,' Anne said, peering over the top of her mug.

'*An Omelette and a Glass of Wine*,' Marnie explained. 'Famous cookery book by Elizabeth David. You'd enjoy it; it's a good read. In fact, I'm sure you'd like all her books. They're classics.'

Anne smiled. This was the kind of conversation she loved, full of promise, opening up new horizons. Just then, her focus shifted. The smile faded. They were approaching another bridge, now close to home. It came into view over Marnie's shoulder and conveyed a message that made her shudder.

Marnie and Ralph noticed the sudden change in Anne's expression and turned to look ahead of the boat. On the side of the bridge was painted a sign filled with hatred and menace. Dripping, where the paint still fresh had run, was a large red swastika.

****

'What the hell's going on, Angela?' Marnie asked.

She and Ralph were sitting opposite Anne and the Reverend Angela Hemingway over lunch at the kitchen table in the farmhouse. Ralph poured wine while they waited for Angela's reply. Typically, she was wearing a clerical grey dress, complete with dog collar. Some people had described her as having a 'horsey face', but she had an attractive and infectious smile that lit up her features. It was not in evidence that lunchtime.

'I think it's fair to say we're facing a major problem.'

'We?' said Ralph.

Angela made a face. 'As luck would have it, it's my turn to chair the inter-faith committee. The bishop thinks the job should be shared around when it's the turn of the Anglicans.'

'And it's you rather than the archdeacon?' Marnie said.

'Yes, well ... I think the bishop takes the view that the archdeacon needs to be ... how can I put it?'

'Assassinated?' Marnie suggested.

7

Angela chuckled. 'I was thinking more along the lines of *reined in*, but your idea has definite merits, Marnie. Oh dear, did I say that out loud?'

'Okay, so tell us about this major problem.'

Angela took a deep breath. 'It could well be as serious as the situation we faced three years ago at the time of the European election.'

Marnie glanced across at Anne, whose expression registered alarm. They all remembered the riots provoked by extreme right-wing organisations which had led to the shooting dead of a charismatic hard-line candidate. Donovan had been a prime suspect at the time. Some local police officers still wondered about his involvement.

Ralph frowned. 'You've presumably arrived at that conclusion from reports you've received in your committee?'

Angela shook her head. 'No. It's much more than that, Ralph. I've seen examples on the streets. And there are other indicators.'

Marnie said, 'So you're convinced it's New Force that's stoking up trouble?'

'Undoubtedly. Their NF symbol has been sprayed on walls in the town, and they seem to be especially targeting immigrant communities.'

'That's no surprise. What is it, Afro-Caribbean and Asian, like last time?'

Angela looked thoughtful. 'Actually, they seem to be more interested in eastern and central Europe.'

'Do we have many of those in this area?' Ralph asked.

'I think the main grouping would be Polish people.'

'What about the Jewish community?' Marnie asked.

'They're relatively small in numbers in this county, but I know their reps on the inter-faith committee are getting worried.'

'Frankly, they're not the only ones,' said Marnie.

Angela raised an eyebrow. 'How d'you mean?'

'The bridge just by our moorings is now decorated with a swastika.'

Angela's eyes widened. 'No ...' Her voice was little more than a whisper.

'It wasn't there when we set off for our tootle this morning, but it was there when we got back.'

8

'Oh my dear lord ...'

'Quite. Tell me, Angela, did you know something like this was going to happen? Is that why you rang me?'

'No, not at all. I never imagined anything would penetrate down here.'

'Why, then?'

'I felt in need of support. You were so helpful when we had the last trouble, you were the first one I thought of ... all of you really. You were a godsend.'

'But what is it you think I could do ... *we* could do?'

'Would you consider being co-opted onto the inter-faith committee, Marnie? We'd really appreciate your insights.'

Marnie smiled. 'Do you have a membership category for agnostics?'

'I mean it. Really. Our next meeting is on Monday afternoon. Of course I realise it's short notice, and you probably have meetings already in your diary ...'

Marnie glanced at Anne and raised an enquiring eyebrow. Anne gave the slightest shake of her head.

'No, I think I'm free then. It's just ... I'm not sure an inter-faith committee is quite my thing.'

Angela looked crestfallen. 'I wouldn't expect you to become a permanent member, Marnie. It would just be while we try to cope with this Easter parade business.'

'What is all that about?' Ralph asked. He reached forward to top up their wine glasses. Angela put a hand over hers and declined.

'We've had word from a reliable source that New Force and their ilk are planning some sort of mass demo over Easter.'

'How reliable?' said Ralph.

Angela hesitated before replying. 'I'm not sure I'm supposed to ... oh, what does it matter? I know I can rely on your complete confidentiality.' She took a breath. 'The police have someone working undercover. They've so to say infiltrated New Force. That's how we know about their plans.'

'Which I suppose means you must be very careful how you treat the information,' said Ralph.

'Absolutely.' She turned her gaze on Marnie. 'Will you join us ... please?'

Marnie shrugged. 'I'm an interior designer, not a ... special agent, but if I can give you a modicum of moral support, then okay. Count me in. I just hope your reliable source has exaggerated the problem.'

'Frankly, Marnie, so do I, but I don't think that's very likely.'

They finished the meal with no more talk of fascists, riots or persecution. Anne made coffee, and they opted to drink it in the kitchen, warmed by the dark blue Aga cooker that was Marnie's pride and joy. Anne was topping up their mugs when Angela's mobile began warbling. She stood and went out to the hall. When she returned minutes later, her face was ashen-grey. She looked close to tears. Marnie stood up and put an arm round Angela's shoulders.

'What is it?' she said. 'Tell me.'

Almost too choked to speak, Angela said slowly. 'That was the police community liaison officer. The reliable source was right. Things are serious, *deadly* serious. Someone's been killed, an old lady.'

'An immigrant?' Marnie said.

Angela nodded, her expression desolate. 'Polish.'

'And it's definitely a hate crime?'

'It seems there's no doubt about it … not the slightest.'

****

The depression that had arrived with Angela Hemingway settled on Glebe Farm for the rest of the day. After supper Marnie tried to absorb herself in a novel, but found she was reading the same paragraph over and over again. Dolly, their sturdy black cat, had curled up beside Marnie on a sofa in the sitting room. Marnie stroked her head absent-mindedly while a soft purring sound filled the room.

Ralph had lit a fire in the wood-burner, but even its comforting warmth failed to cheer them. From the armchair where he was reading an article in *Time* magazine, he looked across at Marnie.

'Dolly's going to end up bald if you carry on like that,' he observed.

'Mm?' Marnie looked up. 'You could be right. Still, she doesn't seem to mind.'

Ralph scanned the room. 'What's become of Anne? I didn't see her go out.'

'Probably just popped to the loo.'

Ralph said, 'I expect you're right.'

But she wasn't.

Anne had opted for an early night to put the gloom of the day behind her. She had nipped out and taken her mobile across the courtyard to the office barn to phone Donovan.

'So, how's it going?' she said.

'Hi, Anne. What time is it?'

'You're bored with my conversation already?'

He laughed. 'Not quite. I've been slogging on all day, trying to finish this essay ... lost track of time.'

'And?'

'Nearly there.'

'Listen, there's something I have to tell you.'

'You sound serious, so I'll refrain from making a jokey reply.'

'Good decision.'

Anne described Angela's anxiety about trouble from the far right. She told him about the so-called *Easter parade*, their shock at finding a swastika daubed on the bridge close to home and the murder of the old lady.

'She was Polish, you said, Anne? And you think that's significant?'

'That's the feeling up here. There's a lot of hatred being stirred up towards immigrants at the moment.'

'She wasn't mugged or anything?'

'She was killed in her own home.'

Donovan considered this. 'Presumably she could've disturbed a burglar.'

'That occurred to me, too,' Anne said. 'But that's not how the police see it.'

'How d'you know that?'

'Angela had a call from them.'

'What's it got to do with Angela?'

'She's on some community committee. There's a police rep on it. They told Angela about the murder.'

'They must have a reason for being so sure it's a hate crime.'

'I s'pose so.'

'Look, Anne, I've got this essay to –'

'Oh, I know. Sorry to interrupt. I just wanted to talk to you. We're all a bit down in the dumps this evening.'

'I was going to say I'll come up to be with you.'

11

'But the essay –'

'Don't worry about that. I'm in the conclusions section. Give me half an hour to finish it and I'll get on the road.'

'But it'll be so late.'

'That's okay.'

Anne checked the office clock. 'Half an hour plus travel time …'

'It's fine, Anne. I'll get it done and be on my way up.'

'Then I'll expect you at midnight.'

'I like the sound of that. See you soon!'

Anne went back to the farmhouse and told Marnie and Ralph that Donovan would be coming. Pleased as they were to hear that, they could neither prevent themselves from thinking that it was all reminiscent of the long hot summer of violence and disruption that had first brought Donovan into their lives.

****

At home in west London, Donovan sat thinking. His life seemed to be haunted by the spectre of fascism. His German grandparents and their children, including his own mother, had only just managed to escape the clutches of Heinrich Himmler by the skin of their teeth. A German great-uncle, a photojournalist, had been 'disappeared' by the Nazis in 1938 while writing a magazine article on the SS involvement in the invasion of the Sudetenland in Czechoslovakia.

Donovan had worked solidly all day to complete his university assignment. After speaking with Anne he had to make a supreme effort to refocus his thoughts on the essay. He took a deep breath, summoned up all his mental energy and buckled down to it. Twenty minutes later he typed the last sentence, reread the conclusions and switched off his laptop.

He stuffed a few essentials into an overnight bag and threw it onto the back seat of his elderly but lovingly maintained VW Beetle. A thought struck him. He dashed back into the garage, took down a box from a high shelf and stowed it in the car. Fastening the seat belt, he started the engine. The last thing he needed at that hour was a fifty mile drive up the motorway. But it had its compensations. What had Anne said?

I'll expect you at midnight.

He smiled inwardly at the thought as he put the car in gear.

Prologue 2
The Southern Front
Voroshilovgrad, Ukraine, 1942

The navigator in the second plane in the flight looked up at the stars. They shone brilliantly, obscured only briefly by smudges of cloud. The moon had not yet risen. Starlight was reflected in the river that bisected the forest below them. The ribbon of water marked out an easy path to guide them on their way to the enemy lines.

Ahead they could barely make out the form of the leading plane. It was a shadow in the dark. In the cockpits the only light available was the faint glow from the instrument panel. On that first leg of the journey they flew at little more than tree-top height, navigating by compass and stop-watch.

The darkness enveloped them like a safety cloak. Enemy night fighters had little chance of locating the bombers, even less chance of shooting them down. The bomber crews clung to that belief, though they knew it was unreliable.

Now the river meandered away, leaving the aviators to fly on using only map, stop-watch and calculation. The aviator's hand shielded the beam of torchlight over the map for three seconds before calling into the rubber tube, the only means of communicating with the pilot.

'Target area six minutes.'

The pilot acknowledged. 'Six minutes.'

Strangely, they experienced no fear. All their efforts were concentrated on the task in hand and on doing their duty.

Chapter 2

When Anne awoke on Sunday morning she felt confused, like waking in the middle of a disorienting dream. She knew there was something she should have remembered, and lay there gathering her thoughts. Taking a deep breath, she turned and examined the other half of the bed. There was no doubt that someone had occupied the space in the night. The duvet was crumpled and turned back. The pillow was scrunched up. There could be only one candidate for the role of occupant, but where was he? It was the case of the disappearing boyfriend.

Anne slipped out from under the duvet, pulled on her slippers and headed for the wall ladder. After using the shower room at the rear of the office below, she quickly donned a sweatshirt and jeans and crossed the courtyard to the farmhouse. It was just on eight o'clock. Marnie and Ralph were in the kitchen preparing breakfast.

'Seen Donovan this morning?' Anne asked.

Ralph looked up from slotting bread into the toaster and shook his head. Marnie turned from the task of spooning ground coffee into the cafetière.

'Not so far. Did you sleep all right?'

'Too well, apparently,' said Anne. 'I seem to have missed him.'

At that moment they heard the front door open, and seconds later Donovan stepped into the kitchen. He kissed Anne and greeted Marnie and Ralph.

'What happened to you?' Anne said.

Donovan smiled. 'I think it's more a question of what happened to *you*. You were spark out when I got here last night.'

'Oh ...'

'So, mystery solved,' said Marnie.

'What happened to ...' Donovan's accent became pure Marlene Dietrich, 'I vill expect you at meednight.'

'Not my finest hour, midnight,' Anne conceded. 'And what about this morning?'

Donovan's levity evaporated. 'I, er ... went out to take a look at the bridge.'

'Our own personal swastika, you mean?' Ralph said.

Donovan nodded. 'I have an idea about that.'

'Shall we discuss it over breakfast?' Marnie suggested.

They stood on the canal bank and looked up at the bridge, a typical Grand Union Canal structure, beautiful in its simplicity and symmetry. Its brickwork dated back to 1793 when the canal was built. Now it looked as if it had been ravaged by hatred and bigotry. Their faces were masks of disgust and contempt with a hint of despair. From then on, that part of their secluded world had been violated, and the thought would forever lurk at the back of their minds. And there was a further consideration.

'I'm not sure we'll ever get that paint removed,' Ralph said gloomily.

'I could pop into Homebase and see if they have some sort of paint stripper,' Marnie suggested. 'We shouldn't give up.'

'You must *never* give up.' The firmness of Donovan's tone shook them all.

'We won't,' Anne said soothingly. 'We'll do our best to find something heavy duty.'

Donovan said, 'You don't need to go to Homebase to get it. I have some in the car.'

Marnie grinned. 'Why am I not surprised?'

'I got it from a builders' merchant a while ago. New Force had sprayed slogans on a wall round the corner from my house.'

'And it was effective?' Ralph said.

'Not bad.' Donovan turned to Marnie. 'Could I borrow *Sally Ann* for a short while?'

Marnie was surprised by the apparent sudden change of subject. 'Er, sure. When would you like her?'

'Now would suit me fine.'

****

It looked like the start of a regular tootle, but not quite. Donovan reversed *Sally Ann* out of her docking area. It was a narrow cutting, roughly the width of a single lock, joining the canal at ninety degrees. From the stern deck Donovan could see down the length of the canal facing south for almost half a mile. Ann meanwhile had jogged past the bridge around the curve in the opposite direction to check for any traffic approaching from the north. She came back into view, signalling all clear.

Donovan guided *Sally Ann* out and manoeuvred her round to swing into mid-channel with the bows pointing northwards. He accelerated slowly up to the bridge, passed through it and brought her to a halt at a narrow point where Anne could step aboard at the stern. She trod carefully; the deck beside Donovan was partly occupied by a large cardboard box.

'Over to you,' Donovan said, offering Anne the tiller. 'Once I'm on the roof, take her back till you're level with me. Okay?'

'Yep.'

Donovan lifted the box onto the hatch, stepped up onto the lid of the gas bottle container and climbed onto the roof. He dragged the box about halfway towards the bows, then bent down to remove from it a folded sheet of bright blue plastic. He spread it out to hang over both sides, reaching down over the gunwales.

'That'll do,' Donovan called out. 'You can reverse her now.'

Anne pushed the heavy gear lever forward and gently eased the accelerator. The boat slid slowly backwards. As it reached the nearest edge of the sheet, Anne set the accelerator to dead slow and shifted the lever into forward gear. When the boat stopped, Anne pulled up the accelerator and pushed the gear lever into neutral.

Donovan had put on rubber gloves and was now standing close to the bridge, slopping liquid from a container into a bucket. He plunged a scrubbing brush into the liquid and began energetically rubbing the paint-stained brickwork. From the stern, Anne heard the occasional grunt as Donovan put his heart into the task. She knew he would regard it as striking a blow against the neo-Nazis.

****

For Marnie and Ralph it was a normal Sunday morning. In the office barn Marnie finalised designs for meetings with clients in the coming week. In his study on *Thyrsis* Ralph was checking the proofs of his latest book: a study of factors that would soon be causing problems for the economy of Japan. It was not unusual for him to be out of step with orthodox thinking.

By the end of the morning Marnie sat back in her chair, raised both arms in the air and yawned.

'Watch out for flies.'

Marnie's mouth snapped shut. She turned to see Anne grinning at her in the doorway. Marnie stuck out her tongue and ruined the effect by laughing.

'You're not supposed to creep up on people like that.'

16

'I'll carry a bell and clank it before entering in future,' Anne said.

'Good idea. How d'you get on?'

Anne perched on the corner of Marnie's desk. 'Donovan's done wonders, though with all the effort he put into it, he may not be able to walk in an upright position ever again.'

'Bad as that?' said Marnie.

Anne nodded. 'It's quite chilly out there, and he's sweating.'

Marnie stood up. 'I think the least we can do is go and admire his work.' She picked up her mobile. 'I'll call Ralph as we go.'

'Already done that,' said Anne. 'He said he'll be with us directly, a nice break from going boggle-eyeballed with proofreading.'

****

The four of them stood on the canal bank and looked up at the bridge. They were in more or less the same positions as the ones they had occupied earlier that morning.

'That's *amazing*,' said Ralph. 'You've done a *wonderful* job.'

Marnie agreed. 'Absolutely.'

'You must be pleased with it, Donovan,' said Anne.

Donovan made no reaction.

'Donovan?' Anne repeated. 'What's up?'

Donovan breathed in and out audibly. 'I'm pleased that the tarpaulin did its job, and none of the liquid spilled into the canal.'

'Or onto *Sally Ann*,' Marnie observed.

'That too, of course,' Donovan added.

'But?' said Marnie. 'I feel a *but* coming on.'

'The swastika's not there any more,' said Donovan, 'which is good, but ...' He inclined his head towards Marnie. '... here's the *but*: every time I pass the bridge from now on, the swastika's the only thing I'll see.'

****

Lunch was curried parsnip soup and crusty rolls which they ate in the farmhouse kitchen. Donovan was unusually silent throughout the meal. Apart from praising the soup, he spoke not a word.

For dessert Marnie placed the fruit bowl in the middle of the table. 'I hope you're not letting that swastika get you down,

Donovan. You did a great job erasing it. I doubt anyone will come back to restore it.'

'And if they do, we can blot it out again,' Ralph added.

Anne said, 'Can you leave your box of stuff with us, so that we can use it if we need to?'

'Sure. No problem.'

And that was it. Donovan chose a small bunch of grapes from the bowl and began eating them without looking up. They knew the signs. He had withdrawn into himself, immersed in thoughts that excluded everyone and everything else. Marnie looked sideways at Ralph, who shrugged and picked an apple out of the bowl. Suddenly, without preamble, Donovan piped up.

'This woman who was killed ... she was Polish?'

'That's what Angela told us,' Marnie said.

'Do you know her name?'

Marnie hesitated. 'Let me think ... Angela did say what it was. Er, I think her surname was Koslowski, first name Katie.'

'Presumably an anglicised short form of Katarzyna,' Donovan said. 'She lived in Northampton?'

'Somewhere near the centre.'

'There's a part of the town they call Little Warsaw, isn't there?' said Anne.

'A far cry from Little Venice,' Ralph observed, cutting a slice of apple.

Marnie said, 'I believe the police think her murder was racially motivated.'

'I expect that's what everyone's thinking.' Donovan said.

'You're thinking fascists, far right, New Force, perhaps?'

Donovan shrugged. 'Probably, but I'd like to see the place for myself.'

'You're not thinking of doing anything rash, are you?' Anne said.

'Like what?'

'I don't know ... like getting involved in something?'

'I'm just curious, that's all.' Donovan looked across at Ralph. 'What did you mean about Little Venice?'

'Only that it's a highly desirable neighbourhood in London, whereas Little Warsaw up here is a rather modest part of town, mainly terraces of Victorian artisans' cottages.'

'An easy target, then,' said Donovan. He lowered his voice. 'Like the Warsaw ghetto.'

'You're seriously thinking of going there?' Marnie asked.

'Yes, today.'

'Is that a good idea? Your Beetle is rather conspicuous.'

Before Donovan could reply, Anne spoke up. 'I could take you in the Mini. It's less noticeable, and I know the area.'

So it was agreed, albeit with some misgivings on Marnie's part. She consoled herself with one thought: what harm could it do?

****

Straight after lunch Anne's bright red Mini climbed the slope of the field track and cruised through the village. The high street was lined with cottages of local cream limestone under roofs of thatch or slate. On their right, Anne and Donovan passed the primary school and a short way further on, the church, which stood opposite the pub, *The Two Roses*.

'Remind me why the pub's called that,' Donovan said.

'I think it's historical,' Anne said, 'dating back to the Wars of the Roses. Elizabeth Woodville married one of the Edwards, the fourth, I think. She was from round here, from a family that supported Lancaster. He was a Yorkist king who fancied her like mad. They got married in secret in the village church where she lived.'

'In the church here?'

'No, let me think … it must've been Grafton Regis.'

They passed the last houses in the village and took to the narrow country road to the dual carriageway. Donovan refrained from speaking along that stretch so as not to distract Anne's attention. After she had pulled out onto the main highway he spoke again.

'How can a king marry in secret? Doesn't seem all that plausible to me.'

'Well, they did, and the other Yorkist nobles were so annoyed, it seemed they wouldn't recognise the marriage. In the end, they had no choice. That brought the Lancastrians and the Yorkists together in a strange way, uniting the two roses. Then when the Tudors won at the end – you know, Richard the third and all that – the county adopted the rose in red and white.'

'Quite diplomatic, really,' Donovan said, 'and highly symbolic.'

Anne agreed. 'It just goes to show opposing sides can come together eventually, if the will is there.'

19

'Doesn't always follow,' Donovan said darkly.

'How d'you mean?' Anne knew the answer as soon as she asked the question.

'There's no accommodation when dealing with Nazis. It's all or nothing.'

****

Anne drove cautiously through the bustling centre of the county town, past buildings ranging from medieval churches to modern eyesores and just about everything in between. She turned right off the main through route, passed a neo-brutalist monstrosity that she identified as a bus station, and took a side road leading into a maze of Victorian terraces.

The plethora of brightly-painted front doors in different styles, satellite dishes, Venetian blinds and new uPVC windows revealed extensive upgrading.

'Is this it?' Donovan asked. 'Little Warsaw?'

'Not quite. I think it's a bit further on.'

Two streets later they paused at a junction beside a corner shop. Donovan swivelled in his seat to read its sign while Anne concentrated on driving. The name above the shop front comprised two words against a background of red and white bands. It read: *Polskie Delikatesy*.

'Something tells me we've arrived,' Donovan said.

Anne turned left at the junction and drove slowly along the street. 'Yes, this is where it begins.'

They rode in silence until the end of the block where Anne turned left and continued their slow patrol. One block later she brought the car to a halt outside a house from which a West Indian couple were emerging with a small child.

'Something tells me we've done Little Warsaw,' Donovan said.

'Yes,' said Anne. 'That was it, more or less.'

'Can we turn round and go through it again?' Donovan asked.

'Sure. Is there anything particular on your mind?'

'Two things.'

Anne rolled her eyes. 'Inevitably,' she said. 'There are always two things with you. Tell me more.'

'Let's see. Just drive.'

Anne performed a three-point turn and drove back the way they had come.

Nearing the corner shop, Donovan said, 'Don't turn, just keep straight on … dead slow.'

Anne did as she was asked, glancing briefly at the side wall of the shop in passing. She gasped. On the left the brickwork was daubed with a huge red swastika, the paint bleeding from the edges. On the right two words were sprayed: *New Force*. Between them stood the slogan: *Polacks out!* Anne glanced hurriedly at Donovan. He was reaching down to unfasten the seat belt.

'Can you stop here,' he said.

Anne braked and pulled over to the kerb. 'What are you doing?'

Donovan leaned over and grabbed his rucksack from the back seat. He pulled open the zip fastener and took out a camera, a black and silver Leica, dating back to before the second world war. It had once belonged to his great uncle, the photojournalist. Despite its age, it had been little used, and Donovan had kept it in perfect condition. 'Give me a minute.' He pushed open the door and climbed out.

Anne watched him as he quickly lined up a variety of shots and climbed back in the car.

'Did you know that was there?' Anne asked.

Donovan shook his head, fastening the seat belt. 'An inspired guess. That end wall was too inviting not to be targeted. Let's get out of here.'

Anne put the Mini in gear and set off. 'Oh god, Donovan. Don't say it's starting all over again.'

Donovan made no reply. Once again he was lost in his thoughts. Anne drove on till they reached the end of the Victorian quarter and arrived back on one of the town's main roads.

'Well, that was it,' she said.' Little Warsaw. What now … home?'

Donovan was frowning. 'No.'

'Where, then?'

'I meant, no, that can't have been it.'

'Yes it was. You saw the shop. It's quite well known in the town. It's in the centre of the Polish neighbourhood.'

'Can we go back?' Donovan said.

'I'll take us round the block if you like, but that was it. I knew exactly where it was.'

Donovan said nothing until they were back among the terraced cottages.

'The woman who was killed ...' he began.

'Was that your second thing?' Anne asked.

'Yes. We saw her house on the television news, right?'

'Uh-huh.'

'The police had a patrol car outside, and there was blue and white tape across the front door.'

'I remember.'

'And it had a square bay window. It wasn't the same style as these.'

'No. Now that you come to mention it ...'

'We haven't seen her house,' said Donovan.

Anne sounded thoughtful. 'You're right. We haven't. That's curious. Perhaps the car's gone, and they've removed the tape.'

'The report said they were keeping the house under surveillance during the investigation.'

'It did,' Anne agreed.

'So where is it?' Donovan asked.

****

Marnie was in the kitchen chopping vegetables for a casserole when the phone rang. She wiped her hands on her apron and picked up the receiver. The line was crackly.

'Can you hear me, Marnie?'

'Just about. Where are you, Anne, Timbuktu?'

'Good guess. Listen, we've got a problem. We can't find the house where Mrs Koslowski was ... you know.'

'Little Warsaw, wasn't it?'

'Well, no. That's the problem. You saw it on the news, didn't you?'

'Sure.'

'Could you identify roughly where it was from the style of the house? Remember, it had a square bay window. It's not like the Victorian terraces in Little Warsaw. They're all flat-fronted.'

'Square bays ... that's more like an Edwardian house. Let me think.'

'We saw the Polish shop. It had been sprayed with graffiti.'

'Like our swastika?' Marnie said.

'Exactly.'

'Perhaps you could ask in the shop if they know where she lived, although ...'

Anne said, 'We did think about that, but thought it would be a bit insensitive, and we might get a hostile reception. Too ghoulish, we thought.'

'You're probably right. I don't know the town well enough to identify the architecture, but I know someone who does. Give me a few minutes. I'll make a call and ring you back.'

Marnie dialled the number of the village shop. Molly Appleton took the call. She had originally been a Northampton girl and at once identified the locality.

'Those sorts of houses are near Abington Park on the way to the Wellingborough Road. I don't know which street it was, but that's definitely the district. When I was at school one of my best friends, Sue Desborough, lived there and I often ...'

When Marnie was able diplomatically to get away, she rang Anne with the details.

****

Donovan was silent for most of the journey back to Knightly St John. This was nothing new. On such occasions Anne left him to his private thoughts. He sat looking down at the Leica cradled in his lap. He had used it to take half a dozen shots of the house where Katie Koslowski had lived and died. When they reached her street they had spotted a police car. Donovan had climbed out of the Mini and taken his shots, keeping discreetly out of the line of vision of the police officer on duty.

They were cruising on the dual carriageway when Donovan said, 'I don't do this out of morbid curiosity. You know that, don't you?'

'Sure I do. I've always thought you used those old cameras the way your uncle did ... your great-uncle.'

'He did it for a living, writing for magazines. My reason's not quite the same. I just want to keep a personal record of what's going on.'

'It's not only for your own satisfaction, though, is it?' Anne said.

'It's in case the images are one day useful as evidence ... like a dossier. I want to get the whole picture ... literally.'

'Donovan, I wonder if the police will get the person who killed her.'

'Hard to say. The British police have a good track record in solving crimes. As far as I know, they never close a murder inquiry.'

Anne signalled and began slowing for the turn-off to Knightly St John. It was Donovan's cue to leave her to drive unhindered. When they reached the high street Anne said, 'You had something on your mind back there. Are you ready to share it?'

'Not really. Whatever it was, it isn't a fully-formed idea, just a feeling that something was wrong ... out of place ...'

'What sort of thing?'

'Dunno. Did you feel anything?'

'I just felt how sad it was for that poor old lady.'

'How old was she?'

'Knocking on for eighty or thereabouts, I think.'

'So why her?' said Donovan. 'Doesn't add up.'

'I wondered if it really was a burglary, and she just got in the way. But Angela said, the police are convinced it was a racially motivated crime.'

'That's what I thought at first.'

'Something's changed your mind?'

'Not sure.'

Anne turned off the high street, through the field gate and down the track to Glebe Farm. As soon as she saw the rooftops of the buildings beyond the trees, she felt happy at coming home. She tried her hardest not to think that the place she loved so much had been violated by the scourge of the swastika.

****

That evening over supper they talked of their various projects. Marnie outlined her plans for recreating the farmhouse garden, and they discussed the merits of a sunroom versus a conservatory. Ralph was encouraged to describe – in brief and comprehensible terms – his new book on the so-called *Celtic Tiger* economy of Ireland. Anne had little to add to what everyone already knew about her college course. All eyes turned to Donovan, who had not contributed a word to the conversation so far. Marnie prompted him.

'So, Donovan, how's your course going?'

'Fine.'

'Is that it?'

'It's okay ... quite interesting, actually.'

24

'What's your main project at the moment?' Ralph asked.

Donovan's reply came as no surprise, but its bleakness jolted them all. 'Mainly thinking about the murder in Northampton and the fact that we have neo-Nazis camping on our doorstep.'

'It does look pretty grim just now,' Marnie agreed.

'Was she alone in the house?' Donovan asked.

They all knew who he meant.

'Funny you should mention that,' said Ralph. 'Her husband was apparently there at the time, but I don't recall anyone talking about him.'

'He was there,' Marnie said. 'They mentioned him briefly on the news. Angela told me he tried to fend off the intruders and got badly injured. I gather he's in intensive care.'

'How was he injured?' Donovan asked. 'In fact how was the old lady killed? Does anyone know?'

Marnie shook her head. 'The police haven't given out any details of the attack.'

'But you said *intruders*. Was there more than one? Is that definite?'

'They used the plural on the news,' said Anne.

Donovan said slowly, 'So if the police are convinced their house was targeted on account of them being immigrants …'

'Not a burglary that turned nasty,' Marnie said.

'Then perhaps …'

'What?'

'Well, how can they be sure it wasn't the husband who was the main target? Has anyone suggested that?'

Prologue 3
The Southern Front
Voroshilovgrad, Ukraine, 1942

The navigator consulted the map with the briefest flash of torchlight, simultaneously checking the stopwatch before shouting into the communication tube.

'Target three minutes.'

Back came the reply. 'Three minutes.'

Even though they were following the lead plane, every bomber plotted its own course; it was all too easy to lose sight of the leader in that impenetrable darkness. Now the little aircraft was climbing steeply to operational altitude, and the crew sensed rather than saw that the other planes were performing the same manoeuvre. They levelled out and homed in on the enemy positions, feeling the craft tumbled and jostled by winds from all sides. The pilot held a steady course and waited. Somewhere ahead the enemy was trying to rest before the next day's assault.

The pilot throttled back, and the plane floated down like a glider, almost silent apart from the rushing of the wind in the stays and struts.

Suddenly, there it was. The lead plane had released a flare. All the crews saw it dangling from its parachute, lighting up the whole landscape. And there was the enemy, the mighty *Wehrmacht*, the enormous military camp spread out before them. Within seconds the searchlights began probing the sky and soon found the lead plane. The next two aircraft lined up to bomb the searchlight positions.

The navigator yelled into the tube. 'Steady on course and altitude.'

If the pilot replied, it went unheard as the enemy fire opened up. The air seemed to shake with the blast from the flak cannons. Tracer shells lit up the night. Now everything was flooded with a blinding light, bright as a fairground. This was the time they all dreaded most, as the guns below turned the sky into an aerial killing ground.

The aircrews had no time for ducking or weaving or even for fear; all their attention was focused on holding a steady line so that the navigators could aim without disturbance.

With their bombs released, the planes turned away, the navigators already checking compasses, plotting the course for home. Their first mission completed, they knew the night had only just begun. Back at base they would be refuelled, re-armed and sent again to the front line to harass the enemy mercilessly, time after time after time, until dawn lightened the sky.

Chapter 3

Marnie, Ralph and Anne had never had problems with Mondays. For all three of them their work was a key part – probably the defining part – of their lives. But on that Monday morning they felt a cloud hanging over them. It was more than just the swastika on the canal bridge, though that had been depressing enough. It was more than the Third Reich-style graffiti sprayed on the wall of the Polish shop and the murder of an innocent woman from that community. The whole atmosphere in the area had been affected – *infected* – by a sense of impending horrors to come.

They had all been surprised when Donovan announced the previous evening that he had to head home immediately after supper because of university commitments. His departure left Anne wondering if their relationship was slowly coming to an end. For once he had not phoned to say he was safely home and to thank her for a pleasant weekend. She had climbed the wall-ladder to her attic room with a weight in the pit of her stomach and had lain awake into the early hours. When eventually she drifted off into a restless sleep, she had dreamt of paint dripping down walls to form pools of blood on the pavement.

When morning came and Walker and Co, interior designers, swung into action, Anne did her best to focus on organising the office diary, the post and the previous week's accounts. As soon as they were sorted, she gathered together her project files for college.

Opening the office door to leave, Anne said, 'I'll be back in time to do the post run this afternoon. You remember you're attending Angela's committee?'

Marnie sighed. 'How could I forget?'

****

Marnie and Angela drove to Northampton in Marnie's Land Rover Freelander. Since moving up to Northamptonshire from London, Marnie had opted for a four-wheel drive so that she could cope with whatever the weather threw at her. It was particularly important in view of the sloping field track she had to negotiate come rain or shine, ice or snow.

For some reason, Angela had cast off her previous anxieties and bubbled over with chatter for the whole journey. Marnie wondered if this was due to an excess of nervous energy in anticipation of the meeting. She let the sound of Angela's voice flow over her, picking up the threads of her conversation in snatches.

'... and naturally my *bête noire* will be in attendance ...'

'The Archdeacon of Northampton?' Marnie said.

'The very same. I'm sure he can't bear the idea of me chairing the meeting.'

'But no Randall?'

'No. As Rural Dean of Brackley this is outside his area.'

At that point Marnie ducked out and left Angela to ramble on.

' ... who represents the Muslim community. He's basically okay, but perhaps I'm biased.'

'Mm?'

'He can't stand the archdeacon either. Rabbi Josephs on the other hand ...' Angela droned on. 'You'll like Monsignor Riley. He's an old sweetie, but a pretty shrewd cookie when it comes to...'

And on and on. 'We might have a rep this time from the Orthodox brigade, Metropolitan Someone-or-other ...'

Marnie found her thoughts wandering. Like Anne, she wondered why Donovan had left so promptly after their meal together. It was unlike him. Had he really left his university project unfinished? Or was there more to it? Anne clearly thought he was cooling towards her, but Marnie could not believe that.

Angela's voice broke in on her musings. 'Do you think it will last, Marnie?'

'I would've thought so. I think they're really fond of each other. But of course you never can tell about these things.'

Marnie became aware that Angela had fallen silent. She glanced sideways at her and found her frowning as if in deep concentration.

'I'm not sure I get your drift there, Marnie.'

'Sorry?' Marnie's turn to feel confused.

Angela said, 'Well, I was asking you about the latest wave of troubles with New Force and the far right, if you thought they'd keep it up for some time. Your answer wasn't quite what I expected.'

'Oh, well, yes ... I mean no ... I mean ... Sorry, Angela, I must've lost my bearings for a moment.'

'So do you think it will go on beyond Easter, or is it just a temporary blitz?'

Marnie stopped herself just in time from saying, *God knows*. Instead, she made non-committal noises and was grateful when the sign came up a moment later for the turning to the town centre.

****

Marnie's misgivings about joining the committee, even on a temporary basis, proved to be well founded. It seemed that every delegate had the same goal: to say their piece. She found herself wondering if they actually listened to – or were even interested in – the views of the others sitting round the table. She realised that sooner or later Angela would probably invite her to speak. Two possibilities faced her: either she could say something anodyne that might at least contribute a vague sense of harmony, or she could spell out her concerns. She was convinced that the far-right trouble-makers could destabilise the whole community. Convinced that nobody apart from Angela would pay any attention to her views, she prepared herself to take the easier path.

A minister from a nonconformist church made the point that the problem had blown over in the past. They should keep their heads in case a strong reaction played into the hands of *these undesirable elements*. When he finished speaking, Angela turned to Marnie.

'Thank you, Mr Cranham. Marnie, I wonder if you have anything to add at this stage?'

The words, *what a load of claptrap*, were forming on her lips, but she restrained herself. Instead she paused to gather her thoughts, looking down at notes she had made during previous contributions.

'Marnie?' Angela prompted.

Marnie spoke slowly and deliberately in measured terms. 'The previous speaker alluded to the failure of New Force and their allies to cause mayhem three years ago. Perhaps we should remind ourselves that exceptional measures were adopted at that time to ensure that large numbers of young people were transported out of town to avoid possible confrontations. Even so, there was rioting on the streets, and we were lucky to avoid serious casualties.'

'Oh now, come on –'

Angela raised a hand to silence the interruption. 'Please, archdeacon, we should let Marnie have her say. She was after all –'

'That was a *gross* distortion of those events.' He pointed at Marnie across the table. 'You cannot compare –'

'Archdeacon,' Angela insisted, 'would you please at least address your comments to the chair.'

The archdeacon ignored her. 'The present situation is in no way comparable with those times.'

'A woman has been murdered,' Marnie said quietly. 'Some would regard that as a serious matter.'

'I hope you're not suggesting –'

Angela was about to call the archdeacon to order when the door opened and a flustered-looking woman entered. All eyes turned towards the newcomer who scanned the room and began advancing towards the archdeacon. Marnie intervened. She stood and pointed at Angela.

'The chairman of the meeting is at that end of the table,' she said in a firm tone.

The woman looked if anything even more disconcerted and veered hurriedly in Angela's direction. She bent forward to whisper in her ear. Angela only just prevented her mouth from dropping open. There was silence in the room as the delegates stared at Angela. She nodded at the intruder, who left without a word.

'Ladies and gentleman,' Angela began, 'I have just been informed that an incident has taken place here in Northampton. It appears that certain premises have been the subject of an outrage. The Polish shop in the town centre has been firebombed.'

A collective gasp sounded in the room. Shock registered on every face. One word was spoken.

'Casualties?' said Marnie.

'Apparently, yes, but no details have yet been released.'

The ensuing silence was broken by mutterings among the committee's members. Marnie spoke again.

'I wonder, chairman, if this latest event has caused anyone to change their mind about the seriousness of the situation.'

Marnie looked across the table. The archdeacon was staring down at his notepad. Angela took the initiative.

'In view of what's happened, I think we might all wish to have a minute of silent prayer and meditation.' She bowed her head. Everyone present followed her example.

Prologue 4
The Southern Front
Voroshilovgrad, Ukraine, 1942

They were on their eighth mission that night when it happened. For this attack their plane had been ordered to take the lead role. With their nerves already jangled they were flying like automata, performing their tasks doggedly with thoughts of nothing but unloading their deadly cargoes and returning to base as best they could.

Gliding into the target area, they knew the flak-gunners and searchlight crews were now fully alert and waiting for them. To maintain at least a shred of surprise, they skirted round the enemy lines and approached from a different angle. The navigator released the flare, and all the planes swooped in to drop their bombs as quickly as they could.

The change of tactics worked well; the enemy on the ground hurriedly had to alter their aiming positions. Meanwhile the aircraft flew over the target area, scattering their bombs widely, satisfied that whether they hit personnel, equipment or supplies, no member of the enemy units would be enjoying any rest that night.

The lead plane turned away from the battle area, pleased to see fires burning throughout the vast encampments, pleased to see that fewer guns and searchlights were now in action. There would be more on other nights, that was certain. The enemy's seemingly endless supplies would guarantee that, but for now they were seriously diminished. But not diminished enough.

The lead navigator was checking the compass to fix the homeward course when a new fire burst across the sky like a flare. One of the bombers had been hit by enemy flak. It immediately burst into flames and plummeted towards the ground. The flyers tried to shut out of their minds the screams of the crew being burnt alive as they fell through the air.

Chapter 4

During the days following the arson attack on the Polish shop, the whole country was stunned by the news of the increasing violence in Northampton and its environs. The authorities did all they could to contain the trouble, with police mobile patrols around the clock, and extra uniformed officers on the streets. The fire and rescue service was on constant standby, with increased numbers of staff on duty at all times. Budget limits were temporarily overlooked in the face of the perceived threat from New Force and its allies.

Down at Glebe Farm the anxiety had an added dimension. Marnie was concerned that the response from the community groups was totally inadequate. Angela was clearly out of her depth, and Marnie was aware of her own shortcomings. She had a business to run, a living to earn. The constraints on her time were severe. And in any case, what could she do?

That Wednesday morning it was reported that the owner of the Polish shop, Mr Florjan Badzinski, had died of his injuries. Marnie, Ralph and Anne heard the news on the radio at the breakfast table. Marnie was exasperated.

'It's all very well praying and meditating, but that won't resolve anything.'

'Don't you think you're expecting too much of the inter-faith committee, Marnie?' Ralph asked. 'Surely only the police and the emergency services can deal with the situation.'

'I suppose so, but the whole community has to come together to resist what's going on. These neo-Nazis want nothing more than a fragmented society. People stood up to them a few years ago, but that was in the summer holidays when things were easier to organise.'

'There's going to be more and more trouble, isn't there?' said Anne.

'Definitely, and this is just the start.'

'Don't be too pessimistic, darling,' Ralph said. 'The security people are pretty good at tackling this kind of disorder. And didn't Angela say New Force had been infiltrated by an undercover police officer?'

'She did, but I don't think that's much consolation to the Koslowski and Badzinski families.'

****

Anne went off to college with a heavy heart. The time she had spent with Marnie at Glebe Farm had brought her happiness and fulfilment. Now, she had forebodings that her life, filled with achievement and promise, was starting to unravel. Marnie's sense of impending calamity was contagious. It took hold of Anne and unsettled her.

Added to this, she had begun to feel insecure in her relationship with Donovan. She had never before had a serious boyfriend, never slept with anyone else, never even looked at other young men in that way. But he had left suddenly without a word at the weekend and made no contact since then. Anne knew that life moved on, that nothing was immutable, but she also knew she was not ready to face emotional upheaval on top of everything else.

It took all her energy to focus on her classes that day.

****

At the end of the afternoon Anne returned bearing a bouquet of daffodils, the biggest she could find at the florists. Marnie immediately began planning a meal designed to boost their morale. For his part, Ralph disappeared into what he called the 'wine cellar'. It was in fact a rack at the rear of the pantry.

They had scarcely dared listen to the early evening news on the radio, but were encouraged that no further atrocities had been perpetrated that day. By the time they sat at the refectory table in the kitchen for supper, the atmosphere at Glebe Farm was visibly improving. This was in part attributable to the starter comprising avocado with prawns in Marie Rose sauce, and in part to their first glass of Chablis.

Ralph topped up their glasses while Marnie was serving the main course of grilled Dover sole with new potatoes, and Anne was placing a bowl of mixed salad in the centre of the table.

Dessert was slices of fresh pineapple topped by Greek yogurt, followed by coffee. By unspoken agreement no one mentioned New Force, the murder of Katie Koslowski, or the fire bombing of the Polish shop. It almost felt as if life had returned to normal.

****

After supper, Anne settled down in her attic room with a book on the Austrian artist and architect, Hundertwasser. She chose him deliberately for the humour and exuberance he invested in all his works. To create a comforting atmosphere she lit a joss stick of snow jasmine and played a tape of the 'Haydn' string quartets by Mozart at low volume. She was reflecting that the day had not ended too badly when her mobile rang.

'Hello.'

At first she heard nothing and was wondering if someone had misdialled when she heard voices in the background. She could not make out what was being said, but they seemed to be speaking a foreign language, possibly German. Their tone was urgent, and the sound quality was strangely unclear, crackly like an old newsreel. She pressed the mobile hard against her ear and immediately regretted it. A rasping hollow ping echoed loudly on the line. She started in surprise. What on earth was that sound?

Anne was reaching for the red button to disconnect when another sound intruded. This time it was a voice, though strangely metallic and somehow disembodied. She strained to make out the words being spoken. It was undoubtedly German, incomprehensible but oddly familiar.

At the end of the message the same indistinct voice changed to English.

'This is U-boat X Null Zwei, requesting permission to berth in line with battle-cruiser *Thyrsis*. I repeat, U-boat X Null Zwei, requesting permission to berth in line with battle-cruiser *Thyrsis*. This is Kapitän-Leutnant Nikolaus Donovan Smith. I repeat, Kapitän-Leutnant Nikolaus Donovan Smith. Over.'

This was followed by another loud ping, then silence. Anne began to laugh. With some difficulty she managed to reply. '*Jawohl.* I repeat *jawohl.* Over.'

The voice returned. '*Danke.* I repeat, *danke.* Over.'

With shaking ribs and suppressed laughter, Anne spluttered, 'Bloody idiot. I repeat, bloody idiot. Over.'

There was no further reply but a loud final ping. The line went dead. Silence.

Anne pressed the red button to disconnect, descended the wall ladder in haste and rushed out to skip through the spinney in the darkness. She found Donovan tying up behind *Thyrsis*, across the entrance to *Sally Ann*'s docking area. She stood looking on with hands on hips until he stepped down from the boat's stern deck and faced her.

'I was wondering why I hadn't heard from you,' Anne said.

'I wanted to give you a surprise.'

'You certainly did that. To get here in this time you must have been travelling almost non-stop.'

'You're always telling me this is the only U-boat on the waterways, so I thought I might as well act the part.'

'Did you get any sleep at all?'

'A few hours each night. That's all I needed.'

'I wondered what the hell was going on.' Anne said.

'By the way,' said Donovan. 'I don't think the High Command of the German Admiralty officially addresses its officers as *bloody idiots.*'

'Perhaps they should,' Anne said.

'Fair point. I'll ask them to bear it in mind.'

With that he opened his arms wide. Anne rushed forward to embrace him, all cares forgotten, if only for the moment. The day had definitely ended better than it had begun.

Prologue 5
The Southern Front
Voroshilovgrad, Ukraine, 1942

The crews of all the bombers felt sick at heart having seen one of their aircraft shot down in flames on their eighth raid of that night. The camaraderie in the regiment was strong, and they all dreaded finding out which of their number had perished. As was their custom, the pilot leaned back and dozed in the front cockpit while the navigator flew the plane on the return leg to base. At the agreed distance to destination, the navigator shouted into the megaphone connected to the pilot's seat by a rubber tube.

'Five minutes to base.'

The reply came back at once; the pilot was not resting, but no doubt reliving the moment when disaster had struck and killed their comrades. The navigator spoke again.

'Airfield ahead, five kilometres.'

Trusting the navigator's accuracy in the darkness, the pilot throttled back and lost height steadily, gliding down clear of the trees that marked the edge of their field. They bounced gently once as they reached the ground and rolled to a halt. They had hardly come to a standstill when the ground crew manhandled the plane into position for refuelling and re-arming with the next load of bombs.

While these actions were taking place, the officer on duty that night, the deputy chief of staff, climbed onto the wing for a report on the mission. The shaking of the pilot's head gave a warning that something had gone badly wrong. Luckily, disasters were rare, but this was war. Everyone knew and accepted the risks. The loss of one bomber was reported. No one would know the identity of the crew until the duty officer had counted all the planes back from that sortie. No other crew members would be informed of which of their comrades was lost until the night's missions had been completed.

While waiting for the other planes to return and be re-equipped for the next mission, the crew of the lead plane were given hot coffee in enamel mugs and a bread roll. No one felt like talking. Twenty minutes later all the aircraft but one were ready to take to the air again. The crews knew that the enemy were expecting them, no doubt as apprehensive as they were. The difference was that the bombers were now more determined than ever to bring the maximum possible grief down on the heads of their foes.

Chapter 5

On Thursday morning Marnie sat alone in the office, working on a design project. Anne had suddenly become much chirpier than in the past few days, and had set off for a morning of lectures in college. It had come as a slight surprise to Marnie when Donovan appeared at the breakfast table, but she was delighted as always to see him. It was no surprise when he announced that he would be accompanying Anne to town, where he had 'things to do'.

Marnie glanced up at the wall clock. It was almost time for coffee. Ralph would be arriving from his study on *Thyrsis* within the next ten minutes. She was about to get up and fill the kettle when the phone rang. It was Angela Hemingway.

'I owe you an apology, Marnie. I'm so sorry.'

'Have you run off with Ralph?'

Angela hesitated. 'No.'

'Anything else, I can forgive.'

'I've been meaning to ring and thank you for coming to the meeting on Monday. I can't think where the week's gone. I'm really grateful to you for your support.'

'That's okay. Is there anything else I can do for you?' Marnie felt like crossing her fingers.

'Er ... well ...'

'Is this a subtle hint that you want to come down for coffee?'

'My goodness, is it that time already?'

'Just about.'

'No, thanks awfully, Marnie. I've got a pile of things to do.'

'So was that it?'

Angela hesitated again. 'Not exactly. Do you remember that woman police officer in uniform at the meeting?'

'Groves, wasn't it?' Marnie said. 'Pamela?'

'That's the one. She's a sergeant, our official police liaison officer. She rang earlier to say she wants to talk to me.'

Marnie spoke slowly, her voice edged with more than a hint of suspicion. 'I'm just wondering where I fit in.'

'Do you think ...' Angela began. 'I mean could you possibly consider ... what I mean is ...'

'When would this be, Angela?'

'Tomorrow, early afternoon.'

Marnie was already bringing the diary up on the computer. 'Sorry, no can do. I'm in Oundle from lunchtime onwards.'

Angela sighed. 'Oh well, worth a try.'

'As a matter of interest, why would you want me to be with you?'

'You've had so much experience in handling the police, Marnie. I don't feel confident about dealing with them.'

'Did she say what she wanted to talk about?'

'No. She was sort of ... cagey.' An intake of breath. 'I've gotta go. Things to do, people to see. Look, I'll let you know how I get on.'

'Thanks,' said Marnie.

After disconnecting, she sat staring at the receiver for a long moment. If *thanks* is the word, she thought.

****

Detective Constable Cathy Lamb had decided to take matters into her own hands. They were after all investigating a double murder plus a GBH and an arson attack. The police had little evidence to go on, so every lead, no matter how tenuous, had to be pursued. The DCI in charge of her syndicate had agreed with her suggestion. He notified the community liaison team that Lamb would be following up a new line of inquiry and sent her on her way.

With a blue light flashing on the roof of the unmarked police Cavalier, Lamb sped along the dual carriageway from her base in Towcester and took the turning for the village of Knightly St John. There was no car on the drive of the vicarage – an unpretentious detached house on the modern estate – and no reply when Lamb rang the doorbell. Her next port of call was obvious.

She drew up outside the church and walked along the gravel path to the entrance. The bird-wire mesh gateway to the porch swung open at her touch. Promising. Lamb closed it carefully behind her and pushed against the heavy medieval main door. Inside, the building was cool and dim, with the faint musty smell common to churches everywhere. From up near the altar came a light clattering sound. She set off briskly along the centre aisle.

But it was not the vicar who confronted her by the lectern, but a middle-aged woman in a floral apron arranging flowers ready for the weekend services. The sound had been a metal watering can tapping against a vase.

'I'm looking for the vicar.' Lamb held up her warrant card. 'DC Cathy Lamb.'

'Ooh, you've not long missed her. She was here not ten minutes ago.'

'Do you know where she went?'

'I don't.'

Lamb frowned. 'You've really no idea?'

The woman shook her head. 'Sorry. Did you have an appointment?'

Lamb stared at her. 'That's not how it works. We don't ask for appointments when we're investigating a murder.'

The woman raised a hand to her open mouth, her eyes bulging.

****

Outside on the pavement, Lamb looked up and down the high street for inspiration. It took five seconds to decide on the village shop as the next target. The local combined grapevine-and-radar-system common to all villages almost guaranteed that Molly Appleton, the proprietor, would be able to trace anyone within a five mile radius.

But on that day it was not to be.

'Any ideas, Molly?' said Lamb.

'If she's not in church, have you thought of trying the school? She is a governor there. She's always in and out on some business or other.'

Lamb winced. The school, yes, a logical if unwelcome suggestion. Unwelcome because it meant an encounter with the Secretary from Hell.

****

Inside the school's main entrance, Lamb was faced with a brightly-coloured display featuring an array of spring flowers – daffodils, tulips, freesias – framed by swathes of primrose yellow net curtaining. The background was a painting by the pupils of a green hill surmounted by three crosses. Above the display was the caption: 'Happy Easter', in large letters, each one a different colour. Below that was the slogan: 'The message of Easter is LOVE for all mankind'.

With that comforting thought Lamb made her way along the corridor and passed through the open door of the school office. Seated at a desk, the school secretary was busy checking a pile of papers behind a nameplate bearing the title, Mrs Valerie Paxton. Lamb flourished her warrant card.

'Good morning. I'm Detective Constable –'

'I know who you are.' The secretary's tone suggested she had not wholeheartedly digested the message of Easter.

'I'm looking for the reverend Angela Hemingway. Is she here?'

'No.'

'Have you seen her this morning?'

'Yes.'

Lamb waited ... and waited. 'When did you see her?'

Paxton considered this for several seconds. 'Earlier on.'

Lamb wanted to roll her eyes, but desisted. It would be unbecoming for an officer in the CID.

'Can you be more specific?'

Paxton shrugged. 'It's been a busy morning.'

'Look, Valerie –'

'It's Mrs Paxton. We use surnames in school.'

'I'm making inquiries as part of a murder investigation. You are obstructing me. I want a straight, precise answer. Do I make myself clear?'

Paxton pursed her lips. 'The vicar left here at fourteen minutes past nine after speaking with the head teacher for eleven minutes and thirty-six seconds.'

Lamb opened her mouth to speak, but closed it without uttering a word. She turned on her heels and left. Listening to her footsteps along the corridor, Paxton scowled. If they're investigating a murder, they should send a senior officer, she thought, not the office junior.

****

Marnie heard a car pull up on the gravel beside the farmhouse and looked up from her work. Seconds later, Angela Hemingway passed the large tinted plate glass window fronting the office barn and knocked on the door.

'Changed your mind about coffee?' Marnie said. 'The kettle's probably still warm.'

'I wouldn't want to barge in on you and Ralph. I know you like to have a break together mid-morning.'

43

'No problem,' Marnie said. 'He's headed off for meetings in Oxford, and Anne's in college, so Dolly and I are running the show together.'

Angela reached down to the stroke the thick-pile black fur of the sturdy cat sitting on Marnie's desk.

'In that case, I'd love a coffee,' Angela said, plonking herself on a visitors' chair. 'It's been one of those days, and it's hardly even got going.'

Marnie crossed the office to the kitchen area at the rear. 'What's the problem, or is it theological and therefore over my head?'

'My meeting in Northampton with the archdeacon's been cancelled ...' Angela paused to reflect on that.

'What's the bad news?' Marnie asked.

'I've got time to fret about what the police liaison officer wants with me.'

Marnie was heaping coffee into the cafetière. 'Why should you fret?'

'It's all this wretched murder business, those two poor Polish people. I can't get it out of my head, Marnie ... so much wickedness.'

Marnie poured hot water into the pot. 'I feel the same, but I can't see what you can do about it. The whole thing's a full-blown police investigation.'

'They must have some reason for –'

Angela was interrupted by the phone ringing. Marnie picked up the receiver from Anne's desk.

'Walker and Co, good morning.'

'Marnie, it's Cathy Lamb.'

'Hi, Cathy.' She mouthed *Cathy Lamb* silently to Angela. 'What can I do for you?'

'Have you by any chance seen Angela Hemingway this morning?'

'She's here with me now. D'you want to speak to her?'

'Look, I'm in the village at the moment. Could I come down and see her at your place?'

'Sure. I'm just making coffee.'

'On my way!'

Marnie hardly had time to add more coffee to the pot when DC Cathy Lamb entered the office and collapsed onto a chair beside Angela. She sighed audibly.

'There are times when I wish we were an armed force. I could've shot Valerie Paxton for resisting arrest.'

Two heads snapped round to stare at Lamb.

'You've arrested Valerie Paxton?' Marnie said in astonishment.

'Well, no not actually. I was speaking figuratively.' She grinned. 'But you'll know I mean it when I ask to borrow Donovan's Luger.'

Angela's jaw dropped. 'Donovan has a gun?'

Lamb nodded. 'Licensed, legal and above board.'

'What's brought this on?' Marnie asked.

'All I did was ask the Paxton woman if she'd seen Angela. Obstructive is not the word.'

'Why d'you want to see me?' Angela asked. 'I'll be getting a persecution complex. I've got Sergeant Groves coming tomorrow. Now you're on my case, Cathy.'

'Not any more, you haven't. I'm here instead.'

'And?'

Lamb shifted in her seat and accepted a mug of coffee from Marnie.

'Not sure how to begin, but ... how can I put this without seeming off the wall?' She paused. 'Do you know how I can get hold of a witch, Angela?'

Marnie snorted. 'I thought you'd already seen Valerie Paxton this morning!'

Lamb stared at Marnie. 'You're not serious, are you? Nothing would surprise me about that woman.'

'I was speaking figuratively,' Marnie said. 'But why are you wanting contact with witches?'

'I'm er ... following a lead.'

'Go on,' said Angela.

'I can't really say more than that.'

'Come off it!' Angela protested. 'You can't just come out with a question like that and not explain what it's about.'

'Believe me, I'd really like to say more, but you know my hands are tied.'

Angela and Cathy sipped their coffee. Marnie looked on in silence, but eventually said, 'Can you really not give us even a small clue about what this is all about, Cathy?'

Cathy shook her head. 'You know I would if I could.'

'And you seriously want to get in touch with a witch?'

'Yes.'

Angela shook her head slowly. 'Sorry. I can't help you.'

Cathy was taking a dejected sip of coffee when Marnie spoke quietly.

'I might have an idea.'

****

It was mid-afternoon when Cathy Lamb returned to Knightly St John by arrangement with Marnie. She had deliberately avoided contact at the station with DS Marriner and DCI Bartlett, keeping her head down, working her way through witness statements. If she revealed the outcome of her first visit to the village, she knew that would be the start of a barrage of jokes about her *witch hunt*.

As soon as Cathy arrived back at Glebe Farm, Marnie suggested they take the Freelander. Angela was already there, as were Anne and Donovan who had returned from Northampton. The five of them piled into the car. Cathy was offered the front passenger seat, while Angela, Anne and Donovan squeezed into the rear.

'Why are we actually doing this?' Anne asked, as they drove up the field track.

There was a pause before Marnie replied. 'It's Cathy's request, but she's not telling us why.'

'Why not?' said Donovan.

Marnie glanced sideways. 'Your turn, Cathy.'

'I can't explain for operational reasons. We don't give out that sort of information.'

'Then we'll just have to guess,' Donovan persisted. 'There are probably two main reasons why you're interested in witches.'

'What a surprise,' Anne murmured.

'What do you mean?' Angela asked.

'With Donovan there are usually two reasons.'

Donovan ignored this. He continued. 'Either you have reason to believe – is that the right phrasing? – that Mrs Koslowski was a witch, or alternatively you think witches, or a witch, were involved in her murder. Now you'll tell us you can't possibly comment.'

'That's right, I can't.'

Anne grinned at Donovan. 'Smartarse.'

Angela suppressed a laugh. Marnie spoke over her shoulder.

'Well at least that's cheered you up a bit, Angela.'

By now they had travelled through the village and reached the dual carriageway. Marnie crossed to the central section to turn right and shortly afterwards took a left turn. They passed a Forestry Commission signpost indicating Knightly Woods.

'I'm still a little in the dark as to why we're doing this,' Angela said.

Marnie pulled into the small car park, which was otherwise empty. 'All will be revealed,' she said.

They were wearing walking boots or otherwise sensible shoes for rough terrain, as advised by Marnie, and they set off initially along a designated footpath. But soon they deviated from the marked trail and began climbing a less clear route between the trees.

Marnie said, 'You'll need to remember this turn-off, Cathy. You have to follow this track by that stunted oak tree. Okay?'

'I've got it,' said Cathy. She stopped, took a small camera from her pocket and photographed the location.

They climbed for the next several minutes, hearing only occasional birdsong against a background hum of traffic in the distance. Nothing else stirred in the woods. Marnie recalled her first visit when she caught a faint whiff of woodsmoke, and there it was again floating on the breeze like a distant memory. By now the intermittent sun was dipping towards the horizon, and soon the light would be fading. Marnie led the group on at a steady pace until they arrived in a clearing. She stopped and waited for the others to reach her.

'This is it?' Cathy asked.

'Yes.'

'If you want to take any shots, I'd do it now,' said Donovan. 'The light's going to diminish pretty fast from now on.'

'Why are we here?' Angela sounded bewildered.

'Witches,' said Marnie. 'This is where they have gatherings, or at least they have in the past.'

'You're sure of that?' Cathy said.

'Yes.'

'How d'you know?'

'I've seen traces of their activity. That was in fact a couple of years ago, but it's the only lead I have.'

Cathy said, 'You see, Marnie, in my line of work we need something tangible so that we're sure of our facts.'

'And what are we expecting to find here?' Angela asked.

Marnie turned to face her. 'Nothing specific today. I just wanted to show Cathy the place, so that she can follow up her enquiries when she needs to.'

Cathy looked doubtful.

While the others were speaking, Anne was mooching slowly around the clearing. She had noticed a change in the ground roughly in the centre of the open space. While most of the area was covered in coarse grass and low weeds, there was a patch in the middle that seemed to be covered in fine soil. At first Anne took this to be a kind of pale sand. Closer inspection revealed that it was in fact light grey ash. She was scuffing it with the side of her boot when something unexpected caught her eye. Squatting down, she parted the ash with her fingertips.

'Stay just as you are.'

When Donovan spoke from the edge of the clearing, the others realised that he had been missing for some minutes. Anne looked round so suddenly that she almost overbalanced.

'Hold it there,' Donovan said.

They heard the click of the camera.

'Okay, you can get up now.'

Anne rose unsteadily. She was holding something in her hand.

'What are you doing?' she asked.

'Thought I'd get views of the whole scene, together with all of you *in situ.*'

'Why are you doing that?' Cathy asked.

Anne spoke first. 'He likes to keep a record of what's going on.'

'What's that you've picked up?' Angela said to Anne.

Anne held up a small object. 'I wonder if Cathy would accept this as evidence.'

Everyone gathered round and saw that Anne was holding the charred remains of an animal's skull. It looked like a goat's.

****

Like Cathy Lamb earlier in the day, Ralph had decided to take matters into his own hands. The Jaguar that he had recently acquired had a built-in phone system. Normally averse to modern technology, he found this fascinating and used it often. That afternoon he pressed the buttons for Marnie's mobile. She took the call on the descent from the *witch ground.*

48

'Where are you?' Marnie asked.

'Can you hear me all right?' Ralph said.

'Perfectly. You're not home already, are you?'

'No. I'm sitting in the car park at All Saints using the car phone.'

Marnie laughed. 'Your latest toy! You're in danger of becoming a nerd, Ralph.'

'Definitely *on grid*.' He paused. 'Does that actually mean anything?' His tone now more doubtful.

'Not sure, but presumably there's a reason why you're phoning me.'

'I have a suggestion. How about an Indian takeaway this evening?'

'Great idea.'

'How many are we for dinner?'

'Four including Donovan.'

'I'll call in at that restaurant we like in Stony Stratford on the way home.'

'You could probably place your order online so it's ready for when you get there,' Marnie said.

'Online?' Ralph sounded dubious.

'Sure.'

Another pause. 'I said *takeaway*, darling. Let's not get carried away.'

****

Ralph arrived at Glebe Farm just over an hour later, bearing brown paper carrier bags filled with eastern promise. He smiled to himself. Anne had lit a sandalwood joss stick in the hall of the farmhouse, and a CD of Ravi Shankar on sitar playing a soothing evening raga floated from the open door of the living room. Across the hall, the door to the kitchen was closed. Anne evidently did not want the scent of the joss stick to conflict with the spicy flavours of the meal.

Ralph's choice of dishes was well received. So too was the selection of German beers that Donovan had by chance brought with him from London.

While they ate, Marnie told Ralph about Cathy Lamb's interest in witches. She mentioned Donovan's suggestion that the police either believed that Katie Koslowski was herself a witch, or had been attacked by a witch or witches. Ralph conceded the logic of that view, but thought it all sounded highly improbable.

To everyone's surprise, Donovan agreed with him. 'I was really just trying to provoke some kind of response from Cathy. You know what it's like with the police. They expect you to be totally frank but never give anything away.'

'I wonder who that reminds me of,' Anne said cryptically.

'I can't imagine,' said Donovan.

'Come to think of it,' Marnie said, raising her glass in Donovan's direction, 'we don't seem to have heard how you spent your morning in Northampton.'

Anne laughed. 'You can be totally frank with us.' She pulled a face.

'Okay. I went wandering about looking for Nazis, fascists and general far-right undesirables.'

Anne's smile vanished. 'You *didn't.*'

'You said you wanted me to be frank.'

Ralph said, 'I take it that your being here in one piece means you failed in your quest?'

'Not entirely.'

'Was that wise?' Marnie said.

'What d'you mean, *not entirely?*' said Anne.

'I walked round the town centre after you dropped me off at college, then headed into Little Warsaw. It's appalling: no one has cleaned off the graffiti on the Polish shop wall.'

'Presumably it's cordoned off as a crime scene,' said Ralph.

'Even so ...' Donovan shook his head. 'You've got to get rid of graffiti straight away. It sets a bad example, leaving it on display.'

'You haven't answered my question,' Anne insisted.

They all turned to Donovan.

'I was surprised that on my previous visit I didn't see any sign of far-right activity in the town. It occurred to me they might have become nocturnal, keeping out of sight till this Easter parade thing comes along.'

'But this time you did see some?' Anne said.

Donovan nodded. 'Unfortunately.'

Anne frowned. 'What happened?'

'I was on my way back to meet you from college, walking along the main road from the centre. There was a lot of traffic, so at first I didn't spot them. A big Carlsberg tanker went by, followed by a bus. Then I saw them on the other side of the road, a group of four or five ambling along, all in black leather.'

'Skinheads?'

'Mostly. One of them noticed me and pointed.'

'Perhaps because you were dressed in black like them?'

'Could be. Then another one made what I thought was a Nazi salute, raising an arm towards me. Too late I realised the arm was holding up one of these new small digital cameras.'

'They photographed you?'

'I think so. It was too late to take cover.'

'Would you recognise them again?' Anne asked.

'Surely one skinhead looks much like another,' Marnie said.

'This was no skinhead,' said Donovan. 'It was a girl, and I'd certainly recognise her.'

'What was she like?' Marnie asked.

'A mass of long black hair, sharp features, loads of make-up, pointed chin, longish nose.'

'Quite distinctive, then,' said Marnie.

'Oh yes, definitely. In fact I can only say she looked like … a witch.'

Prologue 6
The Southern Front
Voroshilovgrad, Ukraine, 1942

The bombers returned to base for the last time that night shortly before sunrise. They had flown ten missions and were exhausted, partly from the fatigue and strain of combat, partly from the mind-numbing stress of seeing their comrades' aircraft falling through the sky like a flaming torch. One crew after another reported to the commander for debriefing, walking to the command hut on legs still trembling from shock and tension.

A tough situation became worse when they discovered the names of the victims of enemy gunfire. Leaving the hut, many of the aircrew stood in a huddle, took off their helmets and bowed their heads. Each knew they could permit themselves only a limited time for regret or sorrow. Tomorrow they would take to the air again on just as many missions. With those planes and that equipment and their skill as aviators, they would stand a fighting chance of coming back alive. But nothing was guaranteed. Their determination to destroy and harass the enemy would sustain them through everything.

Of one thing they were certain. They would be haunted by the images of that blazing aircraft for the rest of their lives, however long or short their lives might be.

Chapter 6

Friday brought mixed fortunes. When DC Cathy Lamb arrived at police HQ everything seemed normal. The other CID officers in the open-plan space greeted her with the usual chorus of casual hellos, barely looking up from their desks. It was only when she sat at her own work station that she realised something was out of the ordinary. A nameplate was standing on the front of the desk. Reaching forward, she turned it round to examine it. The title facing her was: WITCHFINDER-GENERAL. She groaned inwardly and tried to pretend she had not seen it. Glancing quickly round the room, she slipped it into the top drawer of her desk.

Typical unsubtle, heavy-handed police humour, she thought. If she ignored the feeble attempt to belittle her work, she figured it would go away. Determinedly, she drew towards her the serious crimes folder. She would keep her head down and devote all her energies to making progress with the two Polish murders and the arson attack. She opened the folder and discovered a magazine on the top of the wad of documents. At first glance it appeared to be a copy of 'Which?' Magazine. Then she noticed that the heading had been changed. Some bright spark had altered the title to 'Witch?'.

As she was reading the heading, a round of applause broke out across the room. Looking up, she saw through the glazed partitions of his office that even DCI Bartlett was smiling.

She sighed and muttered, 'Ha bloody ha ...'

The other officers were on their feet, giving her a standing ovation much to her chagrin. But it was not for nothing that she was regarded as one of the brightest young detectives in the force. Thinking quickly, she too stood up and laughed heartily at the jokes which were on her. She judged rightly that this action would mark her out as a good sport, one who could take a joke, one of the boys. She joined in the applause, then waved two fingers with both hands at her grinning colleagues.

Mentally, unbeknown to the others, she was thinking of witches, of black cats and potions and wishing she could cast a spell on the lot of them and turn them into frogs. That thought kept the smile on her face.

****

53

For the Reverend Angela Hemingway Friday morning started frustratingly. She had sent out the draft minutes of Monday's inter-faith committee meeting on Wednesday, confident that they gave a simple, clear account of proceedings and would be acceptable to members of all faiths and none. The first item in the post on Friday morning was a letter from the Archdeacon of Northampton, enclosing a copy of the minutes on which he had written his comments and 'required amendments' in red ink. Angela strained to read the minute handwriting, her cheeks gradually turning the same colour as the ink. He had queried almost every point she had made. The two pages of notes were a mass of corrections, together with additional paragraphs on which he 'insisted'.

Angela was on the point of screaming when the phone rang. Suddenly the day became brighter. The caller was Randall Hughes, rural dean for Brackley, the south of the county. He had been a controversial vicar of Knightly St John a few years earlier. Even his critics regarded him with respect as a tough, no-nonsense free-thinker, who was not averse to shooting from the hip. He and Angela were also an 'item', though they did their best to act with discretion to prevent tongues from wagging while their relationship developed.

Angela explained her exasperation about the archdeacon's comments. Randall waited till she reached the end of her tirade before responding.

'You're the chairman,' he said. 'Tell the miserable old sod to get knotted.'

'Er ...'

'Well, not in those exact words, perhaps.'

'So what words would you have in mind, Randall?'

'First tell me this. Do you expect the other members to agree with your minutes?'

'I've already had e-mail replies from three others who accepted them.'

'Then do nothing until everyone else has replied. If the others are all happy, you can just write back and say you feel obliged to accept the majority view and you think you must move on from there. Thank him for his kind attention. Say you'll be taking his comments on board in due course.'

'And how do I do that?'

'You ignore them.'

'I'm impressed,' Angela said. 'All that is covered by *get knotted*. Who'd have thought it?'

'Glad to be of service, but that isn't why I'm ringing. Did Marnie tell you she'd phoned me after your chat with Cathy Lamb yesterday?'

'No, but she did hint that she had an idea. That's all she said.'

'She told me you were trying to find a witch, Angela.'

'You don't mean –'

'Yes. I think I've found you one.'

'You're kidding!'

'No. Do you realise this is the sort of conversation that probably hasn't taken place between members of the clergy since the sixteen hundreds?'

'Tell me more, Randall. I've drawn a complete blank in all my attempts.'

'I know how you feel,' said Randall. 'When you *need* a witch ...'

'Well go on. Don't keep me dangling in suspense.'

'Ooh ... I'll pretend I didn't hear that.'

Angela winced. 'Sorry. I ought to rephrase that. I meant –'

'Don't tell me you're burning to know what I've found.'

'Randall!'

'Okay. This is how it went. I called in at the drop-in centre yesterday evening to see how things were going.'

A few years earlier Randall had acquired a large house in Brackley, where he was rector, and had it adapted to create a refuge for homeless people and itinerants. Most people called them *tramps*. Randall insisted on referring to them as *guests*. Anne had described the place as a drop-in centre for drop-outs.

Randall continued. 'One of the current guests is a young woman we hadn't seen before. You know we never ask questions about their backgrounds or circumstances. But she asked if she could put up one or two posters in her room, as she wanted to stay for a couple of weeks.'

'I thought you didn't allow that because drawing pins and sellotape might damage the walls.'

'That's right, but she was adamant that Blu-Tack wouldn't hurt the emulsion. We experimented on a wall in the office, and found she was right.'

'I'm sure there's a good reason you're telling me all this, Randall. By the way, what's her name?'

'She calls herself Jade. You know we only ask for a first name. Anyway, I offered to help put up her posters.'

'You wanted to make sure they didn't promote something undesirable?'

'Let's just say I was a little curious about them.'

'And this is presumably where the witch connection comes in,' said Angela.

'Celtic shamanism, to be precise.'

'Never heard of it.'

'To cut a long story short, we now have an intro to the world of Wicca.'

'She gave you a contact?'

'Not quite. She thought that if I wrote to one of her friends, I'd probably not get a reply. They've had too many weird approaches from people in the past. She offered instead to talk to someone for me and help with an introduction.'

'Brilliant! Do you think she will?'

'We'll have to wait and see, but I'm hopeful.'

****

Randall's optimism proved to be well founded. He did not have to be patient for long. That same afternoon he received a phone call from the warden at the drop-in centre: Jade had a message for him. He drove round straight away and found her waiting for him in the hallway by the reception office. It was a spacious area with an elegant curved staircase rising to the first floor, a reminder that it had been the home of a well-to-do family in times past. Over the reception office hung a banner in large letters proclaiming, WELCOME.

Jade was sitting to one side on a bench below a framed print of Holman Hunt's painting, *The Light of the World*. It was surmounted by a quote from the Bible:

Jesus said : Behold I stand at the door and knock
If any man hear my voice and open the door I will come in to
him and will sup with him and he with me

This was the only religious reference in the whole building, though there was a small room designated as the chapel down a side corridor. Randall's aim was to make clear that the centre was open to all who needed it, without being too 'churchy'.

Jade stood up when Randall entered the hall. Like most of the guests she liked him. He accepted her as she was. Most of the guests were men ranging from middle-aged to quite elderly. Unlike most of the guests, as far as she knew, she found him physically attractive. He was in his thirties, well over six feet tall, willowy and with a long sensitive, intelligent face topped by dark curly hair. His appearance was made all the more dramatic by his choice of clothes: a long black cassock with buttons all the way down the front. He offered Jade his hand, and his long fingers gripped her firmly and warmly.

'How about a cup of tea in the sitting room?' he said.

****

Later that afternoon Marnie and Anne were sitting together in the office barn, reviewing a design that Marnie had produced for a retired couple. They had downsized to a cottage in the nearby village of Hanford. Having sold their large family home in Northampton, they had a substantial capital nest egg and had decided to treat themselves to the services of an interior designer for the first time in their lives. For Marnie it was a fun project; Anne said it was like playing with a doll's house.

When the phone rang Anne picked up the receiver.

'Walker and Co, good afternoon.'

'D'you want the good news or the bad news?'

Anne mouthed *Angela Hemingway* to Marnie and pressed the button for speakerphone. It was unusual for Angela to talk without any greeting.

'Hi, Angela,' Marnie called out. 'We can both hear you. So what's up?'

'Randall has found us a *witch*.'

'A witch?' Marnie repeated. 'Is that the good bit or the bad bit?'

'It's what we wanted, so it's the good news.'

'If you say so.' Marnie sounded less than enthralled. 'I can't wait to hear the bad news.'

'The bad? Oh well, er yes ... Cathy Lamb's coming. She's on her way now. I said we'd meet at your place.'

'So now you're inviting the police to drop in on me. Thank you, Angela. Yes, I guess that would probably qualify as the bad news. Can I ask why she's coming here?'

A pause. 'Good question.' Angela reflected. 'I think she said she was keen to get away from the police station.'

'So a detective is coming to Glebe Farm for light relief,' Marnie said. 'It's gotta be a first.'

'Well, that's the impression she gave me.'

Marnie sighed. 'We'll soon find out if you're right.'

Hanging up, Marnie turned to speak to Anne, but found she was on her way to the kitchen area.

'Putting the kettle on already?'

Anne turned, her expression inscrutable. 'No. I'm going to hang out the flags.'

****

While Marnie and Anne were occupied with the country cottage project, Donovan was making calls on his mobile at the rear of the office, seated at Anne's vacant desk. Intermittently Anne caught the odd snatch of conversation. She was intrigued to notice that some of the time he was speaking German.

Cathy Lamb and Angela Hemingway arrived almost simultaneously. Activities in the office were immediately put on hold. Anne had already set out mugs and a plate of biscuits, and she gravitated to the kitchen area, gently touching Donovan's shoulder as she passed. While the new arrivals moved chairs together, Marnie took their jackets and hung them on the coat stand. Pulling her chair round to the front of the desk, she turned to Cathy Lamb.

'Presumably you're not really here just as an excuse to get out of the office, are you?'

Lamb smiled ruefully. 'Not entirely, though my patience with being the butt of my colleagues' witch jokes – *non-jokes* – is wearing thin.'

'So what else brings you here?' Marnie asked. Her tone was less than hospitable.

Lamb turned serious. She glanced quickly at Angela Hemingway. 'Sorry. I do realise that you have a business to run, Marnie.'

'I'm sorry, too,' Angela said. 'I shouldn't have suggested we meet here, but –'

'I don't mind you coming, but I'm not personally involved in your investigation, Cathy, and to be frank, I've had enough dealings with police matters to last me a lifetime.'

58

'Are you sure about that, Marnie?' Donovan said. He was carrying a tray of mugs across the office, while Anne followed with the coffee pot and biscuits.

Marnie frowned. 'You think I need more?'

Donovan set the tray down on Marnie's desk. 'I meant about not being involved. What about the swastika sprayed on the canal bridge?'

'*Swastika*? When was that?' Lamb asked in surprise. 'Did you report it?'

'It was at the weekend,' Marnie said.

'I must see this.'

Donovan handed her a mug. 'You can't.'

'Why not?'

'We got rid of it, just as you should've got rid of the graffiti sprayed on the wall of the Polish shop. Leaving it there is just what New Force wants.'

'It's *evidence*,' Lamb protested.

'No it isn't. You could photograph it and remove it. As it stands, it's publicity for the far right and intimidation, possibly provocation, for the whole community.'

'We have rules and procedures.' Lamb was holding up her mug while Anne filled it with coffee. 'And while I'm on the subject, I could remind you that you should not be tampering with signs of criminal activity.'

Donovan passed her the milk jug. 'So arrest me.'

Anne tried and failed to suppress laughter. The others looked at her.

'Sorry,' she said, 'but this does look rather incongruous. Arguing like that while passing the milk jug makes Miss Marple seem like the Gestapo.'

There were smiles all round.

'Shall we just start again?' Marnie suggested. 'DC Lamb, Cathy, what do you think I or we can do for you?'

Lamb sipped her coffee. 'This is really good.' Everyone noticed that her tone had softened. 'The thing is, I need help in handling the witch question.'

'You've got a station full of rozzers,' Marnie said reasonably.

'Who are treating me like I'm some sort of nut case.'

Marnie raised a finger and spoke slowly. 'The answer is definitely no.'

'But I haven't asked anything,' Lamb protested.

'I think you have ... and the answer's still no.'

Lamb turned to look at Angela, whose mouth opened.

'You want me to talk to a *witch*? Cathy, you must be out of your tiny mind. And do you honestly think a witch is going to want to talk to *me*, a *vicar*? It may have escaped your notice, but we don't actually have a great track record at getting on together.'

Lamb slumped in her chair. The others drank their coffee in silence.

'I just thought ...' Lamb began. 'That poor Polish lady and the shopkeeper, Mr Badzinski, not to mention Stan.'

'Who's Stan?' Marnie said.

'Katie Koslowski's husband.'

'Stanislav, presumably,' Donovan said. He pronounced the name like *Staneeswarff*.

Lamb nodded. 'Is that how you say it? No wonder people just call him Stan. Anyway, he's in hospital in a serious condition. He was out of the house when his wife was attacked, but got home just as her assailants were leaving. They knocked him to the ground, kicked him repeatedly and stamped on his head.'

'Ouch!' said Anne.

Donovan winced.

'Prognosis?' Marnie asked.

Lamb shrugged. 'He's in a really bad way. It's so sad. He seems such a nice guy.'

'No doubt his family's rallying round,' said Angela. 'Those communities are usually close-knit. Do they have children?'

'No, that's just it. They had no kids and they seem to have kept very much to themselves. When I went to the hospital the other day a nurse told me he never gets any visitors.'

Angela looked puzzled. 'That's odd. I'm sure at least their local priest would've looked in on him.'

'Do you know who that might be?' Lamb asked.

'Father Novak. He celebrates mass in Polish several times a week.'

'You know him?'

'Yes. He's quite young and keen. I'm surprised he's not been to visit.'

'That really is odd,' Donovan said.

'I know. The Poles do stick together, and the church plays a big part in their lives.'

'I didn't mean that. It just occurred to me that if you wanted to attack Polish people, logically you'd go after them in Little Warsaw.'

'Like Mr Badzinski and his shop,' Anne added.

'Exactly,' Donovan said. 'But the Koslowskis lived outside the Polish part of town and could hardly be regarded as representatives of that community.'

'They may just have been easy targets,' Lamb said.

'Have they had trouble before?' Donovan asked.

Lamb reflected. 'I think skinheads shouted at Mr Koslowski some time ago – *go home, Polack!* Something like that.'

Donovan frowned. 'And they attacked his wife, an elderly woman, and murdered her?' He shook his head. 'Doesn't add up.'

'It's all racist violence,' Lamb said. 'Part of a growing pattern, regrettably.

'Killing someone in her own home is a long way from name-calling in the street.'

Angela was wringing her hands. 'It's all very horrible, but I still don't understand where *witches* come in. I mean, that is what you came to talk about, isn't it, Cathy?'

'Yes,' Marnie said. 'What's all that about?'

'I thought I'd made it clear,' said Lamb. 'I can't elaborate.'

'But you're absolutely certain there's a witch connection,' Marnie said.

'Absolutely. That's why I need help. All I'm asking is that you talk to this witch that Randall's located and get some information from her. Is it really so much to ask, when a woman's been murdered and it's one of the few clues we have?'

Angela looked across at Marnie, who breathed out audibly and closed her eyes.

'I suppose ...' Angela began. 'I mean, since Randall's managed to track one down ... But I'll only do it if Marnie will join me.'

Marnie glared at Cathy Lamb. 'And you expect me to be involved. That's it, is it? That's all you're asking?'

Lamb fidgeted in her seat and took a sip of coffee.

'Why are you looking sheepish, Cathy?' Marnie asked.

They all suddenly realised what Marnie had said and began to chuckle.

'Cathy Lamb, sheepish?' said Anne. 'Surely not.'

Marnie squeezed her forehead and said wearily, 'I wasn't meaning to be funny.'

Lamb shook her head. 'You're as bad as my lot down at the station. But I have to say, there is one other thing.'

At that moment Donovan's mobile rang. He took it from his back pocket, excused himself and went to take the call at the rear of the office.

Marnie stared at Lamb. 'Amaze us.'

Lamb spoke slowly. 'I want to be in on the interview with the witch.'

'Are you kidding?' Marnie sounded incredulous.

'No. I really have to be there.'

'But you've got copper written all over you,' Angela said.

'Thanks a bunch. I'm supposed to be in plain clothes, remember?'

'Even so ...'

'I assume you won't be wearing the dog collar, will you?' Lamb said.

'Absolutely not. I'll wear a dress or jeans or something casual.'

'Then so will I. And that's good.'

'What's good about it?' Marnie said.

Lamb beamed. 'What's good is that you both seem to have agreed to cooperate.'

Marnie and Angela looked at each other, exasperated. Anne on the other hand seemed to be focused elsewhere, her head turned in Donovan's direction. He had now finished his phone call and was slotting the mobile back into his jeans pocket. With a troubled expression he walked slowly back towards the others.

'Who was that?' Anne asked.

For some seconds Donovan did not reply. Anne wondered if he was annoyed by her question. Then he turned to look at her, muttered something and headed for the door. He went out without another word.

Cathy Lamb looked at Anne. 'What did Donovan say to you?'

'He said ... it was the police.'

Lamb stood up as if intending to go after Donovan. She looked bewildered. 'Were they phoning from my HQ?'

Anne looked thoughtful. 'Not unless they speak German in Towcester.'

****

Of Donovan there was neither sight nor sound for the rest of the afternoon. As soon as Cathy Lamb and Angela Hemingway left

Glebe Farm, Anne gathered together the day's mail and set off for the post-box by the village shop. On her way out she detoured to the docking area to check on Donovan's boat, *X O 2*, which she knew was pronounced *Exodos*. He was not on board.

On the way back from the post run, she turned as a car pulled up at the kerb. It was Ralph back from his meetings in Oxford. She climbed in beside him.

'Going my way, big boy?' she said with an impish grin.

'You betcha,' Ralph replied. He accelerated away. 'So what kind of day have you had?'

A pause. 'Interesting.'

'Bad as that?' he said.

'Well, the high point was Marnie agreeing to meet a witch with reps from the church and the police.'

'Interesting,' Ralph said dubiously.

'Like I said. Oh, and the German police have been in touch with Donovan, who hasn't been seen since.'

Ralph swung the Jaguar through the field gate, shaking his head. 'The things you get up to when my back is turned ...'

'Look on the bright side,' Anne said.

'There's a bright side?'

'Sure. There'll be no shortage of things to talk about over supper.'

****

Anne was right. When she and Ralph arrived back at Glebe Farm they met Marnie crossing the courtyard. She kissed Ralph and made two announcements: first, she was going to pack up work for the day, unable to settle following the talk with Lamb and Hemingway; second, she completely lacked inspiration for supper and would be raiding the freezer. The three had no sooner installed themselves in the kitchen than Donovan returned. He tried to lighten the mood with a cheery greeting, but fooled no one.

'Any ideas for supper?' Marnie asked.

'You haven't any more German treats in the car, have you, Donovan?' Anne said.

Her optimism was not misplaced, as Donovan regularly returned from Germany laden with all manner of food and drink. He replied that sadly the cupboard was bare, but offered to go to the supermarket and assemble the basics for *Sauerkraut,*

Schnitzel and mashed potato. Marnie was already rummaging in the freezer.

'How about …' She took out two containers and read the labels. '… swordfish steaks with … *ratatouille?*'

'We could add pasta,' Ralph suggested.

'Any takers?' Marnie said.

The division of labour fell into a well-tried pattern. While Marnie defrosted the frozen items in the microwave, Anne boiled water and weighed out *fusili* pasta. Ralph checked the 'wine cellar' and Donovan began laying the table. As they set about their tasks, Marnie gave an abridged account of the conversation in the office that afternoon. Ralph withdrew a bottle from the wine rack and placed it on the table.

'So when are you going to see this witch?' he asked, adding, 'I can hardly believe we're having this conversation.'

'I'm waiting to hear back from Angela, who's waiting for more details from Randall.'

'And you're really going to take Cathy Lamb along?'

'She insists.'

At that moment the microwave pinged, and Marnie removed the packs. She placed the swordfish steaks in foil wrapping, added some knobs of butter and popped them into the roasting oven. She scooped the *ratatouille* into a pan and set it down on the simmering plate. The pasta meanwhile began bubbling merrily on the boiling plate. With all this activity the atmosphere in the household was improving by the minute.

'Why?' Ralph said.

Marnie looked round at him. 'Why what?'

'Why does Cathy Lamb want to be there, and what is this *witch* connection anyway?'

Marnie thought for a moment. 'Cathy won't say why, or perhaps I'm missing something. What do you think, Anne?'

'No idea. She's not giving anything away.'

'Surprise, surprise,' said Donovan.

'Talking of which,' Anne began, 'what happened to you this afternoon?'

'What did happen?' Ralph asked.

Anne explained. 'Donovan had a phone call in German, then went off without any explanation.'

'Not bad news, I hope,' said Ralph, aware that there had been serious illness in Donovan's family in Germany. 'Your uncle's okay?'

Before Donovan could reply, the phone rang. Marnie took the receiver from the wall mounting. It was Angela Hemingway.

'I've done it again, haven't I, Marnie? I am sorry for lumbering you.'

'That's okay. Are you phoning to tell me you've got the details of our witch?'

'Not yet, but I'm seeing Randall this evening. Perhaps he'll have more news then.'

'Doing something nice?'

'A district meeting to discuss the building maintenance estimates.'

'Your guy really knows how to show a girl a good time!'

'It's not all beer and ciggies being a vicar, you know, Marnie. Actually, there was something I wanted to say to you. I thought it might be nice to visit Stan in hospital. Cathy said he didn't get any visitors and –'

'Weren't you going to ask Father Whatsisname, the local priest?'

'I will, but even so ...'

'And?' Marnie's voice dripped with suspicion.

'I thought we could take him some fruit, magazines, biscuits, anything to cheer him up.'

'We?'

'I thought two friendly faces would be better than one, and you're so much more outgoing than me, Marnie.'

Marnie said she would think it over, but she knew when she was beaten.

When Marnie ended the call, Anne said, 'Lumbered again, Marnie?'

Marnie gave the ratatouille a stir and nodded. 'Honestly, having Angela around is like living with the Spanish Inquisition. My life's not my own.' She pointed at the bottle of wine on the table. 'What is that, Ralph?'

'It's a light-bodied red from Chinon. I thought it might go well with the swordfish.'

Marnie sighed. 'I don't care if it's Albanian hooch. Just pour me a glass.'

65

Chapter 7

Saturday morning was bright and breezy. A pale sun was dodging between clouds as Anne and Donovan made their way across the courtyard to the farmhouse for breakfast. The wind had an edge to it, a reminder that spring could have a sting in its tail.

Donovan turned up his collar against the chill and glanced at Anne. 'I noticed that no one pressed me last night to explain about my German phone call.'

Anne shivered in the cold air and grinned. 'You are allowed some privacy, you know. We're not the Gestapo.'

The hall in the farmhouse was warm and inviting. They hung up their jackets and headed for the kitchen. Anne stopped at the kitchen door and turned to face Donovan.

'Is it something you don't want to talk about, 'cos if it is -'

'It's something I have to talk about. I just wasn't sure what to do about it yesterday.'

'But now you are?'

'Yes.'

They pushed open the door and went in. Marnie was standing facing the Aga.

'Any sign of Ralph?' she asked, half turning. 'He's usually back from his early walk by now.'

'Haven't seen him,' said Anne. 'What's that you're doing?'

'Making porridge. It looks a chilly old day, so I thought I'd warm us up.'

Anne turned to Donovan. 'Do you like porridge?'

Donovan looked sceptical. 'Er ...'

'I don't suppose you have it in Germany, do you?' Marnie asked.

'Well, I am partly British.'

'And you have Irish connections,' Marnie pointed out.

'Is that relevant?'

Marnie indicated the saucepan. 'These are Irish Jumbo oats ... organic, too.'

'Then how could I resist ... or at least have a try?'

'Good for you,' said Marnie. 'On the table I've put out runny honey, various jams and some pouring cream. You can add whatever you want to the basic dish.'

Anne set about making coffee. Marnie looked up at the wall clock as she gave the porridge a final stir. Donovan raised a finger.

'That's the front door,' he said. 'I think Ralph's back.'

'Perfect timing,' Marnie said.

The kitchen door opened, and Ralph stood looking in. They all turned to greet him. As soon as they saw his expression, they knew.

****

Breakfast turned out to be more sombre than Marnie had envisaged. The porridge was a success, but Ralph's news had brought an unwelcome intrusion back into their lives. As soon as the table was cleared the four of them set off through the spinney, leaving the dishwasher chugging away. By the canal they passed *Sally Ann* and *Thyrsis* and walked on towards the accommodation bridge.

'I didn't spot it when I crossed the bridge and headed north,' Ralph said. 'It was only on my way back that I saw what they'd done.'

As before, the group stood on the bank looking up at the bridge: no swastika this time, but a simple hateful message. They were confronted by the letters 'NF' in large red capitals. New Force was set on causing trouble and chaos in the area. On either side of the letters were twin runic lightning-flash symbols, the same emblem used by the SS in the time of Hitler.

Donovan had brought one of his classic Leica cameras. He began taking photographs from a variety of angles.

Marnie said, 'I know you want to keep a record of what's happening, but we really have to let the police see this. Cathy Lamb said it would be regarded as evidence.'

Donovan stopped and turned to face her. She waited for him to speak, but he said nothing. After several seconds he simply nodded and turned back to take two more shots.

Ralph said, 'I suppose we should count this as lucky.'

Marnie looked up at him. 'How d'you work that out?'

Ralph shrugged. 'They could as easily have sprayed the boats.'

'Not as effective,' Donovan said. 'We could just turn the boats round to hide the spraying. Everyone passing sees the bridge. That's why we have to get rid of this stuff as soon as we can.'

'But we let Cathy or her team see it first,' Marnie said emphatically. 'I don't want to get the wrong side of the police ... again.'

****

At *Sally Ann*'s docking area they split up. Ralph headed towards *Thyrsis* to start work. Like many leading players in their field he applied himself every day of the week, though at weekends he sometimes opted to spend only half the day in his study. Marnie and Anne followed much the same routine, striving to establish their business. Marnie remembered someone saying that being self-employed gave you total freedom ... to work seven days a week.

Donovan announced that he had phone calls to make and took himself off to the farmhouse kitchen. Marnie and Anne opened up the office barn, sliding the doors to one side to reveal the large tinted plate glass window like the frontage of a shop, that let daylight in.

'We've got messages,' Anne observed, passing Marnie's desk.

She went round the office, switching on lamps, and set out two vases of spring flowers that she brought from the kitchen area at the rear. The answering machine beeped as Marnie pressed its button. There was only one message that Saturday morning.

'Marnie, it's Angela. I've got details of our witch ... er, the witch ... from Randall. Can we get together? Talk to you soon. Bye!'

Marnie looked at Anne who was hovering at her desk. 'I'm not sure about this.'

'Why not?' Anne asked. 'D'you think it's creepy?'

'It's not that. It's just ... I don't want to get involved in yet another police enquiry. I'm sorry about those poor Polish people, I really am, but what can I possibly do about it? Investigating murders is a matter for the professionals. And as for this witchcraft thing ... How can it possibly have anything to do with me, with us?'

'How do you know we're not going to be the next victims?'

They had neither noticed Donovan come in. He stood in the doorway, his expression grim.

'Why do you think that?' Marnie asked.

68

'I'd have thought that was pretty obvious.' It was a typical Donovan reply.

'The graffiti on the bridge,' Anne said quietly.

'I don't want to go looking for trouble,' said Marnie. 'We've had more than our fair share in the past.'

'That sort of argument let the Nazis have their way in Germany years ago,' Donovan said. 'And in any case, this time the trouble has come looking for you, for all of us here. You don't think by ignoring it you can just make it go away, do you?'

'You seem to think that scrubbing off the graffiti makes the trouble disappear.'

'No, Marnie. I think you have to oppose them in any way that's appropriate. They spray graffiti; we get rid of it immediately. We must never let them think they can get away with anything.'

'And what if they resort to violence?' Marnie said.

Donovan shrugged. 'It's obvious. You know what I think.'

'You think that if someone had assassinated Hitler at the outset ...'

There was no need for Marnie to finish the sentence. They all knew how Donovan felt. His own family had been persecuted by the Nazis in Berlin before the war. For all his restrained manner, they knew he had a will of iron when it came to dealing with the far right.

'So what do you think we should do, Donovan?' Marnie said. 'As if I didn't know.'

Donovan shook his head. 'Whatever you choose to do, I'm afraid I'll be out of the picture, at least for a while.'

'Why's that?'

'Yesterday I checked my answering machine at home. I had a message from the police.'

'Cathy Lamb rang your London number?'

'The locals don't have my number. This was from the police in Germany. They've found my Porsche.'

Anne was wide-eyed. 'In Offenbach?'

'No.' Donovan looked and sounded confused. 'Somewhere near Bonn.'

'I don't understand,' Anne said. 'Bonn isn't near Frankfurt, is it?'

Small wonder that Anne was confused. The last time she had seen Donovan's 1950s sports car it was sliding through snow down a steep bank in an industrial estate. That was in the town of Offenbach opposite Frankfurt. That night the car plunged into the river Main to disappear, she thought, forever.

Donovan said, 'No, it's more than a hundred miles from Frankfurt.'

'What does this mean?' Marnie asked.

'They want me to go and claim it.'

'But I thought you said it was -'

'I know, but now somehow it's turned up in a garage not far from Bonn.'

'How can that be?'

'Marnie, I have no idea.'

'Perhaps there's some mistake,' Anne said.

Donovan looked at her. 'Or perhaps it's a trap.'

'What do you mean?'

'After the car was … lost, I wrote to the police in Frankfurt to report it as missing. I explained that I lived in England. It's possible they think I was perpetrating some kind of insurance fraud.'

'Did you claim it on your insurance?'

'No. I notified the company that it was missing, but made it clear I didn't want to pursue a claim at that time.'

'Why not?'

'I told them I hoped I might get it back one day. But in fact I just wanted to let the matter drop. I wanted to put the whole business behind me. I figured that if it ever was fished out of the river, it would be in such a bad state that it wouldn't be identifiable.'

'But it has been identified,' said Marnie.

'Apparently. So now I have to claim it, and I have to do that in person.'

'Aren't you pleased about that?' Anne said. 'You inherited it from your father, after all.'

'The police are going to ask how much insurance money I received for it. Then they're going to want to know why I didn't actually claim it. Classic Porsches are quite valuable.'

'Awkward,' said Marnie.

'You could say that.'

****

70

While Donovan was packing his weekend bag, Marnie rang Angela who was keen to come to Glebe Farm straight away. Marnie wanted to deal with the witch business before reporting the graffiti to the police. That wish was shared by Angela, who arrived in record time.

Over the inevitable mugs of coffee Marnie, Anne and Angela got down to business.

'So you have a name for this witch?' Marnie began. It sounded like an improbable opening line.

Angela checked her notebook. 'Her name is ... Moya.'

Marnie sat upright in her chair. 'Moya? Like the famous architect? It's not a common name. I wonder if she's related.'

Angela looked blank. 'Architect?'

'A famous London firm after the war,' Anne explained. 'Powell and Moya.'

Frowning, Angela looked down at her notes. 'Er ...'

'You must at least remember the Skylon,' Marnie prompted. 'The Festival of Britain ... 1951?'

'Rather before my time,' Angela murmured. 'Ah yes, here it is.' She looked up at Marnie and grinned. 'Moya ... is her first name.'

'Oh.'

'Yes, she's called Moya Goodchild.'

Marnie chuckled. 'I think I got the wrong end of the stick there. I'm not sure if I'm not a little disappointed.'

'An easy mistake to make, Marnie. I could've made it clear by -'

'No, I mean the name, Moya. I thought a witch would be called something like Esmeralda.'

'Perhaps when she was born her mother didn't realise she'd become a ... Marnie, this is a ridiculous conversation.' Angela laughed.

'Or Hermione,' Anne added. 'Like the girl witch in the Harry Potter book.'

Marnie looked confused. 'The what book?'

'It's a story about children who are witches and wizards ... a new book, just out.'

Marnie raised both hands. 'Okay. Let's get focused. How do we get in touch with this Moya?'

'Send an e-mail?' Angela suggested. 'I've got her address here.'

'Or an owl,' said Anne.

71

Marnie and Angela looked at her blankly.

'Why an owl?' Marnie asked.

'Sorry,' said Anne. 'Long story. You'd have to read the book. It's quite good.'

'An e-mail, then. And who's going to send it?'

'Well,' Angela said tentatively. 'I thought it might be better coming from someone who wasn't in the church.'

Marnie sat back in her chair. 'Now who might that be, I wonder?'

Angela returned to reading her notes and said nothing. Anne broke the silence.

'Shall I draft a message for you to play around with, Marnie?'

Angela looked up with hope in her eyes. Marnie nodded. She knew she was beaten again. In the background Donovan was descending the wall ladder from the attic, the handles of his weekend bag looped over one shoulder.

Much brighter now, Angela said cheerfully, 'So, do you have exciting plans for the weekend?'

'Not exactly,' said Marnie.

'I'm going back to London,' Donovan said. 'But first we'll be scrubbing Nazi graffiti off the bridge by *Sally Ann*.'

'After we've informed the police,' Marnie insisted. 'I only hope DCI Bartlett isn't on duty at the weekend. That's all I'd need.'

'I've got Cathy Lamb's mobile number,' Angela said, flicking the pages of her notepad. 'She asked me to keep in touch with her direct about the witch.'

While the others looked on, Marnie rang the number and pressed the speakerphone button. Lamb answered promptly but said she was not working that weekend. She would call round on Monday morning after her syndicate's briefing meeting. In the meantime no one was to touch the graffiti or interfere with it in any way. Donovan groaned.

'Cathy, it's Donovan. Listen, we've got to get rid of the graffiti pronto. You can't just leave it up there. It's like an advert for New Force.'

'I'm telling you, Donovan, it has to stay until forensics can examine it. It could help us find who did this.'

'I think the letters *NF* are a bit of a clue there, Cathy. What more do you want, a signature?'

'The graffiti has to stay, at least for the time being. It's evidence.'

Donovan muttered something inaudible under his breath. Marnie resumed.

'We'll wait till Monday, Cathy. But I don't feel comfortable having the graffiti so close to home.'

'I'll get down to see you as soon as I can get away.'

'You do that.'

After disconnecting Marnie looked at Donovan's weekend bag. 'You're leaving straight away?'

Donovan nodded. 'I was going to deal with the graffiti like I did before, but now ...'

'Are you taking the boat back to London?' Marnie asked.

'I'd like to leave her here, if that's okay with you, Marnie. I'll leave you the keys in case you want to move her.'

'I'll take you to the station,' Anne offered.

'Great.'

'So you're planning to go to Germany alone?' Marnie said.

'I'm not sure what I'm planning,' Donovan said. 'I'll probably fly to Bonn and take it from there. I may have to see the police in Offenbach or Frankfurt, as that's where the car went missing. It all depends what action they decide to take.'

'You'll probably have a lot of running around to do between the various cities, I'd have thought,' Marnie said. 'Wouldn't it be easier to go by car?'

'Maybe.'

Marnie turned to look at Anne and then back at Donovan.

'Could you use a companion?'

Donovan hesitated. 'Probably best to go by myself in case there's trouble. A companion would be good.' He smiled across at Anne. 'But not if she's seen as an accomplice.'

Anne rummaged in her bag. 'I've got my car keys.'

Donovan stepped forward, kissed Marnie on the cheek, shook hands with Angela and went out. Anne held the door open and followed him. Marnie and Angela watched them pass by the window.

'All very mysterious,' Angela said.

'A long story.' Marnie sighed. 'Some other time, perhaps. Meanwhile, where do we go from here?'

'Well, you're going to contact Moya Goodchild, and I'll see if we can visit Stan Koslowski in hospital. Okay?'

'Did I agree to that?'

'I thought so.'

'Really?'

'Trust me, I'm a vicar. Another thing: I'm going to speak with Father Novak to make sure we're not treading on any toes. He might also be able to give me some background information on Stan and Katie and the Polish community in general.'

After Angela left, Marnie sat wondering how she had managed to get lumbered yet again.

****

Donovan was heaving his bag onto the back seat of Anne's Mini in the garage barn when they heard Angela start her car. Turning, they saw her drive out of the courtyard towards the field track.

'So you really don't want me to come with you?' Anne said. 'Marnie wouldn't mind.'

'Better if you don't. If the police get tricky, you could get implicated.'

'Huh!' Anne rolled her eyes. 'Me, the gangster's Moll. Who'd-a-thought it?'

'I'm serious.' Donovan was grinning. 'There could be trouble.'

'Okay. Did they tell you what happened to the car?'

Donovan shook his head. 'They're like the police here. They don't give much away.'

'You said you'd reported it as stolen.'

'I had to do that in case it was ever found.'

'Yet you didn't claim on insurance. Won't the police think it odd?'

'Probably. I'll have to convince them of my reason for that.'

'Is that what you've been talking about on the phone?' Anne asked. 'I've heard you speaking German.'

'No. Earlier I was ringing round friends and contacts about the far right, some here, others in Germany and Austria.'

'And?'

'There seems to be a concerted effort across Europe to make some sort of mark at Easter.'

'This *Easter parade* thing?'

'In Britain, yes. Apparently it's not just going to happen here, but Britain will play a key role. The neo-Nazis are banned in some countries, so they're looking to the UK as a kind of spearhead. The attacks on the Poles were only the start.'

'I'm thinking you're going to try to stop them, Donovan. Am I right?'

'Absolutely ... assuming I'm not in gaol in Germany on a fraud charge.'

'D'you really think that's possible?'

'Dunno. We'll have to wait and see.'

They climbed into the Mini and drove off.

****

Alone in the office, Marnie decided she would there and then write to the witch, without waiting for Anne to produce a draft message. She switched on the computer and collected her thoughts while it booted up. Just keep it simple, she thought. When the program opened, she began typing.

Dear ... (is that how you address a witch? Too chummy?)

Start again.

Hello Moya Goodchild (that seemed more promising - business-like and not too informal)

I've been given your name by Randall Hughes in Brackley. I understand you are willing to ... (to what exactly?)

Marnie sat back and wondered. Did Angela and Cathy want to talk about witchcraft in general? Why? What did they actually want to know? The police seemed to think witchcraft or witches had a link of some kind with the murder of Katie Koslowski and perhaps also the fire-bombing of the Polish shop. But how could that possibly be? Surely those incidents arose from the actions of the far right groups that were causing havoc across the county. There was so much that did not make sense.

Marnie got up from the desk and went to look out of the window. Across the cobbled yard she admired the simple architecture of the row of cottages that she had carefully restored over the past few years. They had originally had dark green doors - very Laura Ashley - but she soon found the colour too heavy and repainted them in a deep blue that seemed to her both smart and cheerful. She found her thoughts wandering to the shop in Little Warsaw. It too had once probably been someone's prized project. Now it had been violated, burnt out, its end wall defaced with hateful slogans.

Prejudice and hatred she could grasp, but where did witchcraft come into it? Marnie returned to her desk and began doodling on the blotter, puzzling over the witch connection. She

75

was still mulling it over when Anne walked into the office. Marnie shook herself mentally.

'Donovan get off all right?'

'No probs,' Anne said. 'It looks like rain.'

Marnie groaned. 'Bang goes our tootle on *Sally*. Are you disappointed about Donovan going to Germany by himself?'

'Not really. I think I'd only be in the way. What are you up to?'

'Writing to that witch.'

Anne laughed.

'What's funny?' Marnie asked.

'Don't you think it sounds funny, Marnie? It's not the sort of thing we do every day, set up a meeting with a witch.'

'Of course,' said Marnie. 'That's it. Keep it simple.' She looked back at the computer screen and returned to her text, reading it out loud as she typed.

I understand you are willing to meet to explain certain aspects of witchcraft, if that is the correct term. Would you like to phone me to fix a date? My number is ...

Marnie typed in her number and ended with *Best wishes, Marnie Walker.*

'Shouldn't that be *Best witches*?' Anne said, smiling.

Marnie gave her The Look. 'Go and put the kettle on.'

Anne turned and made for the kitchen area. 'I'll go and put the kettle on.'

****

What do you do on a gloomy Saturday afternoon in early spring when rain is falling steadily and you want to relax? Marnie's answer was to make herself comfortable in the farmhouse sitting room, reading a book, feet up on a sofa in front of a crackling fire in the wood-burner. She had borrowed the Harry Potter book from Anne in the hope of learning enough about witchcraft to prepare her for the meeting - if it ever came about - with Moya Goodchild. She soon became engrossed in the story, but quickly formed the opinion that the details about the world of witches and wizards said more about the author's imagination than the realities of present-day Wicca.

Ralph had opted to spend a little more time in his study on *Thyrsis* working on the *Celtic Tiger* book. He was grappling with questions relating to the possible impact on the Republic of greater stability in Northern Ireland following the Good Friday agreement. Such questions were meat and drink to Ralph. Anne meanwhile was sitting up on the bed in her attic room reading a biography of the potter and designer William De Morgan for her college course.

As was her custom, Marnie had brought over the laptop computer from the office. It stood on the coffee table beside her and served two purposes: it was close at hand if she needed to look up any subject of interest and enabled her to access any e-mails that might require her attention.

Marnie was just turning a page of the novel when she heard a distinctive double *ping!* announcing the arrival of an e-mail. She glanced down at the screen and was surprised to see the name Moya Goodchild in the message box. Marnie double-clicked on the box to bring up the message. It was short and to the point.

Hello

Yes, we can certainly meet. You decide where and when. Here if you like.

Blessings,

Moya

Marnie stood and went into the kitchen, taking the phone from its wall-mounting. She dialled a familiar number.

'Angela, it's me. Listen. I've had a reply from Moya. She's agreed to meet us.'

'Brilliant! That was quick. I did wonder if we'd hear from her at all.'

'She says we can go to her place. That might be interesting.'

'Where does she live?'

'Don't know. I'll have to find out. Can we compare diaries for next week?'

'I can tell you straight away that I have Tuesday or Wednesday morning free so far.'

'Okay, I'll offer those dates and get back to you.'

'Marnie, before you go, I have some news for you. Stan Koslowski can receive visitors at any time after the surgeons have done their morning rounds.'

Marnie hesitated. 'So when do you have in mind? Or do you want me to check with Moya first?'

It occurred to both of them that they were starting to refer to Moya as if she was a mutual friend.

'Well ...' Angela's turn to be hesitant. 'I was thinking about tomorrow some time.'

'Angela, tomorrow's Sunday. Isn't that the one day you go to work?'

'I'll ignore that remark,' Angela said primly. She chuckled. 'As it happens I don't have evensong this week, so I was wondering about an hour after lunchtime. What d'you think?'

'Okay, if you're driving ... unless you'll have been knocking back the communion wine.'

'Marnie, you're awful! All right, I'll drive.'

****

Across the courtyard Anne was pulling on a jumper in the attic when her mobile rang. The room was cooler than comfortable, and the increasing chill in the atmosphere was making it hard to concentrate on her book. She pushed her head through the neck of the jumper and struggled to get her arms down the sleeves as she reached for the phone. The screen on the mobile showed Donovan's number.

'Yo! What's up?' Anne said cheerfully.

'Sorry, I seem to have the wrong number. I thought I was phoning somewhere in England, but I'm guessing you must be in ... Alabama? Is that right? Or perhaps Mississippi?'

'Ha ... ha,' Anne said slowly. 'I was only trying to be perky. The day's miserable enough already.'

'Because I'm not there?'

'Because it's rainy, dull and cold, and I'm reading a book that matches the weather. It's trying unsuccessfully to enthuse me about XXXusterware and chemical glazes.'

'Bloody hell!'

'Exactly. So how are things at your end? Clue: it would help if you could say something positive to cheer me up.'

'Well, I've managed to book a flight for Monday. I phoned the police in Bonn, and they said I had to go to Bergheim.'

'Where's that?'

'Not far from Cologne, so I'm flying to Köln / Bonn airport and renting a car for a few days.'

'What's at this Bergheim place?'

'Police HQ for the county.'

'Too far to stay with your family, presumably?'

'Yes, they're about two hundred miles away. I'm going to book a room somewhere, but I thought I'd phone you first.'

'So you're missing me already.' Anne's tone was chirpy.

'Yes, I am.'

Donovan sounded serious. Anne found that strangely disturbing.

****

Marnie rang Angela back ten minutes after ending their first call. She had had a rapid exchange of e-mails with their newfound witch-friend and arranged to meet for coffee at Moya's cottage in the village of Grenton on Wednesday morning.

'She's given me her address,' Marnie said. 'Can't say I've ever heard of Grenton.'

'I know it,' said Angela. 'Pretty place in a scenic part of the county, the Northamptonshire Uplands, over towards Daventry.'

'Her house is called Lark's Cottage in Drover's Lane.'

'Won't be hard to find,' Angela observed. 'It's not a big village.'

They agreed on pick-up arrangements for the hospital visit the following afternoon and hung up. Feeling restless, Marnie went to the kitchen to make a cup of tea. While the kettle was boiling she wandered over to the window. Outside, the rain was falling relentlessly, untypical for Northamptonshire's normally dry climate. But then it was a strange season altogether.

Chapter 8

Marnie tentatively parted the bedroom curtain with one finger on Sunday morning and peered out over the sodden jungle that would one day soon become a charming country garden. At least, that was the plan. Sodden it certainly was, but the rain that had blighted the previous day had passed over. It had now given way to intermittent dapples of patchy sunshine and fleeting shadows of wispy cloud.

Plans for the day began forming in Marnie's mind as she padded to the bathroom, leaving Ralph still sleeping under the duvet. Reaching the bathroom door, she suddenly remembered her promise to Angela Hemingway to visit Stan Koslowski in hospital. She muttered a number of mild profanities to herself as she reached into the shower cubicle and turned on the turbojets.

****

Marnie made a surprising announcement over breakfast. In her opinion they were working too hard and needed a day of rest. Ralph muttered that it proved she had spent too long lately in the company of Angela Hemingway. On the other hand, he did not raise any serious objection and asked what she had in mind. Looking up from a bowl of weetabix, Anne joined in.

'The hot money's on a tootle on *Sally Ann*.'

'That's one possibility,' Marnie conceded.

'It's our usual possibility,' Ralph said. 'Unless for a change you felt like a walk in Knightly Woods?'

'Oh no,' Marnie said emphatically. 'I don't want to go anywhere near witches' circles. It's a quiet life for me.'

'A tootle it is, then?' said Anne.

Marnie was slotting bread into the toaster when she stopped, her hand resting on the handle at the side of the machine.

'One condition,' she said. 'We go south. I don't want to come back facing the graffiti on the bridge.'

'Mm ...' Ralph murmured.

Marnie looked suspicious. 'You're not about to announce that they've sprayed graffiti on this side, I hope.'

'Not exactly, but it did occur to me that it might be worth checking before we settle too firmly on a plan to tootle.'

'Will you check that out?'

Ralph nodded. 'I'll nip through the spinney after breakfast.'

'Didn't you notice when you went for your early morning walk, Ralph?' Anne asked.

'I went up the track and through the village today.'

'Oh?' Marnie said.

'Yes. I don't like seeing the graffiti any more than you do.'

****

Ralph's reconnaissance had revealed no further graffiti on the bridge and so, twenty minutes later, the Glebe Farm trio found themselves chugging along on *Sally Ann* in the direction of Cosgrove. One extra condition had been imposed for the trip by mutual consent: there was to be no talk of witches, neo-Nazis or murders.

With breakfast so soon behind them, for once they travelled without refreshments. They clustered together on the stern deck and took turns at steering. This section of the Grand Union was bordered by trees and meadows on both banks, the setting tranquil and rural. It felt remote, with only occasional views of livestock in the fields and no signs of habitation. Marnie and Ralph made occasional comments about the views, the running of the boat and the inevitable lugubrious heron hunched opportunistically on the bank. Anne on the other hand seemed far distant in her thoughts, as remote in her way as the landscape. With the rain clouds swept aside, the air was fragrant with damp vegetation.

Holding the tiller, Anne took in a long slow breath and exhaled audibly. 'Hundertwasser would love this,' she said.

'Hundertwasser,' Ralph repeated carefully. 'Sounds like one of Donovan's chums.'

'It's this Austrian bloke I've been reading about … artist and architect. I'd never heard of him before. He says his favourite time is after the rain when everything smells fresh and washed clean.'

Marnie and Ralph breathed in deeply.

'He certainly has a point,' Marnie said.

'He also has a boat,' Anne remarked. 'It's called *Regentag*, meaning rainy day.'

'Very apt,' said Ralph.

'Yes, I think he's sailed it all the way to New Zealand. He lives there now.'

Anne lapsed back into silence staring at the ribbon of water before them, glancing intermittently out across the fields.

'Anne?' said Marnie.

'Mm?'

'I'm sure Donovan will be okay. He's a coper. He is as the French say, *débrouillard.*'

'Oh yes, I know. He would say in German, *er setzt sich durch.* He gets through. That's certainly something I've learnt since knowing Donovan.'

'I'm sure you don't have to worry about him,' Ralph said.

'I wouldn't normally, but I just wonder if it's all a bit different this time.'

Ralph thought this time they were being assailed from all sides. But he kept that to himself.

For a few brief seconds Anne closed her eyes and inhaled, filling her lungs with the country air that was now warming as the sun poked through the high clouds. She became aware of an extra tang somewhere at the edge of her senses. Opening her eyes, she realised that Marnie had noticed it too. She had lifted her face and was turning her head like a predator in the wild scenting prey.

'Can you smell something, Ralph?' Marnie said.

'Yes. It's more reminiscent of autumn than spring. Someone burning leaves, perhaps?'

Marnie looked doubtful. 'Not as wholesome, somehow more ... acrid.'

Anne turned to scan the land around them, looking out for any trace of smoke rising.

'Steering, Anne!' Ralph called out.

Anne's head snapped round. They were approaching a long right-hand bend and she was wandering across the canal. She swung the tiller hard over to correct the drift and bring *Sally Ann* back on course. Keeping the boat right of centre, she began the turn, all thoughts of the burning smell temporarily banished.

Marnie and Ralph suddenly stiffened, stepping forward on the deck, straining to focus on something up ahead. Thinking that a boat was approaching from round the corner, Anne hastily reached down and pulled up the accelerator to slow the boat. Ralph shifted his gaze to look at Marnie. He stepped towards her and touched her face.

'What is it?' she said.

Ralph examined his finger tip. 'It's like soot. You've got some in your hair, too.'

'So have you, Ralph.'

By now the odour had become stronger. At the apex of the curve Anne saw the reason why. Fifty yards ahead of them a burnt-out narrowboat lay at its mooring on the towpath side to their left, plumes of smoke still rising from the hulk. The bows of the boat were facing them, and one of its lines had been cut or burnt away, so that the stern had drifted out from the bank. The blaze had scorched off much of the paintwork. No name was visible.

Anne stopped *Sally Ann* in mid-channel some way short of the other boat. It was a pitiful sight. At that moment they spotted movement on the bank. Two men in lycra cycling gear were standing with hands on hips, staring helplessly at the shell. Lying on the towpath behind them were two bicycles. Noticing the arrival of *Sally Ann*, one of the men walked swiftly along the path, cupped his hands round his mouth and called across the water.

'Do you have a mobile phone?'

'Yes,' Marnie replied. 'Have you seen any sign of life hereabouts?'

'No. We only got here a minute ago.' The import of Marnie's question suddenly struck home. The cyclist turned briefly towards the smouldering boat. '*Jeez*, you don't think ...'

Marnie was already pulling the mobile from her pocket. 'Anyone on the towpath?'

The cyclists conferred together and shook their heads.

Anne meanwhile pressed lightly on the accelerator and swung the tiller to point the tail at the bank. As soon as the boat began turning she pushed the gear lever into reverse.

'We're coming in to moor,' she shouted.

'How far are we from that pub by the road?' Marnie called out, pointing ahead.

The first cyclist looked back along the towpath and checked his watch, mentally calculating the distance. 'I reckon about a mile or so ... not much more.'

Marnie hit three nines and reported the incident to the emergency operator. By now, *Sally Ann* was nudging the bank at her stern, and gradually the hull swung into line at the edge of the towpath. Anne moved fluidly, deftly adjusting tiller, gear lever and accelerator to bring the boat closer to the charred remains, stopping ten yards short. Ralph stepped ashore with mooring hooks to make her fast. Anne joined him on the bank while Marnie was talking on the phone and walked along with him for a closer look. The air was rank with the sour stench left by the fire, and their eyes were smarting.

The cyclists seemed to be in a state of shock. As Anne and Ralph came nearer, they turned and bent to pick up their bikes. They began mounting them when Marnie came along.

'You can put those on our stern deck, if you want,' she said. 'Though I'm sure they'll be safe where they are.'

'Why? What happens now?' They seemed keen to be on their away. 'No need for us to hang around, is there … not now you're here?'

'We have to wait for someone to come,' Marnie said. 'The police will be on their way.'

The cyclists looked at each other, perplexed. The second one spoke.

'The police won't think we had anything to do with this, will they?'

'I very much doubt it,' said Ralph. 'This fire happened a while ago, probably in the early hours, at a guess.'

'How did it happen?' the cyclist said. 'I mean, do boats often catch fire?'

'No, they don't.'

'Come on board,' said Marnie. 'You don't want to get cold. Have a cup of tea while we're waiting.'

The cyclists dismounted and began wheeling their bikes towards *Sally Ann*. Anne had wandered away from the others and as Marnie was turning, Anne gestured to her and pointed at the wreck.

'What is it?' Marnie asked.

'Come and look.'

On the side of the hull six letters had been sprayed. Despite the fierceness and extreme heat of the blaze, they remained pale yet clearly visible: POLACK.

****

'So what happened then?' Angela Hemingway asked.

It was later that afternoon. She was sitting in Marnie's Freelander in the car park of Northampton General Hospital.

Marnie had not expected that they would be joined by DC Cathy Lamb who now occupied the rear seat. The discovery of a burnt-out narrowboat had resulted in a call to the detective to return to duty on her day off. She was less than ecstatic about that, but nonetheless keen to get to grips with this latest apparent arson attack.

'We waited for about twenty minutes,' Marnie said. 'I wondered how the emergency people would get there.'

'Motor-bike cop,' said Lamb.

'Correct,' said Marnie. 'I suppose that was the logical response.'

'Then what, Marnie?' said Angela.

'The usual. We each gave a statement. While we were doing that on *Sally Ann* the forensic team arrived. I think they'd walked along the towpath carrying their gear. The photographer got to work straight away, and the others cordoned off the bank. About a dozen uniforms then turned up and began a search of the area.'

'Presumably your statement covered the ground as you've just described it to us,' Lamb said.

Marnie shrugged. 'What more was there to say?'

'Any idea whose boat it was?' Angela asked.

'Not the foggiest.'

'Then I'm ahead of you there,' said Lamb. 'It seems it belonged to a ...' She flicked open her notebook. '... Nathaniel Jackson.'

'That doesn't sound very Polish.' Marnie's tone was sceptical.

'Perhaps he has a Polish wife,' Angela suggested. 'The target didn't necessarily have to be him.'

'I suppose not.' Marnie turned in her seat to look back at Cathy Lamb. 'Is there anything else, or shall we go in?'

****

They followed the signs to the Intensive Therapy Unit, and Marnie tried not to think of the time she herself had been a patient there. They arrived at a lobby at one end of the building. Each floor of this block was glazed from sill height upwards and half a dozen brightly-coloured chairs stood in a row under the windows. To their left were glazed double doors leading to a corridor at the end of which the passage turned left out of sight. There was an intercom on the wall by the doors. Marnie pressed the button and waited. A full minute passed before a metallic voice asked if it could help them.

'We've come to visit Mr Koslowski.'

Marnie held the handle of the nearest door, ready to pull it open when the buzzer sounded. But the buzzer did not sound. The voice asked them to wait. A few seconds later a nurse turned the corner and came towards them. She pressed a button on the wall and pushed open the door.

'Only two visitors are normally allowed,' she said. She was young and slightly built with a Scottish accent and a serious manner. Her auburn hair was tied back in a ponytail.

'I'll wait here,' Marnie said, pleased to have the opportunity to duck out. 'You two go ahead.'

The nurse made no move to let them in. 'I'm afraid you don't understand. Mr Koslowski already has some visitors.'

'We understood he never had any,' said Lamb. 'Do you know who they are?'

'Are any of you members of his family?' the nurse asked.

Lamb pulled out her warrant card and held it up. 'Detective Constable Cathy Lamb, CID.'

The nurse looked confused. 'The police have already seen Mr Koslowski. I really don't think he's well enough to face questioning.'

Angela stepped forward, fingering her dog collar. 'We're not here to question him. We just want to see if there's anything he needs, or anything we can do for him. You could regard this as a pastoral visit.'

If anything, the nurse looked even more confused. 'You're a vicar?'

'Well spotted.' Angela smiled sweetly.

'I didn't know ...' The nurse shook her head. 'Never mind. Look, if you'd like to wait I'll let the other visitors know you're here.'

Cathy Lamb touched the nurse's arm. 'I'd appreciate it if you didn't mention that I'm a police officer.'

The nurse nodded. 'And I'd appreciate it if you didn't try to interrogate him. He's very weak.'

'Deal,' said Lamb.

The nurse closed the door and walked back along the corridor. They took their seats.

Marnie looked at Angela. 'I thought you said –'

'I know, I know, Marnie. That's what I was told. He never had anyone to visit him.'

'That's why we came,' Marnie said. She looked at Lamb. 'Unless you have another reason for being here, Cathy.'

'I just hope that nurse doesn't let it slip that I'm with the police.'

'Then why have you come?' Angela asked.

'It's called using your initiative. I had orders to pitch in on this suspected arson case and I thought it worth checking the Polish connection.'

'So it is definitely arson, then?' Marnie said. 'That's official is it?'

Lamb hesitated. 'Okay, here's the situation. It seems the boat you found was taken from its mooring on the Buckingham Arm in the night.'

'Stolen?' said Angela. 'How could that be possible?'

'You can steal almost anything if you're determined enough. Anyway, that's what happened. The vandals sailed to the secluded spot where you found it, and the rest you know.'

Marnie wanted to correct Lamb and tell her that narrowboats aren't 'sailed', but she let it go.

'At least there were no victims this time,' she said.

'There's no such thing as a victimless crime, Marnie.'

'I meant no one was killed or injured.'

'That's some consolation,' Lamb agreed. 'Nevertheless, it's one more hate crime to add to the list, and in such circumstances you never know where it's all going to end.'

Angela tapped Lamb on the arm and nodded towards the doors. They all turned to see two men coming along the ITU corridor. One was middle-aged dressed in a dark suit, the other much younger, probably in his twenties, wearing the garb of a Catholic priest. They were deep in conversation, and the older man seemed distressed. The priest was doing his best to comfort him.

Angela spoke softly. 'That's Father Novak. I don't know the other man.'

'He looks upset,' Marnie said. 'Perhaps he's a relative.'

Lamb said quietly, 'I heard the Koslowskis didn't have any relatives either here or in Poland.'

They stood up as Father Novak pressed a button on the wall and the men came through the doors. Angela stepped forward and shook hands with the priest.

'Good to see you Pawel,' she said, pronouncing his name like *Parvel*. 'I didn't realise you'd be visiting today.'

'Angela, let me introduce Mr Gorski.' The priest spoke with a strong Polish accent.

'How do you do?' Angela said, shaking his hand. She turned and completed the introductions, using only first names.

'Are you related to Mr and Mrs Koslowski?' she asked.

'No. In fact, I don't think I've ever met them.'

Mr Gorski was a compact man of stocky build and seemed to be in his fifties. His English was fluent and unaccented. Marnie guessed he was a second generation Pole, probably born and brought up in Britain.

'You're obviously upset,' she said. 'Is he in a bad way?'

Gorski nodded. 'Barely conscious. It's tragic. This man was a hero in the war. Did you know that?'

'No. I don't think we know very much at all about him or his wife.'

'Kazimir is President of the Polish Club,' Father Novak explained, indicating Mr Gorski. 'We thought it was time for the community to do something for Mr Koslowski.'

'He and his wife kept very much to themselves,' said Gorski. 'But we felt we couldn't stand by and do nothing after what's happened.'

Lamb looked over their shoulders. 'Here comes the nurse.'

They turned and saw the nurse opening the door to the ITU. She smiled slightly.

'You can come in now, ladies.'

As before, Marnie offered to wait outside.

'It's okay,' said the nurse. 'You can all visit him, but I have to insist you don't stay for more than a few minutes.'

After much shaking of hands, the visitors split up. As the 'ladies' drew nearer to the unit, Marnie felt her insides tighten. In that place she had come close to losing her life and, although she had been unaware of her surroundings at the time, the very thought of the ITU sent a shiver down her spine. They turned the corner and discovered that only three bays of the unit were occupied. Stanislav Koslowski was in the furthest bed, and none

88

of them turned their heads to look at the other incumbents as they passed.

At the bedside the nurse leaned forward and spoke quietly. 'You have some more visitors today, Stan. They'll not stay long. Don't tire yourself.'

She turned to face them with a look that said it all. As the nurse walked away, Marnie made a gesture with her head to Angela. The vicar stepped forward and took a seat near Mr Koslowski's head.

'Hello, Mr Koslowski.' Her voice was a shade above a whisper. 'My name is Angela. I'm a sort of colleague of Father Novak. I hope you're feeling a little better today.'

Angela paused for a reaction. It was slow in coming. The patient looked drawn and grey, but that was not unexpected. Tubes were attached to his arms linked to drip bottles, one of which contained a clear liquid, the other was evidently a blood bag. Beyond his head a monitor registered his readings in jagged lines of varied colours. Mr Koslowski opened his eyes a fraction and turned his head slowly towards Angela. He spoke in a whisper. Angela's mouth turned down at the corners as she looked up at Marnie and Lamb. Marnie leaned forward.

'What did he say?' Marnie asked softly.

'It sounded like a name,' Angela said.

'Katie?' Marnie whispered in her ear.

Cathy Lamb reached for Marnie's arm. 'Be careful. He hasn't been told about his wife.'

'Really?'

Lamb shook her head. 'The medics said he was too weak to take it.' She glanced down at Mr Koslowski. 'He doesn't seem any stronger now.'

The old man spoke again. This time his voice was clearer. He was obviously using Polish, but they managed to catch one word: *Katya*. He repeated it two or three times. Angela moved her head closer to his.

'Mr Koslowski, I'm a friend of Father Novak.' She paused. There was no response. 'I'm Angela.'

'Angela?' he repeated quietly.

'Yes, that's right.'

'Not Katya.'

'No.' Angela looked round in desperation at Marnie. She mouthed, *What should I say?*

89

Marnie murmured, 'You can only play for time.'

Angela nodded briefly and turned back to the patient. 'Katya can't come yet. We're here to see if there's anything you need.'

The silence that followed lasted a whole minute. Lamb moved past Marnie and spoke softly to Angela.

'Ask if he knows who attacked him.'

Angela looked flummoxed. Marnie was shocked.

'You can't do that!' she said, her voice a hoarse undertone. 'He's in no fit state to answer questions.'

'We're here to try to help him,' Lamb insisted.

Marnie shook her head. 'Cathy ...'

Angela seemed completely nonplussed. She was spreading her hands palms up towards the others when Mr Koslowski tried to speak. None of them could understand what he said. Angela moved her head close to his.

'Can you repeat that, please, Mr Koslowski?' she said.

The old man's lips began moving. Angela leaned even closer to listen. Her expression became totally bewildered. Mr Koslowski straightened his head and closed his eyes, sighing deeply and wearily. Angela sat back.

'Did you catch what he said?' Marnie asked.

'Not really. It sounded like ... Aberdeen.'

'Aberdeen?' Lamb repeated. 'Are you sure?'

Angela shook her head. 'No, I'm not, but that's what I thought it was.'

The sound of footsteps heralded the arrival of the nurse.

'Time to go, ladies.'

The four women walked together out of the unit and along the corridor to the exit. Angela asked if there was anything they could bring for him. The nurse thought a little fruit might be a good idea and suggested a few bananas, rather than the customary grapes. When they reached the security doors Marnie stopped and turned to the nurse.

'Is he ... I mean, is he going to ... is he making any progress at all? He seems terribly weak.'

The nurse's reply made Marnie start in surprise.

'He's no worse than you were when you were brought here, Marnie.'

Marnie's eyes widened. She had to swallow before she could speak.

'You know I was here?' she stammered.

'I was on duty when you were admitted. Few people gave tuppence for your chances back then. But look at you now. Quite a transformation, I'd say. You look wonderful.'

Marnie's eyes moistened. She blinked several times, momentarily unable to speak.

'I'm sorry,' said the nurse. 'I didn't mean to upset you.'

'It's okay,' Marnie croaked. 'I'm afraid I have very few recollections from that time. It's all just a painful blur.'

'Of course. But, coming back to your question, we've got him more or less stabilised now, and with any luck he should improve from this point on.'

'Thank *God*,' said Angela.

'And the medical team,' Marnie added.

****

Angela and Cathy Lamb waited while Marnie paid for the parking ticket, and the three of them paused by the Freelander before climbing in. Marnie and Angela stared at Lamb. She grimaced.

'Look, it's my job, okay? It's what I have to do ... find who killed that poor old man's wife and nearly did for him.'

Marnie and Angela swapped glances.

'I'm sure you acted with the best of intentions, Cathy,' Angela said.

'Of course you did,' Marnie added. 'We know that. It's just that ... well, there's a time and a place, you know.'

'Sure I know, but I'm not so sure that Mr Koslowski has that much time. We sometimes have to make tough judgments, Marnie.'

'Okay. Point taken.'

They drove through Northampton, heading for the dual carriageway for Knightly St John. In the centre of town they stopped at traffic lights.

'My god,' Marnie murmured.

'What is it?' said Lamb from the back seat.

'Look at the place. Look around you. What do you see?'

Angela and Lamb did as Marnie asked. Their thoughts had been back in the hospital, but now they surveyed their surroundings. They were in a street of small shops, three of which had yellow paint sprayed on their front windows. One bore

91

the inscription: JEW. The other two were daubed with:
POLACK.

'My goodness,' Angela said, holding her face in both hands.

'Christ!' Lamb muttered.

'If Donovan was here now ...' Marnie began.

'What about him?' Lamb asked.

Marnie's instincts were alerted. She knew that in the past
Cathy Lamb had nurtured suspicions about Donovan's
involvement in violent action against New Force. At one time she
had even tried to have him arrested on suspicion of having
assassinated a leading politician of the far right.

Marnie continued. 'He'd be telling us how important it was to
get rid of graffiti immediately. You can't leave the place looking
like this, Cathy.'

'For once I'd have to agree with Donovan,' Lamb said.

Marnie added, 'He'd also be reminding us that this is what
parts of Germany looked like in Hitler's time.'

'He'd certainly have a point,' Angela said.

The lights changed to green, and they moved off.

****

Back at Glebe Farm Lamb declined Marnie's offer of tea. She
pleaded that she had to submit a report on the hospital visit and
reminded her companions that this was supposed to be her day
off. Lamb went straight to her car and drove up the field track.
Angela, on the other hand, had never been known to turn down
an invitation.

Ralph and Anne joined them in the kitchen, where Angela
made the pleasing discovery that Anne had made a cake.

'That looks wonderful,' Angela said.

'I had a sneaking suspicion that you might be coming in for
tea or coffee,' Anne said. 'No Cathy Lamb?'

'Cried off,' said Marnie. 'People to see; things to do.'

'It's her loss,' Angela observed. 'What sort of cake is it, Anne?'

'The recipe calls it a rhubarb and custard cake.'

'Scrummy!. Rhubarb is one of my –' Angela broke off as her
mobile began ringing. 'Oh, sorry. D'you mind if I ...?'

She pressed the green button and announced herself. 'Oh,
hello Pawel.' She made an apologetic gesture and stepped out to
the hall, closing the door behind her. 'What can I do for you?'

'Would you mind if Kazimir Gorski came to the next meeting of your committee on Tuesday? I hope you don't think it is cheeky of me to ask you that.'

'Not at all. I'm sure his views would be very helpful. Will you invite him, then? No need for a formal invitation.'

'Thank you, Angela. What did you think of Mr Koslowski today?'

'Poor soul. He looked washed out. I'm not surprised they haven't told him about his wife.'

'That will fall very hard on him,' Father Novak said.

'To be honest, Pawel, I thought he looked just about ready for the sacrament. I'm sorry to say that, but you know what I mean.'

'Angela, he looked even worse when they brought him to the hospital. He is more stable now, thank God. I should tell you I administered the last rites on my first visit. Everything since then is ... how do you say? ... borrowed time?

When Angela returned to the kitchen, Marnie was bringing Ralph and Anne up to speed on the hospital visit.

Ralph was saying, 'So you didn't actually get anything out of him?'

'Hardly a word,' said Marnie. 'At least nothing we could understand. He did attempt to speak to Angela.'

'What did he say to you?' Ralph said.

'Well it was odd, really.'

'Tell him,' Marnie urged.

'I thought he said ... Aberdeen.'

They all looked baffled.

Anne said, 'Perhaps he was trying to tell you something ... well, I mean, obviously he was, but perhaps it was a clue about the people who'd attacked him and his wife.'

'They might have been from Scotland, you mean?' Ralph sounded unconvinced.

'Well, it must've meant something.' Anne began cutting the cake.

Marnie examined the tea pot. 'This looks okay to me. Are you ready for tea, Angela?'

'I'm always ready for your tea, Marnie.'

'How did you get on with Father Wotsit? Or perhaps I shouldn't ask.'

'It was just some committee stuff. He wants that chap who was with him this afternoon to come to the next meeting.'

'Good idea.'

'Oh, and there was something else of interest.'

Anne was serving slices of cake onto plates, which Ralph handed round. Angela took her seat at the table.

'What was that?' said Marnie.

'It's about that boat, the burnt-out one you found this morning.'

Suddenly all focus on the cake was diverted as the Glebe Farm residents stared at Angela.

'It seems that the couple who owned it – Mr and Mrs Jackson – are in fact Polish in origin.'

'We more or less knew that,' Ralph said. 'That's why their boat was taken from its mooring. The vandals singled it out for arson.'

'There's something else,' said Angela. 'Mr and Mrs Jackson are Jewish.'

'Father Novak presumably knows them through the Polish connection,' Ralph said.

'Yes. They often go to the Polish Club, which isn't exclusively Catholic. All the Poles like to stick together.'

Ralph said, 'A chance to use their language and talk about matters of common interest, no doubt. I wonder what the Jackson's name was originally.'

'I know that,' said Angela. 'Pawel said they used to be called Jakobovits. They changed it to blend in happily with the local populace.'

'Not much luck there, then,' Marnie said.

Chapter 9

Donovan's Ryanair flight brought him into Köln-Bonn airport mid-morning on Monday. After collecting his baggage he found the Eurauto car hire desk and was soon filtering out onto the local Autobahn system in a red VW Polo. He took the southern ring road round Cologne and followed it westwards away from the city. Twenty minutes later he turned north at the *Kerpen Kreuz* interchange and took the A61, direction Bergheim.

He had booked into a mid-range hotel on the outskirts of town. It turned out to be a pleasant surprise. The *Hotel am Stern* looked like a modern box from the outside, but had a private car park and was clean and bright. The staff were friendly in the formal German style to which he was well accustomed. The receptionist told him his room would not be ready until 3.00 p.m., but he was welcome to leave his bags in the secure luggage store. He accepted the offer to use their rest room facilities, after which he was back on the road. Beside him on the passenger seat lay a copy of a map that he had copied from the Internet. Bergheim was a small town. The police HQ was not hard to find.

Like the hotel, the *Polizeiwache* had a large car park, part of which was open to the public. Like the hotel it looked modern and characterless, but it did not offer the same welcome. Donovan approached the entrance carrying his folder of papers. The first surprise came when he tried the handle. The door was locked. Odd. If this was the HQ of the county police it could surely not be closed on a weekday morning.

He was twisting the door handle for a second time when he noticed a bell-push. He gave it a try. A minute passed during which Donovan scanned the car park for signs of life. In a reserved section there were four cars in the distinctive white and green police livery. Suddenly the door opened behind him. He spun round and was confronted by a woman in police uniform. She was blonde and well built, with three blue stars on her epaulettes. He did not recognise the rank, but it looked impressive. Her expression was stern.

'How can I help you?' she asked. Her tone was not encouraging.

'My car was stolen and has been found near here. The police in Bonn said I should report to this office to claim it.'

'What sort of car?'

'A Porsche 356, 1955 model, black.'

The officer raised an eyebrow and studied him for several seconds. 'A Porsche, you say.'

'Yes. I assumed you'd know all about it.'

She held out a hand. 'ID, please.'

Donovan pulled his British passport out of the back pocket of his jeans and handed it over. The officer looked at it and frowned before taking it from him.

'This is your ID?'

'Yes.'

'It's a British passport.'

Donovan nodded. 'I know.'

'You speak amazingly good German for a Brit.'

'Thank you.'

'In fact, you could be taken for a German.'

Donovan said nothing. The officer examined the passport, studied the photograph and looked carefully at Donovan's face. Eventually she spoke again.

'Nikolaus. That's a German name.'

'My late mother was German, but I was born in England, and that's where I live.'

Without returning the passport, the police officer stepped back and held the door wide. She led Donovan down a short corridor and stopped at a door bearing the nameplate: *H-J Schröder / Polizeihauptkommissar*. She knocked twice and entered. Donovan held back, waiting to be invited further. After a few brief exchanges, the woman officer pushed the door open and gestured to Donovan.

The office in which he found himself was large and contained two desks. Facing him, behind one of these was a burly man in shirtsleeves. The flashes on his shoulders bore three silver stars. But that was not what surprised Donovan the most. The *Polizeihauptkommissar* was the image of the film actor Rod Steiger. Donovan tried not to stare.

'Good morning, *Herr Hauptkommissar*,' he said.

Schröder remained seated, his expression serious. 'You know my rank.'

'It's on the nameplate on the door.'

'Have you had dealings with the police before?' Schröder asked.

'Well, yes of course, when I reported the car as stolen.'

'Otherwise?'

'Never in Germany.'

'What does that mean?'

'I was taken into care by the police in South Africa when we were involved in a road accident. My parents both died there.'

Schröder frowned. 'When was that?'

'About twelve years ago.'

'You were just a child.'

'I was ten years old.' Donovan quickly changed the subject. 'Herr Schröder, may I ask about my car?'

'What do you want to know?'

'I have many questions. For example, do you have it here? How was it found? Where? Who found it? What is its condition?'

Schröder raised a hand. 'Yes, yes. Okay. We also have many questions. In fact we need a statement from you.'

Donovan nodded curtly. 'Of course.'

Schröder gestured towards the other desk in the far corner where an equally burly officer was sitting at a computer. 'My colleague will take your details in the interview room. Go with him now, please.'

The other man rose from his seat and gestured towards the door. Donovan turned and discovered that the woman officer had left. At the end of the corridor, Herr Schröder's colleague ushered him into a small windowless room, invited him to sit at a grey metal table and left without another word.

To Donovan it felt like being under arrest.

Chapter 10

By Tuesday morning Anne was wondering why she had heard nothing from Donovan. It was unlike him not to phone while he was away. It was unlike her to lack the concentration to study for her college course. Aware that her eyes kept straying to the phone on her desk, she was assailed by self-contemptuous thoughts. A girl sits by the phone waiting for her boyfriend to ring: how pathetic is that? But these were strange times, and Donovan could be in a fix.

Marnie had picked up on Anne's mood and came over to stand by her before leaving for the committee meeting.

'Angela will be here in a minute. Are you okay to look after things in the office for the rest of the morning?'

'Sure. No probs.'

'Remember Ralph has a meeting in Cambridge, so it's you and Dolly running the show. I know Walker and Co will be in safe hands.'

'Paws,' Anne corrected her.

Marnie smiled. 'Quite.' She cocked her head to one side. 'I think that's her now.'

'Is Angela all right?' Anne asked. 'She seems a bit stressed these days.'

'Aren't we all? Between you and me, I don't think she's a natural born leader. Having to chair this committee while all this far-right stuff is going on is weighing heavily on her.'

'That's why she's glad to have your support, Marnie.'

'Talking of which, I'd better get going. See you later. Don't let the power go to your head.' In the doorway Marnie paused and looked back. 'Give Donovan my love when he rings.'

Anne was about to speak, but thought better of it. She nodded.

****

There were several new members of the committee, and introductions were made in the entrance hall at the community centre. In the crowded space Marnie recognised Father Novak speaking with Mr Gorski who in turn was shaking hands with colleagues. Marnie was about to remark to Angela on the increased size of the group when she suddenly froze. Angela noticed the abrupt change.

'What is it, Marnie? Are you all right?'

'Over there.' Marnie indicated with her head. 'Next to Mr Gorski. It looks like –'

Just then the person in question turned round.

'It looks like who, Marnie?'

Marnie shook her head. 'No, my mistake. But for a moment I thought it was Donovan.'

Angela followed her gaze. 'Oh yes. I see what you mean; roughly the same height and build, same blonde hair, dressed in black. Obviously not him, but they could be brothers.'

'Any idea who he is?' Marnie asked.

'No, but I think we're about to find out.'

Father Novak had caught their eye and was weaving his way through the throng with Mr Gorski and the Donovan lookalike in tow. On reaching them he half turned towards the two.

'Angela, you know Mr Gorski.'

'Of course. Nice to see you again. And you know Marnie.'

Gorski smiled and they shook hands. He reached towards the younger man and took him by the arm.

'Allow me to introduce my youngest son. This is Dominik, though he prefers to be called Dom these days.'

While shaking hands, Marnie examined the young man without making it obvious. Her initial assessment was substantiated. He was about the same age as Donovan and in almost every respect resembled him, even down to the style of clothes. Angela glanced briefly at Marnie, indicating that she shared her opinion. The group began to make their way into the meeting room.

As before, Angela had asked Marnie to sit on her right at the table. At the previous meeting Angela had taken the seat at the head of the table, while the archdeacon had installed himself at the opposite end. Marnie guessed he regarded himself as sitting at the true head of the table. On the drive into town Marnie had persuaded Angela to adopt a different layout. She should sit in the centre of the long side, rather like a prime minister chairing meetings of the cabinet in Downing Street. The archdeacon, following his normal custom, had taken his habitual place and thus found himself on the periphery. He had recognised this as a shrewd move by Angela and viewed her with new, if grudging, respect.

Among the new members attending, two represented the West Indian Parents Group, and two others came on behalf of the Sikh community. Kazimir Gorski and his son took their places beside Father Novak.

Most of the meeting was taken up by reports of outrages committed by New Force and their cohorts, mainly consisting of widespread racist graffiti and smashed shop windows. Thankfully there had been no further fire bombings. Sergeant Pamela Groves gave a detailed report of all the crimes perpetrated over the past few weeks, which brought groans of anxiety from everyone present. Angela looked close to despair.

Knowing that some degree of leadership was required, Marnie passed a note sideways to Angela. It read simply: *Counter measures? Easter Parade?* To Marnie's surprise and consternation, Angela immediately called on her to speak.

'We now have to decide what measures need to be taken to counter the activities of New Force. Marnie, would you like to begin?'

Marnie swallowed and tried not to look flustered.

'Thank you, Angela. No doubt each member of the committee will have given this some thought.' Marnie knew she was desperately playing for time, but suddenly had a light bulb moment. 'I'd like to kick off by proposing that we recommend the local council to instigate a plan to remove all graffiti with immediate effect. The town is fast beginning to look like Berlin in the –'

Sergeant Groves raised her hand. Marnie stopped and turned to look at Angela, who returned her gaze. Marnie gave the slightest nod.

'Oh, er, Sergeant Groves … you wish to speak?' said Angela.

'I need to remind everyone that we're talking about evidence here,' Groves began. 'Our forensic people –'

Dominik Gorski intervened.

'I'm sorry, sergeant, but that's irrelevant.' He spoke firmly. 'The fact is, we don't need to wait for forensic results to know who sprayed the graffiti. By leaving them in place, we're playing into the hands of the fascists. I'm sure we all hear what you say, but the Polish community believes this committee has its own priorities and responsibilities. I think the chairman should rule on this.'

Angela tried hard not to look confused. Marnie thought it could almost be Donovan speaking.

Dominik continued, 'She should ask for a vote on whether we urge the borough council to take *immediate* action.'

Angela hesitated. Marnie leaned slightly in Angela's direction and murmured, 'Now.'

'Er, thank you, Mr Gorski … Dominik. Can we have a show of hands on that suggestion?'

Every member but two at once raised a hand to the accompaniment of mutterings of agreement. Angela looked round the table. As she did so, the archdeacon slowly raised one finger, while looking down at his notes.

'Thank you,' Angela said. 'Against?'

No response.

'Abstentions?'

Sergeant Groves raised a hand, adding, 'I don't really have a choice, I'm afraid.'

'Understood,' said Angela. 'I'll write to the leader of the council today.' She looked at the agenda, but it offered no help. The only items were reports on problems.

Marnie discreetly tapped her earlier note with one finger.

'Ah, yes … the so-called Easter Parade.'

'We should have it banned by the police.' The archdeacon had spoken. His words were clipped; his tone brooked no argument.

Angela turned towards Sergeant Groves and raised an eyebrow.

'Well, chairman –'

'The correct title is *chair*.' Another peremptory pronouncement from the archdeacon.

'Through which all comments should be addressed, I believe,' Angela said. 'Please go on, sergeant.'

A *harrumph* was heard from the archdeacon.

'We don't really have adequate grounds to ban an Easter Parade as such. There's no tradition of such activities in this country, but they're certainly not illegal.'

This time a derisory snort emanated from the far end of the table.

'You wish to comment, archdeacon?' Angela asked.

'We know perfectly well that this may be a parade, but it certainly has nothing to do with the Christian festival of Easter and all that it represents.'

101

'In terms of love for one's fellow man ... or woman?' Angela said.

'Exactly.' The archdeacon seemed oblivious to the irony in Angela's remark.

Angela turned her head towards Sergeant Groves. 'Pamela?'

The sergeant made a non-committal gesture. 'There will obviously be a considerable police presence on the day, but an outright ban is simply not an option.'

Dom Gorski piped up. 'Then how can we oppose it ...' He noticed Sergeant Groves stiffen. '... without breaking the law, of course?'

Angela hesitated. Marnie exposed the watch on her left wrist and slid her hand forward on the table. Angela took the hint.

'Ladies and gentlemen, I think that's all we have time for this morning. Let's consider Mr Gorski's – Dominik's – question at our meeting next week. That will be our main subject, plus reports of any further actions by New Force and their ilk.'

The archdeacon was heard to clear his throat.

'I declare the meeting closed,' Angela said decisively.

****

On the drive back to Knightly St John, neither Marnie nor Angela said much until they cleared the town traffic. Their spirits were still dampened by the sight of the neo-Nazi graffiti visible throughout the town centre. They were heading towards the western ring road when Marnie spoke.

'You did a good job back there, Angela.'

'You mean driving through Northampton?'

Marnie grinned. 'You know perfectly well what I meant. You chaired the meeting really well.'

'If I did, it was thanks to your promptings.'

'Not a bit. I think you're enjoying being chairman and taking on the archdeacon.'

'The correct title is *chair*.' Angela mimicked the archdeacon's tone as well as his words.

'I've never felt comfortable with that,' Marnie said.

'And you a feminist?' Angela said in mock horror.

'I've never felt comfortable with labels, either, to be honest. I just like to be able to get on and do my own thing. In my field that's not a problem. I can see it can be in yours, Angela.'

'I'm not sure I like being regarded as a *chair*.'

'I can see why your chum the archdeacon likes to think of you in that way,' Marnie said.

'Why?'

'He likes to think you'll bear the imprint of the last person to have sat on you, and he'd want to be that person, no doubt.'

Angela laughed. 'You are awful, Marnie! Still, I can hardly complain. It's you I have to thank for getting me through that meeting.'

'Aided and abetted by Gorski the younger,' Marnie added. 'He's not a shy retiring little flower, is he? Did you know he was coming?'

'No. Did you think he sounded like Donovan as well as looking like him?'

'Absolutely, though he's not as nice looking as Donovan. His features are heavier. But he certainly has very strong views on how to combat the far right, just like Donovan.'

'Good for him,' said Angela. 'Come to think of it, I haven't seen him much lately. Where is Donovan?'

****

Where is Donovan? Anne muttered to herself. She had practically worn the handset thin by staring at it for much of the morning. She had even taken it with her when she went to the loo for fear of missing a call. But there had been no call. By one o'clock, with Marnie surely due back for lunch at any minute, she had a brainwave.

As usual, Donovan had left a copy of his itinerary with her. It included the details of his flights plus the address of the police station in Bergheim. It also included the name and address of his hotel. She ran a finger down the page and stopped at the entry for the *Hotel am Stern, Königsdorferstraße, Bergheim.* Yes! There was a phone number.

Anne had been secretly learning German from a course comprising a book and audio-cassettes. She was keen to strike the right balance, taking an interest in Donovan's life and background, without seeming to take too much of their relationship for granted.

After a deep breath, she pressed buttons on the phone and had a response after two rings. The voice on the other end of the line was that of a young woman, brisk and efficient.

'*Hotel am Stern, Fräulein Walther, guten Tag.*'

Anne replied carefully in German in her best accent. 'Good afternoon, I'd like to speak to Herr Donovan Smith, please.'

The young woman changed immediately to English. 'He's not in the hotel at the moment.'

Anne sagged. So much for her pronunciation. 'Do you know when he's returning?'

'I'm sorry, no. He has booked a room for tonight. More I cannot tell you.'

'Can I leave him a message, please?'

'Of course.'

'Please ask him to phone Anne.'

'Is that Anne with an 'e'?'

'Yes, Anne with an 'e'. He has my number. Thank you.'

'You're welcome.'

They disconnected. Anne with an 'e', she thought. Yes, that's me.

****

Donovan sat back in the chair and put down his pen. He had kept the statement as brief as possible. Now he re-read it and decided it was okay. They must have been observing him, because as soon as he finished writing, the police officer entered the room. He picked up the paper and asked Donovan to follow him.

The *Hauptkommissar* – dead ringer for Rod Steiger – took the statement and read it, gesturing Donovan to sit. He read it twice before setting it down on the desk. He looked up.

'You write excellent German.'

Donovan said nothing.

'Are you in fact German?' Herr Schröder persisted.

'I have a British passport but, as I told your colleague, my mother was German.'

'You still have family in Germany?'

'In Göttingen.'

'You have business colleagues here?'

'I'm a university student. I have no business colleagues.'

'The Porsche was your car?'

'*Was* my car? I thought it had been found.'

'Classic cars are expensive, and you say you are just a student.'

'It belonged to my father. I inherited it.'

104

'And it was insured for quite a lot of money.'

'Insurance is required by law.'

'For how much?'

Donovan shrugged. 'For its whole value at the time of loss or destruction. I have a special classic car policy.'

'And how much did it pay out?'

'I haven't claimed anything.'

The *Hauptkommissar* sat forward in the chair. 'Why not?'

'I informed the insurance company that it had been stolen, but I told them I didn't want to make a claim immediately. I hoped it might be found.'

'You're an optimist, Herr Smith.'

'It seems I was right to be optimistic. The police here in Germany have done an excellent job. I'm very grateful.'

Herr Schröder narrowed his eyes. He looked back down at the statement.

'You say here you were at a meeting in Offenbach and when you left the meeting the car was stolen. Why were you not in the car?'

'I've explained in the statement. I stopped ... to take a leak. While I was behind a tree someone drove it away. Stupidly, I'd left the key in the ignition.'

'You didn't see them?'

'I was behind a large tree.'

'The car was found in the river Main.'

Donovan sat bolt upright. 'So it's ruined?'

'Nearby another car was destroyed in a fire. Two occupants were killed. Can you tell me anything about that?'

'You suspect joy riders, *Herr Hauptkommissar*?'

This time it was the police officer's turn to say nothing. He sat back in the chair, looking speculatively at Donovan.

'Herr Schröder, may I ask you a question?'

Schröder nodded.

'If the car was in the river, how was it found? By whom? What condition is it in?'

'That makes three questions.'

'Yes. I'm naturally curious about it. That Porsche was – is – very dear to me.'

Schröder continued staring at Donovan for some time, the tips of his fingers pressed together. Suddenly he stood up and went to look out of the window. He spoke without turning round.

'A few weeks ago we received information about a car theft ring. This led to a raid on premises where we suspected a gang was doing up stolen cars. Among others we found the Porsche. It had no number plate, but when we checked the list of missing vehicles, we found that the engine and chassis numbers matched the records for your car.'

'Is it ...?'

'The car was not submerged for long. It seems that a man working on a dredger saw the other car explode in flames. That is what caught his attention. He saw also the black Porsche go into the river. He quickly arranged for your car to be brought up. There is a procedure for such things.'

'You haven't mentioned its condition,' Donovan said.

'The car came into the possession of a certain gang who have spent much time and effort preparing it to sell. Therefore both you and your insurance company are in luck, Herr Smith.'

'And may I see the car?'

Herr Schröder raised a finger. 'Not so fast. I have more questions.' He resumed his seat, stared at Donovan again and continued. 'In his statement the man from the dredger said he saw a person come out from behind a tree and walk quickly away. That seems to be in line with your story.'

'My factual account,' said Donovan.

'You didn't report the incident involving the car that burnt out. Interestingly, you don't mention that at all in your *factual account.*'

'I had no means of reporting it. My mobile phone was in the Porsche. I set off on foot through the industrial estate, which was deserted and soon heard emergency vehicles going to the scene. There was nothing I could do to help.'

'You didn't stop to try to assist the men in the burning car?'

'It was an inferno. The whole situation was very scary ... it was obviously a dangerous place. Frankly, I just wanted to get away from there.'

'Were you alone, Herr Smith?'

Donovan's instincts screamed *caution!* 'I had a girl with me. I'd picked her up earlier.'

'What was her name?'

'She said it was Anna.'

'What did you do after your car was stolen?'

'We went into town and spent the night together in a hotel.'

106

'Which one?'

Donovan shrugged. 'I've no recollection of its name. It was quite some while ago.'

'Then?'

'We parted the next day.'

The *Hauptkommissar* looked at his watch. He had spent long enough on this matter. The young man had technically committed no crime, unless he had lied about the insurance claim. That could be checked.

'I have another question, Herr Schmidt ... sorry, Smith. You said you had no business colleagues and yet you were at a meeting in Offenbach. Can you explain that?'

'I was meeting someone in connection with a research project.'

'For the university?'

'No. It was a private enquiry.'

'With whom did you have this meeting?'

'I would like to respect that person's identity.'

'Why?'

Donovan hesitated. 'She was the daughter of an officer in the *Abwehr* in the war, Hitler's intelligence service. I promised I would never reveal who she was. You will understand that that would be a sensitive matter for anyone. Of course, if you insist, I will give you her full name and contact details, but this has nothing to do with my stolen car.'

Schröder frowned. He had to concede Donovan's point. It would not sit well in his report to have insisted on knowing this woman's identity with no justification. He stood up.

'Please return here tomorrow. There may be papers to sign.'

'Papers ... in addition to my statement?'

'This is Germany,' Schröder said with a shrug. 'There are always papers.'

Donovan permitted himself a smile. 'Of course.'

'Then we can release your car, after which you will be able to make arrangements for its transportation.'

'At what time should I return?'

'Shall we say ten o'clock?'

'Thank you, *Herr Hauptkommissar*. Thank you for everything.'

Donovan offered his hand. Herr Schröder shook it and asked his colleague to escort Donovan from the building. When the officer returned he found Schröder watching Donovan drive out of the car park.

'A self-confident young man,' the officer said. 'He called your bluff about his meeting.'

'Yes. He was also cautious never to say too much. He obviously knows more than he says, but there's a limit to how much time we can spend on a stolen car case. Get in touch with the insurers. My guess is that he told the truth about not making a claim. He knew that would be easy to check.'

'You think his story stacks up, *Herr Hauptkommissar*?'

'Most of it … as much as we'll ever know.'

****

When Donovan returned to the hotel that afternoon the receptionist handed him a message slip with his key: 'Please phone Anne'. He decided to call during the evening.

Anne was in her attic room reading when her mobile rang. She snatched it up from the floor beside the giant beanbag.

'Hi. How's it going? Have you seen the car?'

'It's not as simple as that, Anne. There are forms to fill in, statements to sign, la-de-da. I think Germany invented bureaucracy.'

'Are they playing for time, d'you think?'

'The police are playing for something. I'm sure they suspect something's odd, not quite right. Look at it from their point of view. Here I am, a student with a Porsche that goes missing. I don't claim it on insurance. It must seem weird.'

'What can they do about it?'

'Dunno. I'll just have to play it by ear and see what comes up.'

'What d'you think will happen, Donovan?'

He hesitated. 'Well, on the face of it, I haven't actually committed a crime. I've given a plausible reason why I didn't claim on the insurance, and there's no evidence to prove I did anything wrong.'

'Then why do you sound so uncertain?'

'They could start probing into the Mercedes aspect, you know, the car that crashed and exploded. Technically I should have reported it, but I had no way of doing that. I don't think the police can really connect me with that incident.'

'So when will you get your car back?'

'Good question. I think it's evidence at the moment.'

'Against the people who stole it?'

'That's my impression.'

'Then why did they want you to go over if they're not ready to hand it back?'

'I think they may have wanted to check me out and –' Just then the phone on the bedside table began ringing. 'I'd better get that, Anne. Look, I'll ring you tomorrow when I have more news.'

After disconnecting he let the phone ring three more times before picking it up.

'Yes?'

'Sorry to disturb you, Herr Smith, but there is someone here who wishes to speak to you.'

'Who is it?'

'A police officer. Shall I send her up to your room?'

Donovan needed to buy time to collect his thoughts and prepare himself.

'Er, no. That isn't convenient at the moment. You're sure she is a police officer?'

'Oh yes. She's in uniform.'

'Is the hotel bar open?'

'Until ten o'clock.'

'Give me five minutes. Please say I'll meet her there.'

Donovan went to the window which looked out over the car park. Sure enough, an Opel in the white and green police livery was clearly visible, occupying a slot near the entrance. A visit from the police at this time of the evening. This was unexpected. What could it mean? They weren't going to arrest him, that much was clear, not with a solitary woman officer. Nor would they ask politely at reception. An idea formed in his mind.

He hurried to the bathroom and turned on the shower. While the water warmed up he took off his shoes and socks and put on slippers. Pulling off his jumper and shirt he leaned into the shower cubicle, just enough to wet his head. A rapid application of shampoo was quickly rinsed off and rubbed slightly dry. Four minutes and counting. From his sponge bag he took out a 4711 deodorant spray and gave himself a quick blast under the armpits. He pulled the shirt back on and tucked it into his jeans, carefully leaving part of the tail hanging out. While walking down the stairs he used both hands to bring a slapdash order to his hair. He smiled at the receptionist on his way to the bar.

The police officer was not the woman with the three blue stars that he had seen earlier in the day. Judging by her uniform, this was a highways cop. She stood as Donovan entered the bar. Taller than him – he guessed she was not far short of six feet – she had blonde hair tied back in a pony tail and wore a dark green leather bomber jacket with police insignia. A peaked cap lay on the table beside her. He noticed a document case under her left arm.

Donovan offered his hand. 'Donovan Smith. Sorry to keep you waiting.' He indicated his damp hair. 'I wasn't expecting a visitor.'

He hoped he looked and smelled as if he had just emerged from the shower. The policewoman nodded.

She shook his hand. 'Maria Klepp.' She was not smiling, but her gaze was not hostile.

Donovan gestured at the chairs. 'Shall we sit? What can I do for you, Frau Klepp? May I offer you something?'

She sat down. 'Thank you, no.'

Donovan took the chair opposite and waited.

'You had an appointment with Herr Schröder tomorrow morning.'

'Yes, at ten o'clock.'

'That will not now be necessary. There are no more formalities until you take possession of your car.' She opened the document case and removed two sheets of paper. 'Here is your handwritten statement and a typed copy. Please read them both, assure yourself that they are the same text and sign the two pages.'

Donovan did as requested and found the statements identical. He signed and dated both versions, printed his name in full, and handed them back to Officer Klepp. She slid them into the case and zipped it up.

'And when will I be able to take possession of my car?'

'That I cannot say at the moment.'

'Do you know why our meeting is not taking place?'

'Yes, I believe we have spoken with the insurance firm, and they have confirmed what you told the *Hauptkommissar* this morning. We are taking no further action.'

'Okay, but I cannot have my car?'

'Several vehicles remain impounded in the workshop as evidence.'

'I understand. Presumably that could take a while.'

Frau Klepp shrugged. 'We will let you know when your car is available. What is the best way to contact you?'

Donovan reflected. 'I'll probably return to England. You have my mobile number.'

'Yes.' Maria Klepp stood up.

'Thank you for coming,' said Donovan, raising to his feet.

Before he could offer his hand, the policewoman tucked the document case under her arm, picked up her hat, nodded curtly and walked out.

Chapter 11

Wednesday morning was cloudy with a fresh breeze. Ralph left early to catch a commuter train to London where he had a series of appointments: publisher, BBC, external examiners' board at UCL, the usual round. At the breakfast table Anne reminded Marnie that this was the day of her meeting with Moya Goodchild, the witch. Marnie's expression revealed that she needed no reminding. She stood and began clearing the table.

'Leave everything,' Anne said. 'I'll do it. It's time you were going.'

'Thanks, Anne. I'm sorry about this, but are you okay to look after the shop this morning? I'm hoping to be back by lunchtime.'

'If you haven't been turned into a frog,' Anne said cheerfully.

'Please, no jokes. This whole murder business is stressing me out. No one seems to appreciate I have a business to run, a living to earn.'

Okay. I'll hold the fort till you get back. How are you travelling?'

'Angela will be here any minute. We're going in my car, picking Cathy Lamb up from police HQ in Towcester. It's on the way.'

'Good. You'll just have to tell them to hop in.'

Marnie grimaced and poked out her tongue. She was laughing as she went out.

****

From Towcester they took the A5 north and crossed the Grand Union Canal half a mile short of the crossroads at Weedon. The glimpse of the waterway made Marnie long to be on *Sally Ann* cruising off on a voyage of discovery. They turned left onto the A45 at the junction and began the climb towards the Northamptonshire Uplands, crossing the canal once again as they left the village. Angela had the road atlas on her lap and was following the route with a finger.

'We're looking for the turning signposted to Newnham and then Badby,' she said. 'It's not far from there on.'

'That'll be on the left, right?' Marnie said.

Angela blinked. 'Er, I think I see what you mean.'

'The answer is yes,' Lamb added from the back seat.

Marnie was pleased that Lamb was dressed in jeans and a jumper and even more pleased that Angela was similarly kitted out but, like her, in slacks. Although as a detective Lamb wore 'plain clothes', she had taken to heart Marnie's remark that she looked like a copper. For her part, Angela was anxious not to look remotely like a vicar. She had even removed her habitual crucifix, though she admitted she felt naked without it.

'There's the sign for the turning,' Angela said, pointing through the windscreen.

'Got it,' said Marnie.

They made the turn and drove on through attractive rolling countryside of meadows interspersed with wooded slopes, a hilly landscape by the standards of Northamptonshire. As they passed through villages, Marnie noticed that there in the Uplands the limestone typical of the area around Knightly St John had given way to a darker sandstone.

'After Badby we take a right about a mile further on,' Angela said, poring over the map.

'Signposted Grenton?' said Marnie.

'Possibly.'

'Meaning?'

'Well, it could indicate Staverton or even Shuckburgh.'

'Why not Grenton?' Marnie asked, trying to hide her impatience. She was accustomed to precise instructions from Anne, who was a first class navigator.

'It's little more than a hamlet,' Lamb said, leaning forward.

'You're sure this isn't the proverbial wild goose chase, Cathy?'

'Forgive me for pointing out that you arranged this meeting, Marnie.'

'Only because you said you had to investigate the witch connection. You've never explained why. Don't you think now we're almost there, you could at least give us some idea?'

Lamb sighed. 'I've told you before, Marnie, I can't talk about it. You'll just have to trust me.'

'Here's the turning ... I think,' Angela said.

Marnie slowed and lined up for the turn. The new road was even narrower than the one they left.

'Did you see that signpost?' Marnie said.

'Er ... yes.' Angela was checking the map.

Marnie continued. 'It said Flecknoe. Are you sure this is the right way?'

'I think so. If we meet the A425, we might have to turn back.'

Marnie spoke over her shoulder. 'Cathy, if I beat Angela to death, would you have to serve as a witness?'

'Certainly not. I'd be an accomplice.'

Exasperated, Angela protested. 'I'm doing my best. The trouble is the atlas doesn't seem to agree with the roads and … here, Marnie. Turn right.'

Marnie hit the brakes and they all lurched forward against their seat belts. Grenton was signposted as a single lane road with passing places. The good news was it was only half a mile away.

'Oh, Aberdeen!' Lamb suddenly exclaimed.

'Blimey,' Marnie said. 'We've come further than I thought.'

'No, listen. You said Mr Koslowski muttered something about Aberdeen, didn't you, Angela?'

'That's what it sounded like.'

'I mentioned that in my report. I've just remembered. The DCI said Mr Koslowski had said the same thing when he was interviewed in hospital.'

'That's definite, is it?' Angela said.

'He was barely coherent, scarcely audible, but he lost consciousness after that, and they couldn't pursue it further.'

'What the hell's Aberdeen got to do with anything?' Marnie said.

'It means he definitely said it. Angela wasn't mistaken. So there must be a link with their attackers.'

Marnie muttered, 'I give up.'

'We're here,' said Angela. 'This must be Grenton.'

There was no signboard, just a collection of stone houses clustered around a crossroads. Clouds had gathered and, for the first time that morning, it looked like rain could fall at any minute.

'We're looking for Drover's Lane,' Lamb said. 'Lark's Cottage.'

Marnie pulled up at the junction. 'I think we've found it.'

'How can you tell?' Lamb asked. 'There don't seem to be any road signs.'

'Try looking over there.' Marnie pointed to their left to the end cottage about fifty yards away.

The last of the row of cottages, built of the local sandstone under a thatched roof, sported an installation in wrought iron on its end wall. It was in the form of an owl.

'Looks promising,' said Angela.

'Spooky,' Lamb added.

Marnie muttered, 'Maybe Anne was right. Perhaps we should've sent an owl.'

Angela turned to look at her. 'I don't follow you, Marnie.'

'Oh, nothing. It's just something in a book that Anne lent me. Come on.'

They made their way the short distance along the road, turned in at the sign for Lark's Cottage and parked on the drive next to an elderly Land Rover. The front door was on the side of the house and appeared to be made of solid oak. Marnie pressed the bell.

The door was opened by a tall slim woman in her forties wearing blue jeans and a smock that was tie-dyed in shades of blue and green with traces of purple. Her smile was welcoming and friendly but with a tinge of curiosity.

'Hello. Which one of you is Marnie?'

'That's me. I'm glad to meet you, Moya. This is Angela and this is Cathy.'

'Come in. We can complete the introductions inside.' Moya held the door open to let her visitors enter. 'The sitting room is straight ahead of you. You don't need to duck anywhere on this floor.'

Moya followed them into the room which was comfortably furnished with squashy sofas covered with multi-coloured throws. The walls were emulsioned in pale green, and a large Oriental rug covered most of the floor over varnished oak boards.

'Please sit where you like. I was expecting just Marnie, but that's no problem. You're all very welcome. Coffee?'

They murmured acceptance, and Moya turned, announcing that she was fetching two extra mugs from the kitchen. After she went out Lamb spoke in a low voice.

'I'm surprised her crystal ball didn't tell her there'd be three of us.'

Lamb went to take a seat but Marnie stopped her, placing a hand on her shoulder.

'Stop that, Cathy. Moya agreed to see me, and I assured her the subject would be treated with respect. No more snide comments, okay?'

Lamb looked resentful but nodded. Moya reappeared.

'Not sitting down?' she said, placing two mugs on a tray. It was standing on an antique server against the wall.

Marnie held out her hand. 'Thank you for offering to see me, Moya. I'm sorry, I should've made it clear that I'd be coming with friends. I didn't mean to spring a surprise on you.'

'That's all right, Marnie.' Shaking hands, she looked at her two unexpected visitors. 'Angela, was it?' They shook hands.

Lamb stepped forward. 'And I'm Cathy. Nice to meet you.'

They sat while Moya poured coffee and offered mugs and plates.

'I've made some biscuits, ginger nuts. I think they've worked. Sometimes mine are rather chewy. Please help yourselves.'

Marnie was looking round the room. 'Sorry to stare, Moya, but I was admiring your paintings. You like landscapes.'

Moya nodded. 'Anything to do with nature.'

Marnie pointed. 'Isn't that by Tristan Howarth?'

'Yes. It's an original. I've known him since we were at college together. My husband bought me the picture as a wedding present. That was before Tristan became famous, of course.'

'It's beautiful.'

'Yes, but I don't think you've come to admire my pictures, Marnie. Why have you come, in fact? I'm guessing it's not out of idle curiosity.'

Moya was smiling encouragingly at her from across the room. Marnie looked at her companions, knowing that they had come in disguise, concealing their true reasons for being there. Moya had received them in good faith, and Marnie felt guilty at deceiving her.

'I'm going to be absolutely frank with you, Moya. I asked to meet you because there's been a dreadful crime committed and there appears to be a witch connection.'

'What sort of crime?'

'A murder.'

Moya closed her eyes for some seconds, and the room fell silent. When she opened them, she said softly, 'A witch has been murdered?'

'No, at least I don't think so.'

'A witch committed the murder, you mean?'

'Not as far as I know.'

Moya put down her mug and sat back, folding both hands in her lap.

116

'I'm afraid I don't really understand this … witch connection, as you put it.'

Marnie waited for Cathy Lamb to say something, but neither she nor Angela spoke. Marnie took a decision.

'Moya, we're here to talk to you about an elderly lady who was killed recently in Northampton.'

'I heard about that,' said Moya. 'It was on the local TV news. Nothing was said about witches.'

Marnie continued. 'She was Polish and was murdered in her own home. Her husband, also Polish, was seriously injured. It seems to have been a hate crime.'

Moya looked confused. 'I'm still none the wiser. And I don't see where you fit in either, Marnie, unless you're in the police or something.'

Marnie paused to give Lamb a chance to explain, but she remained silent.

'You've been kind enough to invite me into your home, Moya, and you've made me and my … friends welcome. The least I can do is tell you the truth. Cathy here is a detective working on the investigation. She can't – or won't – tell us why she's interested in witchcraft. Is that the right word?'

'Yes, it is.'

'I've known Cathy for a few years and always found her straightforward to deal with, but I can't say any more because I don't know any more. Cathy, it's up to you now to say your piece.'

Lamb looked far from delighted that Marnie had blown her cover.

'Ms Goodchild, do you mind if I ask you some questions?'

They all noticed the change of tone. Lamb was now in detective mode.

Moya shrugged. 'If you think I can help in some way …'

'Does the name Katie Koslowski mean anything to you?'

'No. Is that the lady who was murdered?'

'That's right.'

'I'll think of her in my meditations.'

'Ms Goodchild … er, may I call you Moya?'

'I thought that's how we started out.'

Lamb said, 'I need to understand more about witchcraft.'

'What aspect interests you, Cathy?'

'That's just it. I don't know.'

'Then why do you think the murder has something to do with witches?'

'I'm afraid I can't explain that. It has to remain confidential. Do you know of any groups operating in Northampton?'

'Nothing comes to mind.'

Marnie jumped in. 'Moya, we believe there's a group – would you call it a coven? – in the area where Angela and I live, which is Knightly St John. That's between Towcester and Stony Stratford. Does that ring any bells?'

Moya grinned. 'We don't normally ring bells. We leave that to the Catholics. And yes, a group is called a coven.' She turned to Angela. 'Are you a police officer, too?'

Angela flushed. 'Er, no ... not actually.'

'Just a friend of Marnie's, then?'

Angela glanced across at Marnie, who said quietly, 'Angela is the vicar of Knightly St John.'

'So not really connected with the murder enquiry,' Moya said. 'Then what's your angle?'

The word *Pentangle* floated through Marnie's mind, but she held her tongue.

Angela spoke slowly. 'It's like this. I was approached by the police who thought I might know about witch activity in the area.'

Moya was smiling again. 'I don't think we've had much to do with each other for a few hundred years, have we?'

Angela looked down at her lap. 'Not really.'

Marnie said, 'Frankly, Moya, we're all groping in the dark, as you've probably gathered. Suppose we just ask you about witchcraft in general and your own experience of it?'

'Whatever you wish.'

'So how long have you been a witch? And is that the right term?'

'You could call me a *white* witch or a *green* witch or even a *hedge* witch. Don't worry about the distinctions. The point is my philosophy is entirely benign and rooted in respect for nature.'

'So no dark side, then,' said Marnie.

'Absolutely not. To answer your question, I suppose I first felt inclined that way as a child. It arose from my love of the natural world.'

'And are you also a healer?' Angela asked.

'Not so much in the way you mean. I have helped people with sort of psychological problems, though.'

'Do you belong to a coven?' Lamb asked.

'I'm usually solitary, but I have been to the odd moot. That's an informal kind of gathering.'

'Whereabouts does it meet?'

'Not far from here.' She grinned. 'It meets in a pub on the way to Daventry.'

'Could you ask the members if they've heard of Katie Koslowski?' Lamb asked.

'Okay, though I probably won't see them until Beltane now. We've passed the equinox just recently.'

'Beltane?'

'A festival halfway between the spring equinox and the summer solstice. It falls on the first of May. It's sometimes known as the festival of fire, but it encompasses fertility and the abundance of nature, too.'

'Thinking of fire,' Marnie began. 'In the woods near us we've found a place where fire has been burnt. Someone told us it was a witches' circle. Could that be right?'

'Why couldn't it just be a bonfire?' said Moya.

'There were other things, and they seemed to be set out in a pattern.'

'What sort of things?'

'Some skulls, possibly goat skulls. Also the stubs of black candles.'

Moya narrowed her eyes. 'That sounds like it might be what you've called the dark side ... spell casting, perhaps ... hexing even.'

'Hexing?' Lamb sat bolt upright. 'What can you tell me about that?'

'I've known people who think they've been hexed or cursed.'

'What happened to them?' Angela asked.

'I can give you an example. A woman came to me in a terrible state, said she'd been hexed. She wouldn't say by whom, but she was quite serious and terrified.'

'Could you exorcise her?' Angela said self-consciously, adding, 'or whatever witches do?'

'I was able to help her. First we meditated together. I have a stone circle in the garden – I call it my sacred space – and we sat in it to do that. I gave her a pouch with some herbs to keep by her – sage, lavender and rosemary – and gave her a spell to use. I also gave her a pendant made from the heart wood of an old apple tree in my garden.'

'Potions?' Lamb suggested.

Marnie gave her a sharp look, but Moya did not take offence.

'Yes. I made her a potion of floral water, also of sage, lavender and rosemary, to keep in a dish for when she went through the process of meditating at home. And I gave her some essential sandalwood oil and a burner to heat it in to help her meditate. There were other objects to keep by her and a whole process to go through, but I don't suppose you need all that detail.'

'What sorts of objects?' Lamb asked.

'Oh ... crystals, clear quartz, a candle – white of course – simple things like that.'

'Did all that help?' said Angela.

'Yes. I saw her a couple of months later. She said she felt much happier and was more or less back to normal.'

'That's wonderful,' Marnie said. 'How did she find you, by the way? Did you know her already?'

'I'd never seen her before. She came to me by recommendation. That's how I meet most of my clients. Would anyone like more coffee?' Moya smiled. 'Or I could knock up a small potion?'

Lamb looked wary.

'I'm only kidding. Look, my beliefs are based entirely on the love of nature, the passing of the seasons and good will to all creatures, including humans. I'm very saddened about the Polish lady and I'll remember her in my meditations, even though we never met.'

'And you'll ask around in case you hear anything?' Lamb said.

'Of course I will.'

'Can I ask ...' Angela began tentatively. 'When you have important events, ceremonies and such ... are you ... do you wear clothes ... I mean, special clothes?'

Moya smiled. 'I think what you're getting at is ... are we naked?'

Angela blushed. 'Well, I did sort of wonder ...'

'In the past I may have been,' Moya said. 'We call it being sky clad. But not really these days. Is there anything else you'd like to know?'

'Thank you for being so frank,' Angela said.

'And thank you for your time, Moya,' said Marnie. 'It's been lovely meeting you.'

'I'm not sure I've been able to help you much.'

'It's been very interesting. We're really grateful. I expect we'll think of a hundred more questions after we've gone.'

'Well, you know where I am. Just send me an e-mail ... or perhaps an owl?' She winked at Marnie.

As they made their way to the door, Marnie noticed a broomstick in the hall. Moya saw her glance at it.

'Not a means of transport, Marnie!' Moya grinned. 'I use the Land Rover for that.'

'A witch's broomstick!' Marnie replied. 'How apt. Or do you just sweep the floor with it?'

'It's a besom, used for symbolic cleaning ... and yes I also sweep the floor with it.'

Moya saw an expression bordering on distaste on Lamb's face.

'Cathy, have you never swept the old year out of the house at midnight on New Year's Eve, prior to welcoming in the first foot?'

'Well, yes, I suppose ...' Lamb stammered.

'The old ways are still with us, Cathy. Some of us are just a little closer to them.'

She opened the front door, and they turned to thank her one last time.

Marnie said, 'There is a question I've remembered, Moya. I've always wanted to ask if a witch really does have a familiar. Is that the right word?'

Moya said. 'Yes, Marnie, it is, and I certainly do.'

'Is it a black cat, in accordance with popular belief?'

'You're thinking of the children's stories ... Meg and Mog. Sorry to disappoint you. Black cats don't really feature in our sphere. No, my familiar is a fox.'

'Is it a real one or a sort of imaginary one?' Marnie asked.

'Oh, she's very real ... a vixen.'

'When do you see her?'

'Most days.' Moya raised a hand and pointed into the field beside the cottage. 'See? She's under that tree over there, watching us.'

The three women strained to see across the grass to a belt of trees about a hundred yards away.

Lamb said, 'I can't – oh god, yes. Look, over in the corner. She's just sitting there looking this way.'

'I'll tell her all about you when you've gone,' said Moya.

'I bet she knows already,' Angela replied.

Moya laughed. 'Probably.' She stepped forward and kissed each of them on the cheek.

As they drove off, Angela lightly touched the side of her face. 'That must be a first,' she said.

Marnie glanced sideways and grinned at her. 'Not feeling spooked, are you? A kiss on the cheek from a real live witch!'

Angela looked strangely moved. 'No, but in a way – you'll probably think this silly of me – I almost feel as if all the bad things the church has done to witches in the past have been … if not forgiven, then perhaps slightly expiated.'

'All that from just a friendly kiss on the cheek?' Marnie said.

'I knew you'd think it silly, but –'

'I didn't mean it like that, Angela. I'm glad you and Moya got on okay. That meeting can't have been easy for either of you.'

'To be honest, Marnie, I don't really think I took issue with anything Moya said. Her religion – if that's what it is – is about respecting nature and being good to others. I've come away with the impression that she could never harm anyone, nor could any witch of her kind.'

From the rear seat Cathy Lamb joined in. 'I've come away with the impression that I'm no further forward.'

'Hardly surprising,' said Marnie. 'You don't give anyone the slightest idea what you're looking for or why. Small wonder we can't do more to help you.'

Angela said, 'Was there really nothing of interest back there, Cathy? I noticed you sat up when she spoke about hexing.'

Marnie added, 'And I thought I detected a *frisson* of interest when she talked about the festival of fire. I wondered if you were thinking of what happened to the Polish shop and the Jacksons' boat.'

There was no response. As Marnie retraced their journey back, Lamb sat staring at the countryside passing by. Whatever thoughts she had, she kept to herself.

****

'Come on, Ralph.' Marnie closed the door of the Aga's top oven and stood up. 'You're the brainbox round here. If anyone can work it out, you can.'

Ralph was emerging from the pantry holding a bottle of dry white wine from Greece. 'I think this should go quite well with grilled sardines.'

'Did you hear what I said?' Marnie repeated her previous statement.

Ralph placed the wine in the fridge and turned to face Marnie and Anne. He looked thoughtful, slowly shaking his head.

'In the absence of any other facts, I'd have to agree with Donovan. Either Mrs Koslowski was accused of being a witch and attacked for that reason, or she was being hexed – to use your friendly witch's term – by a witch on the dark side, for reasons we can't deduce. What other possibilities are there?'

'Do they have witches in Poland?' Anne asked. She was cutting an avocado into cubes to go in the salad.

Ralph shrugged. 'Beats me. It's rather outside my field, but I can check with colleagues in the Institute of Slavonic Studies, if you like.'

'Not a bad idea,' Marnie said. She opened the door of the Aga's top oven again and peered inside. 'I've never used the top shelf in the hot oven before ... seems to be cooking them all right.'

Anne said, 'She sounds really nice, your witch. I'd love to have seen her fox-familiar. Was the cottage creepy at all?'

'No. It was ... cottagey, I suppose. The kitchen was big like this one, and she had an Aga ... an old-fashioned-looking cream one with a hot water tap on the front. Must have been installed before the war at a guess. What we saw of the rest of the house was rather charming.'

'But you're no closer to knowing why Cathy wanted to see her.'

'Nope.' Marnie inspected the sardines in the oven again. 'Another minute or so. Ralph, I think we're going to need one of those rapid-ice freezer jackets on the wine to cool it down *rapido.*'

By now Ralph was laying the table. 'Straight away, ma'am. Your merest whim is my most urgent command ... and my constant pleasure.'

Marnie gave him The Look, but he was already moving towards the freezer and missed it. She diverted her gaze in Anne's direction.

'Has Donovan had any further thoughts about the witch angle since we spoke of it before?'

Anne considered the question. 'We know Donovan's views, Marnie, like Ralph said. Otherwise, I don't think he's made any further pronouncements. But I think he's had other things on his mind just lately.'

******

Anne was crossing the yard on the way back to her attic room when the mobile started vibrating in her pocket. It was Donovan's daily update.

'So they haven't thrown you in jail yet. That's good news. How are things in sunny Bergheim?'

'It was drizzling when I left this morning.'

'You *left?*'

'Yes. I'm back in London, been travelling all day. Got a train from Cologne to Brussels, then Eurostar to Waterloo. Just got in.'

'Great! Does that mean I might see you some time soon?'

'How about tomorrow? I could come up in the morning, if that was okay.'

'You won't be too jet-lagged?'

'I'll be fine.'

'So, tell me about the Porsche.'

'Seems they need it a bit longer. It's evidence. It's a drag, but I'll have to go back again to collect it.'

'Is it a complete mess? Have you seen it?'

'No to both questions. Apparently it's been restored by some crooks who wanted to flog it. I've completed all the paperwork, which is what the police wanted. Now it's just a question of waiting for their call. Any news your end?'

'Marnie's been to see her witch lady today.'

'Any results?'

'Don't think so. Marnie reckons Cathy Lamb's floundering. We're no further forward there. Oh, there is one thing, another mystery. They went to see Mr Koslowski in hospital.'

'How's he coming on?'

'Pretty poorly, still in intensive care. But he did try to speak. The strange thing is, Angela thinks he said something about Aberdeen.'

'What?'

'I know. It's weird.'

'She must've misheard him.'

124

'I'm not so sure. Cathy told Marnie that he'd also said something like that to the police when they first tried to interview him. Have you got any ideas?'

'Not off the top of my head. What do Marnie and Ralph think?'

'None the wiser.'

'Witches … Aberdeen?' Donovan said. 'Sorry. I don't get it. I think we'll need Sherlock Holmes *and* Hercule Poirot to sort this lot out.'

'And Harry Potter,' Anne added.

'Who?'

'Never mind.'

Chapter 12

On Thursday morning Marnie enjoyed two full hours working on interior design projects without interruption. It was bliss until a call came in just after ten. As usual Anne picked up the phone. After a brief exchange she covered the mouthpiece and called across the office.

'It's your favourite vicar, Marnie.'

'Can't be. I don't have one. Tell her I've emigrated.'

Anne removed her hand and spoke into the receiver. 'Marnie says she's delighted to hear from you, Angela. I'll put you through.'

When Marnie answered, Angela said, 'I heard every word of that. Anne didn't cover the receiver very well. Where have you emigrated to ... Australia?'

'Not far enough. What can I do for you, Angela?'

'I don't suppose you'll be going anywhere near Northampton today?'

Marnie looked down at her diary. She had a meeting just outside the county town at noon.

'Well ...'

'I'm really sorry to impose on you again, Marnie, but before you can think of an excuse could I just say that Father Novak would like a brief word. I'm seeing him in town for coffee at eleven. Any chance?'

'What does he want?'

'Oh, you know ... a chat about the Koslowskis and what's happened to them.'

Marnie had a vision of the old man lying in intensive care, a pathetic sight, hooked up to a battery of instruments, fighting for his life. She too had once been in that position in that very unit. For all she knew, perhaps she had occupied that same bed.

'Are you there, Marnie? Could you manage just half an hour and a coffee? Please?'

Marnie relented. She tried not to sigh as she replied. 'Which café?'

'Oh that's great! Thank you so much, Marnie. That Italian place in Abington street. You know it?'

'I'll be there at eleven, but I can only manage half an hour.'

'You're an *angel*!'

Marnie thought of saying, 'And you're a *witch*!' but she thought better of it. It would be unkind to witches.

****

The *Caffè Sorrento* was really quite stylish. Marnie was impressed. It boasted all the latest hi-tech equipment with hissing and bubbling soundtrack to match. The shelves behind the bar were laid out with colourful bottles of syrups for flavouring and canisters containing different blends and types of coffee. They made Marnie think of witches' potions. Beneath the shelves a mirror ran the length of the serving area and made the cafe seem larger than it was. The tables and chairs were matt black steel; the walls displayed monochrome photographs from Italian movies of the fifties and sixties. Images of the Trevi fountain in Rome, plus shots of exotic sports cars and Vespa scooters were much in evidence.

When Marnie walked in a few minutes before eleven, Angela and Father Novak were already seated. The priest stood up, smiling warmly, and indicated the small queue at the bar.

'Good to see you, Marnie. Can you tell Kazimir what you'd like. He's buying.'

Marnie asked for a regular cappuccino. When she rejoined the two clerics she noticed five chairs were assembled round the table. A warning bell sounded in her head. Something told her this was not just going to be a brief chat. Marnie remained standing.

'I'll help Kazimir carry the coffees.' she said.

Angela said, 'No need, it's all right. Dom's with him.'

Marnie looked back and for the first time noticed Dominik Gorski in the queue beside his father. She took her place next to Angela.

'I'm so glad you agreed to come, Marnie,' Pawel Novak said in his strong accent.

'That's okay. As I explained to Angela, I'm on my way to a meeting, so I can't stay long. If there's something particular on your mind, perhaps we could get on with it straight away?'

'Of course, as soon as the others join us.'

Father and son arrived with a tray each and distributed the coffees, plus packets of *cantuccini* biscuits, which they spread out on the table. While the others occupied themselves with prising open the wrappings, Marnie spoke up.

'First, thank you for my coffee, Mr Gorski.'

'Kazimir, please.'

'Fine. Can I just ask what we're here to talk about? My time is rather limited and -'

'It's the Koslowskis,' Dom interjected.

Marnie looked at Father Novak. 'And it doesn't matter to you that they weren't churchgoers?'

'No, though it is unusual for Poles, especially with a Polish Pope in Rome. We are a very religious people.'

Dom added, 'We are very proud to have a Polish pope. We call him Jan Pawel, of course.' He pronounced the name like Yan Parvel.

'What else do we know about the Koslowskis?' Marnie asked.

Kazimir said, 'Stanislav used to work for the county council as a highways engineer. I believe he trained after the war.'

'And did you tell me that Mr Koslowski was a war hero?'

'That's right.' Dom got in first. 'He was a pilot in 303 squadron, the Polish fighter outfit. They were legendary. Did you know they had the highest number of kills of any squadron of the RAF in the Battle of Britain?'

'Really? No, I didn't know that.'

'Oh yes, and he later served on the eastern front liberating Poland.' Dom lowered his voice. 'That's where his plane was hit and he had to crash land.'

'You obviously know him well,' Marnie said.

For a moment, Dom looked tongue-tied. 'Er, well no ... not really.'

'But you know a lot about him.'

Father Novak said, 'There are people in the town - men who served in the war in Polish units - who know of his background.'

Dom added. 'I've been learning Polish for some time. I like to chat with the old people, and my girlfriend knows the Koslowskis.'

Marnie sipped her coffee. 'It's strange the Koslowskis didn't join in with the Polish community as a whole. I wonder why not.'

No one rushed to reply. Eventually Dom spoke. 'It was thought they might be ... communists. That's what I've heard.'

'That could explain why they weren't churchgoers,' Marnie said. 'But if they were communists, why did they choose to stay here after the war? Why not just go back to Poland?'

Dom said, 'A lot of people have history.'

'What do you mean?'

'You never know what burdens people might carry with them, what reasons they have for their actions.'

'I suppose not.' Marnie glanced at her watch. 'Look, I don't want to rush you, but I haven't got long. Is there something we can do for Mr Koslowski?'

Kazimir said, 'I'm sure he could use some things, like fruit, orange juice … maybe some XXXucozade.'

'That's a blast from the past,' said Marnie. 'My mum always gave me and my sister XXXucozade if we were unwell as children. But … I don't really think you asked me to come to talk about fruit and XXXucozade. Your concern for Mr Koslowski goes deeper than that.'

'What makes you think that, Marnie?' Angela asked.

'I'm guessing that people assume he was the intended target of the attack. After all, he was better known in the community, more prominent as a well-known war hero and regularly frequented the Polish shop. Would that be right?'

Gorski shrugged. 'Probably. Katie stayed more or less in the background. If the far right extremists were going to attack anyone, it would be him.'

'Or you, papa,' Dom said. 'You're even more prominent with your position in Polish circles.'

'Goodness!' Angela exclaimed. 'Do you think you could be in danger, Kazimir?'

Gorski made a dismissive gesture. 'We're not here to talk about me. Marnie's short of time. Let's use it wisely.'

Marnie looked at her watch. 'Yes, I have to be away in -'

'Father Novak and I have been in touch with the police. It appears the Koslowskis' house was vandalised. The police say they no longer need it to be quarantined. We want to put together a team to help by repairing the damage.'

Father Novak said, 'The community can now go in and assess what needs to be done. We would like very much for you, Marnie, to be involved. As a designer you have much experience in such things. Obviously, we would find the money to pay for any materials needed, and of course we would pay for your time.'

There was a pause which Marnie suspected was intended to give her time to waive any thought of fees. She was the first to speak.

'I'll have to look at my calendar, but I know I can only act as an adviser. I've too many projects running to allow me to handle this as a normal job.'

Father Novak nodded. 'Of course.'

'Now I really have to be on my way.'

Gorski said, 'The house is available to us from now onwards. Just let me know when you want to visit and I'll let you have the key. Here's my business card. Please feel free to call me whenever you want.'

In an automatic reaction Marnie produced one of her own cards and handed it to him.

'I must go too,' said Dom. 'I'll come out with you, Marnie.'

After a round of handshaking, Marnie found herself outside on the pavement with Dom, who was pulling car keys from his pocket.

'Thanks for agreeing to help, Marnie. Can I offer you a lift to the car park? I was lucky to get a space here.'

'No, I'm parked just round the corner, thanks. Is this yours?'

She pointed to a small hatchback. It was a Peugeot 205 GTI, dark blue with a red coachline and shiny alloy wheels. Someone had lavished great care and attention on it. The bodywork was dazzling.

'Yeah,' said Dom. 'I've been doing it up.'

'You've done a great job.'

'Well, I'm lucky. I can get everything I need at trade prices.'

'How's that?'

'Didn't you know? My dad's in the business. He has autoparts shops all over the county. You've heard of Mechaniks ... with a *k*?'

'Rings a bell, now that you mention it. Aren't they on the Wellingborough road?'

'That's his biggest store.'

'Lucky you.'

'You bet!'

They parted company and went their separate ways. Climbing into the Freelander, Marnie thought how similar Dom was to Donovan, not only in appearance, but in their shared enjoyment of cars with character. And they had something else in common, a fierce antagonism towards New Force and all it stood for.

Chapter 13

On Friday morning in the office barn, Marnie could tell she did not have Anne's full and undivided attention. Anne sorted the post, as usual, and attended to the filing and generally kept Walker and Co running smoothly. But each time Marnie looked across the office at her friend, she saw that Anne appeared to be distracted. There was no doubt in Marnie's mind as to the reason for Anne's inattention.

'So you've prepared this month's invoice for Willards, then.'

'Uh-huh.'

'And the filing's up-to-date.'

'Yeah.'

'I heard that Martians landed in Oxford yesterday ... on Gloucester Green.'

'Mm ...'

Marnie smiled to herself, shook her head and returned to the design on the drawing board, muttering inaudibly, 'Funny girl ...'

Shortly after ten Anne got up and walked to the kitchen at the rear of the barn. Moments later the sound of the kettle heating up rattled across the office, accompanied by the clink of crockery. Anne was preparing refreshments for the staff of Walker and Co, plus the builders who had recently resumed external works to the farmhouse that had been put on hold during the months of winter.

In passing with her tray, Anne stopped to place a mug of coffee on Marnie's desk before heading out to the site. As she returned to the office barn, Anne paused in the doorway and cocked her head on one side. With the door half open, Marnie thought she heard in the background a familiar rumbling sound. It was the unmistakeable burble of a VW Beetle's engine.

'I think our visitor has arrived,' Marnie said. 'Just in time for coffee.'

'Seems so,' Anne agreed. 'He must have installed radar in the car. I'll put some more water in the kettle.'

'I'll do that, Anne. You go and meet Donovan.'

'Okay.' Anne set the tray down by the door, leaning it against the wall. As she straightened up, she hesitated. 'Gloucester Green, eh? Quite appropriate really ... Martians ... green ...'

Marnie groaned as Anne set off at a brisk pace.

****

The waters of the canal smelled fresh and clean, and the air was mild and limpid, with not a trace of the mist that had floated over the fields and meadows in recent days. Anne was perched on the roof of the narrowboat *Exodos*, written as *X O 2*, from which vantage point she could look down on Donovan. At that moment he was crouching in the engine compartment checking grease in the stern gland, oil levels in engine and gearbox, distilled water in the batteries. He glanced up at her as he was unscrewing the drop filter to examine it for condensation.

'So have you been to look at the Koslowskis' house yet?' he asked.

'No. The police have only just let us know that people are actually allowed inside.'

'I see the New Force decoration of the accommodation bridge ...' He gestured with his head in its direction, '... is still in place. What about the graffiti in town?'

'Still there, too. Angela's written to the council to ask them to get it all removed.'

Donovan reassembled the drop filter and began to extricate himself from the engine. 'Well, I'm not holding my breath. Have NF added any more?'

'Not sure. You seem just as keen as ever to find out.'

'I am, and even keener to get rid of it all.'

****

Donovan had thoroughly gone over *Exodos* from stem to stern and was planning a tootle to shake out the boat's cobwebs when he had a change of mind. The situation in and around Northampton was preying on his mind. He felt restless at the mere thought of New Force running riot – perhaps literally and soon – in the town and its surrounds. On the way back to the office barn through the spinney he voiced his concerns to Anne.

'Listen, I'm not waiting for the council to make up its mind about getting rid of the graffiti. No one seems to realise they're playing into the hands of the fascists by just leaving it visible. It's a clear message that New Force are calling the shots. We can't have that.'

'What are you going to do?'

'I'd have thought that was obvious. I'm going to make a start on cleaning up the mess.'

132

'But won't that bring you into conflict with the police? Cathy Lamb said we ought to wait till the forensics people have done their work.'

Donovan stopped and turned to face Anne. 'What are they going to find? Do they think the graffiti were sprayed by the Salvation Army, or was it the RSPCA?'

'I agree with you really, Donovan, but wouldn't it be better to work with the authorities rather than go against them? Don't you think a united approach would show solidarity?'

Donovan turned and began walking slowly along the path. Anne fell into step beside him and took his hand.

'Couldn't you at least see what Marnie thinks?'

'Anne, I just feel so frustrated. All the time I was in Germany I kept thinking about the far right and what they were doing here. It's a constant struggle.'

'But everyone's joining in,' Anne protested. 'Look at Marnie. She's on Angela's committee. You know she doesn't really have the time, but she's doing her bit.'

'You think I should sit back and wait for someone else to take action?'

Donovan's tone was mild, but Anne could sense the depth of his feelings. For him it was a just cause.

Anne said, 'All I'm saying is perhaps you could have a word with Marnie. We're all on the same side, after all.'

They arrived at the office barn to find Marnie closing the door behind her. She cheerfully announced that she was pleased with a morning of uninterrupted work and was ready for a sandwich.

'Would you two be okay with that? I've promised to make one for Ralph. He wants to keep on with his proof-reading. With any luck this will be a day when we actually get on top of things.'

'I'll help with the sandwiches,' Anne said. 'But Donovan's fretting about the graffiti. He thinks we ought to clean it up straight away.'

They crossed the courtyard and went into the farmhouse. Marnie said nothing until they were settled in the kitchen.

'I agree with you, Donovan. I don't think we should wait.'

'You don't?'

'Of course not. But there is just one thing ... two things, actually. The first is that the Polish community has been in touch with the police. They're pressing for permission to do a clean-up. We don't want to cross wires with them. The second is

133

that the police have just granted access to the Koslowskis' house.'

'Yes, Anne told me about that.'

'Well, the thing is, the Poles want to get the place sorted out before Mr Koslowski comes out of hospital.'

'You're thinking we ought not to upset the police right now?'

Marnie shrugged. 'We seem to be getting along together, which makes a pleasant change, so ...'

While Marnie and Donovan were talking, Anne was assembling the ingredients for sandwiches.

'Couldn't we make a start by just cleaning the graffiti from the bridge like we did before?' she asked.

Marnie looked at Donovan.

'In the spirit of cooperation,' he began, 'perhaps we could clear that with Cathy Lamb? In the meantime I wouldn't mind checking out the Northampton scene.'

'Okay,' said Marnie. 'Here's a plan. We have a quick lunch, then you and Anne go into town for a look round. I'll get on with my projects while the going's good.'

'Don't you need me here in the office?' Anne said.

'The thing is, I might be able to get access to the Koslowskis' house. It would be useful if you two could check it out while you're there. What d'you think?'

'Fine,' said Donovan.

'Okay by me, if you're sure,' said Anne.

Anne and Donovan set to work making sandwiches. Marnie rang Kazimir Gorski. He agreed to meet Anne at the house and let her in. They had a plan.

****

Within the hour the black VW Beetle was making its way through Northampton's traffic, heading towards the Koslowskis' house. Donovan found it difficult to concentrate on driving, such was the state of the town. Hardly a blank wall was unsullied by slogans and far-right symbols.

'What the hell are they playing at?' he exclaimed.

'New Force up to their old tricks,' Anne said.

'I don't mean them. I mean the *police*, the authorities, the public. How can they tolerate this? The neo-Nazis must be laughing up their sleeves. Ridiculous!'

134

'Well, I suppose it won't be much longer. Angela should hear back from the council soon.'

'You believe that, do you, Anne?'

Anne bit her lip. There was only one true answer. She was relieved to see their turning up ahead.

'Look, that's where we have to go. Next right, then down to the junction and first on the left.'

Muttering to himself, Donovan made the manoeuvres and found a parking space almost outside the house where Katie Koslowski was murdered. They sat in silence staring at the building for a few moments. The police tape had been removed. It looked like any normal home in any normal street. They climbed out together.

'I don't see Mr Gorski anywhere,' Anne said.

'Anne, I'm gonna park round the corner, out of sight.'

Anne was accustomed to Donovan's secretive ways. 'I'd better wait here in case Mr Gorski arrives,' she said.

Anne took up station on the doorstep as Donovan drove slowly away. He had just turned the corner when she saw a car approaching. She had no idea what make of car Kazimir Gorski would be driving, but she was fairly certain it would not be a sporty little *hot hatch*. To her surprise, when the car pulled up, a young man got out, and Anne nearly did a double-take. He was almost a clone of Donovan. He saw her bemused expression and walked up to her.

'I was expecting Marnie Walker,' he said.

'And I was expecting Mr Kazimir Gorski.'

They smiled at each other.

'We must be the B team. I'm Dom, Kazimir's son. Don't tell me. You're Marnie's daughter, right?'

'Not right. I'm her assistant from the office. I'm Anne, Anne Price,'

They shook hands.

'You've come to check the house over for the restoration job?' Dom asked.

'Come to see what's involved, that's all. You've brought a key?'

'Yes.' He reached into his pocket. 'My father couldn't get away. He's with a wholesaler, so I came instead.'

'Nice of you. Are you coming to look round as well?'

'No. I'm on my lunch break. I work in the shop in the college holidays.'

'Have you been inside before?' Anne asked.

Dom looked momentarily confused. 'No. That wasn't possible before. The place has been cordoned off until today.'

He stepped forward and unlocked the door, moving aside to let Anne pass. He smiled at her.

'If I'd known you were coming I'd have ...'

'Baked a cake?'

Dom laughed. 'Something like that, or at least cleared more time in the day.'

'So you're not coming in?'

Dom shook his head and removed the key from the lock.

'I'd better be getting back. Just pull the door shut when you leave. You've got our number if you need anything.'

He shook hands again – very continental, Anne thought – and got back into the car. He blipped the throttle twice – Anne was not impressed – before he drove off down the street rather more quickly than Anne thought wise. She waited on the doorstep, watching the Peugeot till it went out of sight. She had no desire to enter the murder house alone.

Seconds later Donovan rounded the corner. 'Sorry to be so long. Parking here's a nightmare. Mr Gorski's been and gone?'

'Yes. He sent his son, actually. I didn't want to go in ... you know ...'

'Sure. Let me lead the way.'

Their first impression on entering the house was how ordinary it was, the typical suburban home of an old couple. It had fitted carpets, floral wallpaper, potted plants on windowsills, reproductions of Old Masters on the walls. Yet here there was a significant difference. Evidence of dusting powder, presumably for fingerprints, was everywhere. Anne had not expected that. She thought the police would have wiped it away. Yet every hard surface was coated. And something else was not right. There was a tang in the air, a mustiness overlaid with an odour of something rotten, an unsavoury unhomely smell.

Standing in the hall, Anne gripped Donovan's arm. 'That smell. You don't think it could be ...'

'No. I'm sure it isn't. I reckon we'll find some vegetables going off somewhere.'

Anne looked at the closed door on the left of the entrance hall.

'Mrs Koslowski was murdered in the living room, wasn't she?'

'We'll leave it till last,' Donovan said firmly.

Anne put an arm round his waist and spoke softly. 'I'm not sure this was a good idea.'

Donovan took her in his arms and held her close for a long moment.

'We'll just check the place out, get some idea of the damage and what needs doing. No need to stay long. You okay with that?'

Anne nodded and they separated.

'I'll look in the kitchen first,' Anne said.

'And I'll poke around upstairs. You all right?'

'I'll be fine. Don't be long.'

She took a notebook from her shoulder bag. Donovan pulled a camera from his and took the stairs two at a time. Anne breathed in deeply and at once regretted it. She grimaced at the smell and stepped purposefully forward. She stopped almost at once and called up the stairs.

'Donovan, the murderer didn't use a kitchen knife, did he?'

From the landing Donovan replied. 'Don't think so. Don't think I've heard how she was … Look, Anne, if you want me to –'

'No, it's all right. Let's just get it over with.'

Donovan heard Anne's footsteps on the lino in the kitchen. He pushed open the door of the nearest bedroom and raised the camera. There were signs of disturbance, a lamp knocked to the floor, books from a bedside table strewn about, but no serious damage. It was the same in the next room, where he took a few more shots. Evidently the master bedroom was at the rear, overlooking the garden. Through the viewfinder of the Leica the room looked hardly disturbed. There, the only sign of intrusion was the bedspread. It had been thrust up onto the bed. Someone had peered underneath, as if searching for something.

Donovan was about to leave the room when he noticed a collection of photographs on the dressing table. In the centre was a war-time wedding picture. In it, the married couple posed arm in arm. Stanislav Koslowski was lightly-built and wearing Royal Air Force uniform. His bride was more of a buxom beauty, with curly blonde hair protruding from under her headdress.

Donovan spotted her again in a separate photograph. Here she looked a little younger, though just as sturdy. But this time she was in uniform, smiling at the camera, wearing a drab green-brown tunic, her ample bosom displaying an impressive array of medals and decorations. Donovan's eye was caught by two further picture-frames. In each of them those same medals were on show. He studied them closely, but recognised none of them.

He photographed the whole collection on the dressing table, followed by a shot of each individual item. Setting down the camera, he studied the photos of Katie Koslowski. In one, her smile embodied proud defiance, in the other, bridal happiness. Why would anyone wish to harm her, let alone murder her? What had attracted New Force thugs to this tranquil corner of suburbia with such vicious malevolence?

Or was the real target Stan Koslowski? Perhaps something in his past had caught up with him. He was after all apparently a communist, and that would make him a high priority on any far-right hit list. And of course he too had been attacked and left for dead. It was odd, though, Donovan thought. The harmless elderly housewife had been brutally murdered – though how, he did not know – while the perpetrator had not made sure of finishing off her commy husband. Was he disturbed in the act of –

'Donovan! Are you okay up there?'

Donovan walked away from the dressing table and called down to Anne.

'Yes, I'm done. Nothing much to report. I'm coming down.'

He found Anne in the hallway, clutching her notebook, hovering outside the door to the living room.

'I've made a list of things that need repairing or replacing,' she said. 'But I'm not so sure about the decoration ... all these patterned wallpapers. They're not what we'd choose at Walker and Co. Marnie will know what's best.'

'Shall I take some photos down here?' Donovan offered. 'I took several upstairs.'

'A few wouldn't go amiss,' Anne said.

Donovan moved from room to room with Anne, shooting from a variety of angles. He knew she was glad to put off the moment when they would enter the murder room.

'Okay,' Donovan said. 'Just one last room and then we go.'

'Right.' Anne tried to sound resolute, flicking open her notebook. 'Let's do it.'

She had hoped the living room would look no more ravished than the other parts of the ground floor. She was disappointed. Here, the furniture was chaotic, armchairs thrust about, testifying to a violent struggle. The television had been knocked aside, its screen smashed.

Donovan summed it up. 'Katie Koslowski may have been an old lady, but she must have put up one hell of a fight.'

Anne gazed in stunned silence at the disarray. She was moving slowly forward like a sleep-walker when Donovan seized her by the arm.

'Hold it there, Anne! Don't go any further.'

She was about to respond when she saw that Donovan was peering downwards. The carpet was stained with copious deep brown splashes: dried blood. A faint fetid odour rose from the floor. Anne lifted a hand to her mouth, her eyes wide with horror. Donovan turned her towards the door.

'Come on. That's enough in here. I'll take a few shots and we'll go. Just wait for me in the hall. Two minutes max.'

Anne did not resist but willingly did as Donovan instructed. She was stepping across the room when she heard him speak again, this time in a hoarse whisper.

'Bloody hell.'

Anne turned to look at Donovan. He was staring over her shoulder at the wall behind her. She looked round. There, over the fire place, were sprayed in bright red paint four letters, one word: *HEXE*.

****

At Glebe Farm Marnie was pleased to be getting on with her work without interruption or anxiety for the wellbeing of the community. She knew she should feel guilty at such selfishness, but reminded herself she had deadlines to meet. She knew she had contributed her fair share of time and effort to the needs of society in general and Angela's committee in particular.

In the early afternoon she had a surprise call. The strong accent made it easy to guess who was ringing.

'Is that Marnie Walker?'

'Yes. Good afternoon, Father Novak.'

'Pawel, please.'

'Okay, Pawel, what can I do for you?'

'First, I apologise for interruption. I have your number from Angela. Can we speak?'

'Certainly.' Marnie hoped she sounded sincere.

139

'Thank you. I want to tell you I have been to the house of Koslowskis. Angela says you have offered to ... how do you say? ... renew it?'

'Renovate.' This came as news to Marnie. 'Well, in fact I said I'd be willing to help if I can. It depends how much needs doing.'

'You will wish to see the house, naturally.'

Not quite how I'd put it, Marnie thought. 'I've sent my assistant to see what's needed. You say you've been there?'

'Yes. It is in a terrible condition. Much furniture is turned over. There is graffiti on a wall and marks of blood, much blood, on the floor. It will need new carpet there in that room.'

And I've sent Anne there, to a house of horrors!

Father Novak continued. 'It is all very upsetting, not suitable for Mr Koslowski to return to.'

'That's awful.'

'Yes. It is very bad. Can you please visit the house soon and start a programme to renew ... er, renovate?'

'I'll discuss it with my assistant when she gets back.'

'Thank you, thank you so much. I am glad she has been there.'

Not a view Anne will share, Marnie thought.

****

A number of questions ran through Marnie's mind in the minutes following her conversation with Father Novak. How was Anne getting on at the Koslowskis' house? Why hadn't she phoned to let Marnie know what was happening? Was she very shocked at the disruption and especially the aftermath of the murder? What state was she in? Marnie decided to take direct action. Anne took the call as soon as the ringing tone sounded.

'Hi, Anne. How's it going?'

'It's horrible.' Anne's voice was a croak.

'I shouldn't have asked you to go there. I'm really sorry.'

'Most of the house is not too bad, but the living room where that poor lady was ... you know.'

'Yes, I heard.'

'How did you hear?'

'Father Novak phoned me. He told me about the ...'

'The blood?'

'Yes.'

140

'Marnie, that's not all. There's graffiti on the wall in that room. The murderer sprayed *HEXE* in red paint. It looks like blood where the paint has run.'

'Hexe?'

'Yes.' Anne spelled it out: 'H – E – X – E in capitals. It's all red like the graffiti on the bridge by *Sally Ann*'s mooring.'

'Well, that explains why the police were interested in witches, but it doesn't explain why it should be sprayed in their house.'

Anne said, 'Surely, they must think there's some link between Mrs Koslowski and witches in the area. What else could it mean?'

'We'll talk about it later. What are you doing at the moment?'

'Waiting for Donovan.'

'Why? Isn't he there?'

'He's gone to fetch the car. It's funny, he's been gone quite a while. We'll get back as soon as he returns. I must say, I don't like being here on my own.'

'Are you all right?'

'I am now. I felt quite queasy before, but Donovan found some brandy and gave me a drop. I hope he won't be much longer.'

****

Donovan spotted them as soon as he turned the corner. More to the point, they spotted him. Best guess, he was about a hundred yards from the Beetle. He decided to keep on walking and hope they would just pass by on the other side of the road. They had other ideas. The first ominous sign came when they stopped and went into a huddle, glancing across in his direction. Donovan quickened his pace but not enough to draw attention, he hoped.

There were five of them. They had been shuffling along the street, out looking for trouble. Skinheads. Like Donovan they were dressed in black, but there the similarity ended. With their shaved heads, piercings and tattooed arms, they could not be mistaken for anything but New Force vigilantes on the prowl. When they saw Donovan, they knew they had found some prey.

Donovan's mind was racing, considering his options. He was alone, which was a blessing. He would not want Anne to be caught up in whatever these beauties had in mind. He was unarmed, which was perhaps just as well. If he had his Luger with him, in the heat of the moment he might not hesitate to use

141

it. So what was it to be: fight or flight? Donovan sized up the situation and braced himself for what was to come.

The skinheads had made a plan. They began crossing the road. In this quiet street there was no traffic and no passers-by. That meant no witnesses, which suited them fine. They took their time, ambling over. They were in no hurry.

Their self-confidence played to Donovan's advantage, at least initially. They were caught off-guard when he suddenly sprinted away, fleet of foot in lightweight black trainers. The skinheads took off in pursuit, but they were hampered by their heavy boots, which were more suited to kicking a victim than giving chase.

Within seconds, Donovan had gained more than twenty yards on his pursuers. He calculated the distance to the VW, certain he could reach it before they reached him. But fiddling with a key in the lock while they bore down on him was probably a risk too far. And that would make his distinctive classic 1971 black Beetle a known target for the future. Time for quick thinking. Then he saw the others.

About fifty yards away another mob of skinheads was coming towards him. Their interest was no doubt pricked by the sight of him running, with the first bunch in pursuit. This was not good. Options were closing down fast. To make matters worse, he was rapidly approaching a side street and would have to slow in case of traffic. Worse still, the gang ahead of him now had an urgency in their strides. They were scenting blood.

He had no choice but to skid round the corner and charge into the side street, praying that he would not encounter another gaggle of skinheads in hunting mode. They seemed to be everywhere that day. His prayers were not answered. At the end of the street yet another group was mooching along. Damn and blast! The only blessing was that so far they had given no sign of noticing him. He took an instant decision.

The houses in this street were set back behind small front gardens, most of them little more than concrete yards containing dustbins, concealed behind privet hedging. Donovan slid into the nearest one with the tallest hedge and crouched down between two bins. He held his breath and waited.

All too soon the heavy clumping of bovver boots announced the passing – he hoped – of one of the gangs of skinheads. They seemed to be lumbering along at a good pace. Donovan curled into a ball and made every effort to slow his breathing. The boots came and the boots went. Donovan heard the thugs muttering amongst themselves as they hurried by. He collected his thoughts and focused everything on the next move.

The gangs would converge at the street corner and share intelligence, if that word was appropriate to them. As soon as they met, they would realise he had headed that way, and the search of likely hiding places would begin. He was a sitting duck. Donovan knew the best bet was to leave his location when the skinheads were at their furthest point and make a break for it in the opposite direction. He was confident he could out-run them, but aware that he might find himself charging into another bunch along the road.

He was preparing to make his dash for freedom when it happened. The first warning came when he heard footsteps clomping nearer. He huddled down even further. The footsteps came to a halt very close by and he wished for a crack in the ground to swallow him up. Once again his prayers went unanswered. The second ominous warning sound was a faint shuffling from inches away.

Donovan almost cried out when he felt a hand fall firmly on his shoulder. He knew the game was up and turned slowly to face his enemy. But it was not a skinhead who was signalling him to keep silent, nor was it even a man. To his great surprise, Donovan found himself looking into the face of a young woman, but stranger than that, he found himself looking into the face of someone he could only describe as a witch.

****

The clock on the kitchen wall showed that Donovan had been gone for more than ten minutes. Anne cross-checked it with her watch for the *n*th time. *Where the hell was he?* He'd said the car was just parked down the road round the corner. How long could it take to walk a hundred yards and drive back, unless ... Anne tried to restrain her imagination. After all, this was the part of town in which a gruesome murder had taken place.

Anne was standing up to go to the front door when she heard something in the garden, a faint plaintive sound like a whimper. She turned back and walked over to the kitchen window. Peering out, she saw nothing unusual. But there it was again. She realised it was a cat meowing at the door. It was making a tentative sound, not a bit like Dolly's loud confident call. Did the

Koslowskis have a cat? No one had mentioned it. A key was protruding from the lock on the door to the garden. Anne turned it and pulled the door inwards. The cat was sitting on the scraper-mat. It looked up at Anne and immediately backed away.

'It's all right, puss. I won't hurt you. Do you want some milk?'

It was a large black and brown tabby with a round face and yellow eyes, wary of this stranger in its house, if it was in fact the cat of the house. Anne tried again, speaking in her softest tone.

'Don't be frightened. I mean you no harm.'

She took an exploratory step forward. The cat retreated by a yard, still watching her intently. Anne had a sudden brainwave. Leaving the door wide open, she walked to the food cupboard. She knew there was little point in examining the fridge. Donovan had already cleared out a quantity of items that were well past their use-by date and in most cases rotten. In the cupboard she found several tins of cat food and soon located a tin-opener. All the while the tabby observed her from the garden, but gradually coming nearer. Anne took a saucer from a dish-rack and tipped some succulent delicacy labelled 'Chicken Chunks' onto it. She held the saucer out in front of her and advanced slowly, making gentle encouraging sounds as she went. The cat turned a few circles, but came no nearer.

'You are one nervous beastie,' Anne said quietly.

The cat maintained its stand-off while Anne went out onto the small patio. She slowly knelt down and placed the saucer on the flagstones. The tabby inched forward uncertainly, sniffing the air.

'That's his favourite, that is.'

The voice startled Anne. She jumped back, one hand pressed against her chest.

'Sorry, me dook. Didn't mean to give you a scare.'

Anne turned to find a woman leaning over the fence between the houses. She was regarding Anne with a mixture of curiosity and wariness, though her tone was kindly. Anne placed her somewhere in her seventies.

'You took me by surprise,' Anne said. 'I didn't see you there.'

'Are you a relative?'

'Sorry?'

'Are you a relative of Katie and Stan? You look like you could be.'

144

'Do I?'

'Well, your colouring and that ... blonde and pale. Are you Polish?'

'No. No, I'm not.'

'You're not the police. We've seen lots of them round here ... since ...'

Anne relaxed and was glad to have some unthreatening human contact. From the corner of her eye she noticed the cat now moving slowly in the direction of the saucer.

'My name's Anne and I'm with a firm of interior designers, Walker and Co. We're involved in renovating the house after what's happened. I've come to make notes.'

'Oh, I see. So do you know the people who live here?'

'Not at all, but my boss has visited Mr Koslowski in hospital. Is this their cat?'

'That's right. I've been looking after him while they're away.'

The neighbour talked as if the Koslowskis were on holiday, and Anne wondered if the magnitude of what had happened next door had not quite sunk in. The cat meanwhile was now within a few feet of Anne, and she squatted down and held out a finger. The big tabby came forward and rubbed his muzzle against it. Anne ran a hand over his head, and he pushed his big round face hard against her, turning from side to side.

'He seems friendly enough now,' Anne said. 'Probably because you're here.'

'He's always shy,' the neighbour said.

'What's his name?' Anne asked, looking up at the old lady.

'It's on his collar. Can you see? I'm never sure how to say it. I think it must be Polish.'

Anne felt under his chin where a brass disc was attached to a red collar. On one side was a phone number, on the other a single word: Borodin. With a decisive movement the cat disengaged from Anne and advanced purposefully towards the saucer. He began eating.

'I hope I'm not messing up your feeding routine, Mrs ...'

'Betts, Joyce Betts. No, that's all right. He can have his tea a bit later than usual tonight. Not a problem.'

'Good.' Anne suddenly remembered Donovan. 'Well, I'd better be off. Er, could I give you my business card, Mrs Betts? Just in case anything happens or you have any problems.'

As Mrs Betts took the card her face clouded over. 'What might happen? You don't think ...'

'No, I'm sure everything will be fine, but if you have any questions any time, we're in touch with the Polish community. You'll probably see people coming and going as work gets underway, that's all.'

'That's quite reassuring, thank you. Do you know how Stan is? Is he getting better?'

'He's still in intensive care as far as I know. If I find out anything else I'll be in touch. Probably see you from time to time.'

Anne left the tabby contentedly eating his chicken chunks outside and locked up. As she closed the front door behind her she was deeply troubled. Where on earth was Donovan?

****

Marnie was going great guns. The small pile of folders on the right of her desk was gradually but steadily becoming a small pile of folders on the left as the number of projects requiring attention changed to those she had dealt with. A glance at the wall clock showed that she had worked through her coffee break. Soon it would be time for lunch. Where had the morning gone, she wondered, but she did not care. The frustrations of the preceding weeks were fast being blotted out by the progress she was making that day. Settling back to work, the thought crossed her mind that Anne and Donovan would probably be returning any time now.

The positive calm of the morning changed a few minutes later. With Anne out of the office, she was taking phone calls herself.

'Walker and Co, good morning.'

'It's Anne.'

'Hi, how are things –'

'Has Donovan phoned you?'

'Donovan? He's still not back?'

'No. So you haven't heard anything from him?'

'Not a peep. Where are you?'

'I'm in the street outside the Koslowskis' house. I told you when Donovan went to fetch the car *ages* ago. Well, he still hasn't come back. I thought if he had a problem he might've let you know.'

146

'Exactly how long has he been gone?'

'I make it almost half an hour.'

'And your mobile's been switched on all the time?'

'Sure. This is really not like Donovan. I'm worried, Marnie.'

'Okay. Look, I'm coming to get you. I'll bring Ralph and we'll search together. Is the car where you left it?'

'I don't know. He parked it after dropping me off. Before you do anything, Marnie, perhaps I ought to find the car.'

'No, I think I ought to –'

'Really, Marnie, let me go to the car first. Please. I'll be careful.'

Marnie pondered the situation. 'Ring me as soon as you find the car or if – I mean when – Donovan turns up, whichever is sooner. Okay?'

'I'm setting off now.'

'You take care.'

As soon as she disconnected, Marnie rang through to Ralph on *Thyrsis* to put him in the picture. She told him to stand by for a rapid departure.

****

The street was deserted. There was not a single person to be seen. Yet Anne imagined a threat in the air, as if someone was watching her. She rounded the corner and set off in the direction that Donovan had taken.

The whole neighbourhood seemed eerily quiet. Anne feared that at any moment someone might leap out from a doorway and grab her. She quickened her pace, peering into the distance, scanning the area for a sight of the bulbous black form of a VW Beetle.

And suddenly there it was.

Anne spotted it about fifty yards ahead on the other side of the street. She broke into a jog, found a gap between parked cars and skipped across the roadway. Whatever she expected to find, she was either relieved or disappointed. The car was empty; the doors were locked. Of Donovan there was no sign.

Anne reached into her pocket, pulled out the mobile and stared at it. It seemed pathetically lame to call Marnie and report no result. She had only been searching for a couple of minutes. The least she could do was try a little longer. And what would Marnie and Ralph do when they arrived? They would

147

probably split up and search the surrounding streets, by which time Donovan would probably have returned, and they would have had a wasted journey. Anne decided that that was what she would do. She had crossed a side street on her way to the VW. That would be her starting point.

Anne set off briskly. She retraced her steps to turn into the side street, glancing in each front garden as she passed. She had no idea what she expected to find but cast about her in every direction. Suddenly she stopped abruptly. Wide-eyed and open-mouthed she began to advance again at first slowly. Further along the street there seemed to be a bundle lying at the roadside. At first sight it appeared to be a black rubbish sack, but the closer Anne came to it, the more she was certain it was a human form. She accelerated, dreading what she might find.

There was no doubt about it. The blonde hair, the black jacket and jeans. It was Donovan, curled in a foetal position. She threw herself down beside him and gasped at what she saw. The side of his face and hair was bright red. Her hand was trembling as she tested for a pulse. She had seen detectives on television placing fingers on the neck of a victim to determine if they were alive. Her efforts were a total failure. There was not the slightest murmur, which threw her into a panic.

'Donovan! Donovan!' Her voice was a hoarse whisper. She shook his shoulder, at first gently, then with increasing vigour. 'Please, Donovan, wake up!' She knew it sounded silly, but she felt desperate. Anne was pulling the mobile from her pocket when he spoke.

'Anne.' His voice was a whisper, but surprisingly firm.

'Don't worry,' she said. 'I'm calling for an ambulance. I'll get you to A and E. You'll be fine. Just hold on.' Everything came out in a rush of staccato bursts.

'No. Don't phone. Get the car. Bring it here.'

'But –'

'Do you know where it is?' He spoke without opening his eyes or moving.

'Yes.'

'Good. Keys are in my pocket.'

'You need treatment.'

'Just fetch the car.'

'I can't leave you here.'

'Yes, you can. The sooner you go, the sooner you'll be back. Go now.'

Anne bit her lip, filled with indecision.

'Anne, I mean it. Just do as I say. Trust me.'

With an audible sigh, Anne retrieved the car keys, stood up and satisfied herself that the street was deserted. 'I'll be quick.' She sprinted away.

Anne was as good as her word. She was breathless when she skidded to a halt beside the VW, but knew she had made it in world record time. Climbing into the driver's seat she realised she had never driven the car before. But the controls seemed straightforward, no more complicated than her own. Still panting, she fired up the engine, slotted the lever into what she hoped was first gear and eased away from the kerb. Thankful that there was no traffic around, she even managed to find reverse and perform a turn.

The short trip back to Donovan was quick and uneventful. Anne pulled up close by. She leapt out, leaving the engine running, and knelt beside him.

'Donovan, I'm here, but you need help. I have to call –'

'No you don't. We're going back to Knightly.'

'I don't think that's a good idea.'

'Anne, I'm dying.'

'What?' She was totally alarmed. 'No you're –'

'You've left the bloody engine on. I'm choking to death here with exhaust fumes.'

'Oh, sorry! I'll turn it off.'

She rose, rushed to the car and switched off the ignition. As she withdrew from the cockpit she found Donovan on his feet next to the passenger door.

'You drive,' he said. 'Let's go.'

Before she could object, he was in the car fastening his seat belt. Anne got back in. Filled with misgivings, she did as he had asked. Gradually she was becoming aware that something was not what she expected. She had to give her full attention to negotiating the town traffic, but was surprised when Donovan pulled open the glove box and took out a packet of wet wipes. He began rubbing the blood from his face and hair. His clothes were dusty from lying in the gutter, but otherwise he seemed to be functioning normally. Neither them spoke as Anne concentrated on driving the unfamiliar car. The Beetle was not as nippy as the Mini, but felt solid, and Anne knew it was more important to get them home safely than to chat.

Even so, she had a myriad of questions to ask and was completely bewildered by the situation. She permitted herself the occasional glance at Donovan, who seemed content to let her get on with driving without interruption.

When they reached the dual carriageway Anne said, 'Donovan, what's going on?'

'I'll tell you later. For now, just drive.'

****

At Glebe Farm nobody was surprised when Donovan announced that he needed a hot bath followed by a lie down. While Marnie, Ralph and Anne enjoyed a late soup- and-sandwich lunch, Donovan wallowed in reinvigorating Radox suds upstairs in the guest bathroom. He had assured everyone that his wounds were not bleeding or even serious, and he produced a sleeping bag from the Beetle with the request to Marnie that he might rest in a bedroom in the farm house. He promised to tell his story during the evening meal.

He emerged from the bathroom enveloped in a huge white towel to find a ham sandwich, a glass of red wine and a banana on a small tray on the bedside table, with a pink paper heart bearing a simple message:

With love from Anne x

The heart was propped up against a bud vase containing a single daffodil.

****

Unbeknown to Donovan, Marnie popped out in the afternoon to visit the supermarket, leaving Anne and Dolly in charge of the office. Like Donovan, Anne felt that she had been put through a shredder that day, but was happy to man the fort when Marnie explained her proposal for a supper of 'comfort food'.

At the end of the working day the residents of Glebe Farm converged on the kitchen where Marnie and Anne set about preparing the meal. For once Ralph was not preoccupied with choosing a suitable wine. On this occasion he was happy to go along with Marnie's choice of beer as recommended by the supermarket's drinks manager. The beer was German, *Warsteiner*, and the comfort food was Frankfurter sausages, sauerkraut and mashed potatoes with onion gravy. Dessert was apple strudel from the patisserie counter.

Ralph hovered by the Aga taking in the smells of the cooking and declared they really needed comfort food of that sort more often. When Donovan presented himself to join them, he paused in the doorway, took in a deep breath and exclaimed in German, '*Mensch! Würstchen mit Sauerkraut. Wunderbar!*'

'I think we probably get the gist of that,' Marnie said. 'I take it you approve.'

'Absolutely.'

'Genuine German Frankfurters,' Marnie added. 'And I found a German make of vegetarian ones, so Anne can join in, too.'

Donovan grinned. 'Marnie, my cup runneth over ... or should that be my beer glass?'

'So it should. You've had quite a day. How's your injured head?'

'Completely fine.'

'Good.'

'No, I mean that literally. There's nothing wrong with me, nothing at all.'

Three mystified expressions turned his way. Marnie glanced at Anne before replying.

'But Anne's told us what happened. She found you lying, bleeding in the gutter. What part of that didn't she understand?'

'In the gutter, yes ... bleeding, no.'

'But I saw the blood,' Anne protested. 'It was all congealed and horrible.'

'Did you ... really?'

Anne reflected. 'Come to think of it ...'

'What?' said Marnie.

Anne shook her head. 'There was something.'

'Okay, Donovan,' Marnie said, 'I think you should tell us what actually happened.'

'And I think,' Donovan said, 'that we should all have a glass of that excellent beer and nibble some of those pretzels while we wait for the Frankfurters to heat up.'

Donovan began telling his story after raising a glass.

'*Prost!* Okay, so there I was on my way to fetch the car when I ran into a bunch of skinheads. No point trying to take them on,

151

so I legged it down the nearest street. Then another gang came my way and I dived into a front garden and hid by the rubbish bins. I thought I'd got away with it when suddenly a hand grabbed my shoulder.'

'So that's how they got you,' Marnie said.

'Not quite. I looked round and found I was looking into the face of what I thought was a witch.'

'A *witch*?'

'Yeah.'

'What does a witch look like? When we met Moya I thought she looked like any normal person, quite attractive, in fact.'

'Well this one had a sort of longish nose and a rather pointy chin. Also, I was convinced I'd seen her before.'

'When?'

'That day last week when I was going to meet Anne from college. Remember I said a woman in a far right gang took a photo of me from across the street? It was her. I'm sure of it.'

'You were beaten up by a *girl*?'

'Not beaten up at all. She told me to stay put until the others had passed. Then she took out her lip gloss and smeared it all over my face and head.'

'Of course!' Anne exclaimed. 'I thought your blood had just sort of coagulated.'

'It was all her idea,' said Donovan. 'She said once they'd all gone I should lie in the gutter till help came, in case any of them spotted me. They wouldn't want to stick around in case someone reported the incident and the police turned up.'

'Clever thinking,' Ralph said.

Donovan agreed. 'Yes, but also risky, I thought. Still, I couldn't think of a better way out of a dangerous situation.'

'And that's how Anne found you,' Ralph added.

Donovan nodded. 'And here we all are, safe and sound, about to eat one of my favourite meals.' He raised his glass. '*Danke!*'

They all drank. When Anne lowered her glass, her expression was thoughtful.

'I suppose we'll never know who your guardian angel was,' she said. 'Or why she protected you like that.' An impish smile. 'Unless she fancied you.'

'Curled up and cowering between the dustbins,' Donovan said. 'Obviously a woman of refined taste.'

'I wonder …' said Marnie.

Ralph said, 'Are you thinking what I'm thinking?'

'I also wondered about that,' said Donovan.

Anne looked blank. 'What am I missing?'

Marnie said, 'Anne, would you start serving while I make a quick call.'

'Okay.'

Marnie picked up the kitchen phone and went out into the hall. She returned two minutes later with a smile on her face.

'Were you right?' Ralph asked.

'I rang Cathy Lamb direct on her mobile and asked her point blank if the undercover cop working with New Force in Northampton was a woman.'

'And is she?'

'Cathy said she couldn't possibly comment.'

'That's pathetic, but probably understandable.'

'Anyway, I persevered and asked her if the undercover cop was a young woman who looked a bit like a witch.'

'What did she say to that?'

'She was laughing when she hung up.'

'Aha,' said Ralph.

Donovan said, 'I was wondering if she thought she'd seen me before, and maybe she thought I was a Pole.'

'And I was wondering,' Anne said, 'if you wanted your sauerkraut while it was still hot.'

'Good thinking,' Ralph said, opening more bottles of lager.

****

With all the excitement surrounding Donovan's assumed beating, the other events of the day were overlooked. It was not until they were finishing their strudels that Marnie thought to ask about the Koslowskis' house. Ralph suggested they move to the living room for coffee.

Once they were sitting comfortably, Anne began her narration. Ralph had not been party to any of the earlier conversations, so she started from the beginning, describing the condition of the house room by room. She read out notes of what she thought was needed to bring the house up to an acceptable state. When she arrived at the living room, she hesitated.

'Do you want to do this bit, Donovan?'

'No, you carry on.'

153

Anne described the desolation they had found, the scattered furniture, the bloodstains on the carpet.

Marnie said, 'I feel badly about that, Anne. I should've realised what it would be like. I am sorry.'

Anne shrugged. 'It had to be done.'

'Even so …' She looked at Donovan. 'Did you take photos as usual?'

'Yes, everywhere. I'll get them developed and printed tomorrow.'

'There was something else,' Anne said. 'It was horrible … graffiti on the wall. Someone had sprayed *HEXE* in red paint.' She made a face. 'It looked like more blood.'

Marnie said, 'I wonder why they should use a German word.'

'Homage to their Nazi heritage?' said Donovan scornfully.

'Yes,' Marnie agreed, 'and close enough to the English word *hex*, for a curse. Is it the same in German?'

Donovan shook his head. 'No. German uses a different word for a curse. But of course a witch is a *Hexe*.' Like Anne, he pronounced the word like hexer.

'That would be Cathy Lamb's witch connection,' Ralph added.

'No doubt,' said Marnie. 'Though why she couldn't have told us that in the first place, I've no idea.' She looked at Anne and Donovan. 'You had quite an eventful outing. Thank goodness you're both back safely.'

'There was one other thing,' Anne said.

'What was that?'

'I met a next door neighbour, an old lady, and I saw the Koslowskis' cat. In fact I gave him something to eat. He's a lovely big tabby, very tough-looking. I called him Butch because that's how he looked.'

'Did he seem all right? Is someone looking after him?' Marnie asked.

Anne nodded. 'The lady next door, Mrs Betts, Joyce. He certainly looked well nourished … great big teddy bear of a thing.' Anne smiled at the thought. 'He had thick-pile fur like Dolly and he butted my hand hard with his head. He pushed his big round face into my hand when I stroked him.'

'Sounds like you had a better time than me,' Donovan said. 'Butch seems to have become quite a friend.'

'Actually, he wasn't really called Butch. I just thought of him like that. It wasn't his real name.'

'He introduced himself, did he?' said Donovan.

'Sort of. He had a collar with a disc on with his name. He's called Borodin. I thought that quite suited him, too ... a good name for a bear.'

'But rather an odd choice when you think of it,' Ralph said.

'How so?' Marnie asked.

Before Ralph could reply, the phone rang on the table beside Marnie. She picked it up.

'Angela, hello.'

While Marnie was occupied, Anne topped up their coffee cups. The call lasted only a couple of minutes. By the time Anne replaced the coffee pot on its stand, Marnie had disconnected. Her expression was grave.

She said, 'You'll have gathered that was Angela Hemingway.'

'Bad news?' said Ralph.

Marnie took a breath. 'Stan Koslowski came round and was conscious for a while. He asked where was his wife, so they broke it to him. He was very distressed and soon afterwards took a turn for the worse. The consultant has sent for Father Novak to administer the last rites.'

Chapter 14

It rained in the night. The cobbled yard at Glebe Farm glistened in the pale light of Saturday morning. When Ralph went out for his pre-breakfast constitutional he had to choose carefully where he trod on the footpath through the spinney. As he passed, droplets fell from branches onto his head, and the trees smelled washed and clean. Emerging into the boats' docking area, he found *Sally Ann* and *Thyrsis* shining at their moorings. He remembered what Anne had said about the artist Hundertwasser and his love of the colours that glowed after rainfall. Ralph wondered if the artist had ever tried power-walking along a slippery towpath, dodging puddles and patches of mud that invited him at any moment to take an unplanned bath in the canal.

Despite the hazards he had faced that morning, Ralph returned to Glebe Farm refreshed, looking forward to a shower and breakfast. From the hall he could hear Marnie's voice in the kitchen, obviously speaking on the phone. She sounded serious. Ralph stuck his head round the door as Marnie hung up. She was standing by the Aga. Anne and Donovan, seated at the table, were staring up at her.

Marnie said, 'It's all right …not bad news.' She looked towards Ralph. 'That was Angela. She'd just phoned the hospital to ask about Stan.'

'How is he?'

'The medics have got him stabilised. He's sedated but breathing normally again without assistance.'

'That's a relief,' said Anne. 'When the phone rang I feared the worst.'

'Me too.'

Anne continued. 'You know, I don't think they should've told him about his wife, not in his condition. It's too soon.'

Ralph stepped into the room. 'They probably thought they had little choice. The alternative was to lie to him.'

'I think Ralph's right,' Marnie said. 'Once he was awake enough and *compos mentis* enough to ask for her, what else could they do?'

Ralph said, 'I think he had to be told sooner or later.'

'It's all about timing,' Donovan muttered.

Marnie said, 'We all have to face up to hard facts sooner or later.'

****

After that sombre start to the day, Ralph came down from his shower to find everyone making an effort to be cheerful over breakfast. It had started raining again, so to lighten the atmosphere Marnie was preparing scrambled eggs with smoked salmon. The smell of toasting bread pervaded the kitchen. Donovan's contribution to the gathering was to light one of his sculpted German candles. He was blowing out the match when his mobile began ringing.

'Donovan.' He listened for a few seconds before speaking again. '*Herr Hauptkommissar, guten Morgen ... ach so ... ja, natürlich ...*' He placed a hand over the phone. 'I'll take this outside,' he whispered and went out into the hall.

After he closed the door, Marnie said, 'What d'you think that was all about?'

Anne said, 'I expect the *Hauptkommissar* is the police chief Donovan met in Bergheim. You know, Herr Schröder, the one he said looked like Rod Steiger in that film.'

'*In the Heat of the Night*,' Ralph said.

'That's the one. Donovan said Schröder was a tough-looking character.'

Donovan was gone for some minutes. Marnie was beginning to worry that his scrambled eggs might be turning to rubber when he reappeared looking thoughtful.

Marnie said, 'I hope this isn't bad news,'

'It isn't,' Donovan said, taking his place at the table. 'Not at all, though it's rather unexpected.'

They began eating and, between mouthfuls, Donovan explained.

'That first call was from Herr Schröder in Bergheim.'

'First call?' Marnie said.

'Yes. Let me tell you what happened. The *Hauptkommissar* rang to say the Porsche is now available for collection.'

Anne swallowed and said, 'That's great news!'

'So soon?' said Ralph.

'Apparently the case is pretty well wrapped up and I can take the car away. In fact, he seemed keen to get shot of it. I told him I couldn't come at once, and he said he'd be prepared to release it

157

to a responsible member of my family, seeing that I have relatives in Germany.'

'Nobody nearby, though,' said Anne.

'Well, I rang uncle Helmut and explained the situation. He straight away had an idea. It seems Uschi has a new boyfriend who has a quadbike. He races with it - you know, like rallycross - and transports it around on a trailer.'

'That sounds promising,' said Ralph.

'To cut a long story short, I rang the police back. Herr Schröder agreed to them collecting it, provided that uncle Helmut took responsibility in person and completed all the inevitable paperwork.'

'Is he up to it?' Anne asked. 'He's been quite unwell lately.'

'This new boyfriend, Wolfgang, is happy to take uncle Helmut and do all the driving. Uschi will go with them. They'll make an outing of it and probably stop for a nice lunch somewhere.'

'A perfect solution,' said Marnie. 'And when will you go over to bring it back?'

'I'll have to work that out. There are things that have to be dealt with here. We've got enough on our plate right now.'

'You can say that again,' Marnie said.

****

It rained in the morning. Marnie had planned to spend an enjoyable hour tinkering with her pre-war MG sports car. She had looked forward to the regular routine: a complete rub down and thorough check-over. Soon, with spring underway, she would be able to take it out for a run to blow away the cobwebs. But not that Saturday morning. Instead, she and Ralph went back to their respective work stations, both of them keen to stay ahead of the game.

Anne joined her in the office barn and devoted the morning to going over Marnie's latest designs for clients. Donovan spent the time on the phone, firming up on plans for collecting the Porsche.

****

It continued to rain on and off throughout the afternoon, which scuppered any plans Marnie nurtured for a tootle on *Sally Ann*. When she met Ralph, Anne and Donovan for coffee mid-afternoon they all agreed it was a totally frustrating day, but at least they had put in some productive work. Now they were ready for a more enjoyable evening.

Marnie and Ralph had an invitation to a college dinner in Oxford and would stay overnight.

'How about you two?' Marnie asked.

Anne looked quizzically at Donovan. 'Any bright ideas?'

Donovan pondered the question. 'How about the cinema? I think there's a new Mike Nichols film on in Northampton. Might be worth seeing. It got good crits.'

Things were looking up. They had a plan, and to make things even better, the rain eased off late in the afternoon.

****

Soon after Marnie and Ralph left for Oxford, Anne and Donovan set off in the Mini for an early pub supper before the film. They found a slot in a multi-storey car park a short walk from both pub and cinema. The first hint of problems came when they spotted a group of skinheads shambling along the main shopping street. Such gangs seemed to have become a regular feature of life in the town. Everyone knew they spelled trouble.

'They're looking for bother as usual,' Donovan said.

'I'm sure you're right,' Anne replied, 'but we aren't, are we? We're just here for a pleasant night out.'

Donovan's response did not assuage Anne's concern. 'Mm ...' he muttered.

'Why don't we go another way?' Anne suggested cheerfully.

Donovan looked at her. 'Okay. Let's go down here.'

They turned into a pedestrian walkway and then onto a road parallel with the main street.

'There, that's better,' said Anne.

It wasn't. Within seconds they saw another mob prowling some distance ahead. People were wisely crossing the road to avoid contact with them. The skinheads, though, had other ideas. From that moment, the evening started to become interesting, at least as far as Donovan was concerned.

The first sign of trouble came with a cry of pain. Anne stopped walking and held Donovan tightly by the arm. A man on the pavement opposite the gang had gone down on his knees, clutching his head.

'What the hell ...?' Donovan murmured.

'What was it?' Anne said.

159

'Dunno.'

Then Anne's question was answered. A shower of objects flew into the air. The skinheads were lobbing missiles randomly into space. Some of them bounced off the roofs of parked cars, but some found human targets. People began to scatter and run, some of them screaming, cheered on by the far-right thugs.

'Beer cans,' Donovan said. 'Empty, no doubt.'

'What?' Anne was bewildered.

'That's what they're throwing, like grenades. You can see them, look.'

More missiles followed, sped on their way by whooping and cheering from the gang.

'Let's get out of here,' Anne said, tugging at Donovan's arm.

'No, wait,' he said. 'Look there. What's that?'

'I don't want to wait, I just -'

She stopped in mid-sentence. They had both noticed something unexpected. On their side of the road, about thirty or forty yards ahead, someone was creeping along, sheltering behind parked vehicles. It seemed to be a young man, silently stalking the gang, picking up fallen missiles as he went.

'What's he up to?' Donovan said quietly. 'Is he one of them?'

'It's Dom!' Anne said in a hushed voice..

'Who?'

'Dom, Dominik Gorski, Mr Gorski's son. He's the one who brought the key to the Koslowskis' house yesterday while you were parking the car. I told you he did.'

'You're sure it's him?'

'Pretty sure. He looks rather like you … blonde hair, similar height and build, dark clothes.'

'So what's he doing here?' Donovan asked.

They would soon find out. Dom stopped in the lee of a tall van with no windows. He hurriedly peeped round it at the skinheads who were now launching missiles again. Dom stepped back and began hurling the empty beer cans high into the air. In the early evening light they crossed with the cans from the skinheads. Their effect was devastating. Dom's aim was outstanding. They rained down on the thugs whose cheers changed quickly to yelps and shouts of pain and surprise.

'He's asking for trouble,' Anne whispered.

But she was instantly proved wrong. The thugs began turning on each other, throwing wild punches, blaming their mates for aiming badly. Within seconds a violent brawl broke out.

'Our cue to leave,' Donovan said.

Anne needed no second prompting. She pulled Donovan's arm and they began briskly retracing their steps in the direction of the main street. Donovan turned his head for one last glimpse of Dominik Gorski, only to find that he had melted away, his goal no doubt achieved.

'That,' Donovan said, 'is one cool guy. No messing about with him.'

'I thought you'd approve,' said Anne.

'I certainly do. We've found an ally.'

Chapter 15

On Sunday morning Anne had a surprise phone call. She was padding through the office on her way back from the shower when the phone on her desk began ringing. She guessed it might be Marnie letting her know what time she and Ralph would be returning from their overnight stay in Oxford. But she was mistaken.

'Hi.'

'Hello, is that Anne?'

A male voice. She did not recognise it, though it seemed vaguely familiar. 'Yes, it is. Who is this?'

'Dom, Dom Gorski. We met on Friday. Remember?'

'Of course I do. Sorry, I wasn't expecting it to be you. I didn't realise you had this number.'

'My father gave it to me. He has Marnie's business card.'

'Oh, I see. You want to speak to Marnie. I'm afraid she isn't –'

'No. I wanted to speak to you. Is that all right?'

'Sure. What can I do for you?'

There was a brief pause on the line. 'It's a personal thing, really. I was wondering … well, it's like this. There's a good film on in town.'

Anne said, 'Directed by Mike Nichols, I know. *Primary Colors.*'

'That's the one,' Dom said. 'You've heard about it. Would you be interested in seeing it?'

'I went to see it last night.'

'Ah …'

'It was very good.' She added, 'I went with my boyfriend.'

'You have a boyfriend. I should've guessed. Would you mind me asking is it a serious relationship, or …?'

'I think it's pretty serious, yes. We've been together for a while now.'

'And you went to see the film with him. Of course. I hope you didn't mind me –'

'Actually, Dom, that isn't all we saw.'

'Really?'

'Mm. We saw you.'

'Last night?'

'We saw what you did to the skinheads in the town centre.'

This time the pause was lengthy.

'Are you there, Dom?'

'I'm not a hooligan, if that's what you're thinking.'

'I'm thinking you believe in direct action. Donovan was impressed.'

'Who was?'

'Donovan. That's my boyfriend's name. Donovan Smith. He believes in direct action, too.'

'Good for him.'

'Though it can get you into trouble. It can be a risky business, like last night.'

'I'll take my chances.'

'That's for you to decide, Dom. Anyway, thanks for phoning.'

'No worries. Thank you for explaining how things are.'

'That's all right. Goodbye, then.'

'Oh, Anne?'

'Yes?'

There was a smile in his voice. 'I'll remember what you told me, but it doesn't mean I won't keep trying. I'll leave you in peace for now, though. I'm off to meet some friends. We're planning to get rid of the graffiti in town.'

'When?'

'Probably tomorrow or the next day, as soon as we can get our act together.'

Anne said, 'Did you know the vicar here, Angela Hemingway, has written to the borough council to get the graffiti cleaned up?'

'I did know that and I've met Angela. It's probably a very correct way to proceed. I suppose it's what vicars do. I prefer good old direct action, as you call it. We'll be waiting for ever if we rely on the council to do anything.'

****

When Anne joined Donovan in the farmhouse kitchen for breakfast, he told her that Marnie had phoned. She had rung him on his mobile, as Anne's mobile was switched off and the home phone was engaged. Marnie and Ralph would not be back until the afternoon. The Master of Ralph's college, All Saints, had invited them to stay on for lunch. He wanted to discuss something with Ralph.

'I was on the phone in the office,' Anne explained.

'Right.'

'It was Dom Gorski. You know, the chap we saw lobbing beer cans at the skinheads last night?'

'Did you establish that it was in fact him throwing the grenades?' Donovan asked.

'Oh, it was him, all right. But he wasn't phoning to talk about that. He wanted to invite me out.'

'Did you tell him it would mean pistols at dawn?'

'Something like that. I told him I'd seen the film already and I'd gone with you. I also told him we'd seen what he was doing with the beer cans, I mean grenades.'

Donovan smiled. 'I must say, that was pretty cool.'

'He's like you, Donovan. He's all in favour of direct action.'

'Great.'

'In fact, he's going to clean up the graffiti in town.'

'Oh? When's he doing that?'

'Some time in the next day or two, he said.'

Donovan drained the rest of his coffee and looked speculatively at Anne.

'Do you have his number?'

'I can get it from the office phone.'

'Good. I'd like to call your admirer and tell him we'll help – *I'll* help, at any rate – with the graffiti.'

'What about pistols at dawn?' Anne asked.

'That'll keep for another day, another dawn.'

Chapter 16

D onovan wasted no time on Monday morning. He had phoned Dom Gorski on Sunday, after which he felt inspired to get rid of the graffiti from the canal bridge. When he told Anne what he intended to do, she was at first worried that he might get into trouble with the police. But she relented when Marnie agreed to him using *Sally Ann* once again as a platform. She judged that they had waited long enough.

Anne shrugged mentally. *If it was good enough for Marnie ...*

Anne was happy to keep *Sally Ann* in place while Donovan stood on the roof as before and did the scrubbing. She only had to move the boat out of the bridge hole to let other boats come through on two occasions all morning. By lunchtime Donovan's work was done. It was hard to tell that graffiti had ever been sprayed there.

'That stuff you use is really effective,' Anne said, gazing up to admire his handiwork.

Donovan looked pleased. 'It does the trick all right. I've got enough to last me a bit longer.'

'Is it tomorrow that you're meeting Dom and his friends?' Anne asked.

'Possibly, or the next day. It depends on how many can make it. Whatever happens, I'm -'

He was interrupted by his mobile. He recognised the number displayed and immediately replied in German.

'Hi Uschi. How are things?'

'Good news. We've got the car.'

'You're home already?'

'No. We've just stopped for lunch at a place on the Autobahn near Dortmund.'

'So, you've met the *Hauptkommissar*. What did you think of him?'

'Herr Schröder? Tough guy, but okay. Papa signed a load of release papers, presented his ID and other stuff, and that was that.'

'And the Porsche?'

'You wouldn't believe it.'

'Try me.'

'Wolfgang got in and switched on the engine. It started straight away ... sounded really good. Those crooks did a lot of work on it. I think the seats might even be new replacements, and the hood looks like new.'

'Really?'

'*Ja!* And the bodywork was gleaming. You'd be proud.'

'Sounds like they did me a favour.'

'When are you coming to fetch it?'

'Soon as I can. It'll take a day or two to organise things.'

'Okay. I'll meet you at the airport. Just tell me when.'

'Thanks, Uschi, and please thank Onkel Helmut and Wolfgang. I'm looking forward to meeting him.'

When Donovan disconnected, he climbed down from the roof of *Sally Ann* and gathered the groundsheet and cleaning materials together. Anne steered the boat into the dock. He joined her on the bank and helped with mooring ropes.

'Did you understand much of that from what you heard?' he asked.

'A little. You seemed pleased with things.'

They set off through the spinney, carrying the gear between them, while Donovan explained all that had happened in Germany.

'When d'you think you'll be able to travel?'

Donovan grimaced. 'I'll have to go soon, but …'

'But what? It'll be nice to see your family again and great to get your beloved Porsche back. What's not to be glad about?'

Donovan stopped and turned to face her. 'It's just …there's so much unfinished business here.'

****

That morning, alone in the office, Marnie took on one of Anne's roles. At ten-thirty she carried a tray filled with mugs of steaming coffee out to the rear of the farmhouse. There, with winter past, the builders were completing external works while the gardeners were clearing the jungle that would soon, she hoped, be transformed into a country garden. The recent rainy spell had held off, and they were all making good progress. Marnie meanwhile was happily pressing on with her own work without interruption. That was due to change when Anne reappeared shortly afterwards with Donovan in tow.

'Have you heard from Angela this morning?' Anne asked.

'No.'

166

Marnie hoped she gave the impression that that was an end to the subject. She failed. Anne advanced on the kitchen area and poured water into the kettle.

'D'you think -'

'Not really.'

Anne gave Marnie *The Look* and continued unabashed. 'Do you think it's worth urging Angela to follow up her letter to the council with a phone call?'

'Why?'

'I'm sure the archdeacon would. He'd probably camp out on the steps of the town hall until -'

'Okay, okay.' Marnie raised her hands in surrender. 'I'll give her a ring. She's probably busy, though, writing her Sunday sermon.'

'Marnie, it's Monday morning. She's probably having a lie-in after her exertions in the pulpit yesterday.'

With a theatrical sigh Marnie gave in and reached for the phone.

****

The afternoon passed off without serious disruption. There was the odd phone call for Walker and Co, but otherwise all was quiet on the Glebe Farm front. The evening was a different matter. Marnie was on the point of tipping the ingredients for a stir-fry into the wok when Angela rang. She pressed the speaker button so that Anne, Ralph and Donovan could hear.

'Hi, Angela.'

'Hello, Marnie. I hope I'm not phoning at an awkward moment.'

'No, good timing. I was just about to start a stir-fry.'

'Oh, I wouldn't want to disturb you at wok.' She tinkled a girlish laugh. When there was no reaction, she cleared her throat and continued. 'Yes, well, er ... I phoned the council as you asked and the good news is, they will carry out removal of graffiti.'

Marnie said, 'Something tells me that *bad news* is on the way.'

'There is a snag, yes.'

'Which is?'

'The man I spoke to said their budget is over-committed for the current financial year.'

'I take it that means they've no money?'

'Yes,' Angela said. 'He said they could do nothing until the next financial year.'

Donovan groaned.

Ralph said, 'So that's presumably after the first of April.'

'There is a further snag.' Angela's voice sounded strained.

'Amaze me,' said Marnie.

'They have other schemes being held back, apparently, and they automatically get first priority.'

'In practical terms, what does that mean?' Marnie asked.

'His best guess was that the clean-up work would probably not start until … the summer … at the earliest.'

Donovan raised his voice for Angela to hear. 'The work will've been done by then.'

Angela sounded confused. 'I don't see how.'

'I do,' said Donovan.

****

The next call came in while the Glebe Farm four were in the sitting room having coffee. Anne checked the caller ID on the tiny screen of her mobile, but did not recognise the number. She hoped it would not be Dominik Gorski pressurising her.

'Hello?' A woman's voice. She sounded timid, as if unaccustomed to using the phone.

'Hi. This is Anne, Anne Price. Who's calling?'

'It's Mrs Betts from next door.'

'Next door? Oh, you mean next door to the Koslowskis.'

'Yes. Are you the young lady I spoke to on Friday?'

'Yes, that's right, Mrs Betts. How are you?'

'You said I could phone you if I had any problems.'

'Sure. What's the problem?'

'It's the cat.'

'Oh dear.'

'I haven't seen him since Saturday morning, only I don't know what to do for the best.'

'Hold on a moment, please.'

Anne put her hand over the phone and outlined the situation to the others. When she listened again, Mrs Betts was still talking.

'… the other young lady with the funny name.'

'Sorry, Mrs Betts. I missed that.'

'I would ask the other young lady who's been coming here, but I haven't seen her for a while, not since Katie ...'

Anne said, 'There's another girl who comes? Who is that?'

'I think Katie called her Maddie, or Madeleine or something like that. I'm not good with foreign names.'

'Is she perhaps Polish?' Anne asked.

'Not sure, probably. She sounds English, though, but I've heard her speaking something foreign with her young man when he brings her ... used to bring her, to see Katie.'

'Could she be a relative, perhaps?'

'I don't know, dear, but she's been coming quite a lot in the past few months.'

'Have you mentioned her to the police at all?'

'The police? No. Why would I?'

'Well, they might want to know who came to see Mrs Koslowski. Didn't they ask you things like that?'

'They asked me if I'd seen anyone acting suspiciously around the time Katie ... died.'

'What about her young man?'

'Oh, he's very nice, very polite. I've seen him a few times bringing the young lady.'

'What does he look like, Mrs Betts?'

'Very nice. He's got very fair hair and he wears casual clothes but smart ... always nicely turned out.'

'Dark clothes?'

'Yes, I suppose so.'

'And he's her boyfriend?'

'I'm only guessing, but I've always seen them together, so I think he probably is.'

'All right,' Anne said. 'Let's get back to the cat.'

'I am worried about him. He doesn't usually stay out. Likes his food regular.'

'Mrs Betts, I'll come over tomorrow and have a good hunt round. I'm sure he'll turn up soon.'

'I do hope so, dear.'

'Do you have a key to Mrs Koslowskis' house?' Anne asked.

'Yes. I can let you in. If I'm not in when you come, I'll leave a key under the mat outside their door.'

They disconnected and Anne filled in the gaps for the others.

'I'll go over tomorrow,' she said. 'Mrs Betts sounded really worried.'

'We can go together,' said Donovan. 'I want to go anyway to make a start on the graffiti.'

Marnie said, 'I'll come too. I'd quite like a look at the house. There are still things to sort out, like how to phase the work, final choice of colours and how we organise it all.'

'Is there actually a budget for the works?' Ralph asked.

'The Polish community is going to pay for things. Insurance might cover some of the costs, assuming the Koslowskis have a building and contents policy. There are still quite a few questions to be answered.'

Donovan said, 'The questions on my mind are about this so-called *young lady* Mrs Betts talked about. Who the hell is she? And why has no one mentioned her before?'

'You think she could be significant?' Ralph said.

'Who can tell? She must at least be worth questioning about what she knows.'

'Perhaps the police do know about her from sources other than Mrs Betts. Perhaps they've interviewed her already.' Ralph turned to Marnie. 'Worth checking with Cathy Lamb?'

'Could be worth following up. On the other hand, I can't imagine the police would be too overjoyed about me asking them if they've done their job properly.'

'You could get Angela to raise it with Cathy Lamb,' Anne suggested.

Marnie laughed. 'How to win friends ... or rather lose them!'

'Are you expecting to see Cathy any time?' Donovan asked. 'If so, you could casually drop it into the conversation.'

'Let me think about it. Meanwhile, we have a cat to find.'

Chapter 17

A small convoy of vehicles left Glebe Farm on Tuesday morning. In the lead was Donovan's black Beetle, followed by Marnie's dark blue Freelander. The aim was flexibility. Donovan had arranged to meet Dom Gorski and some of his friends by the Polish shop in Little Warsaw. Together they would begin Operation Clean-Up, for which Donovan had brought his box of cleaning materials. But first, he would join forces with Marnie and Anne in the search for Borodin the cat. Anne travelled with Marnie and would spend time with her in the house dealing with the renovation project.

The two cars parked outside the Koslowskis' house, and Anne walked along to ring the bell of the house next door. They did not want Mrs Betts to be alarmed at the sight of strangers in the Koslowskis' garden.

'It's nice of you to help look for the cat,' Marnie said to Donovan as they waited for Mrs Betts to come to the door. 'I remember how upset I was a couple of years ago when Dolly went missing.'

'Glad to help,' said Donovan.

'I noticed you slowed right down when we came along this road, and I did wonder why you were keen for Anne to come in my car rather than ride with you.'

'Was it that obvious?'

Marnie nodded. 'You were checking to see if the cat might have been run over?'

'It had to be a possibility.'

There was no reply from Mrs Betts. Anne returned to Marnie and Donovan, and found the key under the mat. Once inside, they examined the interior, upstairs and down, including cupboards and wardrobes. Marnie glanced briefly into the living room, the murder room.

The search next moved out into the garden. They stood by the kitchen door and surveyed the scene. The Koslowskis were clearly not keen gardeners. The area comprised a lawn, now well overgrown, with a narrow weed-infested flower border on each side. At the far end of the lawn, standing aside in one corner, was a small shed.

'I'll go,' Donovan said.

He walked quickly the length of the garden, reached the shed and found the door unlocked. He opened it and immediately a large tabby cat ran out. It stopped and turned round, looking up at Donovan, who squatted down and held out a finger.

'It's him!' Anne cried out in the background.

The cat spun round, startled. Anne put a hand to her mouth and spoke quietly.

'Sorry, Butch. Didn't mean to scare you.'

The cat was now poised in limbo, motionless, sizing up the next step. He had a stranger confronting him close at hand and someone he may or may not have recognised talking to him from beside the house. He made up his mind when Marnie, ever practical, emerged from the kitchen holding a can of food and a tin-opener. She waved the can in his direction, tapped it with the implement and went back inside. For such a large and bulky animal he moved remarkably quickly, sprinting down the lawn and disappearing indoors.

Donovan and Anne heard loud appreciative meowing as Marnie set down a saucer of food and gazed on in satisfaction at a job well done.

'I wish all our problems could be solved so easily,' she said as Anne and Donovan crept in quietly.

Donovan closed and locked the back door. They moved out of the kitchen into the hall to leave the cat to enjoy his first meal for some time in peace. Marnie was about to speak when there came a faint knocking on the front door. Donovan opened it to reveal a confused-looking oldish lady. She stared at Donovan.

'You don't look the same,' she said vaguely.

Anne came forward. 'Hello, Mrs Betts. Remember me, Anne? You phoned me last evening.'

'Yes, dear. I'm very worried about the cat.'

'No need,' said Anne. 'We found him!' She indicated Donovan beside her. 'This is Donovan. He found him in the shed.'

Mrs Betts studied Donovan, frowning all the while. 'You do look like the other young man, but not so much close up.'

'I think you mean Dominik. He's the same colouring as Donovan. Marnie has just given the cat some food. This is her now.'

Donovan stepped aside for Marnie to be introduced.

Mrs Betts said, 'I don't think we've met before, have we?'

Marnie offered a hand. 'No, we haven't. I'm Marnie Walker and I'm working on the renovation here. You heard Anne say we've found the cat?'

'Oh, that's lovely. Where did you find him? Did he just come home?'

'No. He was in the garden shed.'

'How did he get in there?' Mrs Betts looked bewildered.

'Perhaps the door blew open and he went in to explore,' Marnie said. 'Cats are very curious creatures.'

Anne and Donovan both glanced at Marnie but said nothing. Mrs Betts looked reassured.

'I expect so. Are you going to take him back with you and look after him till Stan comes home?'

The question took Marnie unawares. 'Er, well ...'

Anne intervened. 'I don't think that would be a good idea, Mrs Betts. Cats always try to find their way home when you move them. We live quite a long way away.'

'And he knows you,' Marnie added. 'I think it's best if he stays in familiar surroundings. Is that all right with you?'

'I suppose so. I don't really want the responsibility, but someone has to feed him, and he's quite a nice cat.'

'Then let's keep it like that,' Marnie said, 'if you don't mind.'

****

After Mrs Betts returned home, Marnie and the others reconvened in the kitchen. The cat had finished eating, and Anne set down a saucer of water beside his empty feeding bowl. He sniffed it briefly, ignored it, then settled down to wash.

'I want to take a look at that shed,' said Marnie.

Anne looked sceptical. 'You mean the one with the door that somehow blew open of its own accord?'

'The very same.'

They went back out to the garden and examined the shed. It had a simple latch and no lock or even the fittings for a padlock.

Anne said, 'The Koslowskis didn't seem to bother much with security.'

Donovan pulled the door open. 'Hardly surprising. Nothing in here worth stealing. The mower looks like a museum piece, so do the garden tools.'

'So how did Borodin get in?' Anne asked.

'I'd have thought that was fairly obvious,' said Donovan.

Marnie agreed. 'Someone shut him in.'

Anne said, 'But why would anyone do that, and how did they get into the garden?'

Donovan walked to the fence and pulled himself up like a gymnast chinning the bar. From that position he could see over.

'There's an alleyway at the back running behind the gardens. Any fit person could get in and out over the fence. So that answers one of your questions.'

Marnie joined in. 'As for why they shut the cat in the shed, I expect it was just to be bloody-minded.'

'But it's interesting,' Donovan said. 'Don't you think? They could have done much worse. After all, they murdered Katie Koslowski ... if it was the same people.'

'You're thinking New Force,' said Marnie.

Donovan raised an eyebrow. 'Who else?'

****

When Marnie suggested they split forces, Donovan was not surprised. He knew how protective Marnie was towards Anne, and it was predictable that she would remove Anne from the house which spooked her. Marnie's plan was to make notes for the renovation scheme and then head back to the office. She was happy for Anne to go with Donovan to meet Dom and his friends and help with cleaning-up the graffiti.

Alone in the house, Marnie took a deep breath and opened the door to the murder room. She was keen to get this task out of the way before tackling anything else. Notebook in hand, she systematically moved across the bloodstained carpet, wrinkling her nose at the faint stench of suffering and death. She wrote her recommendations that she hoped one day to put to Stanislav Koslowski. All her choices were in a modern idiom but close enough to the house's original colour scheme not to be too great a divergence. Carpet, walls, curtains; the style she proposed would bring everything together with, she hoped, a new feeling of serenity. Casting a brief glance at the red-sprayed *HEXE* on the wall, she shuddered and moved on.

The more she examined the house, the greater became her curiosity about its occupants. She especially returned again and again to the question of why anyone would want to kill a harmless elderly lady. From room to room Marnie went, writing on her notepad, compiling suggestions. Works would be mainly confined to the ground floor, but nevertheless Marnie climbed the stairs if only to get a more comprehensive feel for the house and those who lived in it.

Marnie wondered about Katie Koslowski. What was her character, her background, her Polish roots? What animated her? Why no children? Was it from desire or misfortune? Who in fact was she? The more Marnie thought about it, the more improbable it seemed. She returned to the idea that the real intended victim might have been her husband. Perhaps all would be revealed when Stan was well enough to talk. Perhaps he would be able to identify or at least describe his attacker.

Marnie stepped into the main bedroom and wandered over to the photos on the dressing table. There was Katie, smiling out of her wedding photograph and an even prouder smile as she posed in uniform. The young Katie looked like a well-built country girl with her mop of fair hair and round face. Marnie had no idea what the uniform denoted, but the look of pride in the face of its wearer was evident, as was the row of medals across her substantial chest. Marnie's gaze shifted to the small framed collection of medals. Did they belong to Katie or her husband? She stooped forward until her nose was almost touching the glass to study the medals and the photo of Katie. Yes, they were certainly hers. So what had she done to earn them? Katie's bearing made Marnie think they were not simply campaign medals but genuine awards for service. But in what?

It was all questions and no answers. Katie would never speak again, never reveal her secrets or her past. As for her husband, who could tell what the future held for him? Leaving the bedroom, Marnie froze. A thought had occurred to her. Are the police providing security for Stan Koslowski in hospital?

****

When Donovan parked the Beetle in Little Warsaw he found a group of three young men already hard at work. They were making a pretty good job of removing the graffiti from the end wall of the Polish shop.

'The one on the stepladder is Dominik Gorski,' Anne said, unfastening her seat belt. 'Dom's the one everyone thinks looks like you.'

Donovan nodded. 'Yeah, at a glance, I suppose. And he's the one who asked you to go out with him?'

'That's him. Perhaps you should make it paint brushes at dawn.'

Donovan chuckled. 'Good idea. Let's go and meet him and his ... seconds.'

Anne and Dom made introductions. She noticed that her suitors eyed each other as surreptitiously as they could. It intrigued her to think that two young men both found her attractive. She had always regarded herself as a skinny insignificant-looking girl, but perhaps they saw her in a different light. For her part, Donovan had been her only serious attachment so far, and her only lover, and she was happy to keep it that way.

Dom shook Donovan's hand warmly. 'Glad to meet you, Donovan, and glad you could come to help. I think we've got to get rid of this crap straight away. The authorities have allowed it to pollute the town for far too long.'

'Absolutely,' said Donovan. 'Couldn't agree more. Where shall I start?'

Dom pointed to the far corner of the wall. 'How about over there?'

'Fine. I'll get my stuff.'

'What about you, Anne?' Dom said.

'I'll work with Donovan.'

'Great.'

The team set to and quickly made progress. After scrubbing for twenty minutes Donovan noticed that a small group of skinheads had formed across the road. He sidled over towards Dom and murmured, 'Don't look round, but we've got company.'

'Where?'

'Other side of the street ... six of them, New Force, I think.'

'Time to bring up reinforcements,' said Dom.

'What d'you have in mind?'

'The local law gave me a number to call in case of bother. I'll give 'em a ring.'

'We'll just carry on working,' Donovan said.

Dom walked round the corner and disappeared out of sight. Donovan was already calculating how effectively a wide paintbrush loaded with detergent gel would serve as a weapon. He glanced quickly over as he dipped the brush into his bucket, but the skinheads made no move. They just stood there watching in menacing silence. Donovan wondered if they too were waiting for reinforcements. He turned his back on them and began applying the detergent to the brickwork, ready to defend himself at the first hint of trouble.

But the approach from behind that actually happened took him completely by surprise. It was the voice of a young woman speaking rapidly in a foreign language. Donovan spun round to find he was being addressed by an attractive girl of about twenty, petite and with shoulder-length dark hair. She stopped talking and stared at him in evident surprise.

Donovan said, '*Przepraszam, nie po polsku.*' He was guessing that the girl had spoken to him in Polish.

She now looked no less bewildered as she opened her mouth to say something and then closed it without a word.

'What was that, Donovan?' Anne said.

'I just apologised for not speaking Polish,' he said. 'I've no idea if it sounded right.'

'Your pronunciation was very good,' the girl said in unaccented English. 'But I thought you were someone else.'

'You took me for Dominik Gorski.'

'I did.'

Just then a police car rounded the corner about a hundred yards away and drove quickly towards them, blue lights flashing but no siren. When everyone turned to watch it, Donovan saw the skinheads diving rapidly down a side street. Dom came round the corner and smiled as the patrol car cruised past. His smile turned to surprise when Donovan suddenly dropped his brush and sprinted off down the side street. The cleaning party were frozen to the spot, wondering whether they should follow, but Donovan was back in a trice, pulling a notebook from his leather jacket. He took out a pen and scribbled something hurriedly.

'Your local cops didn't waste any time getting here,' he said.

Dom said, 'They must have been nearby. It took nearly fifteen minutes last time I had to ring them. Why did you chase after the skinheads?'

'Just a hunch. I wondered if they had transport nearby.'

'And did they?'

Donovan nodded. 'BMW, dark grey. I got it's number. You never know when it might come in handy.'

'I suppose not. I see you've met Magda.' Dom turned and kissed her on both cheeks. 'Let me introduce you properly.

Magdalena Paluch, this is Donovan and Anne. Anne's firm is dealing with the renovation of Stan and Katya's house.'

They all shook hands.

'Dealing with the renovation,' Magda repeated. 'What does that mean?'

Anne said, 'We're going to redecorate the house.' She lowered her voice. 'Or at least the parts that were damaged when Mrs Koslowski was murdered.'

Magda grimaced. 'So you're a firm of decorators?'

'Interior designers. The Polish community wants to carry out a scheme, and we're planning it for them.'

'Did you know Mrs Koslowski?' Donovan asked Magda.

'Yes, quite well.'

'I'm sorry. This is a sad time for you and all her friends and family.'

'She had no family, except for Stanislav,' Magda said. 'That's why I used to visit her ... to help with things.'

'Well,' said Dom. 'It looks as if our skinhead friends have gone. Shall we get on with our work?'

Magda looked up at the wall. 'You've done a great job here,' She turned to Dom. 'I know how much it means to you.' Looking round at Donovan and Anne she added, 'Dom is a great patriot for Poland. It's wonderful that you're all working together. You don't have Polish connections, do you?'

'None,' Donovan said. 'But we have something else in common. We don't have time for fascists.'

'I hope to go and live in Poland some day,' Dom said simply.

'Permanently?' Anne said.

Before Dom could reply Magda intervened. 'I tell Dom it's a pipe dream, but he says he's serious.'

'Would you all like to go?' Anne asked. 'I mean all your family?'

Dom shook his head. 'My parents aren't keen. They were after all born here. They say England's their home. They didn't even bring me up to be bilingual.'

'But he speaks pretty good Polish nonetheless,' Magda said.

'I've been taking courses for a few years now,' Dom confirmed.

'Do you all speak Polish when you're together?' Donovan asked, taking in the whole group.

Two of the three shook their heads. One said he spoke a little.

'So you practise with Magda,' Donovan said to Dom.

178

'Yes, but we only met quite recently. I've mainly practised with the older generation. That's how I met Magda.'

'The *older* generation?' Anne said, smiling. '*Magda?*'

Dom grinned. 'I didn't mean it like that.'

Magda said, 'He met me through knowing the older Polish people in town. Katya was one of them, so we had mutual friends.'

Dom clapped his hands. 'Okay. Shall we press on?'

'Let's go for it,' said Donovan, 'before our skinhead friends come back.'

****

During the afternoon Marnie rang Anne to let her know she was returning to Glebe Farm. She was happy for Anne to stay on in town with Donovan. The Clean-up Group carried on for another hour or so. They managed to finish the end wall of the Polish shop plus a fair amount of other graffiti around Little Warsaw. At the end of the afternoon Donovan drove the Beetle through the slow-moving post-school traffic and headed out of town.

Once they were settled on the dual carriageway Anne said, 'So what did you make of them?'

'Our Polish chums?' said Donovan. 'Nice bunch. Can't be easy for them, really.'

'How d'you mean?'

'Well, they're not fully one thing or the other, are they? They've got Polish names, go to Polish shops, probably go to Mass in Polish on Sundays. But then they're also sort of English. Most of them don't speak Polish. One of them even had a Northampton Town FC scarf round his waist.'

'Is that the same for you, Donovan? I mean, with Britain and Germany?'

'You forgot about Ireland. Remember my dad was half Irish.' Donovan chuckled. 'I'm just a mongrel. But my position's a bit different.'

'You're bilingual … English and German.'

'Yeah. And there's my family in Germany.'

'Hey, you spoke Polish to that girl, to Magda. Where did that come from?'

'I've got a few words, the odd phrase. We have Polish shops in my part of London and one or two Polish neighbours in Germany. I picked up a few things.'

'I was impressed.'

'Don't be. It's nothing.'

They fell silent for a minute or two before Donovan spoke again.

'By the way, I'm not going to mention the German side of my family to Dom and his friends. Some people don't realise there were lots of Germans who weren't fans of Hitler and his mob. And most Poles are in this country because of the last war.'

'D'you think the people we met today would hold it against you?'

'You never can tell. I wouldn't want to spoil my friendship with Dom and the others.'

'I can see that,' Anne said. 'You two really hit it off, didn't you?'

'He's a great guy. We have a lot in common.' Donovan smiled, reached over and patted Anne on the knee. 'Even if it does come to pistols at dawn.'

****

The clean-up group agreed to meet the next day to continue the good work. Before splitting up they stood in a circle and bumped fists together, each of them muttering one Polish word they all knew: *Solidarność!* The 'solidarity' movement in Poland in the 1980s had made that word famous worldwide. Dom drove Magda home in his Peugeot after the session, and carried on to his parents' house in a prosperous middle-class suburb.

He liked Magda. She was witty, good-looking and fun. She also had a serious side that he respected, and she made him believe the feeling was mutual. She would always occupy a special place in his affections.

Dom also liked the new girl on the block. Anne was unlike any girl he had met before. He was attracted to her impish features, her slim boyish figure and especially the way she moved, that fluid effortless walk, combined with a kind of natural grace. But more than that, she was possessed of an intelligent sensitivity that shone through even when she was not speaking. One glance told him how attached she was to Donovan, but who could tell what the future held?

Dom was musing in this manner as he made his way through the traffic that was now gradually building up. That no doubt explained why he failed to notice the BMW keeping its distance a few cars behind him. Where he turned, it turned. Where he drove, it followed.

****

Marnie thought it always felt strange when they had meals as a threesome after Donovan had left. Almost as soon as they arrived back at Glebe Farm, Donovan announced that he would have to set off for London. He needed to pack and have a relatively early night as he was catching a flight to Hanover the next morning. Marnie and Ralph wanted to know how the clean-up had gone. Donovan left it to Anne to give them all the details.

Then he was gone, leaving only his cleaning-up box in the garage barn and a gap they all felt in their different ways.

While they ate supper, Anne gave a full account of their afternoon. Over coffee in the sitting room Marnie outlined her thoughts about Katie Koslowski. She described the medals and the uniform, the happy wedding photo and her own sadness at how their marriage had been so brutally destroyed.

'And I really wonder if Stan was meant to be the victim. After all, who'd want to kill an ageing housewife?'

Ralph steepled his fingers. 'There's no particularly obvious reason for wanting to harm an ageing *male* pensioner, either. And what's the relevance of the *HEXE* on the wall? Witches are usually regarded as female.'

'Perhaps there's a simpler angle,' Anne said. 'They were Polish and could have just been easy targets.'

Marnie nodded. 'I can see all that, but I take Ralph's point about the *HEXE*. After all, that's not Polish.'

'There's a lot more to this than meets the eye,' Ralph said.

He stood and was topping up the coffee cups when two phones began ringing simultaneously. Marnie and Anne reached for their mobiles like gunslingers on the draw in a Western movie. Anne walked through to the kitchen to take her call, while Marnie stepped out into the hall.

****

Anne checked the tiny window on the mobile. The caller's number seemed familiar, but she could not place it.

'Hello? Anne Price.'

'Anne, it's Dom, Dominik Gorski. Have you got a minute?'

'Sure.'

'I just wanted to thank you and Donovan for helping with the clean-up this afternoon. I don't seem to have a number for him, so I thought I'd ring you.'

'That's fine. We were pleased to join in.'

'And you'll pass my thanks on to Donovan?'

'I will, certainly.'

'Actually ...'

'Yes?'

'I wanted to say something to you.'

'Really?'

'I wanted to tell you that I do understand about your relationship with Donovan. I'm not going to pester you.'

'That's good.'

'But I would just say this. If ever things change between you –
'

'What about *your* relationship, I mean with Magda?'

'What about it?'

'It seemed to me she wasn't just another member of the clean-up group.'

'No. Well, you know ... things can change in life, can't they?'

'I suppose so.'

'That's all I'm saying.'

'Okay.'

'Thanks for listening, Anne. And thanks again to both of you for helping today.'

'You're welcome.'

After hanging up, Anne stood quietly for a few moments. In her imagination she saw a misty meadow in the early morning, with dew covering the grass. Two young men in black trousers and white shirts were standing with their backs to each other, each holding an old-fashioned flintlock pistol that pointed upwards. They stepped forward for ten paces before turning and firing. She saw the flashes from the muzzles, smoke pouring from the barrels of the guns. She saw one of them fall to the ground, but could not see who it was. Pistols at dawn, she thought. Blimey!

****

When Anne returned to the sitting room, Marnie looked up at her.

'I was just telling Ralph. That was Angela on the phone. When I got back this afternoon I rang to tell her about the cat being shut in the shed. We both thought it was a minor incident, but Angela decided to tell Cathy Lamb about it anyway. It seems the police are taking it quite seriously ... another intruder on the premises. They're going to keep a close eye on the house.'

Ralph said, 'Presumably they know that you and Anne will be visiting it from time to time, plus people doing work on the premises.'

'Angela told Cathy all about the renovation project,' Marnie said. 'And I mentioned the person Mrs Betts called the *young lady*, so they're aware of her if she comes back.'

Anne said, 'That must be Magda, the girl I told you about who was there today ... Dom's girlfriend. I don't know if she will be going back to the house again. I think she just went to visit Mrs Koslowski.'

'Why was that?' Ralph asked. 'Could they be related?'

Anne shrugged. 'No. Mrs Betts said she helped her with things. I don't know what, exactly. Do they know about Dom being involved?'

'Oh yes,' Marnie said. 'They certainly know Dom. In fact, Angela said Cathy let slip something about him. That time Donovan was chased by skinheads and one of them, a woman, intervened ...'

Anne said, 'Smeared him with lip gloss to look like blood and left him lying in the gutter?'

'Don't tell me,' said Ralph. 'She was the undercover cop?'

Marnie nodded. 'Apparently. Angela said Cathy didn't put it in so many words but it was obvious what she meant.'

Ralph looked thoughtful. 'And the undercover officer thought at first she was rescuing Dominik Gorski?'

'Could be.'

Marnie noticed that Anne seemed no longer to be listening. She was staring ahead into space.

'You okay, Anne?' she said.

'Mm? I was just thinking. For once I'm quite glad that Donovan's out of the picture for a while.'

'You think the skinheads might mistake him for Dom and go after him again?'

Anne shook her head. 'No, not that. It just occurred to me that Donovan and Dominik seem like two of a kind. Even their names

183

make them sound like a double act. It worries me to think what they might get up to if they put their heads together.'

'Both on the same wavelength,' said Ralph.

'Definitely.'

Marnie said, 'And you think they might both be obsessed with the same idea?'

In her mind, Anne heard pistols firing, saw muzzle flash, smelled cordite.

'I do,' she said, 'in more ways than one.'

****

Dom picked Magda up from home after supper, and they drove to a country pub. It was a favourite haunt of theirs and had the advantage that it seemed to be out of range of the skinheads.

They had both changed out of the clothes they had worn on the clean-up mission. When Magda removed her jacket, Dom thought she looked terrific in an embroidered cream smock and skinny jeans. She smelled good, too. He thought he really should try to find out what perfume she used. It had a warm musky tang that suited her brilliantly and he bore it in mind for a future birthday or Christmas present, assuming they were still together then.

The next day would be a work day, so they left the pub shortly after ten and were back in town barely ten minutes later. Dom parked the Peugeot not far from Magda's house and walked with her to her front door. Like him, she lived with her parents, and like him she had a vacation job in her father's business where she worked outside university term time as a bookkeeper. There was no question of him going inside with her, so they kissed on the doorstep and she waved him off. He waited until the door was closed before retracing his steps to the car.

The lighting in the street was concealed somewhat by the new foliage of the trees that lined the road, creating a dappled effect of shading on the pavement. Dom had both hands in his pockets as he strolled along. He was just thinking he could still taste Magda's lipstick when he thought he heard a sound like rustling leaves behind him. He stopped and looked round, but there was nothing to see. Putting it down to a breeze in the branches of the trees, he resumed his walk. He was only a few paces from the car.

****

184

Sitting up in bed that night, Anne was reading about the artists of the Bloomsbury Group in the inter-war years. They did not feature formally as part of her syllabus, but she had become interested in them while reading about their contemporaries like Le Corbusier in France and Frank Lloyd Wright in America. She wondered if Donovan would phone. Concentration was an effort.

And of course, he did phone, though only for a brief chat before turning in. Anne brought him up-to-date on Marnie's phone call from Angela. He was intrigued to have it more or less confirmed that his female New Force saviour had been an undercover police officer, and that she might have mistaken him for Dom.

Minutes after ending their conversation, Anne heard the door of the office barn open. She pricked up her ears. A soft voice reached her from down below.

'Anne, are you awake?'

'Sure.'

Footsteps were followed by the creaking of the ladder. Marnie's head appeared through the trapdoor space across the room. As soon as Anne saw Marnie's expression she knew that something awful had happened.

Chapter 18

Donovan was frustrated by the long interval between check-in and take-off, a wait of well over an hour in the departure lounge of Heathrow's Terminal Three. He considered the possibilities facing him. The duty-free shop held no attractions. That left the bookshop and the cafe. He decided to tackle them in that order.

He was browsing the bookshelves when the mobile began vibrating in his back pocket. He fished it out, saw the caller's number on the screen and smiled.

'Hi. Missing me already?'

'Donovan.' Just one word, but Anne's tone conveyed a wealth of meaning.

Donovan's smile vanished. 'What's up?'

'It's Dom.' This time it was only two syllables, but Anne seemed too choked to go further.

'Anne, what's happened? What is it? Talk to me.'

'They ... they got him. He's ...' She stumbled again.

'Listen, take a deep breath and tell me all about it. Take your time. This is New Force, right?'

'Yes.'

'And?'

'They attacked Dom last night.'

'How is he?'

'He's in hospital ... in intensive care ... seriously injured ... unconscious.'

'How injured?'

'Concussion ... broken arms ... a broken leg ... internal injuries.'

'God almighty! Is he going to be all right?'

'They said it depends.'

'On what?'

'He got kicked in the head, hard. Oh, Donovan, he could have brain damage.'

'Bloody hell! Look, perhaps I should come back.'

'No. You've got things to do. Get the car sorted out first.'

'But -'

'There's really nothing you can do here, nothing for Dom. That's for sure.'

'I know what I'd like to do ... those *bastards!*'

'That's how we all feel, but Cathy says we have to let the police handle things.'

Donovan fell silent, his mind racing over the options. He imagined Dom, mangled and in pain, lying helpless and comatose in a hospital bed. More than anything he wanted to avenge him, wanted to bring fury down on his aggressors. He could have *screamed* with anger. Then he noticed other passengers staring at him, giving him strange looks.

'Donovan, can you hear me?'

'Yeah. I'm here. I just don't know what to do for the best.'

'Here's Marnie,' Anne said. 'She wants to talk to you.'

'Hi, Donovan. We're all pretty shaken and we really didn't want to worry you, but we felt it wasn't right not to tell you what's happened.'

'I appreciate that, Marnie.'

'Anne's right. There's nothing any of us can do to help Dom for now. So you must get your business completed in Germany, and we'll keep you posted while you're away. Can you live with that?'

Donovan paused. There was so much he wanted to express. He said simply, 'Okay. I suppose that'll have to do. Thanks, Marnie.'

'You have a safe journey and give our regards to your family. We'll be waiting for you when you get back, Donovan. Bye for now.'

'Yeah, bye Marnie.'

****

By the time his flight touched down at Hanover, Donovan was calmer. His initial fury had given way to a controlled anger and a resentment that he was temporarily out of the picture as far as New Force was concerned. More than anything, he regretted not taking more direct action against them. Cleaning up their hateful graffiti was one thing; wiping the floor with them was a quite different matter.

It was only while waiting in baggage reclaim that he realised he had given not a single thought to his family or even to the reason for returning to Germany. He could feel the tension in his body. Breathing in steadily and deeply, he hunched his shoulders, then exhaled and relaxed them. He blinked his eyes and loosened up his face muscles. At the moment when he noticed that one or two people on the other side of the carousel were staring at him, his bag popped up onto the conveyor band. He stepped forward, grabbed it and made for the Nothing to Declare exit.

As soon as he emerged into the arrivals hall, a hand went up from the small crowd at the barrier. Uschi was smiling and waving. Beside her a tall clean-looking young man was grinning. It was the warmest of welcomes and just what Donovan needed.

****

It took Marnie a while to find a parking space at Northampton General Hospital, but she persevered and just managed to slot the Freelander into a narrow gap. It was at the furthest end from the building housing the intensive therapy unit. She set off with Anne and Angela along the familiar path to the ITU.

They climbed to the second floor and were surprised to find Kazimir Gorski sitting close to the entrance doors. He seemed to have aged visibly since they last saw him. His eyes were sunken and his skin had a grey pallor. As soon as he saw the women approaching he leapt to his feet and stuck out a hand. He kissed each hand offered to him, which Marnie thought at first was typical Polish gallantry. She soon realised that it was also a way of avoiding speech at least for a few moments.

'I'm so sorry about Dominik,' Marnie said softly. 'How is he?'

Kazimir shrugged as if the weight of the world was on his shoulders. 'I had to come out. The consultants are with him. They've been examining him for over twenty minutes. It feels like hours.'

'Has he regained consciousness?' Angela asked.

'No.'

There was a finality about Kazimir's reply that sent a chill down their spines.

Anne spoke in a half-whisper. 'But he will get better, won't he? He's young and strong ... and very determined.'

Kazimir looked at Anne as if he had never really noticed her before. 'I'm glad that's what you think.'

'I do. I mean it.'

Kazimir stepped forward and took Anne in his arms. Marnie noticed a single tear fall on her shoulder. As they moved apart, footsteps were heard along the corridor. A nurse came and opened the door.

188

'Dominik is free now,' she said. 'We can't really have four visitors round the bed, I'm afraid.'

Marnie said, 'Perhaps Angela could go with you, Kazimir?'

Angela was taken aback. 'Oh, I think you should go, Marnie. Really.'

'Okay.'

As they walked down the corridor, Marnie took Kazimir by the arm. The thought came to her that Dom's mother was not there.

As if reading her thoughts, Kazimir said, 'To lose a wife is a dreadful thing, but to think you may also lose a son is unbearable.'

She squeezed his arm. 'Time to have positive thoughts.'

'Yes. Yes, absolutely.'

They rounded the corner and approached the row of curtained-off bays. Marnie was pleased to see that Dom had been installed in the next bed to Stan Koslowski.

Kazimir said in an undertone, 'Very soon they'll be referring to this unit as the *Szpital Kliniczny*.'

'The what?'

'Polish term for a hospital.' Kazimir indicated the beds of Dom and Stan next to each other.

'I see what you mean.'

Marnie was alarmed to see how badly injured Dom was. She had expected all the usual paraphernalia of intensive care, but the extent of his dressings came as a shock. One leg was raised in traction. Both arms were bound up and lay across his chest. His head was bandaged down to his eyebrows. Dom looked as if he had been hit by a train. His eyes were closed; he gave no sign of knowing that he had visitors.

Kazimir said to the nurse, 'He's still unconscious?'

'Yes. The surgeons are keeping him sedated for a while. It's best that way. We want to stabilise him before bringing him up.'

'Will he hear us if we speak to him?'

'It's hard to tell, but it won't do any harm.'

The nurse moved a chair nearer to the bed so that Marnie could sit beside Kazimir.

'May I sit with you for a while?' she asked.

In reply Kazimir reached over and squeezed her hand. 'I'm so glad you came, Marnie.'

'Of course I'd come. We're all very upset by what's happened.'

'It's very kind, considering you hardly know my son.'

'Tell me about him … if you feel like it.'

'Where to begin?'

'If it's not too painful, can you tell me what happened to him?'

Kazimir winced, and Marnie regretted asking.

'Not if it distresses you,' she said.

Kazimir sighed. 'The police told me he was attacked in the street last night. He'd just seen his girlfriend home and was walking back to the car. That's when … They must have followed him.'

Marnie said, 'Tell me about Dom in happier times.'

Kazimir collected himself before speaking.

'Dominik is my younger boy. He has an older brother who's away at the moment, working for a firm in New York. Dom's a student at Leicester University, studying mechanical engineering.' Kazimir smiled to himself. 'He takes after me that way.'

Marnie said, 'He certainly loves that car of his.'

'Oh yes. He's lavished attention on it. It's better now than when it was new.'

Another similarity with Donovan, Marnie thought.

'And he's been learning Polish, I gather.'

'Yes. Perhaps we should have brought him up with both languages, but his mother and I wanted to be integrated fully into this country. We were both born here, after all.'

'It's understandable for him to want to be in touch with his roots,' Marnie said.

Kazimir nodded. 'There's no doubt about that. He's become very patriotic for Poland. I think he's got that from all the old Poles in town. He loves spending time with them and hearing their stories. He knows much more about the old country and what it did in the war than I do. I think that's one of the reasons why he's so opposed to these fascist thugs who seem to be all around us these days.'

'Yes,' Marnie agreed. 'He's determined to stand up to them.'

Kazimir was silent for a long moment. Then he said, 'And look where that's got him.'

****

For Donovan, eating lunch in a typical German home, chatting with his uncle and aunt, his cousin and her boyfriend, made

190

Knightly St John seem a million miles away. It felt like he was leading a double life, especially as the family used his German forename, Nikki, short for Nikolaus. Aunt Gabriele served potato soup in fine china bowls by Rosenthal. Uschi handed round white bread rolls, while uncle Helmut poured glasses of Riesling from Rheinhessen. A candle burned in the middle of the table, on which the Sunday best WMF cutlery had been laid out.

Uncle Helmut seemed in better health and spirits than he had been in months. The trip to Bergheim, and even his dealings with *Hauptkommissar* Schröder, had brought a welcome change to his routine. He was happy to tell Donovan all about the journey, the police procedures, the reclaiming of the Porsche and his surprise at how well it had been restored by the criminals.

By the time they moved on to *Wienerschnitzel*, Wolfgang was regaling them with stories about his disastrous outings, racing his quad bike. Donovan found himself relaxing and laughing at the tales of crashes, breakdowns and general mayhem that Wolfgang enjoyed on the off-road tracks.

'Wolfgang,' he said, 'I don't think I would have let you collect my Porsche if I'd known what a disaster zone you were!'

Uschi laughed. 'I had my fingers crossed behind my back when Wolfgang drove the car onto the ramp.'

Donovan covered his eyes with one hand. '*Mein Gott!*' he said in mock horror.

In deference to uncle Helmut's heart condition, aunt Gabriele had refrained from making what she would regard as a serious dessert. Instead, she produced a fruit salad with the option of whipped cream as a topping for her guests.

After lunch Wolfgang offered to drive Donovan round to his parents' home where the Porsche was safely stored in the garage beside the quad bike. Uschi joined them, sitting in the back of Wolfgang's Golf GTI. It was a short drive to what Wolfgang described as a modest suburb of Göttingen not far from the university's North Campus. On arrival Donovan learnt two things about Wolfgang. The first came when he saw his house and its street. It was a far from modest environment, with comfortable detached houses in attractive grounds.

The second was when Wolfgang pressed the remote control to open the garage doors. Wolfgang's father had vacated his place temporarily to house the Porsche. Donovan was amazed at the high standard to which the crooks had restored his car. But his gaze was instantly drawn to the adjacent bay. There, the quad bike was stored under its cover, tucked in behind a Fiat 500, which was presumably Wolfgang's mother's car. The rear wall was fitted with rows of shelves. They were lined with trophies great and small, all of them won by Wolfgang at quad bike racing. Uschi laughed out loud to see Donovan's expression.

****

Kazimir Gorski left the hospital to get back to his business after half an hour at Dom's bedside. When he stood to leave he hugged Marnie warmly and thanked the nurses for caring for his son. In reply one of them offered to invite the 'other two ladies' to join Marnie in the unit. Accompanying Kazimir to the exit, she mentioned that the ITU staff were under orders to contact the police as soon as Dom regained consciousness and might be able to answer a few questions.

While waiting for Anne and Angela to join her, Marnie walked round Dom to look at Stan Koslowski in the next bed. He had been sleeping throughout her visit and did not seem to have changed from the other time she had seen him. An awful premonition came to her that he would never fully recover. She dared not think what might become of Dominik.

****

Donovan could scarcely believe it. Even the interior of the Porsche smelled like new. The seats had either been replaced or reupholstered. The hood was certainly new, as were the floor carpets and mats. Under the bonnet the engine had evidently been steam cleaned, and all the wiring replaced. It seemed strange to Donovan to feel gratitude towards the very people who had taken the car and made it ready to sell at a substantial profit. Ironic really, he thought, considering that he was the one who had crashed it into the river, albeit unintentionally.

Wolfgang told him his father was happy for the Porsche to occupy the garage space used by his Mercedes until he wanted to take it back to London. He gave Donovan the keys and was not surprised when Donovan said he could not wait to drive it. Nor was he surprised when Uschi asked to go along for the ride.

The car started at once, and the engine sounded sweet and mellow. They rolled at a steady pace towards the ring road and then up to the north-south Autobahn. There, Donovan permitted himself the pleasure of opening up the little car and watching the speedometer climb to a hundred miles an hour. He shouted out with joy and could have driven to the North Pole, such was his elation. He was reunited with a prized possession handed down from his father, which he thought he had lost forever.

As they drove, Uschi tilted her head back to feel the wind rushing through her hair. Donovan reached across and took her hand in his. She smiled at him, glad to be sharing his happiness. With both hands back on the steering wheel, Donovan drove more sedately on the home stretch.

'Thank you, Uschi,' he said. 'And thanks to Wolfgang for all he's done.'

'You must tell him that yourself,' she replied.

'I will. I surely will. He's a great guy. You two seem happy together.'

'Yes, but it's early days.'

'I wish I had the time to get to know him better.'

'You will, Nikki. Do you have a friend like him in England?'

Donovan considered the question. 'Not quite. I'm mainly with Anne and the others when I'm not studying.'

'I can understand that. You've always been rather a loner.'

'There is someone though with whom I'm becoming friendly,' Donovan said. 'It's strange, he's so like me. He looks a bit like me and wears the same sort of clothes ... has a car he's been working on.' He laughed. 'He even fancies Anne!'

'That's not so surprising. She's a very pretty girl, and really nice, too.'

'I know.'

'Could that be a problem between you and this new friend?'

'I don't think so, though I don't take Anne for granted.'

'That's good, well said.'

'Thank you, *Mutti.*'

Uschi thumped him on the leg and laughed. By now they were approaching Wolfgang's street, and Donovan pulled up outside the garage. Wolfgang must have been watching for them, as he came out of the house immediately.

'How was it?' he asked Donovan.

'*Wunderbar!* It goes better than ever.'

'Great.' Wolfgang looked across at Uschi. 'Look, I've got to go into town now to collect my mother. She went in with Papa this morning. Shall I see you later?'

193

'Come round when you can.'

'Okay. And Nikki, you can use our garage for the Porsche whenever you wish.'

'Thanks for everything, Wolfgang.'

Wolfgang reached into the car and they shook hands.

'You're really welcome. See you later.'

On the way home Donovan asked Uschi if she had any plans for the afternoon. She explained she had set aside the whole time to finish painting some eggs for the Easter tree. He could help if he wanted. It would be just like old times when they were children. They were turning into their street when Uschi had a sudden thought.

'The plants!'

'What plants?' Donovan asked.

'I have to water the plants for our neighbour across the street. He's coming home tomorrow. I want the soil to be nice and moist when he returns so he can see I've looked after them.'

'He?'

'An old man, widowed. He lives alone. He's been visiting his son in Munich. You can help me with the watering if you like. He's got a fair collection of house plants.'

'Sure.'

Uschi added, 'He keeps them because they were favourites of his late wife.'

'Glad to help.'

Back home, they went in to fetch the keys for the neighbour's house. When Uschi told her parents they were both going over, uncle Helmut looked pensive for a moment, but said simply, 'Have fun.'

As they crossed the road, Donovan said, 'I don't think I've met this old man. Is he new round here?'

'He moved here last year from Berlin to be near his daughter.' Uschi turned the key in the lock. 'His flat is on the ground floor. That's why he chose it.'

'To avoid going up stairs on account of his age?'

'Oh, he's quite fit really, but he was wounded in the war. His right leg is rather stiff.'

Uschi unlocked the door to the flat and switched off the burglar alarm. The space was easily big enough for a single occupant, even with the neighbour's heavy furniture, typical Old Germany. Uschi started opening the built-in window shutters, and Donovan followed suit. She explained it was her first task on every visit to tilt open the tops of the windows to air the rooms. Light began pouring in.

With that first task completed, Uschi went into the kitchen and brought out two brass watering cans. She handed one to Donovan.

'I'll start on the window sill in here,' she said. 'Do you want to tackle the ones in the dining room?'

'Fine.'

'Don't forget there are some small ones on the sideboard. Easy to overlook.'

They parted company and went off to their respective zones.

'The old boy certainly likes his plants,' Donovan called through. 'I've never seen so many.'

'Nor me,' said Uschi. 'They were his wife's passion. They're not my taste. Do you like them?'

There was no reply.

'Nikki?'

Still no reply. Curious, Uschi walked to the dining room and found Donovan standing by the sideboard staring down at its surface.

'What's the matter?' Uschi asked.

Donovan pointed at the sideboard without speaking. In the centre was a heavy ornate silver tray. It looked to be solid silver of the finest quality and was highly polished, a treasured possession. Uschi had never really paid it great attention. Her main concern was normally to deal with the plants, then lock up and set the alarm. There were markings on the tray that she had never noticed before. She noticed them now. Below Donovan's finger was an engraved signature, one of several etched into the surface. The one at which Donovan was pointing stood out with startling clarity:

Adolf Hitler.

****

Marnie drove home with a heavy heart. The sight of Dominik lying heavily bandaged and in traction in one bed, with Stan Koslowski comatose in the next had depressed them all. The atmosphere in the car was sombre, and no one spoke on the journey back to Knightly St John.

When they dropped Angela off at the vicarage, she stood on the pavement and looked into the car, utterly miserable.

'Thanks for the lift, Marnie. You know, I'm not sure I can cope with all this violence and hatred. It's all so ...' She shook her head in despair.

Marnie said, 'You will cope, Angela ... somehow. We all have to find a way. We just have to stick together and try as best we can to see it through.'

'I suppose so. As a Christian I ought to have more faith, but when you see those poor people lying there ...'

'Angela, d'you want to have supper with us this evening?'

'That's nice of you, but Randall's coming round. I think I need to talk things over with him.'

'Good idea.' Marnie smiled. 'And if you really want cheering up, you could invite the archdeacon to come as well.'

Angela pulled a face and nearly smiled. 'What were the words of the song in *MASH*, that old television series ... *suicide is painless?*'

****

When Donovan and Uschi returned from their plant watering expedition, Donovan had the impression that uncle Helmut was watching him, though trying not to make it obvious.

'Everything in order?' asked Helmut.

'Fine,' said Uschi, 'though Nikki made an interesting discovery.'

'And what was that?'

They both looked at Donovan.

'I think you can guess what it was,' he said.

Uncle Helmut narrowed his eyes. 'The tray?'

Donovan nodded. 'The tray.'

'I wondered if you'd notice it.'

'It's funny,' said Uschi. 'I've been over there lots of times, but I've never noticed it. I just want to get everything done ... the watering, the blinds, the windows, the burglar alarm ... there's a lot to think of.'

'One glance,' said Donovan, 'and it struck me in the face. And to think, that tray was no doubt given to your neighbour by Hitler himself. He held it in his own hands. It's enough to make anyone shudder.'

'I'm sorry,' uncle Helmut muttered. 'I should have said something about it, or suggested that you didn't go with Uschi.'

Donovan said, 'Who is this neighbour and more to the point, what was he to receive such a gift?'

'His name is Ekkehart von Karlsdorff.'

'Sounds like an old Prussian aristo.'

'That's exactly what he is. He came originally from Brandenburg.'

'Uschi told me he'd been wounded in the war.'

'He served some time on the eastern front, I understand.'

Donovan hesitated before asking his next question. 'And was he … a Nazi?'

'No.' Uncle Helmut's reply was immediate and emphatic.

'You sound very sure about that.'

'Like a lot of aristocrats, he abhorred Hitler and everything he stood for.'

'Yet he fought in the war and for some reason received a magnificent solid silver tray signed by the Führer and all the High Command.'

'That was something special, Nikki.'

'Namely?'

'I believe everyone promoted to the rank of general received such a gift.'

When Donovan spoke his voice was almost a whisper. 'My god, I've been watering the plants of one of Hitler's generals. I can hardly believe it.'

****

A gloomy atmosphere had pervaded Glebe Farm following the hospital visit, but it dissipated gradually in Anne's attic bedroom that evening. The time was approaching for a call from Donovan. She knew the sound of his voice would cheer her up, but the reality was not quite what she expected. He rang on the dot of nine.

'Hi!' she said. 'How was your day? Did you get the car back all right? Is it okay?'

'The Porsche's fine, if anything better than before.'

'Great. So you've had a good day.'

'Well …'

'Problem?'

'Not exactly. How would you react if I told you I'd been watering the plants of one of Hitler's generals?'

'I'd guess they were on his grave and that you then danced on it. Am I right?'

'I was being serious.'

'No you weren't.'

'Listen, uncle Helmut and aunt Gabi have a neighbour who served in the war.'

'And he really was a general?'

'Yep. Uncle Helmut says he was never a Nazi, just a patriot. Apparently he was no fan of the *Führer*.'

'So where do the plants come in?'

'I went over to help Uschi with the watering. The old guy's been away, and Uschi's been keeping an eye on his flat. Can we change the subject? Tell me about your day. It has to be better than mine.'

'Don't hold your breath,' Anne said.

'What's happened?'

'It's Dom. We went to see him today. Oh, Donovan, you wouldn't believe it. He's completely messed up. It's awful.'

'You mean worse than we feared?'

'I'm afraid it is. It's one thing to know he's badly injured, but to see him ...'

'Must be grim,' Donovan said.

'Because of his broken leg he's in traction. Both his arms were broken -'

'Bloody hell!'

'There's more. He's got three broken ribs, and his head injuries are worst of all. They don't yet know the extent of the damage, apart from obvious concussion.'

'This is terrible. I'm coming back as soon as I can.'

'Donovan, there's really nothing you can do. I thought you might want to spend Easter with your family in Germany.'

'And spend all my waking hours worrying about what's going on around you? You must be joking. At the very least I can show some support, especially for Dom and his family.'

'Dom's father was at the hospital. He looked shattered. We're all feeling pretty low.'

'All the more reason for me to come back.'

'You must do what you think's right, Donovan. I know you will, anyway.'

'There's one other thing we haven't mentioned, Anne. There's this so-called *Easter parade* thing that the fascists are planning. What are we going to do about it?'

'I'm not sure there's very much we can do.'

'Yeah ... well, we'll see about that.'

Chapter 19

An atmosphere close to panic was settling over Northampton in the few remaining days before the Easter Parade. New Force and their cronies were now mounting regular patrols of the streets of the town. Angela Hemingway had called an emergency meeting of the inter-faith committee to take place on Thursday morning, though she admitted to Marnie and Anne in the car on the way there that she was at a loss to know what good might come of it. Desperation was in the air.

Marnie had arranged to drop Anne off at the hospital and collect her after the meeting. Thus it was that Anne sat on the back seat of the Freelander with a bag of bananas in her lap, a gift for Dom. Once again, Ralph had volunteered to man the office with Dolly in support, while making notes for the next chapter of his book on the economic boom in Ireland.

As they headed for the town centre, Anne was dismayed to spot at least two groups of skinheads roaming the streets. As usual, people were crossing the road to avoid passing them on the pavement. In fact, although the skinheads looked just as menacing as before, they were not now causing problems to anyone during the hours of daylight. It was as if they had changed their tactics to avoid giving the police any opportunity to confront them. Anne knew that after dark it would be a different matter. Many people were staying at home in the evenings for fear of violence.

Marnie stopped close to the hospital entrance. Anne got out and made her way through the complex of low-rise blocks to the ITU. As she reached the door into the building, it was held open for her by another young woman. Anne glanced over to thank her and to her surprise found she was facing Magda Paluch, Dom's girlfriend.

Anne smiled at her. 'Hi. I think I can guess where you're going.'

For a few seconds Magda looked confused. 'We've met, haven't we?'

They both stepped inside.

'I'm Anne. We met at the great clean-up.'

Magda was still frowning. 'The great ...?'

'By the Polish shop. I was with Donovan.'

Enlightenment. 'Yes! Of course you were. Sorry. You look so ... smart in that dress. I didn't ... You're here to see Dominik?'

Anne held up her bag of bananas. 'You guessed.'

Anne could tell that Magda was trying to make up her mind about how she felt at finding another girl on her way to seeing her own boyfriend. To try to improve things Anne said, 'Your boyfriend and Mr Koslowski are in a really bad way. I'd like to do whatever I can to help improve morale. My boyfriend would be coming too, but he's away visiting his family at the moment.'

It did the trick. Magda softened. 'Your boyfriend is Donovan, yes?'

'That's right.' Anne gestured towards the staircase. 'Shall we go up?'

Magda hesitated then raised her bag and pulled out a bunch of bananas. She grinned. 'Great minds ...'

Anne laughed. 'Come on, let's see if they're any better today.'

Climbing the stairs, Magda said, 'You're an interior designer, is that right?'

'I'm a sort of apprentice designer, working with Marnie Walker. I'm also a student. How about you?'

'I'm in my first year at uni.'

'Are you at Leicester, like Dom?'

'No, London, University of Westminster, studying Polish and Russian.'

'Wow! Sounds quite exotic. It must be really hard.'

They stopped as they reached the entrance to the ITU.

'Not really,' said Magda. She pressed the bell by the door. 'I've been brought up to be bilingual in Polish and English, and I've done Russian at school since I was thirteen.'

A nurse turned the corner along the corridor almost at once and came briskly towards them. Anne recognised her from the previous visit. She was small and trim with a purposeful air, and Anne thought she might be partly Chinese. She opened the door and stood aside to let them enter.

'You've come to visit Dominik?'

'Yes,' they said in chorus.

'Then he's a lucky young man.'

'Relatively speaking,' Anne said, 'considering where he is.'

'Naturally,' the nurse said. 'Though I think you'll find him improved today.'

'That's wonderful!' Magda exclaimed.

'Relatively speaking,' the nurse said, glancing at Anne.

****

Angela was struggling to keep the committee in order. This time it was not just the archdeacon who was causing problems. Every member seemed to want to have their say. Everyone tried to talk at once, and Marnie had the distinct impression that no one was listening. At the height of the tumult Marnie tapped on the side of her water glass with a pen. It had the desired effect, at least for a few moments. The silence gave Angela the chance to dive in and attempt to control proceedings.

'Archdeacon, I believe you wish to speak.'

'Indeed I do … and I've been waiting for some time.'

'Please go ahead.'

'It's quite clear that the whole situation has got out of hand … has been *allowed* to get out of hand. I want to know what measures the police will be taking during the so-called *Easter Parade* to ensure that law and order are maintained.'

Angela gestured to Sergeant Groves who spoke up.

'I can assure the archdeacon that officers will be in attendance in large numbers. We will certainly –'

'Riot police?' The archdeacon interjected. 'An armed response unit?'

'Archdeacon, please!' Angela exclaimed. 'Kindly let Sergeant Groves finish her point.'

Groves was clearly exasperated. 'We are not a police state. The police maintain order by consent, not with the use of firearms or excessive force.' There were groans from all round the table. Undaunted, Groves persisted. 'It might help if the community nominated stewards, rather like our special constables and community support officers –'

'Vigilantes?' said one delegate.

Kazimir Gorski said, 'Our young people are already involved in cleaning up graffiti … with no help from the authorities, I might add.'

One representative wondered if a unit from the army might be called in. Another lamented the lack of an equivalent to the National Guard in America. No one seemed to be listening to anyone else. As the noise level rose again, Angela looked in desperation in Marnie's direction. To the surprise of everyone present, Marnie abruptly stood up. The assembly fell silent.

'Marnie?' Angela said. 'You wish to add something?'

Marnie looked thoughtful. 'It's interesting,' she began. 'Everyone seems to think someone else should be doing something. There's always a risk if you take things into your own hands that –'

'You think you can come up with a better idea?' The archdeacon, inevitably.

All eyes were on Marnie as she stood looking round at the delegates. Eventually she said, 'Perhaps I can ...'

****

The nurse was right. Dominik had improved markedly, though he was a long way from better. He still looked drawn and pale, but managed a faint smile when Anne and Magda presented themselves at his bedside. Anne thought it was ominous that the curtains round Mr Koslowski's bed were drawn together.

Magda leaned down to kiss Dom, hesitated, then pressed her lips gently to the corner of his mouth, opposite the side where a nasty split had been stitched up. When Magda withdrew, Anne contented herself with patting the fingers of one hand that protruded from his dressings.

'You're looking better today, Dom,' Magda said. She sounded almost convincing.

'I think you'll live,' Anne said, smiling, 'With any luck.'

'I aim to.' Dom's voice was hoarse but not weak. 'Have you two come to fight over me?'

Magda said, 'We've come to help you get better.'

She produced her bunch of bananas and looked round for a fruit bowl. Anne held up her bunch, grinned and placed them on the trolley beside the bed.

'Someone's going to have to unzip these for you,' Anne said.

Dom laughed, though it obviously caused him some discomfort. 'I was right. You have come to fight a duel over me ... bananas at dawn.'

Magda was still frowning, but Anne said lightly, 'Is there anything you'd particularly like ... apart from a front row ticket?'

Dom shook his head. 'There's not much I could do with anything if I had it. You could tell me what's going on in town. I'm really cut off in here. Is there any action?'

'Don't worry about that,' Magda said. 'Just concentrate on getting well again.'

'But I do worry. Those thugs tried to kill me, and they nearly succeeded. I need to know what's happening in the world outside.'

Anne said, 'The inter-faith committee is having a meeting at this moment. They're talking about ways of resisting whatever New Force throws at us.'

'Has anyone else been hurt?'

'Don't think so.'

'That's at least something.'

Anne glanced at Magda, who was visibly upset at the sight of Dom's condition.

'Look,' Anne said. 'I'm going to head off. I only wanted to find out if there was anything you needed. Right now, I think you two should have some time together. Take care and –'

'My car,' Dom croaked.

'What about it?'

'I left it in the street. I'm worried those bastards might know it's mine.'

'That doesn't matter,' Magda said. 'The main thing is –'

'No.' Dom was insistent. 'I don't want them to vandalise it.'

'It's only a car,' Magda said firmly.

Dom looked distressed. Before he could speak, Anne said, 'Whereabouts is it?'

'It's just along from where Magda lives.'

Anne said to Magda, 'Can you take care of it?'

Magda looked at a loss. 'The houses in my street don't have garages. We have to park on the road.'

Anne turned back to Dom. 'What needs doing?'

Dom turned his head towards the bedside trolley. 'My keys are in there, I think. Can you get the car away ... somewhere safe?'

'Can't your father get it for you?'

'He could, but he's got a lot on at the moment.'

'He's probably at the committee meeting,' Anne agreed.

'I expect he is. He's also supposed to be out all day commissioning a new store in Kettering, meeting contractors. Then there's a Chamber of Commerce dinner tonight. He's getting an award.'

'Can't the car wait until he's finished?' Magda asked.

Dom looked pained. 'I don't trust that lot ... those fascist pigs.'

Anne opened the door on the trolley and found the keys. 'Leave it with me. I'm not used to souped-up cars, but I'll do my best.' She gently touched his shoulder. 'I know it's your pride and joy.'

On her way out through the unit Anne passed the nurse who had admitted them.

'You were right about Dom,' Anne said. 'You're all doing a great job. Are you the nurse in charge here?'

'No.' She sounded surprised and pointed at the badge on her chest. 'I'm just a trainee in this unit.' She looked around at the groups of nurses attending to each patient. 'One of these teams will converge on Dominik shortly. I join them as part of my training.'

'I see.' Anne indicated Mr Koslowski's section. In a low voice she said, 'Is that a bad sign?'

The nurse looked at Anne thoughtfully. 'You're not a relative, are you?'

'Mr Koslowski doesn't have any relatives, as far as I know.'

The nurse drew Anne aside, ushering her away down the aisle.

'The consultant is with him, giving him a thorough examination. That's why the bay is closed.'

'Am I allowed to ask how he is?'

The nurse's mouth turned down at the ends. 'I can't really discuss his condition.'

'But it's not good,' Anne said. 'I understand. Is there anything we can get him? He has no one else.'

'He gets everything he needs here.'

Something in the nurse's tone made Anne's eyes well up. She stifled a sob. The nurse placed a comforting hand on her arm.

'That poor man,' Anne said. 'I hate to think of him being shot and ending his days like this.'

The nurse looked momentarily puzzled. 'He wasn't shot. He was stabbed.'

'Oh, I didn't realise. I must've misunderstood. What was it, a kitchen knife?'

The nurse shook her head. 'Something long and thin like maybe a stiletto.' She stopped abruptly. 'I'm not supposed to talk about this. If staff nurse Leach heard me, I'd be in dead trouble.'

'Don't worry. I won't snitch on you. And it's not the sort of thing I'll be chatting to anyone about.'

'I'm only talking to you because you're related to Dominik, aren't you? You've got the same colouring.'

Anne smiled. 'You're not the first to notice.'

The nurse glanced down the aisle. 'The other girl visiting?'

'Dom's girlfriend, Magdalena.'

'I thought so. I must say, you Poles certainly stick together.'

Anne thought it best not to disabuse her. With a smile, the nurse left to go about her business. Anne headed for the exit, her mind buzzing. Stabbed! And not with a kitchen knife grabbed in the heat of the moment. Whoever had killed Mrs Koslowski and wounded her husband was not a disturbed burglar. This was no opportunistic attack. All their worst fears about the far right thugs were true. The assailant went to their house armed and prepared to kill.

As Anne reached the exit door she heard rapid footsteps. She turned to see Magda hurrying towards her.

****

Donovan had at first been surprised to discover that all the documents for the Porsche were intact and in remarkably good condition. They had doubtless been protected in the car's glove box in their plastic wallet.

Wolfgang invited Donovan and Uschi for coffee at his home that morning, which gave Donovan the opportunity to retrieve the car's papers. He wanted insurance policy and AA booking reference numbers in order to confirm his channel crossing. The MOT certificate had long expired, but he decided to overlook that detail until he was home again. He hoped no one would be checking it on the journey back to London.

They got into Uschi's car to drive over to Wolfgang's house. Before starting the engine, she turned to look at Donovan.

'Do you want to tell me what's bothering you?' she said.

'What do you mean?'

'Nikki, I've known you all my life. You're like a brother to me. You can't conceal anything from me. It isn't just that business with the general's silver tray, is it?'

Donovan sat staring ahead before turning to meet her gaze. 'It's ... a lot of things, Uschi. And that tray reminded me of troubles back in England.'

'With Anne?'

'No, no. With New Force, the fascists … causing trouble again. And there's been a murder … an old Polish lady. She seems to have been denounced as a witch.'

'A *witch*?' Uschi sounded incredulous. 'That's why she was murdered?'

'It's not impossible. And there's going to be trouble over Easter. I keep feeling I ought to be there.'

Shaking her head, Uschi switched on the engine and put the car in gear. 'If you want to get back, I'm sure Wolfgang's parents would be happy to store the Porsche until you can come for it.'

As they drove across town, Uschi imagined how Donovan was feeling. Perhaps more than anyone in the family, he seemed to carry all the problems of the world on his shoulders.

While they were at Wolfgang's house, Uschi's mobile buzzed. Aunt Gabi had had a phone call from Herr von Karlsdorff, to let her know what time his train would be arriving. Uschi had arranged to meet him at the station and said she ought to be setting off. Wolfgang said she had time in hand, but she explained she wanted to take Donovan home first. She guessed correctly that Donovan might not wish to form part of the general's welcoming party. Not wanting to seem boorish, Donovan said he would be glad to help with the old man's luggage when Uschi returned with him.

****

Magda and Anne walked out of the building together and headed towards the hospital's perimeter road.

'I thought you'd have stayed longer with Dom,' Anne said.

'That was the idea, but the surgeon came to check Dom over, so that was that. As I was leaving, the nurse said something odd, Anne. She said she'd just said goodbye to Dom's relative. She must've meant you.'

'I know. She assumed that because of our colouring. It sometimes happens with Donovan, too. We get taken for brother and sister.'

'But he's your boyfriend, you told me.'

Anne grinned. 'Absolutely. He's definitely not my brother … far from it.'

Magda looked flustered. 'Oh, sorry … I …'

'I didn't mean to embarrass you, Magda.' Anne decided it was time to change the subject. 'Where are you going from here? Can we offer you a lift home? We're going your way, if we're collecting Dom's car.'

'We?'

'Marnie's picking me up. She's sent me a text message. The committee meeting's over. She'll be here any minute.'

'Oh it's all right, thanks. I'm going into town, back to my father's office … just a short walk. I'll wait with you, though.'

'Okay. Can I ask you something?'

'Sure.'

'You knew the Koslowskis, didn't you?'

'I think I only met Stan once or twice, but I knew Katya quite well.'

Anne said, 'Mrs Betts next door said Mrs Koslowski had a frequent visitor, someone she called a *young lady*. That was you?'

'Must have been.' Magda looked upset. She lowered her voice. 'I don't think she knew many young people.' The last words were almost choked away.

'D'you mind me asking how you came to know her?'

Magda swallowed. 'Dom knew Stan through his father. He was a customer in the shop here in Northampton. We bumped into them once in the shopping centre, and I saw Katya later by herself. I liked her. We got on well together and I used to go and visit. She was an interesting person, when you got to know her, *very* interesting. It was a chance to use the language, too. We both enjoyed that.'

'You must miss her,' Anne said lamely, wishing she could say something to help.

Magda nodded. They stood together on the pavement for a few moments in sad silence. Magda's focus shifted to a point beyond Anne.

'There's a car signalling to stop,' she said. 'Is this for you?'

Anne turned and saw Marnie's Freelander pulling up at the kerbside.

'Yes.' She kissed Magda on the cheek. 'Let's keep in touch. See you around.'

Anne made to step back, but Magda held on firmly and hugged her tight. She spoke quietly.

'Thank you for visiting Dom, Anne. It's really nice of you.'

'We're your friends,' Anne said.

Magda released her. 'Yes, you are true friends. In fact, I think you and Donovan are honorary Poles.' She smiled for the first time that day. 'And not just for your colouring.'

'We're glad to help. I'd better go. Marnie's waiting.'

Magda hugged her again, turned and walked quickly away. Anne stepped across the pavement and climbed into the Freelander behind Marnie and Angela.

'Sorry to hold you up, Marnie.'

'That's okay.' Marnie waited while Anne fastened her seat belt. 'That looked like an emotional little scene just there. Everything all right with Dom?'

'Much improved. He's awake and talking. In fact, he asked me to do something for him. He's worried about his car, afraid the New Force mob might damage it.'

Marnie drew away from the kerb in a gap in the traffic. 'What does he want you to do about it?' she asked.

'He's given me the keys, wants me to get it away. D'you think we could take it back to Glebe Farm with us?'

'I suppose so. We could stick it in the barn next to Ralph's car. Do you know where we can find it?'

'I know where it is, near Magda's house. The only thing is …'

'What's up?'

'It's that Peugeot GTI … what you might call a *hot hatch*. I think it would be a bit of a handful for me.'

'Okay,' Marnie said. 'I'll drive it and you can follow behind in the Freelander.'

'That works for me. Thanks, Marnie.'

Angela said, 'Anne, you didn't mention Mr Koslowski. Any news of him?'

'I didn't get to see him, but I don't think he's any better.'

'That's so sad,' said Angela.

'Can I check something with you both?' Anne asked.

'Go on,' Marnie said.

'Do you know how Mrs Koslowski was killed?'

There was no reply. Marnie glanced briefly at Angela who swivelled in her seat to look back at Anne.

'Why do you ask that, Anne?'

'Well, I don't think I've heard anyone say how she died or how Mr Koslowski was wounded.'

Angela said, 'I don't remember the police giving out any information about that. Do you know?'

Anne said, 'I've just found out they were stabbed. For some reason I thought they'd been shot.'

'Shot?' Marnie sounded surprised. 'Why did you think that?'

'No idea. It was just an impression I had.'

Marnie stopped the car as traffic lights turned to red. She looked round at Anne.

'How do you know she was stabbed?'

'A nurse just told me. She wasn't supposed to, but it sort of slipped out.'

Marnie turned back to watch the lights.

Angela said, 'The killer probably just picked up the nearest implement in the kitchen.'

'Apparently not,' Anne said. 'The nurse thought they were stabbed with a long thin blade, probably a stiletto.'

Angela shuddered.

'So not a lashing out on the spur of the moment,' said Marnie. 'The whole thing seems to have been premeditated.'

'And that explains the graffiti on the wall,' Angela said.

Marnie agreed. 'Yes, but it doesn't explain what it means.'

****

Donovan received a phone call from Uschi just as Herr von Karlsdorff's train was arriving at Göttingen station. He was watching for her returning with him and straight away crossed the road to bring in the old man's luggage while Uschi helped him up the steps and into his flat. Donovan followed behind them and had the bags in the hall before the general had a chance to notice him. He was back in his uncle and aunt's house barely two minutes after leaving it. It was fine by him. He certainly had no desire to wait to be thanked or, even worse, to be introduced.

When Uschi returned not long afterwards she made an announcement.

'Herr von Karlsdorff accepted your invitation, Mutti.'

'That's good,' said aunt Gabi.

'Invitation?' Donovan sounded suspicious.

Aunt Gabi explained. 'I thought it would be nice to invite Herr von Karlsdorff to lunch, but when we spoke on the phone he said he would like to have a rest after the journey. From Munich to here is a long way, and he had an early start.'

'So what's this invitation that he's accepted?' Donovan asked.

'He's coming for coffee instead,' Uschi said. '*Kaffee und Kuchen* at four o'clock.'

Donovan was silent. Aunt Gabi squeezed his arm.

'He's all right,' she said. 'He's not an ogre, just a very elderly man.'

'Who happens to have been one of Hitler's generals,' said Donovan.

'But not a Nazi, darling, and we can't live our lives in the past. We have to move on. He's well into his nineties now, a real old-fashioned gentleman. You'll see.'

'I shall look forward to meeting him,' Donovan said. He hoped he sounded convincing.

Uschi smiled at him.

****

Anne tapped Marnie on the shoulder. 'Here, I think. Next turning on the right.'

Marnie signalled and made the turn. Ominously, they spotted skinheads about fifty yards ahead as soon as they pulled into the side street. There was a gang of half a dozen of them. They were not just out for a stroll but walking purposefully, as if they were on a mission. As the Freelander got nearer, one of them gave another a mighty push so that he stumbled off the pavement directly into Marnie's path.

At the last moment the one who had pushed, seized the arm of the other and dragged him back. For a second this caused great hilarity, and the gang guffawed with laughter. Then it suddenly changed as realisation dawned. The Freelander had neither slowed nor swerved. Marnie had kept going without lowering her speed or changing direction. Raucous laughter became shouts and jeers. Fists were waved, and the skinheads speeded up, chasing the Freelander as it approached the T-junction at the end of the street and would have to slow and stop.

Inside the car, Angela had gasped and pressed a hand to her chest. She had winced when the skinhead seemed about to be run over. What alarmed her even more was Marnie's expression. Her jaw was set, her face grim. In the rear, Anne had both hands up to her mouth and for a moment had stopped breathing. She spun round to look out of the rear window.

'They're coming after us, Marnie!' she cried.

'Hold on to your butts,' Marnie said determinedly.

211

Angela, who as a vicar was unaccustomed to being urged to hold onto her butt, felt like praying, but even she was feeling antipathy towards the skinheads.

'What are you going to do, Marnie?' she asked.

'Dunno, but it seemed the right thing to say.'

'They're not dropping back,' Anne said.

They were almost at the junction.

'Which way here?' Marnie said.

'Left. Then we just have to look out for Dom's Peugeot.'

'Give the keys to Angela,' Marnie said.

'To me?' Angela was alarmed.

Marnie said, 'As soon as I stop, Angela hand me Dom's keys. Anne, you be ready to take over here.'

'I'm ready.' Anne released her seat belt.

Marnie hardly paused at the T-junction. She swung the car to the left and hit the accelerator. The road was clear, though there were several parked cars on both sides.

'There it is!' Anne felt like the whaler in *Moby Dick*.

She reached forward and pointed up ahead, passing the Peugeot's keys to Angela who was trying to remember to breathe. The good news was that Dom's car had clear space in front of it. The bad news was that it was facing towards them.

'Here's what we do,' Marnie said in haste. 'I'll stop alongside Dom's car. Anne, you get into the driving seat here as fast as you can. Then wait while I get in the Peugeot. Let the skinheads get near to you, then take off slowly at first, then go like a bat out of hell.'

'Got it,' Anne said firmly.

'I do hope this is a good idea,' Angela said softly.

The others paid her no attention. She went back to thinking about holding onto her butt and praying. It was a novel situation.

'They're rounding the corner,' Anne called out.

Marnie braked hard and pulled up just short of the Peugeot. Before the car had stopped, Anne was out of the back, tugging the driver's door open. Marnie leapt out and had the key in the Peugeot's door lock as Anne's butt hit the driving seat of the Freelander. She hastily adjusted the rear-view mirror and saw the skinheads racing down the middle of the road. Glancing to her right, she saw Marnie stretch out across the front passenger seat. She began slowly pulling away.

By now the skinheads were within twenty yards of the Freelander. Anne accelerated gently, then more solidly, then she pressed the pedal hard down and took off. The skinheads still came on and were some way past the Peugeot when Marnie switched on the engine and roared off in the opposite direction. This left the skinheads in total bewilderment. They spun round and came to a sudden halt, cannoning into each other.

As they staggered in confusion and annoyance, cursing in the roadway, they looked on helplessly as one car disappeared round a corner at one end of the street, while another sped away into the distance and beyond their reach.

****

Donovan felt increasingly uncomfortable as the time approached for Herr von Karlsdorff to arrive. At one minute to four he looked out of the kitchen window and saw their neighbour cautiously descending the steps outside his block of flats. He crossed the road at a steady unhurried pace, head held high, his back as straight as a ruler. Tall and clean shaven, with short iron-grey hair, he wore a dark suit, white shirt and navy blue tie. Oddly, Donovan found himself wondering what he had been wearing when Hitler shook his hand and presented him with the silver tray. It was of course obvious: full dress uniform; only the best would be good enough for meeting the *Führer*.

The bell rang as the clock in the hall struck four. Donovan could not help smiling to himself. Uncle Helmut and aunt Gabi received their guest together at the door and showed him into the dining room. The table was set with a cloth that had belonged to Donovan's grandmother: crisp white with a pattern of small flowers in pastel colours. In the centre of the table a chunky white candle burned, surrounded by a ring of painted eggs nestling in greenery.

Donovan stood as they entered the room. Herr von Karlsdorff's grip was firm and cool when they shook hands, and he inclined his head in a slight bow, which Donovan surprised himself by emulating. He wondered if Uschi was going to drop a curtsy in the old manner, but she simply shook hands and smiled.

They took their places at the table, and aunt Gabi busied herself with cutting the larger of the two cakes she had made for the occasion. Uschi poured coffee.

'So you are the nephew of whom I have heard so much,' Herr von Karlsdorff said to Donovan, his accent Prussian, clipped and precise. 'I must thank you for bringing in my luggage this morning. It was kind of you. You didn't wait to be thanked.'

'Not at all. You're welcome.'

'I hear you have come on a mission.'

'A mission?' Donovan said.

'To retrieve your Porsche. You are a lucky young man to have such a car.'

'Yes, inherited from my late father.'

The old man nodded slowly. After a pause he said, 'I knew him slightly, you know.'

'My father?'

'No.' The hint of a smile. 'Dr Ferdinand Porsche. We met several times. He was a remarkable man, very talented.' Donovan's brow dipped. Herr von Karlsdorff continued. 'You seem surprised.'

'I must admit I am rather.'

'I met him at receptions and quite a few technical meetings. He designed armoured vehicles for the *Wehrmacht*, and I was a *Panzer* officer. You weren't aware that he designed the Tiger tank, for example?'

'I didn't know that, Herr von Karlsdorff.'

'One of the most famous German names nowadays,' said the general. 'Ironic, really.'

Donovan was aware that no one else was speaking. The others at the table seemed to be observing the conversation with interest, even fascination.

'A household name,' Donovan agreed.

'Yes, indeed, but oddly he was not born a German at all.'

'No?'

The general shook his head and took a sip of coffee. 'Porsche was born a Czech, though of German origin way back. That's why he trod a careful path.'

'I'm sorry, I don't quite follow.'

'You know that Porsche was naturalised as a German citizen eventually. Did you know he was a member of the National Socialists and even of the SS?'

Donovan felt sick at the thought and could not speak.

The general continued. 'But anyone who knew him knew he had no interest in politics, none at all. I never once saw him in

214

any kind of uniform, nor did he wear a party badge in his lapel to my knowledge.' In an abrupt change of direction, the general turned towards aunt Gabi. 'Excellent cake, Frau Hartmann, I congratulate and thank you.'

'You're very welcome, Herr von Karlsdorff.'

The general turned back towards Donovan. 'I forgot to thank you for also watering my plants. Ursula told me you had been most helpful.'

Donovan inclined his head. 'My pleasure, Herr General.' Donovan almost bit his tongue. The title slipped out by accident.

'It's a long time since I was addressed in that way.'

'I apologise if I cause any offence.'

'No, no. I was a general only for a very short time. But then you know that, I think. I suppose you saw the silver tray?'

'Yes.'

'With the date on it?'

'I did notice it.'

'By that time in 1945, the army was running out of generals. I was one of the youngest in the *Wehrmacht*. It was remarkable. You see, in common with many upper-class officers, I was never a Nazi, never interested in politics, especially that brand.'

'Was that always your career?' Donovan asked.

'It was almost expected of my class in old Prussia, that we would join the military. For the first war I was just a boy, though by the end of it I had become a cadet and so eventually joined the army. That meant I missed out the Hitler Youth and all that nonsense. But I had relatives who fought in the 1914 war, uncles, cousins. My father held the rank of major in the Guards Grenadiers.'

'And he was wounded,' Donovan observed.

The others stared at Donovan, wondering how he knew that. The general sat back in his chair and studied Donovan for several seconds.

'That's very observant of you,' he said at last. 'You saw the medals.'

'I watered an African violet beside the frame containing them.'

'Ah, yes. And you recognised what they were. That is unusual.'

Donovan said, 'He received the Iron Cross second class and the Hindenburg Honour Cross with Swords, both of them awards for bravery in battle.'

The general raised an eyebrow. 'And you recognised the silver wound badge. No doubt you also saw the medals from the second war?'

Donovan nodded. 'They were yours, I presumed.'

'They were.'

'You received a Knights Cross of the Iron Cross with oak leaves and the German Cross in gold.'

The general gave Donovan a further appraising look. 'You interest me, young man. You are more knowledgeable than most people of your generation, yet your manner tells me you have reservations.'

Uncle Helmut intervened hastily. 'I'm sure Nikolaus means no offence, Herr von –'

The general raised a hand. 'No offence is taken. I am pleased to have this conversation. Most young people have consigned us old war-horses to the dustbin of history. They regard us not with interest or understanding, but with contempt.'

'I have no right to judge anyone,' said Donovan.

'I respect that,' the general replied. 'I have to say to you that I was a good soldier. I'm not ashamed to have fought for my country. But I was deeply ashamed of the ruffians who had taken over our government.'

'You didn't approve.'

'Absolutely not. I deplored the Nazis, but I would never surrender to the Red Army, to the Bolsheviks.'

'You fought on the Eastern Front.'

'Yes.' The general's eyes lost focus as he conjured up the images from his past. 'You cannot imagine the horror. I saw my men freeze to death in the front line. In normal circumstances we should have defeated the Russians everywhere, as we did at Kiev under von Rundstedt in Army Group South. That was the greatest victory in modern military history. But later everything went against us. Bad planning. We were ill-prepared for winter warfare.'

He fell silent, staring ahead. No one spoke. The family concentrated on *Kaffee und Kuchen*, while Donovan felt guilty that he had brought the conversation to this point. He could not look his relatives in the eye, but knew he had to do something to move things along. Then he had a moment's inspiration. Reaching into his pocket, he produced two photographs and placed them beside the general.

'I wonder, sir, if you know these medals.'

The general moved the photos closer. As he did so, his demeanour changed. From his jacket he took out a pair of glasses and slid them onto his nose. His interest was piqued, and curiosity showed in his face.

'Mm ... interesting. Yes, yes.'

'You know them, Herr General?' Donovan asked quietly.

'Where did you get these photographs?'

'I took them in England, in the house of a Polish couple.'

The general shook his head. 'No.'

'Excuse me?'

'No. These are not Polish medals. These are Russian.'

'*Russian?* You're sure of that?'

'Quite certain. See here, this one with the gold star. It's the medal of the Hero of the Soviet Union. I have seen it many times. Now this one with the flag and the red and white ribbon is also easy to recognise: the Order of the Red Banner.' He looked at the second photo. 'Ah yes ... Here we have the Order of the Patriotic War. A lot of the Russian military received it, but this version with the gold and red star design is the First Class award, denoting exceptional bravery in action. You see it has been awarded twice. This final medal is the Order of the Red Star, very easy to recognise.'

'And they are all Russian, you say.'

'Without doubt. And I'll tell you something else. Whoever won these will have earned them by acts of outstanding valour. This was a great fighter, whoever he was.'

Donovan sat back in his chair, his mind a jumble of conflicting thoughts. Aunt Gabi meanwhile offered a slice of the smaller cake to her guest. The general readily accepted. As Uschi rose to serve more coffee she glanced with curiosity at Donovan, but he failed to notice. He was a thousand miles away, lost among images of another time, another place.

****

Marnie enjoyed driving Dom's hot hatch on the way back to Knightly St John from Northampton. The little Peugeot had plenty of oomph and handled well. Dom had tuned the engine to give even more power than the GTI spec produced by the manufacturers, and the suspension had obviously been tweaked to improve the roadholding. Her only regret was the smell inside the car which made her feel nauseous, and which she attributed to a large cardboard box resting on the back seat. She had the beginnings of a headache by the time she reached home.

She braked to a halt outside the barn at Glebe Farm and tipped the driver's seat forward to reach into the rear. She dragged the box out and gave it a sniff. *Ugh!* It contained a number of tins and sprays, rags and tools. It was evidently Dom's graffiti cleaning gear, and it exuded a powerful chemical odour, much stronger than Donovan's. Marnie took in several gulps of fresh air. She decided to park the car with windows open to air the interior and store the box separately in the barn. She set it down on the floor at the end, before driving the Peugeot in.

Marnie was climbing out of the car when Anne and Angela drew up in the Freelander. Anne parked it in its usual space in the opposite garage barn.

'You got away all right?' Anne said. 'No trouble with the skinheads?'

'No trouble at all. How about you?'

Anne grinned. 'Left'em standing!'

Angela said, 'It was quite exciting.' She had a gleam in her eyes. 'Mind you, I can't say I wasn't a bit scared. They did look rather fierce.'

'That's the idea.' Marnie turned to Anne. 'Don't let me forget. I've taken a box of stuff out of the Peugeot and put it in the barn over there, in front of Dom's car.'

'Okay. What's in it?'

'The cleaning gear from Hell, I think, plus some other stuff, tools and such. It has a horrible, really strong chemical smell. In fact, it's given me a sick headache. Would you mind if I left you to it for a little while? I'm going to take a couple of pills and have a lie-down.'

Marnie had a hand on her forehead as she walked away.

****

In Göttingen the conversation round the table had moved on to more mundane subjects. Aunt Gabi enquired about the general's visit to his son in Munich. Herr von Karlsdorff explained that he took it in turns to spend Easter with his son one year and his daughter the next. They now had grandchildren, and he enjoyed sharing eggs and special treats with both branches of his family. He would be spending Easter this year with his daughter and her family who lived not far away.

When they had all eaten their share of cake and finished their coffee, Herr von Karlsdorff thanked his hosts for their hospitality and asked to be excused.

'I'm afraid these days I have to take things rather gently,' he said.

'And you've had a long train journey already today,' said aunt Gabi. 'Would you like Uschi to accompany you back to your flat?'

'That is kind of you, but I think I can manage.' He hesitated and added, 'Though on reflection that might not be a bad idea. And perhaps your nephew would also do me the honour?'

This request surprised them all. They crossed the road together and Uschi lent the old man a steadying hand on the small flight of steps up to the building, while Donovan opened the front door. In the entrance hall the general opened the door of his flat and turned to face them.

'Thank you both. Will you sit with me for a few minutes?'

'You're welcome,' said Uschi. 'And we'd be delighted.'

They made their way to the living room where the general pointed to large armchairs. 'Please have a seat. A schnapps, perhaps?'

Uschi and Donovan declined the offer. The general poured himself a shot and took the sofa opposite. He raised the glass towards his guests.

'*Zum Wohl!* He downed the spirit in one gulp and set the glass down on a side table. Looking Donovan straight in the eye he said, 'You surprised me with your knowledge of medals from past times. Are you a student of military history?'

Donovan shrugged. 'I've read some books. The medals you won are well documented. If you were in Army Group South on the Eastern Front you will surely have earned them.'

'I did not want to talk further about those times with your family. We all have our memories, and I know nothing of their background.' He looked across at Uschi. 'Excuse me saying this, Fräulein Hartmann, but if members of your family had been favourable towards the National Socialists, I would not want to embarrass them. And talking about the war can in any case be painful.'

'No one in our family supported the Nazi party,' Donovan said. 'I can assure you of that.'

'Yet you show a keen interest in the conflict, as well as some knowledge of military matters.'

'Yes, Herr General, but like you I am mindful of the difficulties in bringing up old memories, especially concerning the Eastern Front.'

'My boy, at my advanced age memories are practically all I have. It was a hard time, and I saw many dreadful things, but I accept what I was given and I am grateful for what I have.'

Donovan said, 'It's good not to have regrets.'

'Oh, I have regrets, and many of them, but I can say with some little pride that I am ashamed of nothing in my past. Nothing.'

Despite himself, Donovan was warming to this old warrior. The long bony hand that he had shaken that day had long ago been gripped by Adolf Hitler, yet this man sitting across from him now did not strike him as a monster.

The general said, 'Those medals in the photographs you showed me. Do you think they may have been stolen or possibly taken as trophies by partisans?'

'No.'

'You seem very definite about that.'

'I saw them being worn on a uniform in another photo standing beside those on the table.'

'And do you know who he was, this highly decorated Russian?'

Donovan's confusion returned. 'Herr General, I don't doubt your knowledge of military matters, but could these decorations not have been earned by a Pole in the war? They were allies of the Russians at that time, of course.'

The general stared into the distance, into the past. Slowly he shook his head.

'One perhaps, but so many ... and earned by one man? I think that would be unlikely for a Pole. I'm certain this was a member of the regular Soviet forces who had seen active service over some time. No one earns those awards in an afternoon.'

Donovan said quietly, 'It doesn't make sense.'

'Do you know this man?' the general asked.

Donovan looked up. 'That's just it. The medals weren't worn in the photo by a man, but by a woman.'

Uschi interjected. 'And she was murdered recently by far-right factions in England.'

The general turned to Donovan. 'They thought like you that she was Polish?'

Donovan looked doubtful. 'It's possible they may even have thought she was German. Nothing seems to make sense.'

'Why German?' the general said. 'I'm becoming increasingly confused here.'

Donovan said, 'They sprayed *HEXE* on the wall in her house. Why they thought she was a witch I have no idea.'

This seemed to shock the general, who stared at Donovan for some seconds, then leaned back in his seat and stared up at the ceiling. Donovan and Uschi looked on in silence. When the old man spoke again his voice seemed to come from far away.

'Astonishing,' he muttered quietly to himself. 'I haven't thought of them these past fifty years or more.'

'This seems to have struck a chord with you, Herr General,' Donovan said.

'Yes, yes indeed.' The general's voice was distant. 'I think it could probably mean only one thing.'

****

Anne was curious. She walked with Angela to where her car was parked beside the farmhouse and waved her off up the field track. Instead of going back to the office barn she retraced her steps to take a look at Dom's hot hatch. Uncharacteristically, Marnie had left the keys in the ignition, a sure sign of how unwell she must have been feeling. Anne swung the door open and climbed in.

The little car felt different from any other car she had known. She had been for numerous rides with Marnie in her 1936 MG two-seater, which was an out-and-out sports car by any yardstick. But the Peugeot was from a different era. The seats gripped Anne snugly. The instrument panel was dominated by a large rev-counter, clearly visible through the spokes of the chunky leather-bound steering wheel. The gear lever was stubby with a polished wooden knob. The whole thing felt low-slung and purposeful.

The one sour note was a strange odour. What had Marnie said about a box of cleaning materials and tools? Anne swivelled round to look on the back seat, but recalled that Marnie mentioned taking the box out and storing it in the barn. Even so, and despite the windows being open, the smell hung in the air. No wonder Marnie had felt nauseous.

Anne took the keys from the ignition and climbed out. Her nose led her to a shelf on the end wall. The box reminded her of the one Donovan used for his materials, but Dom's must have been a degree more powerful still. Anne took a brief sniff and blew out through her lips. Muttering that Dom should try a change of aftershave, she locked the car doors and headed for home.

****

General Ekkehart von Karlsdorff fixed Donovan with his gaze and with a grim smile said something that took his visitor completely by surprise. 'Do you believe in witchcraft, young man?'

Donovan was startled by the question. 'I ... I don't think I can have heard you correctly, Herr General.' He stumbled over the words.

Herr von Karlsdorff now seemed enfolded in his memories. His eyes seemed to lose their focus, wandering over visions from a bygone age.

'The successes of the first campaigns boosted our confidence. I was a colonel in Army Group South in Operation Barbarossa. They were hard battles in Ukraine, but our commanders were brilliant, our men superb. Kiev was our greatest victory, but later many of our units became low in morale, fatigued, demoralised. Often when we engaged the enemy we had been awake for night after night.'

The general paused to reflect. Donovan said, 'Bombardments from Russian artillery?'

'No. We were subjected to constant harassment from the air.'

'But I thought the *Luftwaffe* had air supremacy.'

'In many ways, yes. But the Reds carried out bombing raids at night. Their bases were too far away for our artillery to reach them and too far for advance parties to attack them behind their front line.'

'You had *Flak*, though.'

The general nodded. 'And we shot down some of their planes, though very few. When we examined them on the ground we found they were nothing but flimsy little biplanes that were obviously designed for crop-spraying or training. We understood then why the Luftwaffe could not deal with them.'

'Too slow to hit?' Donovan suggested.

'Exactly. Their *maximum* speed was slower than the *stalling* speed of Messerschmitt or Focke-Wulf fighters. And locating them at night ...'

Donovan said, 'Must have been almost impossible.'

'Correct. To us it seemed an insult to be thwarted by such insignificant machines of plywood and canvas. But the pilots, they were anything but insignificant. When we found the few planes that we had brought down and pulled out the bodies of the dead aircrew, we found they were ...women.'

'All of them?'

'Every single one of them. *Women!* Even that's an exaggeration. Most of them were nothing more than young girls.'

'That's extraordinary.'

'I saw one of the planes myself once. Our gunners had brought it down, shot off the tailplane. It crashed into trees near my regiment. The pilot and navigator can't have been much more than nineteen or twenty ... just girls.'

'They were killed?'

'Yes, but here's the extraordinary thing. You might not believe this, but the navigator had a kitten in the cockpit with her. The girls died but the little cat survived.'

'They must have been incredibly brave,' said Donovan.

'Absolutely. One night, one of our fighters managed to shoot down four of their planes. I saw them blazing through the sky like flaming torches. The crews must have died horribly. There were no more raids that night. But the next night there were more attacks than ever before.'

The general handed the photos back to Donovan who studied them, wondering what acts of courage Katie Koslowski must have performed to earn such awards.

The general added, 'Afterwards we learned that many of them flew over *eight hundred missions!* ... sometimes almost twenty missions in a single night. We hated them for what they did, but grudgingly we had to respect them.'

'I've never even heard of them,' Donovan said.

The general looked at him. 'No one knows about them these days. But I can tell you, young man, they played a huge part in our losing the war on the eastern front. Their campaign took them almost to the gates of Berlin.' He shook his head. 'They were as brave and fearless as any combatants in that dreadful war.'

'I'm sorry, Herr General, but there's something I don't understand. I don't see where witchcraft comes in.'

'Witchcraft?'

'You asked me if I believed in witchcraft.'

The general nodded slowly. 'So I did. That's what we called them, you see, those redoubtable fighters. Officially they were the 588th Night Bomber Aviation Regiment. Later we learnt they had been promoted to the distinction of a Guards regiment, the 46th "Taman". To us they became known simply as *die Nachthexen* ... the Night Witches.'

Chapter 20

‘I t's Good Friday,’ Marnie announced as Ralph came into the kitchen for breakfast the next morning.

‘It's good any day,’ Ralph said with a twinkle in his eye, ‘according to the old joke. *To the woods, to the woods ...*’

‘Okay, we get the picture,’ Marnie said.

Anne, who was pouring orange juice into glasses, gave him The Look. He raised both hands in surrender and went over to the toaster.

Marnie said, ‘Not sure we'll need toast. As it's officially a bank holiday I've popped some croissants in the oven.’

‘Great. Does that mean you're planning to take the day off, and why you worked late last night?’

‘Not really. In fact, I've got some more phoning to do this morning.’

Anne was now pouring hot water into the cafetière. ‘I was hoping we might go for a tootle on *Sally Ann*. It seems ages since we took her out for a run.’

‘That's the plan,’ said Marnie.

‘I'm confused now,’ said Ralph. ‘Work or tootle: which is it to be?’

‘Both. But I have to make some more calls before I'm sure. I'll know better by lunchtime, but meanwhile I suggest you both pack for a journey.’

Ralph said, ‘How enigmatic.’

Anne said, ‘We're going on an extended trip?’

‘I hope so. That's the idea.’

‘And you're phoning round to let others know about it?’

Marnie bent down to slide the tray of croissants out of the oven. ‘Yes.’

Ralph said, ‘Then for Angela's sake, don't forget the immortal line in that old joke.’

Marnie looked suspicious. ‘What immortal line?’

Ralph grinned. ‘*I'll tell the vicar ...*’

Marnie made as if to throw a croissant at him, but then thought better of it.

****

By morning break time Marnie's plan was laid. Three weekend bags were lined up in the hall of the farmhouse ready to go, and the Glebe Farm trio had already changed into their cruising gear. Over mugs of coffee in the kitchen, Marnie outlined her plan.

'I got fed up with the way everyone on the inter-faith committee expected someone else to take action, so I decided to try a different approach. Last night and for much of this morning I've been phoning round everyone I knew in the area who had a boat. Naturally, some had already made plans for the Easter break, but quite a few either had no particular plans or were willing to be flexible.'

'What do you have in mind?' Ralph asked.

'To make the trip down to Northampton and there have our very own Easter parade.'

Marnie waited while Ralph and Anne let this sink in.

'The idea being?' Ralph said.

'That we pack in as many boats as possible, deck them out with all the bunting we can lay hands on and get the good folk of Northampton to join us down by the canal for a celebration … a fun Easter Day out.'

'So, away from the town centre,' said Anne. 'Is that the idea?'

'That's the idea.'

Ralph looked sceptical. 'And that would achieve what?'

'It would take attention away from what New Force and their cronies have in mind.'

'Like when we organised the summer outings for kids a few years ago,' Anne said, adding, 'the first time we met Donovan.'

Ralph said, 'Marnie, I don't mean to be a wet blanket or sound negative, but are you convinced that a load of narrowboats dressed all over, so to say, will be a great attraction to the townspeople?'

'I haven't properly explained everything, have I? I also rang all the committee members and asked them to be involved. They were to contact everyone in their own networks and publicise the event on the grapevine. The same went for the boat owners and any of their friends and families. I asked everyone to get people to bring picnics, with enough food and drink for themselves and more besides to share with others. Some of the social clubs have occasional liquor licences, and they'll be setting up temporary bars on the canalside. Best of all, one man I spoke to had a connection with a firm that does bouncy castles. They always have a spare in case of accidental damage.' Marnie looked at her watch. 'They should be arriving round about now.'

'Phew!' Ralph said. 'No wonder you've been burning up the phone lines.'

'Oh yes, I nearly forgot. One bright spark from Stowe Hill marina suggested we all take as many Easter eggs as we could lay hands on to give out to the children.'

Anne piped up. 'We could organise a *massive* Easter egg hunt.'

'That's a good idea,' Marnie said. 'So what d'you both think?'

Ralph was enthusiastic. 'Terrific idea.'

'If it works.' Marnie said.

'Have you publicised it?' Anne asked. 'There's the local radio station, *two* TV stations. Probably too late to get anything in the papers?'

'I thought of that. Trouble is, if New Force get wind of what we're up to, they'd be bound to come down and cause trouble … try to disrupt everything.'

'That crowd of people would make an ideal target,' Ralph agreed.

'So how do we all make our way there without being spotted?' Anne asked. 'If New Force attacked the boats they could block the whole canal system going into Northampton. It'd be mayhem.'

'I thought of that, too,' said Marnie. 'In fact, I took a leaf out of Donovan's book.'

'We fit gun turrets and torpedo tubes?' Anne suggested.

'Exactly. But apart from that.'

'You're thinking we should make the journey by night?' Ralph said.

'I'm thinking we'd all converge on Gayton Junction, just as if we were going for a normal tootle. From there, the ones who'd had the shortest journey would make their way down the Northampton Arm like any casual boaters. The rest -'

'The armada,' said Ralph.

'The armada,' said Marnie, 'would follow on, beginning their descent after dark. By some time on Saturday most of the craft would be in place. Sunday morning we'd have Anne's egg hunt for the children, followed by our own Easter parade of boats, and then the picnic would begin.'

Ralph steepled his fingers, looking thoughtful. 'Playing devil's advocate … New Force would be bound to find out about the event … by the way, do you have a name for it?'

'Wouldn't it just be the Easter Parade?' Marnie said.

Ralph shook his head. 'Isn't that rather too close to what New Force are planning? We wouldn't want there to be any confusion.'

Anne said, 'I know! What about the *Sally Ann* Rally?'

'Well … I suppose it would just be our own shorthand for it,' Marnie said.

Ralph nodded. 'No harm just calling it that amongst ourselves, then we wouldn't confuse it with the New Force event.'

'What a thought!' Marnie exclaimed.

'How did you leave it with the others?' Ralph asked.

'The plan was to make a start this afternoon, unless I phoned round to call it off. Well, are we up for it?'

Ralph said, 'Just one reservation. I'm still bothered about security. The New Force mob could well notice people making their way down to Midsummer Meadow.'

'I've thought of that,' Marnie said. 'Sergeant Groves from the committee is arranging for a few police cars to be parked strategically and conspicuously along the Bedford Road. There'll also be some uniformed officers and a number of Community Support Officers patrolling the area. How about that?'

'Good thinking, Batman,' said Ralph.

'Spot on!' said Anne.

'Then let's go for it,' said Marnie.

****

It was too early for them to set off that morning. Not wanting to cause excessive congestion around Gayton Junction, Marnie and Co opted for departure later in the afternoon. They had a cruise of some hours ahead of them, so Marnie and Ralph went to check that *Sally Ann* was suitably prepared for the journey. As they left the office, Marnie remembered that she had left Dom's car in the barn with its windows open. She suggested to Ralph that they go and check that it was okay.

'You're not worried that someone might have damaged it, are you?' Ralph said.

'No. So far New Force haven't penetrated this far in. But it might be a good idea to close the windows. We don't want pigeons getting in and nesting.'

They picked up the Peugeot's keys from the hall table where Anne had left them and set off to the garage barn. They found the car in good order, and the chemical smell inside had largely dissipated. Suddenly Marnie had a brainwave. She skipped across the grass to the opposite garage barn, rummaged in the rear and came out with a large bundle that Ralph recognised at once.

'My old cover for the Volvo?'

'You don't use it on the Jaguar, so what about covering Dom's car with it? We don't know how long we'll be looking after it for him. A shame if it got covered in dust.'

'Why not?' said Ralph.

They closed the car's windows, and Marnie locked the doors. Together they pulled the cover over the top. Once in place, the Peugeot was invisible.

Anne had stayed behind in the office to make sure that everything was tidy enough to leave and to arrange for neighbours in one of the cottages to feed Dolly in their absence. She was filing correspondence when her mobile rang. To her surprise she saw that the caller was Donovan; it was early in the day for him to ring her.

'Hi, Donovan. Everything all right?'

'Everything's fine.'

'How's Germany?'

'It was okay when I left it this morning.'

'You've left? You seem to be making a habit of surprise departures.'

'I set off at crack of dawn. I was desperate to get back in time for Easter and I managed to get a channel crossing at short notice online. Just wanted to let you know I hope to be with you tomorrow.'

'But we won't be here. There's been a development.'

'Trouble?'

'No, listen. I'll tell you what Marnie's thought up.'

Anne gave a brief outline of the plan for the *Sally Ann Rally*. When she finished there was silence on the line.

'Donovan?'

'Are you serious?' he replied.

'Yes. Why not?'

'You're going to take on New Force with Easter eggs, a float past of boats and a picnic?'

'That's the idea.' Anne's confidence in the plan started to evaporate.

'My god ...'

'Sounds like you don't think it's a great plan.'

'Understatement.'

'But, Donovan, we've got to do something. We can't just let -'

'When are you setting off?'

'Later this afternoon.'

'How late?'

'Not sure ... maybe ... four or thereabouts? We want to reach Gayton Junction when it's dark.'

Another silence on the line.

'Donovan?'

'Listen. Can you check over *Exodos*? You know where I keep the spare keys. Can you make sure she's ready to go?'

'Why?'

'I'm coming up straight away. I'll join you. Marnie and Ralph can travel together. You can come with me.'

'But, Donovan, that's crazy. You must be *miles* away, and you've already had a long drive from Germany.'

'Don't worry about me. I'll be fine.'

'Where are you exactly?'

'Just in a queue waiting to leave Dover harbour. I can be with you in three hours max.'

'You'll be exhausted, and we're going to travel through part of the night.'

A pause. 'Okay, here's a plan. If you'll wait for me, you can drive *Exodos* for most of the trip. I'll work the locks and in between, if I need a rest, I can lie down for an hour or two in the cabin. What d'you think?'

'Donovan, what would you say if I said you were mad?'

Donovan grinned. 'Guess. Gotta go.'

****

Anne had a busy afternoon. Despite her misgivings, she did as Donovan asked and checked over the boat. She was not surprised that he had left *Exodos* in perfect condition: batteries topped up on the trickle-charger, fuel filters clear, stern gland hand-tight, engine and gearbox oil levels up to the mark, both gas bottles full, plenty of diesel in the tank. No probs, she thought.

Her next mission was a trip into town to visit Dom, her last chance for some days, and to see how Mr Koslowski was progressing. She faced this journey with some trepidation, not only because of her concerns about the two in intensive care, but her dread at the possibility of running into gangs of skinheads.

The town was ominously quiet. Anne knew that for some historical reason Northampton did not keep Good Friday as a bank holiday. She expected it to be business as usual in the county town. But that day it seemed almost as if the place was holding its breath, waiting for something to happen. The only outward sign of recent troubles was the presence of the far-right graffiti that Dominik, Donovan and their friends had not yet removed.

On the way through the village Anne had called in at the shop and bought a bunch of grapes for Dom. She knew it was a cliché, but the choice in the shop was limited: grapes or grapefruit. No contest. Leaving the Mini in the hospital car park, she made her way up to the intensive therapy unit. At the top of the stairs she saw Magda sitting in the waiting area. She looked anxious, but her face lit up as soon as she spotted Anne coming towards her. To Anne's surprise, Magda leapt to her feet, kissed her on both cheeks and hugged her warmly.

'Everything all right?' Anne asked when Magda released her grip.

'Yes. The consultant's doing rounds. We have to wait a while.'

'You had me worried,' Anne said. 'You looked so down in the dumps.'

Magda sagged. 'It's this place. It always depresses me. I keep thinking of all the suffering. There's poor Mr Koslowski lying there. I'm sure it's only the equipment that's keeping him alive.'

'It's really that serious?'

Magda nodded. 'I'm pretty sure. They won't tell me anything about his condition, since I'm not family, but ...' She shrugged. 'And then there's Dom. He's always been so full of life, but even he hasn't been himself for the past week or two, longer than that when I think about it.'

Anne tried to sound sympathetic. 'He's really very concerned about New Force and the like, isn't he?'

'Sure. And I think he had prior knowledge of what was coming. He seems to have been bothered about it for ages.'

'I know what you mean, Magda. Donovan's the same. He can be quite … what's the word? … obsessive about these extreme right-wing thugs. His family suffered a lot under the Nazis, you know.'

Magda frowned. 'His family? Why was that?'

Anne wished she had not mentioned Donovan's family. She said simply, 'Oh, you know, the war and all that.'

'So much misery,' Magda said. 'You wouldn't believe what Katie and Stan went through.'

'Really?'

'Oh my goodness! Do you know they *walked* into Germany from Poland in the last weeks of the war. They were desperate to reach the Allies and get away from the fighting. From *Poland!*'

'My god,' Anne said quietly. 'How do you know all this?'

'I've been helping Katya with her memories.'

'You mean like her *memoirs?*' Anne said.

'She calls them just a collection of memories. She's been through a lot. You wouldn't believe it.'

'So how have you been helping her?'

'I've been translating them into English to publish a book. She wants young people to know what it was like back then in the war. So many of our generation only know English, and her English wasn't good enough for translating. It was good for me too because -'

Before Magda could go on, they heard the door open and looked round to see a nurse standing in the entrance. It was not the trainee they had seen on their previous visit. This woman looked to be in her forties and was wearing dark blue scrubs. At first sight, Anne thought she might be a surgeon, but saw that her badge identified her as Senior Ward Manager Drew. Her expression was grim, her demeanour severe.

'Sorry to keep you waiting,' she said in a flat tone. 'Who have you come to see?'

Magda said, 'Dominik Gorski.'

'I'm afraid that won't be possible.'

Anne almost jumped as she felt her hand gripped tightly by Magda.

'Is he all right?' Anne said, struggling to get the words out.

'Yes, but he's sleeping. He's just had an examination, and it seems to have tired him.'

Magda let out a sigh. 'So no prospect of him going home, then?'

The nurse shook her head. 'He has multiple injuries, so he'll be staying in this unit for some more days. Depending on his condition we'll then move him to a ward.'

'But he is going to be all right, isn't he?'

'He's reasonably comfortable, all things considered.' Drew had an afterthought. 'Oh yes, there is one thing. He seems to be fretting about his car.'

'Tell him not to worry on that score,' Anne said. 'We've got it safely tucked away in our garage.'

'Thanks,' said Drew. 'He'll be relieved to know that.'

Anne said, 'And Mr Koslowski? How is he today?'

Sister Drew considered this question. 'No change.'

'I've brought Dom some fruit,' Anne said, holding up the bag. 'Could you possibly take it for him, if we can't come in?'

For a moment, Anne thought Drew was going to refuse, but she accepted the bag and looked in it.

'I have some too,' said Magda. 'Would you mind?'

The nurse took the second bag and said, 'The poor boy.'

'What is it?' There was fear in Magda's voice.

With the same serious expression, Drew said, 'I think he'll be risking a grape overdose at this rate.'

Anne laughed gently at the nurse's joke, but there was something in her eyes that betrayed a deeper feeling.

'Tough day?' Anne said softly.

Drew looked at her for a long moment, then made the slightest movement of her head.

Anne reached forward and gently touched the nurse's elbow. 'Thank you for all you're doing for our friends.'

Drew gave a hint of a smile, before closing the door and walking away.

****

Despite her concern at Donovan becoming fatigued, Anne was looking forward to seeing both him and the Porsche. She recalled an exciting journey in it when she and Donovan had travelled to Germany. It was the time when the car 'disappeared', and no one, least of all Donovan, expected to see it ever again. Anne was up in her attic room when Donovan arrived. Its walls were of solid stone with only a narrow glazed slit at the gable end for a

233

window, so she had no indication of his return until the office door opened and he called her name. She descended the wall ladder and was in his arms in record time.

'You're later than I expected,' she said. 'I was starting to worry about you.'

'Slight change of plan. I called in at home to get a few things.'

Anne grinned. 'Socks and undies?'

'More or less.'

'Porsche okay? I'm dying to see it.'

'A pleasure deferred,' said Donovan.

'What does that mean?'

'I've left it in London. Came up in the Beetle. I needed to bring a few things with me.'

'For the boat?'

'Sort of. When are we leaving?'

'Any time now,' Anne said.

'Then we'd better get ready.'

The weekend bags were already stowed on *Sally Ann* and *Exodos*. Unusually, when Anne offered to help Donovan with his bag, he accepted. He had left the VW beside the garage barn as its slot was taken up with Dom's Peugeot under its cover. After pulling his weekend bag from the front luggage compartment and giving it to Anne, he reached into the car and took a large cardboard box from the back seat. Anne suspected it contained the haul of goodies that Donovan habitually brought back from Germany, but it was firmly sealed with tape. She had to restrain her curiosity.

Arriving at the bankside they found Marnie and Ralph giving *Sally Ann* a final once-over. Donovan laid his box on the ground, hugged them both and declared himself fit and ready for departure. As they were anxious to get underway, the four of them went into a huddle for a hasty last-minute briefing. Donovan and Anne quickly hopped aboard *Exodos* which was moored across *Sally Ann*'s dock. Donovan carried the box through the study area at the front of the cabin and set it down on the floor beside his mountain bike. Wasting no further time, he and Anne manoeuvred the boat clear so that Marnie could reverse and turn in mid-channel to steer northwards.

On *Exodos* Anne skipped along the gunwale to the bows to wave Marnie and Ralph off. She was happy that Marnie's plan was now in progress, happy too that *Sally Ann* was passing under the accommodation bridge that was now completely cleansed of New Force graffiti. Yet behind her smile she wondered what awaited them all at journey's end.

Back on the stern deck, Anne took over the tiller from Donovan. He kissed her and went below to rest. They had an hour of uninterrupted running ahead of them, all of it in daylight. Anne kept *Exodos* around fifty yards behind *Sally Ann*, far enough back to avoid the exhaust fumes. Up ahead she could see Ralph steering while Marnie was constantly on her mobile, looking like a military commander. But the thought brought Anne no comfort. Could they really be going into battle?

****

Donovan slept right through the seven Stoke Bruerne locks. Marnie and Ralph arrived at the first in the flight as a lone boat was preparing to enter the chamber. Looking back beyond *Exodos*, Ralph spotted another craft coming up some way behind. Anne saw it too and signalled to Marnie and Ralph to go through in company with the other boat.

She was pleased when the following boat arrived to find that she recognised the crew, a middle-aged couple from Cosgrove. She had seen them many times before and had often admired their smartly-painted fifty-seven footer. For their part, they were intrigued by the unusual appearance of Donovan's boat with its matt dark grey paintwork, and even more so by the strange name it bore. Anne explained that *X O 2* was pronounced *Exodos*, meaning Way Out in Greek, and that her boyfriend had chosen it when he dropped out of a university course.

The newcomers suggested that they take the whole sequence of locks 'breasted-up' together, and the husband of the couple offered to handle the locking while the 'womenfolk' steered the boats. Anne gratefully accepted.

Donovan was still sleeping when Anne and her newfound friends exited the top lock in Stoke Bruerne village. There, Anne parted company with her lock partners who were stopping off for refreshment at one of the local inns. Easing past the boats that lined much of the length of the canal towards the Blisworth tunnel, Anne zipped up her jacket and pulled on a hat in preparation for the long damp passage before her. The air grew noticeably chilly as they approached the portal, and Anne reached into the cabin to switch on the headlamp and navigation lights, realising that she had never before braved the tunnel solo.

Donovan had made a thorough job of equipping his boat for such journeys. He had not only installed a powerful headlamp that lit up the way ahead for about fifty yards, but had supplemented it with two further lights that shone to either side at an angle, illuminating the walls lining the tunnel. This arrangement increased Anne's confidence, but after a while she began to experience the disorientation brought on by navigating in such a confined space. Despite her best efforts she misjudged her steering, and the side of the boat clouted the tunnel edging with a resounding clang.

Struggling to bring *Exodos* back into midstream, she suddenly saw the opening of a ventilation shaft in the roof. From its gaping mouth a torrent of water was gushing, and there was no way to avoid being drenched. Hunched at the tiller, Anne braced herself and pulled up her collar, grimacing in anticipation. As the aperture drew near she heard the downpour cascading onto the bows and roaring along the roof of the boat. She closed her eyes, no longer caring whether she thumped the edging or not.

And then it crashed down onto the stern deck. The full force of the waterfall landed only for two seconds or so, while Anne gritted her teeth. Opening her eyes, she was astonished that she was untouched by the deluge. She found herself looking into the face of Donovan who was holding up a vast golf umbrella over them both and grinning at her.

'Shouldn't you be looking where you're going?' he said loudly over the boom of the engine and the echo of the tunnel.

'I thought you were -'

Donovan grabbed the tiller and threw it first to one side and then to the other. The boat corrected itself, narrowly missed hitting the side wall and resumed its position down the centre of the tunnel.

'I was,' Donovan said. 'But then I was woken by the alarm clock.'

'Alarm clock?'

'It sounded strangely like a rather loud metallic clang.' He was still grinning.

'Ah, yes ... Sorry about that. How are you feeling?'

'Awake. And thanks for letting me doze. I must have been out for the best part of two hours.'

'You must've needed it.'

Donovan retracted the umbrella, shook it over the stern and dropped it back into place inside the cabin door. Anne stared ahead, concentrating hard on keeping the boat on course in the confined surroundings.

'That was nifty footwork with the umbrella,' she said. 'I was braced for a soaking.'

'More ventilation shafts to come. Keep a lookout. You okay with steering or d'you want a break?'

'I'm fine. You can lie down again if you want.'

But by now Donovan had his second wind and was content to perch on the stern rail while Anne steered. When *Exodos* emerged from the tunnel it was still daylight. They travelled only a short distance, after skirting round the village of Blisworth, before they came upon the first row of boats lining the canal, waiting for cover of darkness before making the descent to Northampton. Anne had never seen so many craft on that stretch of the waterway. It looked as if a fleet was assembling for action. Somewhere ahead Marnie and Ralph on *Sally Ann* were already moored. Groups of people, the crews from the boats, were standing chatting on the towpath. There was an atmosphere of anticipation, of camaraderie, of a joint undertaking. A fleet really was assembling for action.

****

Donovan was the first to wake up. The rumble of diesel engines coming to life nearby brought him up to the surface. He had been dozing fully clothed in the sleeping cabin, with Anne beside him. When they first lay down after mooring she had wanted to question him about his visit to Germany, but they had both succumbed to weariness and soon their eyelids were drooping. He eased himself from the bed trying not to disturb Anne's slumber, but she sensed movement, and he heard her taking deep breaths.

'Are you getting up?' Her voice was faint.

'Time to move out,' he said quietly. He parted the curtain over the port hole. 'It's dark outside. The others are on the move. I can hear engines. You can stay there if you want. I'll get us going.'

But Anne was already sliding across the bed, yawning. 'We'll do it together.'

237

The boats ahead of them were pulling away as Anne and Donovan untied the mooring ropes while the engine warmed up. With Donovan at the tiller, Anne pushed the bows away from the bank and walked quickly back to step aboard at the stern as Donovan pushed on the accelerator and *Exodos* moved smoothly off. Although darkness had come down he only switched on the navigation lights, relying on his night vision rather than the powerful headlamps. Marnie had briefed everyone to use as little light as possible. Each boat left behind only the faintest glow from a solitary cabin light. To some it seemed an unnecessary precaution, but Marnie had argued that when confronted by an organisation like New Force it was wise to take no chances.

Anne and Donovan made slow progress. The whole fleet was queuing along the main line as far as Gayton Junction where they would head off towards the north-east. When their turn came, Donovan swung *Exodos* into the Northampton Arm, and they crawled snail-like past the boatyard and round Gayton Marina. To any passer-by observing the scene it would have seemed a strange nocturnal procession as boats filled the waterway, nose to tail. But at that time of night there were no passers-by. Secrecy was the basis of Marnie's plan.

An interminable amount of time seemed to elapse before they reached the top lock of the Rothersthorpe flight. Donovan hopped ashore and worked the paddles to bring up the level in the chamber with Anne manning the tiller, holding the boat in mid-channel waiting for the gate to open. While the narrow lock filled, Donovan strolled to its far end and stared ahead into the night. As far as the eye could see there were boats in every lock descending step by step ahead of him, in each one a pale light shining faintly like a line of fireflies. With a jolt he realised that they reminded him suddenly of the films he had seen of torchlight processions at Nazi rallies before the war. His thoughts strayed to old General von Karlsdorff, the horrors of the eastern front and the daring missions of the Night Witches.

He was summoned back to reality by a call from Anne. Even in the darkness she had seen the white-painted end of the balance beam start to move. The entry lock gate was swinging gently open. The chamber was full, and it was time to advance.

Chapter 21

Ιn Northampton the canal merges into the river Nene as it ambles through the south of the town. When the sun rose on the morning after Good Friday none of the boaters whose craft thronged the areas known as Midsummer Meadow and Beckett's Park was up to see it. That whole part of the town's waterways was packed with narrowboats of all shapes and sizes that had slipped in during the early hours. Now the crews were tucked into their beds catching up on lost sleep.

It was almost lunchtime before any sign of life appeared among the boating fraternity. One of the first to be up and about was Marnie, soon to be followed by Ralph who set off for his habitual morning walk with rather less gusto than usual. The weather was mild that day, with intermittent clouds scattered across a blue sky. A number of the boaters took advantage of the spring warmth to enjoy a late breakfast on deck or on the towpath.

Anne and Donovan were also 'early' risers, and they made their way along the towpath to find *Sally Ann*. Ralph returned from a shorter walk than usual and reported that there were boats double banked down the river as far as the eye could see. The four of them had a hasty breakfast, and Marnie took her half-empty coffee mug out, so anxious was she to review the fleet. As soon as she appeared on the bank she was surrounded by boaters keen to receive instructions for the day. Her message was simple.

'Today we just take it easy. Keep everything quiet. We don't want to be noticed yet.' She nodded at a man she recognised. 'It's Graham, isn't it?'

'That's me.'

'You've brought the bouncy castle?'

'All set up, ready to go.' He pointed over his shoulder. 'It's beyond those trees over there. We can start now, if you like.'

'Thanks but no. Everything has to kick off tomorrow, mid-morning. Timing's important.

'Fair enough,' said Graham. 'You're the boss.'

'What about us?' It was a man that Marnie did not recognise. She smiled at him. 'You are?'

'Billing Brass. We're the band. Some of us have got boats, so we're here already.'

'The others?'

'Coming tomorrow. What time d'you want us here?'

'Ten o'clock all right?'

He nodded. 'I'll pass the word along.'

'We're here, Marnie, all present and correct.' A cheerful voice. It was the man from Stowe Hill marina who had suggested bringing Easter eggs for the children.

'Great,' Marnie said. 'And fully armed with eggs?'

'Absolutely, and with more besides.' He looked very pleased with himself.

'Oh?' Marnie tried to keep the anxiety out of her voice. She was not overly keen on anyone freelancing where New Force was concerned. 'And what might that be?'

'Fireworks.'

Beside Marnie, Ralph, Anne and Donovan exchanged glances. Donovan in particular looked intrigued.

'I see,' said Marnie.

'Not a problem, is there?' Stowe Hill man asked.

Marnie looked thoughtful. 'I don't suppose you know if you need a licence for that kind of thing?'

The man looked doubtful. 'I hadn't thought of that.'

Donovan said, 'It would only be some individual letting off a few fireworks for personal pleasure, surely.'

'But in a public place,' Ralph said. 'Wouldn't it count as a display of some kind?'

Another boater piped up, pointing at Donovan. 'I think he's got the right idea. A few fireworks let off on the towpath for personal enjoyment. Where's the harm in that?'

Eventually Marnie said, 'Presumably you'd let them off at dusk to get the full effect?'

Donovan said quietly, 'What time will the police go off duty?'

There were grins all round, though some of those present looked uncomfortable.

Marnie said, 'Look, the idea is just that we've come to have fun. There are eggs and a bouncy castle for the kids, plenty of food and drink, a float past, a band, a party atmosphere. We're here to forget about New Force and all they stand for. If someone wants to let off a few fireworks, there's probably no harm in that.'

There were murmurings of approval all round, or nearly all round. The group dispersed to return to their boats to complete decking out the bunting. Marnie and co turned back along the towpath.

Anne said, 'Do you want any help with the bunting on *Sally Ann*, Marnie?' She turned to Donovan. "There's enough to deck out *Exodos* too.'

'We'll manage,' said Marnie, adding, 'I think ‑ at least I hope – everyone is happy.'

'Some of them struck me as a bit wobbly,' Donovan observed. 'And I'm sure some people will be worrying about New Force.'

Marnie agreed. 'Can you blame them? I wish I hadn't mentioned New Force just then.'

They stopped and looked back at the assembly. Boaters were busy, rigging up their bunting. The scene was relaxed and purposeful, though one or two groups were huddled together in conversation on the towpath.

Anne said, 'On the whole it all looks calm enough.'

'Well, we're here now,' Marnie said. 'We're doing what we can – what little we can – to tackle New Force in as peaceful a manner as possible. I take it as a good sign that things are calm, as you say, Anne.'

They resumed their walk in silence. Marnie was mentally crossing her fingers that things would turn out right. Anne was trying hard to keep thoughts of the skinhead gangs out of her head. Donovan's mind was in another place, as usual. As for Ralph, he could not rid himself of the thought that this might be the lull before the storm.

Chapter 22

Easter Sunday, to Marnie's relief, was another fine day, even warmer than Saturday had been, good picnic weather. Up bright and early, she made her way along the rows of moored boats, offering words of encouragement about the day ahead. Anne tagged along while Ralph took his morning power-walk and Donovan made some phone calls. The previous evening had passed peacefully to everyone's relief. So far they seemed to have escaped the notice of New Force.

At ten o'clock the band struck up. The first families began to arrive, setting out their picnic rugs and in some cases even tables and chairs. The first customers for the bouncy castle scrambled on board with squeaks and laughter. Things were looking good.

Shortly afterwards two groups of visitors arrived, one welcome, the other unexpected. First on the scene came Magda with a small number of young Poles that Anne recognised from the graffiti-cleaning parties. They spotted Anne and Marnie and hurried over to them with smiles on their faces and bags of goodies in their hands. Magda embraced Anne warmly and introduced her companions. They held up their bags.

'Genuine Polish picnic!' Magda exclaimed, laughing.

Anne grinned. 'Does that mean you've got vodka in there?'

Magda adopted an expression of mock horror. 'For shame, Anne. What an idea!'

They were laughing together when Donovan joined them. He embraced Magda and shook hands with the others.

'I've been trying to phone you, Magda,' he said. 'No reply. I wanted to ask if you had any news of Dom or Mr Koslowski.'

Magda fumbled in her shoulder-bag. 'I keep doing that. I forget to switch it on or I leave it on and the battery runs down.'

'I'm really sorry not to have had the chance to visit Dom,' Donovan said. 'I've been away. Would you say hi from me when you see him?'

'Sure. He'll be glad to hear from you.'

'So do you have any news?' Anne asked.

'I visited them yesterday. I think Dom is making some progress, though he now accepts he'll be immobilised for some time. They're moving him out of intensive care and onto a different ward, which is a good sign. But as for Stan ...' She waggled a hand in the air.

'That's too bad,' said Anne. 'I feel so sad about –'

Before she could finish the sentence they were interrupted by the arrival of a man who rushed up to Magda, breathless from running. He began speaking to her in rapid-fire Polish. Noticing the blank faces of the others, he spread his palms and addressed the group in English.

'So sorry to barge in. Please excuse me.' He turned to face Magda and continued in English. 'I've only just heard about Dominik. This is dreadful. Do you have news of him?'

Magda looked at the others. 'I should introduce Mr Jackson –'

'Nathaniel, please,' he interrupted, still breathing heavily.

Magda said, 'Okay, Nathaniel. I should also explain that he and his wife have been away and only just returned.'

'After our boat was destroyed we were so dismayed we went off to Israel for a vacation.'

'Yours was the boat that was burnt?' Anne said, wide-eyed.

'You heard about that?' Nathaniel said.

'We were the ones who reported it to the police.' She indicated Donovan. 'My boyfriend made the actual 999 call.'

Nathaniel glanced at Donovan and did a classic double-take.

'Are you Dom's brother?'

'Friend,' said Donovan.

'Well, you couldn't find a better friend. Dom's a hero. You know that? If anyone can stand up to these hooligans, he can.'

'I'm sure you're right, Mr Jackson. We're on the same wavelength. We've been working together.'

'And did you organise all this?' Nathaniel made a sweeping gesture with his hand.

'No. You see that lady over there ... dark hair, blue jacket, black jeans? She did, Marnie Walker. This was her plan.'

'*That* is Marnie Walker? I've heard a lot about her.'

'How did you get here, Nathaniel?' Magda asked.

'We came with friends on their boat. We haven't been able to replace ours yet. We've got to sort out insurance and such. It's a nightmare.'

Donovan's attention was gradually shifting along the bank to where Marnie was locked in conversation with another group. He nudged Anne and said quietly, 'Who's Marnie talking to? Do you recognise them? They seem to be carrying equipment.'

'Never seen them before.'

Donovan said in a normal voice, 'Excuse me, please. Nice meeting you Mr ... Nathaniel.'

He set off across the grass with Anne in tow.

That second group of visitors turned out to be a small team from the BBC's local radio station. As they drew nearer they heard Marnie speaking.

'... which is why we didn't contact you beforehand.'

A smart young woman in a black trouser-suit seemed to be in charge of the group. She said, 'You organise a major community event like this and you don't want it publicised? That's gotta be a first.'

'But you take my point,' Marnie said. 'Announcing this to the media could bring New Force troublemakers down on our heads. That's the last thing we need. Anyway, how did you find out about us?'

'A tip-off.'

'From whom?'

'We don't reveal our –'

'Oh, come off it! This isn't Watergate.'

The BBC woman said, 'Okay. We were doing some interviews about Easter with ... prominent religious leaders. That's all I'll say.'

Marnie's eyes narrowed. She glanced at Anne. 'The bloody archdeacon!' She turned to the BBC journalist. 'Why did he do that?'

'He probably thought you wanted people to know about the event. It is logical.'

'Not when you're trying to conceal things from the damn' Nazis,' Marnie said bitterly.

'Well, we're here now and this is where all the Easter action is, so ...'

Marnie sighed. 'But if you go out live and word gets back to New Force we'll be sitting ducks down here.'

'Oh, we won't be broadcasting live. Our live event this morning is the big Easter service in All Saints' church. It's being taken by the Bishop of Peterborough with the All Saints choristers and various other choirs performing with them. That starts soon and it'll be going on for an hour or so.'

'So when's your stuff going out?'

'We can make it a feature on the six o'clock news.'

Marnie shrugged. 'Right, we'll press on.'

The BBC crew set off across the grass, lugging their recording equipment. As Marnie and co looked on, a young woman dressed in black ran up to the lead journalist and pointed off towards a cluster of boaters.

'Lining up people to interview,' Donovan said.

Marnie nodded. 'That's how she started with me.'

'Did you agree?' Anne asked.

'We didn't get that far before she twigged she wasn't welcome.'

'Might not be a bad idea to give them an interview,' Donovan muttered.

Marnie was surprised. 'You think so?'

'Maybe. The time might come when we'll want to put out some information.' Donovan nodded over Marnie's shoulder. 'Don't look now, but here comes the God Squad ... including your favourite churchman, I think. At least I'm guessing the crusty old gent in clerical garb with Angela and Randall is your pal the archdeacon.'

Marnie turned her head. 'Yep, that's him.'

'Are you going to say anything to him, Marnie?' Magda asked.

'Too late now. The damage is done.' She lowered her voice as the priests came nearer. 'But if New Force do attack us, guess who's going in the front line of our defences?'

Anne tried to stifle a laugh, but it turned into a hiccup. Donovan patted her on the back. Marnie was just about to greet the approaching clerics when she closed her mouth, cocked her head on one side, shut her eyes and listened.

'What is it?' Anne said.

'Listen.'

By now the three priests had joined them, and they all stood together, concentrating. The archdeacon spoke first.

'I can't hear anything. But then my hearing isn't what it used —'

Marnie raised a finger. 'There ... quite faint ... carried on the breeze. Can you hear it?'

They were straining intently when they became aware of a gathering around them. A party of mothers and children had arrived. Seeing Marnie and the others apparently locked into some kind of trance, they held their peace and waited.

Marnie said hesitantly, 'To me, it sounded like drums beating.'

245

'Got it,' said Donovan.

'Oh yes ...' Angela agreed.

It was only then that Marnie noticed the mums. 'Hello,' she said. 'Looking for me?'

'Are you Marnie?' one of the mums asked.

'Yes.'

'Only we were wondering about the Easter egg hunt. People have been talking about it, and the kiddies have been wondering. Have the eggs been hidden already?'

'Sorry. I'm a bit behind schedule ... had some interruptions.'

'You see, they've got big eyes and ... well, you know.'

Marnie half-whispered. 'You don't want them to see you-know-what going on.'

'Exactly.'

'Bring the kids over here.' They all turned to look at Donovan as he spoke. 'Mums too, but not dads. Okay? Mums and children. Follow me.'

The mums looked at Marnie.

She said, 'Yes. This is Donovan, our friend, one of the organising team. You can go with him. It's all right.'

Donovan began walking away. Anne made to follow, but he turned to her and said in a low voice, 'Ask Magda to help you get the boaters hiding the eggs as soon as we've gone. Then catch up with us. Just you by yourself.'

'But how will I find you?'

'Go to where you hear drums beating. I'll be there somewhere.

A straggle of mothers and children fell in behind Donovan up the gentle slope away from the river, as he turned and gestured to them to keep up. The children formed a ragged line and skipped after him, with their mothers tagging along. They made a merry troop of followers. Marnie and the others looked on while Anne enlisted Magda's help to prompt the hiding of the eggs.

'Is this part of the plan, Marnie?' Angela asked cheerfully. 'Where's he taking them?'

Angela noticed as soon as she asked the question that Marnie's expression was dubious.

'I have no idea,' Marnie said slowly. 'But you know what this reminds me of? The Pied Piper of Hamelin.'

Hearing this, Ralph quoted Browning's poem, 'All the little boys and girls, With rosy cheeks and flaxen curls ...'

Angela said, 'And we all know what happened to them.'

'Good lord!' said the archdeacon.

****

The racecourse in Northampton was a total misnomer; it had not witnessed horse racing for almost a hundred years. The course had been abandoned on account of the large number of fatal accidents that had occurred, largely because of its tight bends. In past times it had been used for over a century for public executions, and in two world wars it had served as an army camp. On that particular Easter Sunday it was the scene of another bellicose gathering. New Force had chosen it as their assembly area.

Over two hundred skinheads, plus some scary-looking girlfriends, began gathering together in preparation for their so-called Easter Parade. Many of them had weapons concealed about their persons, such as flick-knives, stilettos, hammers and even pepper-spray canisters. They were looking forward to a pleasant morning on the rampage. Several members of the mob carried banners sporting the red NF lightning-flash logo in a white disc on a black background. A dozen or so were carrying drums suspended from their shoulders by thick leather straps.

New Force had a definite hierarchy but no single leader. Thus it was that by a general shuffling consensus among the top dogs, a signal was given to move off. As they formed into a procession and sloped along the pavement beside the racecourse, the drummers started up. The 'parade' moved onto the road with banners held high and a steady, heavy, throb beating out.

There was no traffic on the streets in the town centre that Easter Sunday morning, and the skinheads soon noticed that there were no pedestrians to be seen either. Apart from the rhythmic pounding of the drums, their surroundings were engulfed in an eerie silence. No people lined the Kettering Road to watch them pass; no curtains so much as twitched. There was not a single face to be seen looking out from a window. Most shop-fronts were boarded up. Northampton had become a ghost town.

At the front of the procession where the banners were most concentrated, the ad hoc leadership was growing suspicious. They began to put the word around: prepare for a police ambush. And an ambush came, but when it came it had nothing to do with the police, and when it came there was nothing the skinheads could do about it.

The Kettering Road merged with other roads around a triangular garden. Beside it the citizens of the town had long ago erected a statue to one of its favourite sons, a free-thinking member of parliament. At that very point came the first sign of life. Across the road that joined on the left stood a line of spectators, but this was no jostling irate public held back by ranks of sturdy police officers. There was not a blue uniform to be seen, nor anyone but a single row of mothers and children, almost all of them smiling and waving, some of the younger ones even giggling. Most of the children were holding daffodils. No one noticed that the adjacent garden was lacking any spring flowers in its borders.

The faces of the marching throng registered bewilderment as they surveyed the on-lookers who greeted them with such enthusiasm. The mob trudged on. This was not the reception they had expected. The next junction was a crossroads, and here it was the same story. On either side mums and children welcomed them with apparent joy. Along the pedestrianised main shopping street clusters of mothers and their young peered out from shop doorways, many of them waving brightly-coloured handkerchiefs, some holding daffodils. Astonishingly, the townsfolk were treating the march of the skinheads as a spring festival, a regular Easter parade.

The rabble was now proceeding at a less resolute pace, many of them falling out of step with the beating of the drums. Even some of the banners were now looking decidedly bedraggled. At the end of the street the procession arrived at the central square surrounding All Saints' Church, and there they were met by a welcoming party that blocked their way on all sides. The skinheads came to a halt, the banners were lowered and the drumming fell silent. Strangely, sweet music floated faintly and surreally on the air, emanating from inside the church. Mothers and children, some of them no bigger than toddlers, crowded round and applauded. One little girl, the epitome of Browning's child of Hamelin with 'flaxen curls', ran forward unprompted and offered the thuggiest of the far-right thugs a single yellow daffodil. For want of a better idea, he stooped down bemused and took it from her hand.

'Aw, bless …' The sound came unbidden from a gaggle of scary New Force girlfriends.

Some members of the mob looked back in the direction from which they had come and saw that the street was deserted. Those who had cheered them on were now no longer in place.

With one final cheer and burst of applause, the spectators quickly dispersed, leaving the crowd from New Force standing alone and unheeded in the middle of the road.

****

'I think everything's in place, Marnie.' It was the leader of the Stowe Hill marina contingent who had joined up with Anne and Magda to organise the hiding of the Easter eggs.

Marnie said, 'Now all we need is some children to come and find them.'

'Didn't I see them all going off with that young chap, your Anne's boyfriend? Was that all part of the plan?'

'Your guess is as good –'

'Oh look, here they are now.' He pointed up the slope to where a multitude of mums and kids could be seen swarming across the grass, with Donovan in the vanguard.

'So not all drowned in the river Weser,' Marnie muttered. She pronounced it like *Vayser*.

'Drowned?' said Stowe Hill man. 'Is that what you feared?'

'Of course not. They'd never reach the Weser from here.'

'Er … I suppose not.' Bewilderment was etched into his features. 'Where is the Weser exactly?'

'Never mind.' Marnie cheered up. 'Come on, let's get started. I bet those kids are ravenous.'

Typically it fell to Anne to gather the children around her and set them off with whoops and squeals of delight on their egg hunt. While Anne was explaining the ground rules to an attentive throng, Marnie and Magda sidled up to Donovan.

'What was that all about?' Marnie asked. 'Where did you whisk them off to?'

He kept a straight face. 'I just thought it would be nice for them to see the Easter parade.'

Magda looked scandalised.

Marnie was incredulous. 'You what? You mean the skinheads … New Force … the neo-Nazis?'

Donovan turned to face her, his expression deadpan. 'No one organises a procession better than the National Socialists, Marnie. Surely you knew that. Haven't you seen the Nuremburg torchlight –' He could remain serious no longer, and his face cracked into a grin.

Marnie thumped him in the ribs. 'Idiot! Seriously, where did you take them?'

'Actually, Marnie, I was being serious. As we went up to the road I passed Sergeant Thingy from your committee.'

'Pamela Groves, the police officer?'

'That's the one. Well, I said we were getting out of the way while the eggs were hidden and asked her about traffic control. She said the streets in the centre were all cordoned off. That gave me an idea. It was quite safe for the children, so I split the group into batches and told the mums where to go and to get their children to wave and cheer the Easter parade. I said the people parading were in fancy dress to look like goblins.'

'You didn't think that was a bit risky?'

'Not really. The skinheads weren't going to attack little kids. Anyway, it worked like a charm. I said as soon as the parade was over, they'd get their eggs.'

'Did you hear the drums beating?'

'Yeah. I kept well out of sight, but I gather the kids loved it, thought the goblins were hilarious. There's no greater weapon than being laughed at, especially by people who can't be touched. When Anne arrived, I got her moving the groups of mums and kids into place. Worked like a charm.'

Marnie embraced him warmly and whispered in his ear, 'Donovan, there's something of the night about you. The word *ruthless* springs to mind.'

As they separated, he said, 'As far as I'm concerned, Marnie, the words *Easter eggs* come to mind. I hope those greedy little monsters don't scoff the lot.'

As they were grinning at each other, Marnie noticed that Magda was frowning.

'Hey, what's the matter?' Marnie said. 'That's the best outcome we could ever have hoped for.'

'I know, Marnie. It's just ... I can't help thinking ...'

'What is it?'

Magda shook her head. 'That load of skinheads. It's great that Donovan outwitted them ... brilliant. But I can't help thinking

250

that there in that mob is probably someone who murdered Katya and all but murdered Stan. It's just so horrible.'

Marnie put an arm round Magda's shoulders and said quietly, 'We have to take one step at a time. It's all we can do.'

'They almost did the same to Dom,' Donovan said bitterly. 'I don't forget that, either.'

Nearby the radio crew was interviewing an old lady. Evidently they had reached the end of their piece, as the journalist shook hands with her, and the rest of the crew began moving away in search of fresh targets. Seeing Marnie, the old lady walked over.

'Hello. I believe you're the person who's organised all this.' she said.

Marnie made a self-deprecating gesture. 'Well, it's not only me, but I'm involved, yes.'

'It's wonderful. I'm having a *lovely* time. That's my picnic rug over there.'

'Looks like you've brought enough to feed an army,' Marnie said.

'That's the idea. I live by myself now, so I brought plenty of homemade food to share. I've already met lots of really nice people, and they've promised to come and help eat my picnic at lunchtime. Thank you so much for what you've done.'

'You're very welcome.'

The old lady glanced over Marnie's shoulder. 'I think the wireless people are coming this way. I'd better go so they can talk to you as well.'

'Oh, I shan't be –'

At that moment Donovan took Marnie's arm. 'I think you should,' he murmured.

With a friendly wave, the old lady went on her way. Marnie turned to Donovan.

'Why? I don't want to push myself forward. I'd prefer to stay in the background.'

'I can understand that, but this is only radio. You won't be visible.'

'So why is it a good idea?' Marnie asked.

Donovan reflected for a moment, then suggested a form of words to Marnie. By then the young woman in the black trouser-suit was upon them with her crew following on behind.

'Can I really not persuade you to say a few words, Marnie?' she wheedled.

Marnie glanced at Donovan, who gave an imperceptible nod.

'Well, perhaps really just a few words.'

'Great!'

Marnie answered a few brief questions about the day's events and how they brought the community together. With another glance at Donovan, she ended her interview with a simple statement.

'I think it's fair to say that the main Easter event in town this year is definitely on the waterways.'

And that was it, all perfectly painless. As Marnie was shaking hands and thanking the BBC people for coming, Angela Hemingway joined them. At the sight of this new arrival, the radio journalist's face lit up.

'Could I ask you to –'

Angela held up both hands. 'Oh, no. I'm just a hanger-on.'

'But didn't I see you doing something down there? You were surrounded by boat people.'

'We were performing a small ceremony we sometimes do at boating events.'

'Ceremony?' the journalist repeated.

'It's called the blessing of the boats. It's sort of traditional before a float past and, as it's Easter ...'

'I'm sure our listeners would like to hear about it.'

Angela perked up. 'I'm sure they would. In fact, you ought to talk to that man down there, the one with grey hair and steel-rimmed glasses.'

'He's a vicar, isn't he?'

'No,' Angela said portentously. 'He is no less than the Venerable the Archdeacon of Northampton.'

The journalist looked impressed. 'And you think he'd be happy to –'

'Absolutely. He's the senior churchman here today.'

The radio crew bustled off in pursuit of their eminent quarry. Marnie turned to Angela.

'Do you think the archdeacon will agree?' she asked.

Angela nodded. 'Loves the sound of his own voice. I just want him to say something positive about what's happening here today.'

'You think he'll do that, Angela?'

Angela shrugged. 'There's gotta be a first time for everything.'

****

The Easter egg hunt was a great success. But of course it would be. And every parent was relieved that not a single child threw up, even after multiple goes on the bouncy castle. The brass band performed suitably nautical music with brio as the float past of boats took place. There were cheers for the colourful spectacle from the picnickers on the bank, and they in turn were admired by the parading boaters. The scene provoked a comment from Ralph who was at the tiller on *Sally Ann* as they took their place in the pageant. He pointed to the groupings with tables, chairs and in some cases even tablecloths.

'It looks just like Glyndebourne!'

The crew of the good ship *Sally Ann*, supplemented by Magda, were at that moment enjoying their own food, and they raised their glasses as they cruised by in a toast to the bankside diners. The response was instant. A hundred or more glasses were raised in reply. The other boaters followed suit, and soon a ragged series of blasts on boat-horns rang out across the park. It was a festival atmosphere, and even the Venerable the Archdeacon of Northampton looked cheerful. Moderately.

With a smile on her face, Marnie extended her wine glass for a top-up from Anne. As she did so, she caught sight of Donovan who was perched on the wooden lid of the gas bottle container. Like her, he was sipping chilled rosé wine, but there the similarity ended. He was lost in his thoughts. Seeing her looking at him, he stepped across to her.

'Can we have a word?' he said.

'Sure, in fact I've been meaning to ask you something.'

'Go on.'

'Those words you asked me to say on the radio, about the main Easter event this year being definitely on the waterways ... were they supposed to convey some special message?'

'What did you think that might be, Marnie?'

'Not sure.'

'Did it give an impression, d'you think?'

Marnie shrugged. 'Only an idea of what we were doing.'

'When?' Donovan asked.

Magda was overhearing this exchange and chipped in. 'Over the Easter weekend, no?'

253

'Yes,' said Donovan.

'That was it?' Marnie looked puzzled. 'But that's what we are doing ... aren't we?'

****

When the afternoon came to an end everyone agreed the day had been a success. As the shadows lengthened, the sky began clouding over, creating ideal conditions for fireworks. It was a relatively modest display but it nicely rounded off the day's events. The spectacle attracted appreciative 'oohs' and 'aahs' from the audience, who were happy with their day out in gentle spring warmth in the open air.

As soon as the display ended, the children were taken home. They were satisfyingly stuffed with Easter eggs, and generally worn out by over-excitement and over-indulgence. Their parents were less overwhelmed but pleasantly weary as they fastened their offspring into car-seats or installed them in buggies. The members of the brass band retired to a local hostelry to wet their whistles, while the bouncy castle provider sought out Marnie for instructions about the next day's activities. Stowe Hill man organised an excellent round of litter-picking with a small army of fellow-boaters armed with black plastic rubbish bags.

Marnie invited Magda to join the crew of *Sally Ann* for an early supper, but she had to decline the offer. She had arranged to visit Dom in hospital. Visiting hours in the ward were stricter than in the ITU. With hugs for all her friends, she left with the promise to Donovan that she would give Dom his best regards.

While Marnie and Ralph prepared the evening meal of pasta with ratatouille, Donovan and Anne made their way along the line of moored craft to speak to all the crews. By the time they returned, Ralph was opening a bottle of Valpolicella, and the table was laid.

Donovan accepted a glass from Ralph, took a sip and said, 'Anne, do you think you can manage *Exodos* by yourself?'

'Aren't we getting a bit ahead of ourselves?' Marnie said.

'Always wise to plan ahead.' Donovan turned to Anne. 'Well? What d'you think?'

'I'll do my best, but if she runs into an iceberg, explodes or hits a mine, don't blame me.'

Ralph said, 'Or I can run *Exodos*, and Anne can go with Marnie on *Sally Ann*.'

254

'Sounds good,' said Donovan. 'Okay with you, Anne?'

'I knew I'd got you worried,' she said, raising her glass in Donovan's direction.

Chapter 23

I t was inevitable that word would get back to the skinheads that an alternative Easter event was being held by the waterside. One of them had heard some woman on the radio talking about it. She had stupidly blown any chance of keeping things secret. New Force were not going to make the same mistake a second time. One of the ringleaders said that if the opposition wanted to hide behind little kids and women's skirts, it was their funeral. They all had a good laugh about that.

As before, the mob assembled on the 'racecourse', but this time there were no drums and no noise to give them away. It was just after ten-thirty on Easter Monday, a bright spring morning, that a motley rabble of well over two hundred set off towards the green banks of the river Nene. They were looking forward to terrorising the burghers of Northampton and leaving their mark on an Easter that no one would ever forget. An atmosphere of tension and menace hung over them as they hustled down quiet residential streets where not a soul witnessed their passing.

Reaching the Bedford Road, the leaders were surprised that no police cars or officers were visible. They stopped to confer, gesturing to their followers to spread out. Surely, they reasoned, their prey would not be daft enough to attempt the same tactics that they had used on Sunday. They would have to be mad as well as stupid. Or perhaps, one of them surmised, that day's activities were starting later. Whatever. New Force were in place; there was no turning back. The signal went out to advance. The first unhurried steps soon turned into a loping run. The skinheads burst through the trees with a roar designed to put the fear of god into anyone who heard it.

But no one heard it. The onward rush reduced to a stagger and diminished to a halt. Before them lay only the empty banks of the river with not so much as an ice cream wrapper to reveal that anyone had celebrated anything in that place. There was not a boat to be seen, nor a jogger or even a casual stroller taking the air that morning. The massed ranks of New Force stood and gaped.

****

Marnie was still tired when she woke up. Daylight was showing round the edges of the curtains in the sleeping cabin on *Sally*

Ann. Beside her, typically, Ralph was out for the count, the top of his head protruding from the duvet, his breathing slow and rhythmic. How did he do it? To be fair, he had managed Donovan's boat single-handed all the way up the Rothersthorpe flight of locks during the first part of the night. They had only crawled into bed in the early hours after finding a mooring place among all the other boats somewhere near Gayton Marina.

Marnie padded out of the boat's rudimentary bathroom and made her way past the still somnolent Ralph to the galley. She recalled that it had been Donovan's idea. It had been his outrageous plan to quit the venue in town after only one day and make a getaway at dead of night. The initial reaction of some of the other boaters had been dismay. After all, the trek down the long flight of seventeen locks – eighteen for those who had to look further for a mooring beyond Town Lock – was not undertaken lightly. To make the journey again so soon afterwards was daunting.

Donovan had insisted it was the wisest stratagem but could only work if everyone took part. He clinched the argument by reminding the others that anyone who remained behind might find themselves confronting New Force who would be out for revenge. Watching the faces of their fellow-boaters, Marnie understood the wording that Donovan had asked her to use in her radio interview. Did it give the impression that the boat gathering was taking place all weekend? On balance she thought it did, and that was exactly the impression Donovan wanted her to give.

Marnie was brought back to the present by a soft tap on the window and looked up to see Anne passing. She had retired to sleep on *Exodos* after partnering Marnie up from town. Ralph had found a slot for Donovan's boat about fifty yards from *Sally Ann*. They had agreed to meet for breakfast once they were all more or less conscious. Marnie went to unbolt the door to the stern deck to let Anne enter. The door led down into the sleeping cabin, and the sound of the hatch sliding back caused Ralph to stir. Under tousled hair two bleary eyes appeared over the top of the duvet.

A muffled voice was heard. 'It can't be that time already.'

'Rise and shine, my darling,' Anne piped up chirpily. 'Time from brekkie!'

257

Marnie grinned and led the way to the galley / saloon. With a coordination born of long practice, they set about preparing breakfast together. In the background they heard Ralph stumble into the bathroom.

'You're horribly cheerful this morning, Anne,' Marnie said. 'And he's my darling. I saw him first.'

'Fair enough.' Anne desisted from pointing out that Ralph, in his forties, was old enough to be her father. Instead she made reference to the real man in her life. 'There's something strange about Donovan, Marnie.'

'And you've only just noticed? I'm agog.'

'No, seriously. When we tied up last night I gave the boat a check-over as usual and noticed something. D'you remember that big box he was carrying on Friday?'

'Vaguely. What was in it?'

'No idea. He put it in the study area with his mountain bike.'

'I don't recall seeing the bike.'

'He stores it in the study when he's on the move. It's been there all along.'

'Okay,' said Marnie. 'So?'

'They're not there now, box or bike.'

Marnie slid some bread under the grill. Anne poured orange juice into three glasses. She left the fourth glass empty.

'I take it Donovan didn't join you in the night.'

'No. I haven't seen him since we left Northampton. I was helping you get *Sally* prepared, and Donovan went off to check the other boats were all okay. It was already getting dark when Ralph went aboard *Exodos*, and in all the general activity I didn't see Donovan after that.'

'We all knew he wasn't coming with us,' Marnie said. 'That much was clear. But what his plans were … who knows?'

Anne sighed. 'Our resident man of mystery.'

'He didn't tell you what he had in mind, Anne?'

'Nope. There was just so much going on to get all the boats turned round and heading off in the right direction, I didn't have time to give it much thought. I half expected he'd join us somewhere on the flight.'

'That would explain the bike,' Marnie observed, 'but it doesn't explain the box.'

At that moment Ralph made his appearance. He had washed and dressed and generally looked moderately presentable, if not totally awake.

'You didn't see what became of Donovan, did you, Ralph?' Marnie asked.

'I didn't. I expected to at some point, but he never showed up.'

Marnie stared at Anne. 'I hope he's all right.'

'Oh, he will be,' Anne said confidently. 'You know him.'

Marnie nodded. They all knew Donovan. But this time there was New Force to contend with. They had probably murdered Katie Koslowski and severely injured her husband and Dom Gorski. Now if felt as if Donovan had been dropped behind enemy lines with no back-up and – not daring to try to contact him by mobile in case that put him in danger – no means of communication. Marnie thought it wise to keep those thoughts to herself.

****

There was no doubt about it: the whole riverside area was deserted. The skinheads went out in search parties in all directions but found nobody. The banks of the river were vacant, with not a single boat anywhere to be seen. A decision was needed. Lie in wait? Come back later? The whole pack huddled together in one solid group, arguing and shouting. The consensus, if you could call it that, favoured a tactical withdrawal, leaving a few scouts in position to report back to the others if and when people appeared. What bothered most of them was why there were no boats around. They had expected a boating event to have … well, boats. It didn't add up.

And then it happened.

One minute they were yelling at each other, their voices growing louder and louder as the protagonists tried to out-shout each other, the next minute they were engulfed in a wave of fiery explosions. Blast after blast hit them. Starbursts flared in their midst. Thunderflashes crashed in on them. It was chaotic and terrifying, confusing and alarming. The assault lasted only a minute or two, but to those caught up in the turmoil it seemed to be never-ending.

In the rush to get away, several of the skinheads were trampled under the heavy boots of their mates. It was a miracle that no one was seriously burnt or injured. The horde took flight in panic like survivors in retreat from a battlefield, dazed by the cacophony of detonations, shrouded in swirling smoke, their nostrils tingling with the acrid stench of gunpowder.

Worst of all, they had no idea where the onslaught was coming from or who was attacking them. Staggering up to the main road, some looked back to see if they could identify their assailants and judge if they were being pursued, but over the field hung a pall of fog that only added to their confusion. Later, some would recall an impression. It was no more than that, but in the distance they fancied that they had seen someone on a bike pedalling away at speed along the towpath.

****

Donovan was well beyond the first lock and even past the perimeter of the Carlsberg Brewery site before he eased off. He skidded the mountain bike to a halt and looked back, panting. There was no one in pursuit. He pressed on at a pace that was less frenetic, confident that he could ride steadily at that rate all the way up to the top of the Rothersthorpe flight.

He was almost in sight of the bottom lock when he passed the first boat he had seen that day, coming towards him. He subconsciously registered it as a fifty-seven foot semi-trad, obviously well maintained, with gleaming dark blue paintwork and a middle-aged couple in the stern. Seeing Donovan, they raised their coffee mugs in salute. He acknowledged with a wave and slowed to a stop when the boat veered over in his direction. The man on the boat cupped his hands and shouted over the sound of the engine.

'Careful at lock fifteen! Branch down right across the towpath.'

Donovan waved in thanks. As he was flicking the pedal up to move off, he spotted movement in the distance back down the path. Skinheads! Surprised, he tensed and raised himself from the saddle, scarcely able to believe his eyes. They were some way away, but he saw three of them clearly. Two were running at a strong pace, one straggled along behind. They reminded him of Orks from Tolkien's *Lord of the Rings*. He set off at once, the bike swaying from side to side as he pressed down hard on the pedals and gave it everything he had.

Barely two minutes later he saw the lock ahead. Drawing nearer, he saw the branch that had fallen across the towpath.

Branch? It was a whole bough, and it was blocking his way. Donovan dismounted and laid the bike on the ground. He ran up to the bough and began dragging it aside, not without difficulty. It was a fair weight but springy and still partially attached to the main trunk of a tree. He tugged hard to tear it free, but it resisted all his efforts. Again and again he struggled with it, first pulling it one way, then in the opposite direction. All the while his thoughts were focused on his pursuers. Were they still pressing on? Could they have so much stamina?

The answers to these questions soon became clear. Gasping for breath, Donovan stared back down the towpath. The skinheads were alarmingly close; they must have been tremendously fit. His only consolation was that now there seemed to be only two of them. At their present rate they would be on him in a matter of minutes.

He knew the simplest strategy would be to race on, confident that he could outrun them. But he knew nothing of their abilities. Perhaps they were dedicated marathon runners, regular joggers or fitness addicts who spent hours working out in the gym. And what if his gears slipped or the bicycle chain came loose? At least there at the lockside he was not being caught in the open. At least there he had some possibility of concealment. But was that enough?

Donovan's head was spinning, sluggish with fatigue and uncertainty. The bough was still obstinately joined to the main body of the tree. He knew the skinheads would soon have him in sight. Perhaps they might not even know for sure that he was ahead of them. Perhaps they would give themselves as far as the first lock of the flight before turning back. Then he remembered the couple on the boat. The skinheads would surely ask if they had seen their 'friend' on his bike.

Donovan forced himself to put his brain in gear and formulate a plan. It was desperate and uncertain, but the best he could devise in the circumstances. Beside the lock the ground fell away sharply into a ditch filled with undergrowth covered in fresh spring foliage. He quickly seized the bike and set it down by the lock. Dragging back the fallen bough, he pulled off one of his trainers and laid it on its side on the ground next to the bike. Then he took one last look down the canal and squeezed himself behind the bough, squatting out of sight, or so he hoped.

He waited, hearing only the beating of his heart and the rumble of traffic on the nearby ring road. His breathing had returned almost to normal when he heard them coming. They really were amazingly fit, he thought; definitely Orks!

'Hey!' one shouted. 'What the hell's this?'

'Beats me,' said the other.

Donovan risked a glance from his hiding place. The two men were gasping, staring down at the bike. Neither spotted him behind them. The discarded trainer clearly intrigued them. They moved closer to the lock and peered over the edge. The water in the chamber was at its lowest level, left that way by the passage of the boat.

Donovan knew it was now or never. He eased himself up, took firm hold of the bough and rushed forward, thrusting it out in front of him. The skinheads heard a rustling sound and turned. They hesitated in their surprise for little more than a second, but that delay was their undoing. They collided with each other in their haste to avoid the charging bough. It caught them both in the chest and, despite their efforts to fend it away, it knocked them off balance. They toppled backwards and plunged, arms and legs flailing, down into the lock chamber with a satisfying double splash. Donovan was already grabbing his trainer and slipping it on when he looked down and saw them floundering in the murky water. The lock must have had a drop of around six feet from its highest level. Sadly, Donovan thought, the rungs set into the side walls extended far enough down for the reluctant bathers to reach and haul themselves out. But then what?

Donovan left the bough on the pathway and ran back to his bike. Mounting it, he wondered if the drenched skinheads would have the heart to continue their pursuit or would turn back, tails between their legs. The thought did not trouble him for a second as he pedalled firmly on his way without a backward glance.

****

The third skinhead was bent double half a mile down the towpath, wheezing and suffering from a sudden onset of cramp in the left leg. The other two had ignored him and pressed on. There seemed to be no way to alleviate the excruciating pain. He tried grasping the muscle firmly in his hand and kneading it. It felt like a ball of iron. Eventually, he crashed down onto his side, stretching the leg and groaning in agony.

Minutes passed and still there was no relief. He elbowed his way upright and struggled to his feet, letting out a cry of pain. He was hobbling along the towpath when he heard the sound of an engine nearby. Glancing up, he saw a dark blue boat approaching with a woman at the tiller. She eased the boat closer to the bank and called across.

'All right, love?'

He pointed to his leg. 'Cramp. I'll be okay in a minute.'

'Your friends are a long way in front of you,' the woman said.

'Friends?'

'Aren't you with the other two?'

The skinhead realised that in black T-shirts and jeans, they must have looked like a team of some sort.

'Oh, yes.' His voice was contorted into a croak.

'You'll have to hurry if you want to catch them up,' she said cheerfully.

'Bugger that!' he muttered.

The boat was by now leaving him behind, so the woman did not hear his reply. With a jolly wave, she steered back into mid-channel. It was just then that the cramp began to ease off, and the skinhead took a firm decision to turn round and hobble back.

****

Exceptionally, it was after breakfast that morning that Ralph decided to set off on his usual walk. It was a custom he had acquired as early as his student days when he relished the near-deserted streets of Oxford with only the occasional milkman or postman on their rounds for company. In all seasons and in all weathers he strode out, pounding the pavements and byways of the city, returning in time for a shower and a college breakfast and the start of the academic day. The practice had stayed with him all his life. He had always valued it as the stimulus that woke him up and helped him to hit the ground running, or at least walking.

On that Easter Monday, hours later than usual, he opted to walk back down the towpath in the direction from which the boats had travelled, largely in the hope that he might run into Donovan. He was descending the steps beside one of the middle locks when he caught sight of a figure approaching at some speed on a bicycle. In black clothes and moving quickly, it was unmistakeably Donovan. Momentarily Ralph lost him when the

263

cyclist approached a lock and was unsighted, only to pop up at the next level and leap onto the saddle. He exuded a sense of urgency as if being pursued, but Ralph could see no one following him, though his range of vision was restricted by the lie of the land.

Ralph stopped and waited. Almost immediately Donovan saw him and waved, still pedalling hard. He reached Ralph moments later and braked to a halt.

'You look well and truly puffed,' Ralph said. 'Everything okay?'

'Fine.' Donovan was wheezing from his exertions. Briefly, he looked back over his shoulder. 'It went fine, Ralph. Couldn't have gone better. I'll tell you all about it later. For now, I'm keen to get on.'

'You think you're being followed?'

'Don't think so, not now, but you can't take chances with that lot.'

'Shall we walk back together? The boats are moored up near the marina.'

Donovan nodded and began pushing the bike as they fell into step with one another.

****

After the hectic activity of the past two days, the rest of the journey back to Knightly St John felt like a holiday, a leisurely springtime cruise, with mild weather and splashes of sunshine between high thin puffs of cloud. Marnie took the helm on *Sally Ann* as they cast off, pulled out onto the mainline at Gayton Turn and headed south in company with other boats in line astern. Anne and Donovan followed behind on *Exodos*, with Donovan taking it easy while Anne steered. Donovan rang Marnie and suggested that she should hold back and let *Exodos* overtake. Marnie agreed, but only understood his suggestion when they entered the Blisworth Tunnel.

Making the passage, Marnie was amazed at the illumination provided by Donovan's powerful lights. They were so bright she scarcely needed to use her own on *Sally Ann*. Once through the tunnel, a few of their fellow-travellers tied up in Stoke Bruerne for lunch at the hostelries in the village, but Marnie and Ralph pressed on. They pulled over after making the descent of the

Stoke Bruerne flight just long enough to prepare sandwiches and spritzers.

Donovan was now feeling refreshed and took over the tiller on *Exodos* for the final run in tandem with *Sally Ann* back to base. As they were casting off, a line of boats cruised past. Seeing Marnie and the others, the crews waved and cheered. The two Glebe Farm boats swung into line behind them. A sense of great camaraderie was in the air, like a victorious fleet returning to its home port after battle.

On the stern deck of *Sally Ann* Ralph put an arm round Marnie's waist while she steered.

'I must say I'm glad that's over,' he said. 'Quite a relief.'

Marnie nodded. 'I'm curious to find out what Donovan was up to this morning. Though with him, sometimes it's best not to ask.'

'Me too. I'm sure he'll tell all this evening. Whatever it was, I hope the New Force lot have gone and that they don't come back.'

Initially Marnie did not reply. She was concentrating on taking a long right-hand bend in the canal. Eventually she glanced round at Ralph.

'There is just one thing that bothers me,' she said.

'Only one?'

'One main thing.'

'I think I can guess,' Ralph said.

Marnie slowed as they approached a narrow bridge.

'If they really have left town, which I certainly hope, it probably means we'll never find out who murdered Katie Koslowski.'

****

It was late in the afternoon before they reached Glebe Farm. They decommissioned *Sally Ann* and *Exodos*, trekked through the spinney and dumped their weekend bags in the hall of the farm house. As usual they congregated in the kitchen, and Anne on auto-pilot put the kettle on. Marnie announced that she had no idea what they might eat that evening and welcomed any suggestions. Donovan at once said he had brought some wine and beer back from Germany. That was a start. Ralph offered 'peasant food', and everyone accepted his proposal of *revuelto de gambas* – a flavoursome blend of eggs, prawns and garlic, which was almost his signature dish. When Donovan went out to fetch his box of provisions from the Beetle he discovered a cake that his aunt Gabriele had made. The meal would be complete.

But first, Donovan declared, he needed a break. He took himself off to Anne's attic room where he dozed for a few hours, leaving the others impatient to hear his account of the events that had taken place that morning

****

When they were eventually seated at the refectory table for dinner, Marnie proposed a toast. She began promisingly enough. 'To …' But then she hesitated. 'What should we be drinking to, if in fact anything?'

Ralph said, 'A successful mission?' Surviving the Easter weekend? Or perhaps we'd better hear what Donovan has to say about this morning before we decide.'

'Come on, Donovan,' Anne chivvied him. 'We're all bursting to know. Spill the beans.'

'Okay.' Donovan said. 'That box I took along, it was full of fireworks.'

'Fireworks?' Marnie looked surprised. 'But you didn't add them to the display on Sunday.'

'That was never the plan. I originally bought them as a collection last November. A shop in Uxbridge was selling them off as a special offer post-Bonfire Night. I was going to bring them up here to let them off at midnight on New Year's eve. It's an old German custom. But then you and Ralph went to stay with your sister straight after Christmas, and you, Anne, went to spend Christmas and New Year with your family.'

'I owed them a visit,' Anne said quietly.

'Sure. So that's why I flew to Germany to spend that time with my family. I couldn't take the fireworks with me obviously, so I left them in London.'

'This is all very interesting,' Marnie said, 'but what about this morning?'

'I'm coming to that. So, on the drive up from Dover I remembered the fireworks and decided to fetch them from my place. That's why I changed cars and came in the VW – more space for everything.'

'You mean you planned to use them against New Force right back then?' Marnie said.

'Not at all. I just thought we could have them for Easter. I never imagined deploying them as 'artillery' at that point.'

'Is that what you did?' Anne said.

'After the boats had all gone, I set out the fireworks in bushes scattered around one side of the park. Nothing was certain, but I hoped New Force would react to the bait in Marnie's interview and come down to the riverside, thinking they could disrupt the rest of the festivities.'

'And that's what they did?' Marnie asked.

Donovan nodded. 'Your interview did the trick.'

'So where did you spend the night?' Ralph asked.

'Under a bush. It was cold and *very* uncomfortable. I'd wedged a load of Roman candles in the soil and set out rockets at a low angle between them. Also, I filled my pockets with 'Thunderflash' super-bangers. When the skinheads turned up, I lit a taper and rushed between the fireworks, hiding behind bushes. Then I lobbed the bangers as hard as I could in their direction.'

'Did it work?' Ralph said.

'Some of the rockets just hit the ground halfway, but some went the distance. Others flew off over the trees. The Roman candles, though, were very effective, and the bangers ... you should've seen them ... and *heard* them.'

'Didn't the skinheads see you?' Marnie asked.

Donovan shook his head. 'The smoke from the fireworks was like a thick fog in seconds, and I don't think they even realised at first where the attack was coming from. As soon as I'd thrown the last Thunderflash I ran for the bike and took off.'

'They didn't chase you?' Anne said.

'I thought they hadn't seen me and I made the mistake of easing off after a while. That's when I spotted them. I'm not kidding, they were running like the clappers.'

'So you had to speed up,' Anne said. 'No wonder you were worn out.'

'That's not how it happened. At one of the locks the towpath was blocked by a bough that had come down. I tried to break it off from its tree, but it wouldn't come. By then the runners were getting close, so I pulled it to one side and hid. When they saw the bike by the lock, they looked into the chamber, and I rushed them, bough and all. It swung like a spring and crashed into them ... knocked them over the edge.'

'Were they injured?' said Marnie.

'They could've drowned,' said Anne. 'Or got Weil's disease.'

Donovan said, 'Funnily enough, I didn't stop to enquire after their health.'

'Then what?' said Ralph.

'I was in no doubt about what they'd do to me if they caught me. We all know what they did to Dom. With the fireworks and then the ambush at the lock, I hoped I might've done serious injury to whichever of them had killed Katie Koslowski and left Stan fighting for his life. It was a matter of indifference to me if I'd inflicted pain and suffering on the people who'd injured my friend. It's what they deserved.'

****

That night Donovan lay beside Anne in her big comfortable bed with one arm round her thin body. He found it hard to fall asleep. Listening to Anne's slow rhythmic breathing, he felt himself trembling inside, no doubt the aftershock of the violent events of the day. At any time things could have gone hideously wrong and, for all his bravado and daring, he recognised that he had known real fear. He knew that like Dom Gorski, his luck could easily have run out. His stomach churned as he thought of Dom lying in his bed of pain, bandaged and in traction.

Slowly, gradually Donovan's own breathing began to settle down, and sleep started to overcome him. As he drifted off, the last images that came into his mind were the explosions that had laid flat the ugly rabble of New Force. He wondered if that was how the German army had felt when attacked relentlessly and without warning by the Night Witches.

Chapter 24

A n unmarked police car drew up beside the house at Glebe Farm shortly after nine o'clock on Tuesday morning. It was a plain grey Vauxhall Cavalier, a bread-and-butter sort of vehicle, but Marnie recognised it straight away and guessed it could spell trouble. Swivelling in the chair at her desk, she looked across the yard to see who might be emerging. Anne and Donovan, on the other side of the office, heard the car arrive and noticed Marnie's reaction.

'It's Cathy Lamb by herself,' Marnie said. 'Donovan, I think it would be a good idea if you scooted up to Anne's room. Probably best if she didn't find you here.'

Donovan was halfway up the wall-ladder before Marnie had finished the sentence. His feet were disappearing from view as DC Cathy Lamb knocked and entered. Marnie stood up to meet her, and they shook hands.

'Can we offer you coffee?' Marnie said.

'It's a bit early for me, thanks, Marnie.'

'Then at least have a seat.'

Lamb took the chair opposite Marnie's desk and gave a friendly wave to Anne across the room; both good signs in Marnie's view.

'So, if you've not come to take advantage of our coffee, what can I do for you?' Marnie tried to sound light-hearted.

'You organised an event in Northampton at the weekend.'

'Yes, on Saturday and Sunday. I was part of the team that organised it. I can't claim all the credit. It was a community event run by the inter-faith committee, which included your colleague Sergeant Groves.'

'You said you were there on Saturday and Sunday?'

'That's right. We left after the festivities on Sunday night.'

'You weren't there on Monday?'

'No. We had to travel back. We have work to do.' Marnie indicated the papers on her desk. 'We told the police we were leaving.'

Cathy looked thoughtful. 'It takes so long to get here from Northampton?'

'It does on a narrowboat. Apart from the mileage there are more than twenty locks to get through, not to mention the Blisworth tunnel.'

Cathy nodded slowly. 'Did everyone leave at that time?'

Marnie shrugged. 'As far as I know.'

'You haven't asked why I'm interested in Monday, Marnie.'

'Why are you interested in Monday, Cathy?'

'There was an incident … a number of people were taken to A and E.'

'What happened?'

'They seem to have been injured by fireworks.'

'You mean they found some that hadn't gone off and picked them up?' Marnie said. 'Never a good idea.'

'Several people suffered minor burns, others had impact injuries. There were twenty-seven people treated in hospital. I take it your event included fireworks?'

'Not as such, though some of the boaters had brought a few. That was actually after the event, as you call it … late on Sunday afternoon as dusk was falling.'

'Nothing later? You're certain of that?'

'As certain as I can be. Cathy, can I ask you a question?'

'Go on.'

'Why are you involved and why are you here?'

'That's two questions.'

Marnie said nothing. Lamb paused and continued.

'I know you were one of the key organisers and I wondered if you could shed any light on what happened, that's all.'

'I can assure you, Cathy, we were long gone by Monday. And you might like to know that I'll not be involved with any further activities of the inter-faith committee. That was strictly a temporary arrangement to please Angela Hemingway in the run-up to Easter.'

Lamb looked from Marnie to Anne and back again. 'No Donovan? I expected to find him here.'

Marnie shrugged. 'Really?'

Lamb sighed. 'Do you know where he is?'

Marnie smiled. 'He's probably upstairs in the attic, hiding.'

Across the office, Anne grinned.

'Marnie, I'm serious. I take it, he was at your Easter boating event?'

'On Saturday and Sunday, yes.'

'Not on Monday?'

'I told you, we all travelled back together on *Sally Ann* and *Exodos*.'

270

Lamb looked thoughtful. 'When you see Donovan, will you give him a message from me? Tell him we'd like to talk to him about the Easter event. Get him to call in at the station, would you?'

'I'm sure he'll be delighted to see you, Cathy.'

'I'm sure he will. Don't forget.' Lamb stood up and turned towards the door. 'Okay. I'd better be on my way. Marnie, if you do hear anything about it, I want you to let me know.' She raised a hand to her brow and peered up at the sky through the window. 'Oh, was that a pig flying over Glebe Farm?' She waved to Anne and opened the door. 'Bye!'

'I'll come out with you,' Marnie said.

Standing in the doorway, Lamb said, 'You know, the archdeacon will be *so* disappointed that you've left that committee.'

'Really? Why?'

'Sergeant Groves says she's convinced he's got the hots for you, Marnie.'

Marnie laughed, and in the background Anne joined in. Marnie closed the door behind her and crossed the courtyard to Lamb's car.

'Any sign of the skinheads, Cathy? Are they still around?'

Lamb gave Marnie a pointed look. 'You mean the ones that are still capable of walking?'

'I'm serious.'

'Why are you so interested in them? Something on your mind?'

Marnie leaned up against the police car. 'There is something that bothers me. If they disappear, we may never find out who killed Mrs Koslowski. Can you tell me if you're following up any leads?'

Lamb looked pained. 'You know I can't ...' Seeing Marnie's expression, she relented. 'Look, we've got no evidence and no witnesses, but -'

'So it's hopeless,' Marnie said dejectedly.

Lamb touched her arm. 'I was going to say, when it comes to murder we never give up. The case is never completely closed. Who knows what evidence might turn up in the future?' .

****

271

At coffee time Ralph walked through the spinney from his study on *Thyrsis* and found a discussion in full swing when he entered the office barn. Anne was in the kitchen area pouring hot water into the coffee filter, while Marnie and Donovan were standing by the photocopier. Marnie looked round as Ralph came through the door.

'Perfect timing, Ralph,' she said. 'We're just making plans for the week.'

'That's good.'

'Not quite,' said Marnie. 'The good bit is that Donovan will be staying till the weekend.'

'Great. And the not-so-good?'

'He's talking about going off to Northampton to finish cleaning up the New Force graffiti.'

Ralph looked baffled. 'What's wrong with that?'

Donovan said, 'Marnie thinks there might still be some gangs of skinheads lurking around and they could be out for revenge after what happened to them over the weekend.'

'She may have a point,' Ralph said.

'I think they've gone. That's why I've agreed to meet Magda and some of the others this afternoon. We're aiming to get all the graffiti removed as quickly as possible. We want to expunge every trace of them.'

'Expunge,' Anne said, carrying a tray of steaming mugs. 'That's a good word.'

'Isn't it?' Donovan agreed, taking his mug from the tray. 'I regard it as unfinished business. I also want to look in on Dom. Haven't seen him for days. He'll think I've forgotten about him.'

Anne said, 'Don't forget you have to go to the police station in Towcester to see Cathy Lamb.'

'What's that about?' said Ralph.

'Cathy was here this morning,' Marnie said. 'She was asking about what happened to the skinheads on Monday ... wants to ask Donovan if he knows anything about it.'

'Marnie skilfully avoided telling her any direct lies,' said Anne.

'I'd have no compunction about telling direct lies,' said Donovan. 'Not in this case, at any rate. The only thing is, she might've spotted my car.'

'No, she didn't,' Marnie said. 'I went out with her to make sure she didn't snoop around.'

Donovan laughed. 'You sneaky thing! You're getting as bad as I am.'

'Impossible.'

'Could you spare me for the afternoon, Marnie?' Anne asked. 'I'm well up to date with my work.'

'Only if you promise to keep an eye on Donovan ... make sure he doesn't get into trouble.' .

****

After a snack lunch Donovan and Anne walked round to the garage barns. Marnie and Ralph tagged along for a breath of fresh air before settling down to an afternoon at their desks. When Donovan carried his cleaning-up box out from the barn he remarked that he would soon be out of materials. Marnie remarked on the similar box she had removed from Dom's car, and Anne offered to retrieve it.

'I'm sure Dom wouldn't mind you using some of his stuff,' Marnie said. 'It's all in a good cause.'

'You bet,' said Donovan.

Anne helped him load both boxes onto the back seat of the Beetle and they set off for town in relatively good spirits. .

****

Anne looked anxiously about her as they drove through Northampton, but there were no gangs of skinheads to be seen on the streets. The town seemed to be returning to normal. The only group of people they saw were the young Poles outside the Polish shop in Little Warsaw. Its end wall was still pleasingly free of paint. They climbed out of the VW to be met with the usual round of hand-shakes plus a hug each from Magda.

'So where do we start?' Donovan said.

Magda pointed down the street. 'There are some graffiti along there and a few more round by Katie and Stan's house.'

'Okay, we'll deal with those.'

Anne said, 'You're not going to do cleaning dressed like that, are you Magda? That's a really nice jacket you're wearing.'

'No. I'm not stopping, just came to say hello. Then I'm off to see Dom in hospital.'

'We were hoping to visit him, too.'

'Ah ...' Magda looked embarrassed.

'Not a good idea?' said Anne.

'It's just … well, he's got aunts and uncles coming up from London today. It could get crowded.'

'Too many visitors,' Donovan said.

Anne added, 'So we'd probably not get to see him.'

'I'm really sorry. I'm only popping in myself for a -' Magda checked herself in mid-sentence. 'Oh, there was something I meant to tell you. Dom was asking about his car. He was quite concerned about it.'

'It's fine,' Anne assured her. 'We've got it at Glebe Farm.'

'He knows that,' Magda said. 'I already told him. I think he's worried it's in the way. He was pretty agitated, in fact.'

'No need. Tell him it's safe with us.'

'He'll be relieved to hear it.' Magda stepped forward and kissed Anne on the cheek. 'I'd better be going. Good luck with the clean-up.'

'Give Dom a hug from us,' Donovan said.

'But not too hard,' Anne added. .

****

That evening Anne and Donovan took turns in the shower. They had worked solidly in the afternoon for more than two hours scrubbing off graffiti and now they scrubbed their bodies to get rid of the smell of paint stripper. Pink and sparkling, they arrived in the farmhouse kitchen to find asparagus ready and waiting, with baked salmon in the Aga. Ralph was opening a bottle of white Orvieto as they came through the door.

'We're not smelly now, I hope,' Anne said. 'Are we?'

'Positively fragrant,' said Ralph. 'How did it go?'

'My arms are dropping off with all that rubbing. I don't know where Donovan found the energy to keep going, the way he did.'

Donovan shrugged. 'Sheer bloody-mindedness. I'm determined to get rid of every trace of New Force before the week is out.'

Marnie began serving the asparagus. 'There can't be much more to do, surely.'

'Maybe a few bits and pieces. We'll check the whole town tomorrow. With any luck I might not need to get any more of that heavy duty paint stripper. I've used up all mine, and there's just a drop more of Dom's left in his box.'

'Well planned,' said Marnie. 'Let's eat.'

Donovan lit a chunky white candle and placed it in the middle of the refectory table while Ralph was pouring the wine.

'You haven't told us about how you got on with the Porsche,' Ralph said.

Donovan grinned. 'I recommend German car thieves. They did a great job restoring it … better than I could do.'

'No problems with the police?' Marnie asked.

'Not really. They have more important things to do. I was quite relieved.'

'So all in all a successful visit,' said Marnie.

'Yes …' Donovan looked wistful. 'And I made a new friend.'

'Oh? Who was that?'

'A guy called Ekkehart von Karlsdorff.'

'Quite a handle,' said Ralph. 'What does he do?'

'He's retired now, quite elderly, but he used to be …' A pause for effect. '… one of Hitler's generals.'

Marnie and Ralph stared at him. Donovan grinned, pleased with the result of his delivery.

'You're not serious?' Marnie said.

'Uh-huh.'

Marnie turned to Anne. 'Did you know about this?'

Anne nodded. 'I must've put it out of my mind. It's just too weird.'

'How did you meet him?' Ralph asked.

'I watered his plants, invited him for *Kaffee und Kuchen* - or rather my aunt did - and afterwards we had a nice little chat.'

'Blimey!' said Marnie. 'You don't do things by halves, do you?'

'Nice little chat?' said Ralph. 'I can't imagine you had much in common.'

'Absolutely not, though … in fact there was something. Have any of you ever heard of the Night Witches?'

Marnie and Anne shook their heads. Their expressions suggested they were not sure if they wanted to know about them.

Marnie said, 'Something tells me they probably aren't warm and cuddly.'

'Not like Moya Goodchild,' Anne added. 'She was a nice witch.'

'Not a bit,' said Donovan. He noticed that Ralph was sitting with his fingers steepled and a faraway look in his eyes. 'Does the term mean something to you, Ralph?'

'Rings a faint bell … not sure why …'

'You did say *Night Witches*, not white witches?' said Marnie.

275

Ralph said, 'I know. We had a colleague in the Russian department who had an aged aunt who had a connection with something like that.'

'Okay,' said Donovan. 'Let me explain. The general told me about them.'

'Why?' said Marnie.

'It just cropped up in conversation when he told me about his time on the Eastern Front.'

'So why Night Witches?' said Marnie.

'Well, first of all, they only attacked at night … obviously. Their old biplanes were so slow they couldn't use them in daylight. Machine gunners would pick them off like wild geese. The lead plane of the formation would drop flares to light up the target area. Then the following pilots would switch their engines to idling speed, so they'd just glide in, virtually silent. The soldiers on the ground would only hear the wind swishing through the struts of their wings ·'

'Witches' broomsticks,' said Anne.

'Exactly. And then bombs would start falling out of the darkness. They attacked again and again all night long, attack after attack.'

'Terrifying,' said Marnie.

'For aircrew and soldiers in equal measure,' Ralph said.

It was time to move on to baked salmon with noodles, and after their plates were filled Marnie changed the subject.

'While you two were out, I had a chat on the phone with Kazimir Gorski. A few of his friends are going to make a start on renovating the Koslowskis' house, so I said I'd join in. We're going to have a chat about the budget and begin stripping the walls in the living room.'

'Is that okay?' Ralph asked. 'The police are in agreement?'

'Yes. Kazimir had discussed everything with the Northampton authorities, and they gave the go-ahead.'

'Are we up to date with everything in the office?' Anne asked.

'Sure. And most of our clients are away this week, in any case; Easter hols. We're fine.'

Ralph said, 'How will you know what Mr Koslowski wants by way of design, colour scheme, all that kind of thing?'

'Initially, we'll just be doing preparatory work. I'm hoping we'll be able to talk to him some time soon.'

276

Anne and Donovan shared the same image in their heads: an old, gaunt man, ashen pale, lying in a hospital bed, hooked up to an array of machines that were keeping him alive. They both hoped Marnie wasn't being over-optimistic.

For Donovan, another image persisted, this one from Germany: an old, gaunt man, walking steadily with a firm stride, his back ramrod-straight, at ease with his lot in life, a survivor.

Chapter 25

Wednesday morning, and they were back in Northampton. Marnie climbed out of the Freelander and stood on the pavement outside the Koslowskis' house, staring up at the sky. Ominous clouds were gathering to the west. Beside her, Anne and Donovan followed her gaze upwards.

'It's looking very black over Bill's mother's,' Donovan said in a strange quasi-northern accent.

'That's a rather gnomic utterance,' said Marnie.

'Where did you get that from?' Anne asked.

'A bloke in my year at uni. He's from Nottingham. I think it must be a local saying.'

'And it means?'

'Looks like rain.'

Marnie said, 'I think he has a point. You'd better get started before you're rained off. Where are you meeting the others?'

'Usual place: Polish shop in Little Warsaw. We'll sort out what we're doing and spread out from there.'

'Will you be seeing Magda?' Marnie asked.

Anne said, 'We might. It depends what else she's got on.'

'Well, if you do, invite her to come for supper.'

'Okay. When?'

'Any time from tonight onwards, or whenever.'

****

They spotted Magda as soon as they turned the corner and approached the Polish shop. This time, she was dressed for action in an old jacket and jeans and was in a huddle with a group of four or five young men, the usual crowd. When they got out of the car they were swamped in the now customary round of hugs and handshakes.

Everyone was running low on materials, but one of the Polish boys announced that he'd already been round the town on his motorcycle and there were only a few traces of graffiti remaining. He gave directions to the group, and they split into pairs before heading off.

Before leaving, Anne took Magda by the arm. 'Are you free to come to supper at our place some time?'

'That would be lovely. When d'you have in mind?'

'Marnie said any time that suits you from tonight onwards.'

278

'I visit Dom most evenings, but as it happens he's got another truckload of relatives coming tonight.'

'So you're free?'

'If it's convenient for you. What time?'

'Seven?'

'Fine.'

'Do you have transport?' Donovan asked.

Magda nodded. 'I can borrow my mother's car.'

Anne pulled a notebook from her bag and wrote down directions to Glebe Farm, then rang Marnie and gave her the news.

****

The boy with the motorcycle was right, which was just as well. There were only a few walls decorated with graffiti left in town, and by the time Anne and Donovan had eradicated their share, they were down to the last dregs of paint-stripper.

'I think that's about it,' Donovan said, pressing the lid back on the empty can.

'So what now?' Anne peeled off her rubber gloves.

'I fancy a bit more stripping.'

Anne flashed him the heavy eyelids, coaxed her thin body into her most vampish shimmy and, with her huskiest Marlene Dietrich voice, murmured, 'Vot you have in mind, big boy?'

Suppressing a grin, Donovan said, 'I was thinking of the wallpaper in the Koslowskis' living room.'

Anne maintained the same accent and pose and the same husky tone. 'I lurve it ven you talk dirty.'

Donovan guffawed, causing passers-by to turn and look.

****

Marnie had acquired a small team since setting to work in the Koslowskis' house. Two of the young Poles had finished their graffiti-cleaning nearby and come to help. She had given them the task of removing wallpaper in the rooms on the ground floor. While Marnie was scraping the paper in the living room, she was asked to move her car so that a skip could take its place. It had been provided by a local Polish builder who knew Stan Koslowski and was keen to help with the renovation project. The Polish boys immediately began lugging armfuls of stripped wallpaper out to dump in the skip, keeping the floors clear.

Anne and Donovan arrived just as rain started falling. They jogged along the pavement from where Donovan had parked and ducked into the hallway moments before the first tentative drops became a downpour.

'You were right about Bill's mother,' Anne observed. 'Eventually.'

Marnie stepped out into the hall. 'So, three new volunteers.'

Anne and Donovan looked momentarily bewildered. Marnie pointed to the floor behind them. The Koslowski's cat scuttled in and shook his fur, spraying water in all directions. Anne squatted to stroke his head, and he pushed firmly against her palm.

'Just like Dolly,' Anne said. 'She always does that.'

'Come to help?' said Marnie.

Donovan nodded. 'That's the end of the graffiti. And we've run out of fluid, so that's us done for the day.'

'What about Dom's cleaning materials?'

'All gone. So what can we do here?'

Marnie surveyed the scene. 'When it stops raining, you could dump all that stripped paper in the skip outside.'

'I'll get on with that,' Donovan offered.

'Good. And when you've done that, perhaps you could get the Polish boys to help you pull up the carpet. It can go in the skip as well. We can't keep it, not looking like that.'

Donovan stared down at the floor. The ominous dark brown stains in blotches across the carpet in the centre of the room made him shudder.

Marnie pointed to a bucket of sudsy water and asked Anne if she would dampen the end wall to prepare it for stripping. Donovan gathered an armful of paper from the floor and carried it out to the skip. He returned, slightly damp, and bent down to scrape together another bundle. As he did so, he picked up one small piece and studied it.

'Everything all right?' Marnie asked.

'Mm ...'

'What is it?'

Donovan turned the paper over so that she could see. The scrap was about the size of a paperback book. It had a broad stripe of red paint splashed across it. It was part of the word *HEXE*, smeared on the wall by Katie's killers. Anne wandered across to look over Donovan's shoulder.

'How horrible,' she muttered. 'I suppose it was meant to look like blood.'

Donovan made no reply. He stooped to pick up the next pile of paper for disposal. Neither Marnie nor Anne noticed him slipping the scrap with the red paint into his back pocket. Donovan was walking through the door when a rustling sound captured their attention. Marnie had just scraped strips of paper from the wall, and the cat was frolicking among them, flicking pieces up in the air, then pouncing on them as they fell to the ground. It was a cheering sight at a sombre moment, and it brought smiles to their faces.

****

Marnie felt as if she had already had a long day by the time she drove home. She was pleased with the progress they had made and was looking forward to seeing Magda that evening. Back at Glebe Farm, she flopped into an armchair with a mug of coffee and regaled Ralph with everything they had done in Northampton. Most of his day had been spent working on his new book while guarding the phone in the office barn. He had just two messages for Marnie from clients. Equally pleased with the completion of editing a substantial chunk of his writing, he had rounded off the day by putting two bottles of Prosecco in the fridge. Marnie gave that decision her approval before she set off for a soak in the bath.

Magda arrived a few minutes after seven, and they took their places at the refectory table for a simple supper. For such occasions Marnie kept in the freezer a stock of meals that she had pre-prepared. That evening they had a broccoli quiche with minted peas and new Jersey Royal potatoes. They began with fresh avocado topped with tomato water ice.

During the meal they reviewed progress and learned that everyone's cleaning materials had been used up. Best of all, Magda was certain there were now no traces of New Force to be found anywhere in the town. While they were working they received a visit from the police. Sergeant Pamela Groves had reported that the skinheads had left the area. At that point Ralph raised his glass of sparkling wine and proposed an ironic toast to absent friends.

'You were working in Katie's house, Marnie,' Magda said. 'How did that go?'

'Most of the ground floor rooms have been stripped. We'll start on lining them tomorrow. Kazimir's confirmed the budget. We're ready to press on.'

'What about the design?' Magda asked. 'How can you choose the colours?'

Marnie nodded. 'Good question. Do you think Stan will be able to guide us on what he'd like?'

Magda frowned. 'I really don't know. I looked in on him yesterday. He's … it's not looking good.'

'Did you see Dom?' Donovan asked.

Magda perked up. 'I did. He's on the mend, though he feels very frustrated.'

Donovan said, 'It looked like a bad fracture. Is he in a lot of pain?'

'I think they're controlling it pretty well now.'

'That's something at least. When d'you think we'll be able to visit him again?'

'Soon, I hope. I gave him your good wishes. He was pleased to hear from you.'

'They really hit it off, those two,' Anne said. 'They have a lot in common.'

Marnie said, 'We seem to be taken over entirely by Poles these days. We even got a helping hand from Katie's cat today.'

'Helping paw,' Anne corrected.

Magda said, 'How d'you mean?'

'Puss decided to join in the fun,' said Marnie. 'He was jumping about on the strips of paper as they fell from the wall … very playful.'

'Puss?' said Magda.

Donovan said, 'Anne calls him Butch on account of his size.'

'But you know that's not his real name.'

'Oh, I know that,' Anne said. 'It's just I'm not sure how to pronounce it. On his collar it's spelt B-o-r-o-d-i-n, but I'm not sure if the stress is on the first 'o' or on the second.'

Ralph said, 'In England, I think most people would probably stress the first 'o' just lightly, but that's not how it's really pronounced, of course.'

'So how should it be pronounced?'

The reply came in a three-part chorus from Ralph, Donovan and Magda. They all pronounced it like Barradean.

Anne laughed. 'Blimey! I was well off target. I think my Polish is a tad rusty.'

'Actually, Anne –' Magda began.

'Aberdeen!'

All eyes turned towards Marnie.

'Sorry, Magda,' she said. 'Didn't mean to cut across you, but that's what Mr Koslowski must have been saying.'

'When?' Magda asked.

'It was when he was first taken to hospital. Angela – you know, the local vicar – said he tried to speak. She thought he'd said 'Aberdeen'. I think he was pronouncing the cat's name like *Barradeen*. He wanted to make sure he was properly looked after.'

'That could explain it,' said Donovan.

'Odd choice of name, though,' Ralph said. 'The composer had no links with Poland as far as I'm aware.'

'Perhaps they just liked his music,' Marnie suggested.

Anne said, 'Mrs Betts, their next door neighbour – in fact the person who first told me about you, Magda – said he was Katie's cat. It's rather touching that Stan should think of that when he was so badly injured.'

Marnie agreed. 'And that name quite suits the cat. It's rather charming.'

'Charming, certainly,' said Ralph. 'But it's still strange. Borodin was a devoted Russian patriot, a member of a group of composers, all dedicated to patriotic music that reflected Russian themes.'

'It's obvious, isn't it?' Donovan said. 'She wasn't Polish at all.'

There was a moment of silence while that thought sank in.

'Katie was Russian?' said Marnie.

Magda replied. 'Yes, she was.'

'You were translating her *memories*, as she called them,' Anne said. 'You told me that in the hospital. I thought you were translating them from Polish, but you also speak Russian, don't you?'

'That's right. Katie told me the war had had a traumatic effect on her and on Stan, too. I saw this clearly in her diary, her *memories*. It's one of the reasons she didn't want to mix with the other Poles. She wanted to draw a line and put the past behind her.'

'She served in the war,' Marnie said. 'I saw a photo in the bedroom of her in uniform.'

'Yes, in the 588th regiment.'

'Night bombers,' said Donovan. 'They later became the 46th Guards regiment.'

Magda was astonished. 'How do you know this? No one I know has ever heard of them.'

'Someone I met in Germany told me about them.'

'That's extraordinary. So you know how brave they were.'

'I do – phenomenal.'

'Can you tell us about these *memories*?' Marnie said to Magda.

'Katie – you know we call her Katya – wanted to write about her life so that people would one day understand what she and the others went through in the war and at the end. She hoped that some day her story might be published if possible, though not in her lifetime. She didn't want any personal publicity.'

'The story of the Night Witches,' Donovan said, 'told by one of their number.'

'Yes,' said Magda. 'And what incredible people they were. Katya flew *hundreds* of missions, and that wasn't unusual. Can you imagine how awful it must have been? The stress must have been tremendous.'

'But Stan was in the RAF,' Marnie said. 'So how did they meet?'

'Katya crash-landed in Poland near the end of the war with engine failure. She thought it was probably hit by a bullet. The Germans were retreating, so they weren't bothered about finding the plane. Katya's pilot was killed, and she herself was injured. She dragged herself into a barn for shelter and found it was already occupied. Stan had taken refuge in there. He was a fighter pilot, you know.'

'Hurricanes,' said Ralph. 'Polish squadron in the RAF.'

'That's right. He was on a reconnaissance mission when he was shot down. He spoke some Russian, and they teamed up to try to reach the allies. The Red Army was advancing, and Katya would have been safe, but she feared for Stan. In his strange uniform they might suspect him of spying on their formations and shoot him out of hand. Those were dangerous times, and the Red Army could be trigger-happy.'

'How did they travel?' Marnie asked.

'They walked.'

'*Walked?* How far?'

'From central Poland all the way to the middle of Germany. They were picked up by the British army. By then, Stan weighed around forty kilos, six stone or so, and Katie even less.'

'It was a miracle they weren't killed or captured,' Marnie said.

'It was chaos everywhere. They mainly moved by night and slept by day. Luckily it was early summer and they were able to find things to eat, though only just enough for survival.'

'I can understand why they chose to come to Britain,' Ralph said.

'Katya told me she couldn't face going back to Russia without Stan. Everything over there was in turmoil, so here was the obvious choice. Stan already had connections in England from his war service.'

Ralph said, 'Yet they never fully integrated into the Polish community.'

Magda shook her head. 'No. They were neither religious – in fact Katya had been brought up as an atheist and a communist – and she was a patriotic Russian.'

'Like Borodin,' said Ralph.

'I suppose so. Katya thought it best to keep that aspect of her life private.'

'Though she was happy to share it with you, Magda,' said Marnie.

'Yes.'

'She knew she could count on your discretion.'

'Absolutely.'

Chapter 26

I t was still looking very black over Bill's mother's when Marnie set off for Northampton after the rush hour on Thursday morning. Anne was riding shotgun while Donovan occupied the rear seat together with a box containing rolls of lining paper, packs of paste powder and colour charts for emulsion and gloss paint. Once again Ralph and Dolly were in charge of the office.

They travelled the now familiar route to the Koslowskis' house and found something new on their arrival. Two red and white bollards marked out a space beside the skip that adorned the front of the house. As Marnie's Freelander approached, one of the Polish boys stepped out from the front door, picked up the nearest bollard and signalled to Marnie to pull in. As she parked, he greeted her with a smile and a bow.

'These Polish guys have a lot of charm,' Marnie murmured.

'Haven't they just?' said Anne, turning to wink at Donovan. 'I think the English could learn a lot from them.'

'What about the half German, quarter English, quarter Irish?' Donovan said.

He did not wait for an answer but hopped out and lugged the box of decorating materials into the house. He was passed by another of the Polish boys carrying a huge armful of stripped wallpaper to dump in the skip. Seeing Marnie, he called out.

'That's the last of it now, Marnie. What next?'

'Lining the walls next. Donovan's got all the stuff.'

The team assembled in the living room, and Marnie was organising the programme for the morning when Magda came in. She stared about her in wonder.

'Wow! You've made *fantastic* progress here.'

The walls were down to bare plaster, the carpet was gone and the furniture was stacked out of the way, leaving the walls free for action.

'This is one of my favourite times,' Marnie said. 'It's a blank canvas. This is where the scheme begins to take shape.'

'You've got a whole army,' said Magda.

Marnie smiled. 'Our own Polish squadron, certainly. Anne and Donovan are in the kitchen mixing paste in a bucket, then it's go-go-go.' Marnie looked Magda up and down. 'Do I infer from your smart clothes that you won't be joining us today?'

Magda looked embarrassed. 'Really sorry, Marnie. I've got to work. In fact I've just popped out to see how it was going and let you know you can visit Dom this evening. I promised to tell you when you could.'

Marnie's heart sank, though she tried not to show it. The thought of driving back into town that evening after a day of physical toil was unappealing, but she could feel the call of duty, and she had not been to visit Dom for some days.

'It'll be good to see him again. Will you be there?'

'Sure. And I have a special request from Dom.'

'Don't tell me ... he has a yearning for seedless grapes.'

Magda grinned. 'Not quite. He's still fretting about his car. Could you possibly bring it back?'

'His car? What, now? He won't be driving for ages yet.'

'No, but he hates imposing on you.'

'Tell him not to worry. It's under cover and we're happy to look after it.'

That embarrassed look again. 'Marnie, he really is bothered about it. I don't know why ... or perhaps, I do. I think he just lies in bed all day fretting about things. They go round and round in his mind, you know?'

Marnie nodded. 'I can understand that. It happened to me when I was nearly ...' Marnie could not bring herself to say *murdered*. '... when I had a stay in hospital myself. Okay. When shall we deliver it and where?'

'If you can drive it to the hospital this evening, I'll take it from there.'

'Will do.'

'By the way, he's in Grafton Ward. It's well signposted. Oh, and don't be late. The nurse in charge is very strict about visiting hours and numbers. She's quite a dragon!' .

****

Marnie was impressed. The little band of volunteers - her 'Polish squadron' - buckled down to their tasks like a production line. She herself had taken on the work in the living room - the murder room - with Anne and Donovan. The atmosphere in the house was light-hearted, but as the morning wore on Marnie became aware of a strange phenomenon. Whenever any of the Poles came into the living room, they lowered their voices. Their whole demeanour changed on entering a place of tragedy and mourning.

Towards lunchtime Marnie noticed that Donovan was missing. She turned to Anne. 'What's become of Donovan?'

Anne shrugged. 'I thought he'd popped to the loo, but he's been gone a while.'

'Not like him to disappear,' said Marnie. 'D'you think he's all right?'

'He's been very quiet all day. But then, he's never much of a chatterbox, is he?'

Marnie put down her pasting brush. 'I'll just go and check. Won't be long.'

She went along the hall and looked in on the young men in the dining room. 'You're doing great work in here. Have you got all you need?'

'We're fine,' one of them said.

'Have you seen Donovan lately?'

Another said, 'I thought I heard someone go upstairs a few minutes ago.'

They all cocked their heads on one side. Overhead there came the faintest sound of footsteps. Marnie went out and climbed the stairs. She found Donovan in the main bedroom, studying the photographs, holding one of them and staring at it, his concentration intense. Marnie tapped lightly on the door. Donovan spoke without turning round.

'I'll be down directly.'

Marnie crossed the room to stand by his side. In the photograph the young Katie faced the camera proudly in her uniform with medals prominently displayed.

'She deserved better than she got,' Donovan murmured.

'She did,' Marnie agreed.

Donovan sighed. 'To think she survived the years of war and danger only to end up slaughtered in her own home by some mindless thugs.' He turned to look at Marnie. 'We'll probably never know who they were.'

Marnie put a hand on his shoulder and said softly, 'I'll see you downstairs.'

'I'll be right there.' .

****

Ralph was impressed. Marnie's account of all they had accomplished on the renovation astonished him. Added to that, he was more than pleased with the progress he had made with his own work. With scarcely an interruption all day, he had completed editing the final draft of the new book and caught up with his correspondence. The only false note on an otherwise perfect day came when he pointed out that it was almost the weekend and suggested they open a bottle of best Bordeaux to go with their evening meal. Marnie grimaced and raised a hand.

'Not for me, I'm afraid. I forgot to say I'm on hospital visiting duty this evening, plus moonlighting as a car delivery driver.'

'You're going to see Dominik?' Ralph said.

'You guessed. So it's mineral water for me tonight.' She noticed Ralph's expression. 'But I think you should have the Bordeaux. Give it a trial run, but save some for later. I'll probably be in need of it when I get home.'

'Presumably we can't all go?' Ralph asked.

They were in the kitchen with mugs of coffee, seated at the refectory table. The gentle warmth of the Aga was comforting in the cool spring evening.

Anne said, 'I'd like to go with you. Good to see Dom again.'

'What about Donovan?' Ralph said. 'Where is he, by the way?'

Marnie glanced round towards the door. 'I think he said he'd be stowing the cleaning materials away.'

'It's a wonder you've got any left,' said Ralph. 'With all the scrubbing they've been doing this week –'

At that moment Ralph broke off as they heard the front door open and close. The kitchen door swung in, and Donovan's head peeped round it.

'Where d'you want me to put Dom's stuff, Marnie?'

'Where is it now?' she asked.

'Out here. I've brought it in.'

'Oh, leave it in the hall, would you? It's very smelly.'

'Not as smelly as it was,' Donovan said. 'I've dumped the cleaning fluid tins and some of the rags and brushes in the bin.'

'So what's left?' Marnie asked. 'Can't be much.'

'There are a few things he'll want to keep for the car ... tools, chamois leathers, paint, polish ...'

'Okay. Leave it there for the time being. Are you coming in to see Dom tonight?'

'Absolutely.'

'Then perhaps you'd put the box back in the garage on our way out.'

Donovan shook his head. 'No. On second thoughts I'll take it back now and put it with my things.'

'Supper's nearly ready,' said Anne.

'I'll be quick.'

Donovan was back in the house before Ralph could open the bottle of sparkling mineral water. Marnie was cutting a large pizza into slices - another treasure from the freezer - as Donovan took his place at the table.

'What colour is Dom's car?' he asked.

Marnie slid a generous slice of Pizza Marguerita onto his plate. 'Dark blue, quite an attractive shade, almost like teal or petrel. Haven't you seen it?'

'No, it's all covered up.'

'You'll be glad to get your Beetle back into its slot,' said Ralph.

'I don't begrudge Dom my place in the garage. He's certainly earned it, poor devil.' He looked across at Marnie on the other side of the table. 'Is it all blue or is there some red on it?'

Marnie reflected. 'Yes. There is some red. It's got those lines round the waist ... what d'you call them?'

'Coachlines?' said Ralph.

Marnie nodded. 'That's the stuff.' She looked at Donovan. 'Why d'you ask?'

'Just curious.'

'He loves that car,' Anne said. 'He's like you with your old Beetle and your old Porsche. His Peugeot's absolutely immaculate. He keeps it like new.'

'Does he work on it himself?' Donovan asked.

'Certainly does.'

Ralph added, 'Did you know he studies mechanical engineering?'

'I didn't know that. For all Dom's become a good friend, there's still a lot I don't know about him.'

Anne looked down, concentrating on cutting a piece of pizza. She had her own memory of Dom's earlier conversation on the phone ...

I'll remember what you told me, but it doesn't mean I won't keep trying. I'll leave you in peace for now, though

... and she wouldn't be sharing that with Donovan. .

****

290

Donovan had his first sight of the Peugeot when he helped Marnie remove the cover in the garage barn. Marnie reversed it out, and Donovan walked round inspecting the car on all sides. He agreed with Anne's verdict: it looked as good as new, in fact better. It had non-standard chrome alloy wheels and impressive chrome tailpipes on the exhaust system. The suspension looked as if it had been lowered slightly to improve the roadholding. If Dom had done the work himself, Donovan had to admire his skill.

Marnie climbed out of the car with a troubled expression. 'I forgot it was low on fuel. We'll have to stop for petrol on the way into town.' She looked at her watch. 'Better get a move on. Don't want to be late.'

'The nearside front tyre looks as if it could use some air,' Donovan remarked. 'We'd better check everything over when we get to the filling station. You get going. I'll follow in the Beetle.'

It took only a few minutes before they reached the Shell station. There was still enough daylight to see to check the tyre pressures; Donovan removed the valve caps while Marnie dealt with fuelling. By the time she had squirted twenty litres of Super Unleaded into the tank, Donovan had removed all the caps and was checking the water in the radiator and the windscreen washer bottle. In the latter he added some fluid from his own supply which reminded him that in their haste to get away, he had left behind Dom's box of materials. There was no time to worry about that; it could wait for another day. He was quick and efficient bringing the tyres up to the correct pressures, but he knew Marnie was champing at the bit to be on the road again

****

Marnie enjoyed driving Dom's little road rocket. It took her back to the days of her Rover 220 GTI. She made good speed on the way to the hospital, but knew they would have limited time to see Dom. With luck she found a single space in the car park and hurried towards the entrance, following signs to Grafton Ward. Magda was standing inside the door, trying not to show impatience at Marnie's late arrival.

'Really sorry, Magda. We had to stop for fuel, tyres and -'

'No need to apologise, Marnie. You're here safely. That's the main thing.'

Marnie held up the car keys. 'Before I forget.'

Magda kissed her on the cheek and hugged her lightly. 'Thank you for all you're doing. It's wonderful. And Dom will be so grateful, though he seems rather tired this evening. But now you'd better get going. Have you come alone?'

Marnie glanced around. 'No. Donovan and Anne are here somewhere. They sent me on ahead from the garage. They're probably still searching for a parking –'

'No. Here they come.'

With the briefest of hugs, Magda shooed them on their way. 'First floor, second ward on the left. Hurry!'

As they rushed up the stairs they found that some people were already leaving. Visiting hours were almost finished. On entering the ward they were confronted by a stern-looking nurse. Pointedly, she looked at her watch.

'Five minutes,' Marnie gasped. 'We've had a difficult journey.'

The nurse relented and stood aside. 'I'll be counting.'

Marnie had no doubt about that. They found Dom at the end of a row of four beds, still in traction and looking glum. His face lit up when he saw his visitors and he eagerly embraced Marnie and Anne, followed by a warm handshake from Donovan.

'I'm sorry we're so late,' Marnie said.

'We had to do things to the car,' Donovan explained.

'Oh?'

'It was low on fuel, the tyres needed pumping, the washer bottle needed topping up.'

'Of course. I'd forgotten. Who got the fuel?'

'Twenty litres,' Marnie said. 'I put in Super Unleaded. Was that right?'

'Perfect. My wallet's in the cupboard there. Please –'

Marnie shook her head. 'Forget it. Glad to help.'

'No, really. I can't let you do that.'

'It was worth it for the fun of driving it.' Marnie frowned. 'One problem was, I took it up to a hundred and then found ... I couldn't get it into fourth gear.'

Dom's jaw dropped. As he stared at Marnie, she broke into a grin.

'Kidding!'

Dom laughed. 'I suppose this is as good a place as any to have heart failure.'

'Sorry. But it really was fun to drive.'

'Did you get the news about New Force?' Donovan said.

'Is this another wind-up?'

'No, I'm serious. We've been told by the police they've left Northampton.'

Anne said, 'Donovan blew them up.' Her expression was serious.

Dom laughed again, then stopped abruptly. 'You're serious, aren't you?'

'Yep,' she said.

'Nothing to do with me,' said Donovan. 'At least, that's the official line. The trouble is, now they've gone we'll probably never find the bastards who did this to you.'

'Never mind,' said Dom with some bitterness. 'I couldn't identify them, anyway. Let's face it, it could've been much worse.'

They all knew what he meant. They were turning that thought over in their minds when the nurse appeared at the end of the row.

'*Hier kommt die Hexe*,' Donovan muttered under his breath.

Dom laughed gently, 'Yes, a good name. She looks just like a witch.'

He looked sharply up at Donovan who smiled and said quietly, 'We'd better go before she turns us all into frogs.'

Marnie and Anne embraced Dom and apologised for coming empty-handed. Dom shook his head slightly, unable to speak. He offered a hand to Donovan, and they both gripped firmly. Donovan touched Dom's shoulder as they left the ward.

Chapter 27

Friday began badly. Marnie and Anne were working in the office while Donovan was sorting out the boxes of cleaning materials in the garage barn. Ralph was ensconced in his study writing the preface to the new book. It was a normal day until the phone rang. Anne lifted the receiver, sounding businesslike as ever. She called across to Marnie.

'It's for you ... Mr Gorski. He's sounding rather downbeat.'

Anne pressed the button and transferred the call.

'Good morning, Kazimir. How are you today?'

'Marnie, I have bad news.' His tone was flat.

Marnie guessed immediately. 'Mr Koslowski?'

'I'm afraid so. Stan passed away in the night. They've just phoned to tell me. It seems he had a massive heart attack. There was nothing anyone could do.'

'I'm really sorry. It's so sad. And they phoned you. You're the hospital's sole point of contact?'

'We know of no family. They've notified the police, of course.'

'Oh yes. So now it's a case of murder ... a double murder.'

'Frankly, Marnie, I have no idea right now what ought to be done. The hospital staff have asked for instructions. I'm at a loss.'

'I suppose an undertaker should be contacted, rather than going ahead with the renovation project,' Marnie said.

'No.'

'But how do we know what will happen to the house?'

'We don't know, Marnie. All we do know is they had no relations, at least none that we've ever heard of.'

Marnie had a brainwave. 'Perhaps Magda will know. She spent a lot of time with Katie.'

'I just phoned her. She knows of no living relatives.'

'You really think we should go ahead with the house, Kazimir?'

'It's all we can do. Look, Marnie, there's no problem with finance.'

'Oh, I wasn't thinking about my –'

'I know you weren't, but we have a budget and a plan. At some point the house will no doubt have to be sold. Best if it's in good order. Let's get the work done. The Polish community will pay for everything including your fees and expenses. Nothing has changed in that regard.'

'I must say I do feel rather awkward about this.'

'Please, Marnie ...'

Marnie thought for a few moments. 'Very well. I was going to order carpet today and buy more decorating materials.'

'Just go ahead as before, if you would. We leave the design to you. You'll know what's best.'

'I suppose it can't do any harm.'

'Good. That's settled, then. Meanwhile, I'm going to ring round the solicitors in town to see if anyone has been instructed about their estate. Ah ...'

'What is it?'

'I'm just thinking, Marnie. Perhaps one of them has left a will. D'you think you could have a look when you're there?'

'For a will?'

'Yes. Perhaps you could check in cupboards and things. Did they have a desk?'

'Not that I recall. There's a dressing table upstairs, and I'll check the drawers in the kitchen.'

'Will you be going there today?'

'This morning.'

'If I hear anything I'll ring you on your mobile. You have my number?'

'I do.'

After ending the conversation Marnie spent a few seconds collecting her thoughts. When she looked across the office at Anne, she saw her looking desolate with tears running down her cheeks.

****

Marnie broke the news to Ralph on the phone and went out with Anne to tell Donovan. They found him searching through his and Dom's boxes of cleaning materials and putting further items in a rubbish bag. Although Stan's death came as no great surprise, Donovan's reaction was more emotional than Marnie had expected. Without a word, he picked up one of the boxes and carried it with head bowed into the garage barn. When he returned for the second box he made no eye contact.

Standing between the rows of barns, Marnie spoke to Anne in a half-whisper. 'He's taken it really badly.'

'I'm not surprised,' said Anne in a hushed voice. 'He'll be thinking that Mr Koslowski is another victim of the Nazis. You know how he hates them.'

At that moment Ralph came round the corner of the nearest barn.

'Dreadful news, Marnie,' he said. 'You're going into town, is that still the plan?'

'Kazimir thinks we should finish what we started.'

'I wish we could.'

It was Donovan who had spoken. They turned to find him standing behind them.

'I'm talking about the renovation of their house,' Marnie said.

'I know, but I'm not.'

'Are you leaving straight away?' Ralph asked.

Marnie turned back. 'That's the idea. I don't like imposing on you all the time, Ralph, but –'

'No, it's fine. I can get on with my work just as easily in your office. There are hardly any calls. People are still away for Easter. You get off. It's important.'

While Marnie was climbing into the Freelander, Anne said to Donovan, 'You won't forget you're supposed to go to the police station?'

'Yeah.'

'It's no big deal, Donovan. They just want a brief statement.'

'Sure. I'll call in on my way to town.' He looked Anne in the eye. 'I promise.'

The Freelander eased out of the garage. Anne kissed Donovan on the cheek and climbed aboard. Marnie turned the car and headed for the field track leading up to the village. There was something about Donovan's demeanour that bothered Anne. She could feel his anguish, aware of her own sorrow. From her seat beside Marnie, she twisted round and looked back. Donovan had not moved from where she had left him. She began raising a hand to wave, but lowered it when she realised he was not looking in her direction. Instead, he seemed lost in thought, his gaze drawn to one side as if staring vacantly with eyes unseeing into the garage barn.

****

The atmosphere in the Koslowskis' house that morning was sombre. The usual group of young Poles had turned up for duty, but there was none of the cheerful banter of previous days. In every part of the house voices were hushed, behaviour restrained. The team were already waiting when Marnie and Anne arrived with the day's supplies from the D-I-Y superstore. There were handshakes and hugs and an understood shared grief that united them all. Marnie organised the programme, starting with rubbing down of woodwork ready for the first undercoat. She had come to admire the conscientious approach of the young men and their dedication to the work. She realised that they were pleased to have individual rather than collective jobs; nobody felt like talking. Magda did not appear that morning.

While Anne was rubbing down the window frames in the living room, Marnie set about searching for any legal documents. She began in the kitchen, knowing that many people kept important papers in the most-used room of the house. Almost at once she hit the target. In amongst a pile of insurance policies she found a cluster of bank statements. She hesitated, trying not to read the lines of figures, embarrassed at intruding into the private life of two victims of murder in their own home. Closing the drawer, she took out her mobile.

'Kazimir, it's Marnie. I've found some bank statements. Did you know they banked with Barclays, the town centre branch?'

'I didn't. That's really helpful, Marnie. Look, I'm in a meeting at the moment. I'll try to call round later in the day. Is that okay with you?'

'I'll be here. We're making good progress.'

Afterwards, Marnie went from room to room with an encouraging word for each of the Polish boys. Finally she called in on Anne.

'How's it going?'

Anne shook a hand in front of her. 'My wrist's about to drop off, but apart from that ...' A sudden change of subject. 'Heard anything from Donovan?'

'Come to think of it, no, nothing.' Marnie looked at her watch. 'He's been quite a while.'

'Worth phoning him? Shall I give him a ring?'

'It might be awkward if he's still in with the police. Perhaps we should give him a little more time. He'll contact us if he needs to.'

'Okay,' Anne said, but she did not sound convinced.

Marnie resumed her search and was about to climb the stairs when she noticed a drawer in the hall telephone table. She opened it and found an address book. She took it upstairs and sat on the bed in the guest room to read it. What first struck her was how few names it contained. Marnie flicked quickly through from A to Z to see if there were any addresses in Poland or Russia, hoping to find at least one relative in either country. Nothing. There were electricians, a plumber, a travel agent and a taxi service. There was a vet, a dentist, a doctor's surgery, a chiropodist and an optician. Marnie rejoiced to find an entry for a named person, but it was only Mrs Betts, the next door neighbour, with her phone number. She was resigned to a fruitless outcome when she reached the W section and found Wilson and Hartland, solicitors. Success! Again she rang Kazimir Gorski. The call went straight to voicemail.

'Kazimir, it's Marnie. Please ring me. I've found an address book with the name of some solicitors. Bye.'

After hanging up, Marnie went along to the Koslowski's bedroom and crossed to the dressing table. She was pulling open its drawer when the doorbell rang. The drawer contained nothing of interest, so Marnie closed it hurriedly and walked out onto the landing. She heard voices in the hall below and went down the stairs to find Anne and Magda hugging each other inside the door. Hearing her descend, Magda broke free and looked up at Marnie with moist eyes.

'Come on,' said Marnie. 'Let's make some coffee. It's all just too much right now.'

They had barely set out the mugs in the kitchen when the bell rang again. Marnie left Anne spooning out instant coffee and headed for the door.

'Donovan, at last! We thought the police had thrown you in a dungeon.'

'Sergeant Marriner said there were things we had to talk about.'

'Come through,' Marnie said. 'You're right on time for coffee.'

There were too many people in the house to assemble in the kitchen, so Anne and Magda carried mugs to the team in the hall. For the first time that day a murmur of conversation was heard in the house, though voices were still subdued. In the kitchen Anne opened the questioning.

'So what happened, Donovan?'

Donovan shrugged. 'I went to the station and when Cathy Lamb came out I thought it would just be a few questions about the weekend and then I'd be off. It didn't turn out that way.'

'Why not?'

Donovan sipped his coffee. Marnie was not the only one who thought he might be playing for time.

'I ... sort of ...expressed some opinions ...'

'You didn't reveal what you really did on Easter Monday, did you?' Anne was horrified.

'Not really, but I think I said more than I should have. Anyway, they invited me in – if that's the word – and got me to make a full statement.'

'About the Easter weekend?' Marnie said.

'About everything that's happened up here.'

'Has that caused problems?'

'Maybe ... too soon to know, really.'

'Why did you do that?' Marnie struggled to keep reproach out of her voice. 'You're usually so ... careful ... enigmatic even.'

'I suppose I wanted to get to the bottom of all the violence. I felt frustrated that so much hurt has been done, and no one has been brought to book ... yet.'

Marnie, Anne, Magda and Donovan drank their coffee in unison. They all felt the same powerlessness that there was not a single person in the frame for the two murders, let alone a prime suspect. The police had just allowed the perpetrators to melt away. And then there was Dominik, savagely attacked and left with injuries that could keep him in hospital for weeks to come. The damage to his leg alone could leave him with a permanent disability.

Marnie's mobile began ringing.

'Kazimir, hi.'

'I'm sorry, Marnie, I'll not be able to get away. It's almost lunchtime and I'm way behind on everything I have to do today. Could you please give me the name of those solicitors?'

Marnie flicked open the address book and read out the information.

It had been a long morning, but Marnie felt she was getting somewhere. Stan's death hung over them all, but at least they had the consolation of knowing that his affairs were in safe hands. Some order was beginning to take shape amidst all the chaos. On the other hand, there was Donovan. Marnie could not prevent herself from thinking that once again he had strayed into murky waters.

****

The working party split up at the end of the afternoon, promising to meet again on Saturday. They had produced outstanding results, with most of the ground floor walls lined and most of the woodwork undercoated. The day had been sombre but positive. Everyone knew they had done their best for Stan and Katie.

Arriving back at Glebe Farm, Marnie and the others were cheered to find that Ralph had produced a simple supper: jacket potatoes with fillings from his 'peasant food' repertoire followed by Greek yogurt with honey. The aromas that greeted them in the kitchen were very heaven.

After the meal they all opted for an early night, and Marnie tidied the kitchen while Ralph took a shower. Something was bothering her. It had been niggling away at the back of her mind all afternoon, and try as she might, she could not grasp it.

Ralph was sitting up in bed when she entered their room. 'What's troubling you, Marnie?'

'What makes you ask that?'

'You've got that look. When we were living on the boat I knew it meant you'd be going to stand by the stern doors to gaze out over the water.'

'You know me too well.'

'So what is it?'

'That's just it. I don't know. No matter how I try, I can't put my finger on it.'

'Clear your mind. In the shower, just empty your mind of everything. Be aware of nothing but the hot water on your body and the scent of the shower gel. It might help.'

'Worth a try,' Marnie said, but privately she was unconvinced.

Ralph was still sitting up reading a novel when Marnie emerged from the bathroom a short while later, wrapped in her white fluffy dressing gown, rubbing her hair with a towel.

'Feeling any better?' he asked.

'More relaxed than I was, that's for sure.'

She felt her hair, turned to hang the towel on its rail and pulled the light cord. Smothering a yawn, she stretched both arms and padded across the room to sit on the bed. Slowly she peeled off the dressing gown and slipped under the duvet. Ralph

300

closed the book and turned off his bedside light. He was rolling over to kiss Marnie when she exclaimed.

'I've got it!'

Without hesitation Ralph replied, 'I was hoping you might be about to share it.'

Marnie was so concentrated, she did not even give him The Look.

'It's the medals.'

'That's what was bothering you?'

'Yes. Your mind-clearing method worked. It was Katie's medals. They're not there any more. Someone must've taken them.'

Chapter 28

Saturday was a strange day, though it began well enough. At breakfast Ralph suggested they eat out that evening. He had read a good review of a Thai restaurant in Stony Stratford, and he offered to book a table.

The Glebe Farm four travelled to Northampton in Marnie's Freelander, stopping off at the D-I-Y store for more supplies on the way. Ralph was impressed with all the work carried out in the house so far and offered to join Anne in gloss painting the living room. And so the day passed as the days before, with everyone pressing on and results clearly showing, hour by hour.

The only absentee that morning was Magda who was needed in her father's office, her vacation job. She had arranged to look in on Dom briefly that morning to take him a carton of fresh orange juice. The dragon-nurse who was the ward manager had agreed to only the shortest of visits.

Kazimir Gorski rang Marnie mid-morning with the news that he had spoken with the solicitor who had dealt with Stan and Katie. The lawyer had confirmed that she had had preliminary discussions about writing their wills, but the process had not been completed. This would lead to numerous complications. Kazimir had offered to meet the solicitor to try to resolve matters in the absence of any other party willing and able to get involved.

While Marnie was speaking with Kazimir, Ralph phoned the Thai restaurant and booked a table for four at eight o'clock. Their only other fixture that day was a visit to the hospital in the afternoon.

****

There were going to be no mistakes with visiting time that day. They had left Ralph in charge of works at the Koslowskis' house, and Marnie, Anne and Donovan piled into the car and set off in good time. Marnie was determined that they would be punctual, but when they drove into the hospital car park it seemed as if everyone in the town had the same idea. It was gridlock. Minutes dragged by with the Freelander stuck solidly in an immobile queue.

'I think I should let you two out,' Marnie began. 'We're going to be stuck here for ages if –'

'They're moving!' Anne exclaimed.

Marnie shifted into gear to roll forward, but the traffic only advanced one car's length. Instead of accelerating, Marnie hurriedly looked over her shoulder and swung the wheel hard right to turn into a side row. It offered just enough width to perform a multi-point turn, after which she pulled back onto the main spine road and headed back for the exit.

'Are we giving up?' Anne asked.

'No. I'm going to find somewhere to park on the road. We can walk in from there.'

The plan was good, but only in theory. They encountered streets nose-to-tail with parked cars. The only clear spaces were marked with double yellow lines. Marnie was on the point of giving up when she saw a van pull away from the kerb fifty yards ahead. She sprinted along the street, switched on the indicators and reached the space just as a young woman in a Mini Cooper was lining up for a do-or-die attempt to leap in first. Something about the body language of the Freelander and its more imposing size deterred her at the last minute. She glared at Marnie and drove on.

It was a long walk back to the hospital, and all three were breathing heavily by the time they arrived on the campus. They were in sight of their goal when Donovan's mobile vibrated in his pocket. He stopped abruptly to take the call.

'What's up?' Marnie asked, swerving round him.

'Mobile,' he said. 'You two go on. Don't wait for me. I'll catch you up in a minute.'

Anne looked back at him with an expression of concern as she and Marnie continued on their way. Visiting time was half over before they swept into Dom's ward. Seeing them, the staff nurse in charge pointedly checked the time on her watch. Marnie smiled politely and nodded at her in passing.

As they reached Dom's row the ward lit up, with spring sunshine pouring through the windows. When Dom spotted his visitors his face lit up just as brilliantly.

'You're obviously in better spirits today,' Marnie remarked, as she and Anne kissed him on the cheeks.

'Absolutely I am,' he said. 'And I feel so much better at seeing you both.'

'Donovan's following on behind,' said Marnie. 'He'll be here any minute.'

'That's great. And I've got Magda coming this evening.' He laughed. 'My lucky day! Please … sit down.'

'It's good to see you looking so well.'

'I'm coming on, but in any case I generally feel better in the afternoon. By evening I'm starting to flag.'

'Are you in much pain?' Anne asked.

Dom made a face. 'Comes and goes. They give me stuff if it gets bad.'

'Talking of which,' Marnie said. 'We've brought you some stuff.' She reached into her bag and produced a bunch of grapes and a bag of bananas. 'They won't help with pain control but they might cheer you up a little.'

At that moment Donovan arrived, looking over his shoulder. He shook Dom's hand, and they exchanged pleasantries.

'Everything all right, Donovan?' Marnie asked.

'It's that nurse – *die Hexe* – she's watching me, I'm sure.'

Dom said, 'Probably suspects you're smuggling in a bottle of gin.'

'Is that a subtle hint?' Marnie said. 'We'll get a message to Magda, see what she can do.'

'Uh-oh,' said Anne. 'Don't look now but I think one of us might be asked to leave. Are you allowed three visitors at a time?'

'Not sure,' said Dom.

They turned to see a junior nurse approaching. 'Excuse me,' she said. 'Is one of you Mr Donovan?'

'I'm Donovan.'

She handed him a folded sheet of paper. 'I've been asked to give you this.'

Donovan thanked her, took the paper and stepped away to read it.

Dom looked worried. 'What can this be?'

Marnie and Anne exchanged glances, both equally baffled. Anne walked across to where Donovan was standing.

'Everything all right, Donovan?' she said quietly. 'Not uncle Helmut, is it?'

Donovan looked up as if noticing her for the first time. 'What? No, it's nothing like that. I'll tell you later.'

He walked back to Dom's bed in silence, his expression troubled. Anne knew better than to question him further. She thought it best to change the subject.

'We were all very sad about Mr Koslowski,' she said.

304

'Yeah.' Dom winced. 'That was bad. Magda in particular took it very hard.'

While Anne was commiserating with Dom, Donovan passed the paper to Marnie without saying a word. In an attempt to brighten the atmosphere, Anne asked Dom if he would like some fruit, and he accepted a small cluster of grapes. Marnie finished reading the note and handed it back to Donovan.

'Those grapes seem a small reward for all you've done for the community, Dom,' Marnie said.

He said modestly, 'No more than anyone else would do.'

'No, but seriously,' Marnie insisted. 'You did more than everyone. You know you did.'

'Well I only –'

Donovan interrupted. 'Personally, I think you deserve a medal.'

Anne looked quizzically at him. Donovan stepped closer to the bed and dropped something on the cover close to Dom. He stared down at it with a puzzled frown and was astonished to see that it actually was a medal. Dom laughed as he picked it up, but immediately his grin turned to bewilderment. He looked up at his visitors. Before he could speak, Donovan dropped another medal on the bed cover, then another and another. Anne craned forward.

'Aren't those ...' She turned to face Donovan. 'They are, aren't they? They're Mrs Koslowski's medals from the bedroom.'

Donovan nodded and reached inside his jacket. He said to Dom, 'And I thought you might like a photo or two to brighten up the ward.' He pulled out a picture frame and set it up on the bedside table. 'Here's another one to cheer you up.' The first photo was of Katie in uniform. The second was the wedding photograph.

'I don't understand,' Dom said in a half-whisper. 'Why are you giving me these? I hardly knew them.'

Donovan said, 'My original idea was just to keep them safe in case anyone broke in and took them. That was before I worked it out.'

Dom looked totally bewildered. 'Worked what out? I don't know what you mean.'

'I think you do.'

They heard an intake of breath. Anne was staring wide-eyed at Dom in disbelief.

In a quiet voice Donovan said, 'Tell me, Dom. Why did you kill Katie?'

Dom was aghast. 'What on earth are you talking about? I don't know where you got that idea, but it's madness.'

'I think you do know, Dom.'

Dom shook his head, distraught, his eyes welling up. 'How can you say such things? You are my true, dear friend. Everyone says we're like brothers.'

With infinite sadness Donovan said, 'Believe me, it gives me no pleasure to say this to you.'

Dom looked pleadingly at Marnie and Anne. 'You must know he's wrong. Can't you reason with him?'

'You mean you didn't do it, Dom?' Marnie said.

'Of course I didn't. If I had done such a thing there'd be proof, evidence. You know that.'

Donovan said, 'Katie was stabbed to death in her own living room.'

'Yes,' Dom agreed. 'By a stiletto. We all know that. I don't possess such a thing. Only thugs like those skinheads would have –'

'The long screwdriver in your box of equipment is like a stiletto,' Donovan said in an even tone.

'No!' Dom looked again at Marnie. 'The fact that one tool is long like a blade doesn't prove anything, does it?'

'I suppose not,' she conceded.

Dom looked relieved and turned his gaze back to Donovan. 'You see?'

'I'm sorry,' Donovan said.

Dom attempted a smile. 'That's all right. It's easy to jump to – '

'The screwdriver is at the police forensics laboratory. It's being tested.'

Dom was dumbstruck. He swallowed hard.

Marnie repeated Donovan's question. 'Tell us, Dom. We have a right to know. Why did you kill Katie?'

Dom seemed unable to speak. Donovan prompted him.

'We now know she was a Night Witch, a *Nachthexe*. You found that out from talking to Magda. Magda helped Katie by translating her *memories* and regarded her as a hero. She naturally told about that. But for some reason, you saw things differently. Why was that, Dom?'

Marnie added, 'Surely the Red Army was allied to us in the war. They were on our side against the Nazis.'

Dom was silent for so long they thought he was not going to speak again.

Eventually he gave a long sad sigh and said in the quietest of voices, 'Some allies! Huh! They killed thousands of Polish officers at Katyn and elsewhere. They murdered them in cold blood. Then they subjugated Poland as part of the Soviet empire.'

'But not Katie,' Marnie said. 'She never had anything to do with the Katyn massacre. She only fought to defend her country against its enemies.'

'I felt sick when I learned she was part of the Red Army,' Dom said. 'For me they were barbarians, just as bad as the Nazis. Surely *you* can understand that, Donovan.'

'Not all Germans were Nazis,' Donovan said. 'Not all Russians were war criminals.'

Dom muttered, 'I can't help how I feel.'

'Katie was no barbarian,' said Marnie. 'She was an old lady ... never harmed any Pole in her life. Yes, she took part in the war, but she was shot down while her army was liberating Poland from the Nazis.'

'I can't believe you don't understand,' Dom said. None of them responded. He continued. 'So what are you going to do about it?'

'Nothing,' said Marnie.

Dom could hardly believe his ears. 'Really? You mean that?'

Marnie shook her head. 'I think it's time for us to go.'

'And you're really not going to do anything?'

'No,' said Marnie.

'Thank you,' said Dom. 'I knew you'd understand when you thought about it.'

Marnie turned to walk away with Anne beside her. Only Donovan stood still, frowning, his gaze averted. Suddenly, Marnie stopped and looked back at Dom.

'It seems you have some more visitors,' she said.

Dom looked beyond them. 'I can't see anyone.'

Marnie and Anne moved aside to allow Sergeant Marriner and DC Cathy Lamb to pass. Before leaving, Donovan looked down at Dom, lying helpless in bed with his leg suspended in traction.

'Don't run away,' he said.

Marriner and Lamb were advancing on Dom when the ward manager – *die Hexe* – adopted her sternest countenance and strode forward to inform them that the visiting hour was at an end. Simultaneously they produced warrant cards and walked past her. Dom looked up at them with a curious expression.

'Who are you?' he asked.

'Friends of Marnie,' said Lamb. 'We've brought you something.'

'For me?'

Lamb held up a plastic bag. Inside it Dom could see his long screwdriver.

'I can't leave it with you, I'm afraid,' Lamb said. 'You see, this is an evidence bag. The tool came from your box of cleaning materials.'

Dom shook his head. 'Anyone could have put it there.'

Marriner stepped forward. 'It only has one set of fingerprints on it. We'll be taking yours shortly to see if they match. There are also minute traces of blood which exactly match the blood on the carpet in Mrs Koslowski's living room. They also match samples taken from Mrs Koslowski.'

Once again Dom was speechless. Marriner spoke again.

'And the paint sprayed on the living room wall matches exactly the paint from your can, with more fingerprints to be checked.'

He held up two more evidence bags. One contained the spray can; the other, a scrap of wallpaper with a stripe of red paint. It was the scrap that Donovan had collected.

Dom flopped back on the pillow with his eyes closed. He was only vaguely aware of the charge for murder being intoned by Sergeant Marriner.

'... you do not have to say anything, but it may harm your defence if you do not mention when questioned ...'

****

It should have been a normal enjoyable Saturday night eating out, but the four from Glebe Farm looked as they felt: weary and a little shell-shocked. After collecting Ralph from the Koslowskis' house, they had returned to Knightly St John to shower and change their clothes. The atmosphere in the Freelander on the way home was downcast, and Ralph had the good sense not to ask questions that he guessed would be unwelcome; time enough later, he thought.

The restaurant was small but well-appointed, and the welcome from the owner was warm with a touch of Oriental formality. They were passed on to a diminutive graceful waitress wearing a tunic and long skirt of shimmering blue, who led them to their table with effortless elegance. Once they were settled with drinks and menus they began to relax for the first time that evening. Ralph waited until everyone had chosen their dishes and placed orders before he spoke.

'I hope you all think I've been patient long enough. I really don't want to press you, but ...'

Marnie reached across and took his hand in hers. 'It's been quite a day, darling.'

'Yes, I've gathered that. And obviously something has happened that's knocked the stuffing out of all of you.'

Marnie looked Ralph in the eye and said quietly. 'We know who killed Katie and Stan.'

'I guessed that. The same people who injured Dominik?'

'It was Dom, Ralph. It was Dom who killed them.'

Ralph's expression was inscrutable as he absorbed the news. 'Obviously you wouldn't say such a thing unless you were certain. How did you find out?'

Marnie nodded across the table at Donovan.

'A number of pointers,' he said. 'One was a piece of wallpaper, and another the fact that Dom's car is blue.'

'Go on,' said Ralph.

'It was unlucky for Dom, in more ways than one, being attacked and immobilised like that. It meant he had no chance to get rid of the evidence.'

'And how did you find it?'

'Initially by chance when I was sorting out our boxes of cleaning materials. I was surprised that his box contained a spray can of red paint. I thought perhaps his car was red – up till then I hadn't seen it – but Marnie said it was blue. Then I thought maybe he'd had a red car some time and done a paint job on it. But it was obviously a new can, and then it struck me. It was the same colour exactly as the graffiti on the wall of the living room.'

'And elsewhere round the town?' Marnie said.

309

'Yes, but I'm sure that had nothing to do with Dom. I figured he used that as a smokescreen. I wanted to dismiss it all as a coincidence, but then I saw the long screwdriver and it made me think. I remembered that Anne said the nurse told her the stabbings had been done with a blade like a stiletto.'

'Both could have been just coincidental,' said Ralph.

Donovan nodded. 'Sure, and I didn't want to believe that Dom had done it. I really regarded him as a friend, more than just a friend in many ways.'

'An ally,' Marnie suggested.

'Yes. We were allies.'

'What convinced you that Dom was the murderer?' Ralph asked.

'You remember that very strict nurse? Magda referred to her once as a dragon. When I spoke to Dom, I said, *Hier kommt die Hexe* – here comes the witch. He said *yes, she looks like a witch.*'

'And HEXE was sprayed on the living room wall,' said Marnie.

'Exactly. I wonder how many Brits know the German word for a witch.'

Marnie said, 'But you suspected that Dom knew it from Magda, and she in turn learnt it from Katie Koslowski.'

'That's what I thought. And then that conversation I had with old General von Karlsdorff came to mind. He told me about the *Nachthexen*, the Night Witches, how they flew their flimsy little plywood planes time after time against the strongest army in the world and helped defeat them. Heroes, all of them.' Donovan's voice cracked, and it was some seconds before he could continue in little more than a whisper. 'No wonder Katie had earned the highest medals of the Red Army.'

'Presumably you explained your suspicions to the police when you went in to give your statement about the Easter weekend?' Ralph said.

Donovan nodded. 'While I was there I told them what I thought. They asked for evidence, of course, and I had Dom's box in the car. They rang me today just as we arrived at the hospital and wanted to know when I could give them a formal statement. I told them where we were, and Cathy Lamb confirmed what I'd suspected. She said she'd be in touch. Later she sent a message to say she'd be coming to the hospital straight away to charge Dom.'

'You did the right thing,' Marnie said. 'You yourself said Katie deserved better than what happened to her.'

Ralph added, 'And you were right to say the Night Witches were heroes. They were truly amazing.'

Sadness weighed down on them, and Anne reached for Donovan's hand under the table. She squeezed it gently.

'I suppose it was the witching hour when they flew on their missions,' Anne said. 'Would that be midnight?'

'Sounds like something from Shakespeare,' said Marnie.

'Hamlet,' Ralph said. 'I did it for A level English Lit. Actually he never wrote 'witching hour'. It's a misquotation that's stuck.'

'What did he write?' Marnie asked.

'I think it was ... let me see ... "'Tis now the very witching *time* of night, when churchyards yawn and hell itself breathes out contagion to this world". I think that's right.'

'Creepy,' said Anne. 'But what about Mr Koslowski? He wasn't in the Red Army.'

'Wrong place, wrong time,' Marnie said.

Donovan agreed. 'I think he turned up unexpectedly, and Dom felt he had no choice but to kill him.' He added, 'I suppose in a sense you could say Stan was the last Polish victim of the Katyn massacre.'

They all fell silent as the waitress returned, smiled and topped up their wine glasses. Seconds later their first course arrived. The food was beautifully served, each plate decorated with a carrot artistically carved in the form of a rose. The loving care in its preparation stood in stark contrast to the horrors that had beset them those past weeks.

Suddenly and without a word, Marnie took hold of the hands of Ralph and Donovan. Across the table Anne reached for their other hands. As if at a given signal they bowed their heads and closed their eyes. Diners at other tables who noticed this supposed they were saying some form of grace before eating. But Marnie and Ralph, Anne and Donovan were casting their minds back to another time, another place. They were hearing the rushing of wind in the struts of biplanes as the broomsticks of the Night Witches brought terror into the hearts of their enemies. They were seeing the mass graves of the victims of the Katyn massacre. They were thinking for those few moments of

Yekaterina and Stanislav Koslowski, fervently wishing that they were now resting in eternal peace.

About the author

When not writing novels, Leo is a linguist and lexicographer. As director of The European Language Initiative he compiled and edited twelve dictionaries in fifteen languages, including English, since the first one was published by Cassell in 1993.

They include the official dictionaries of the National Assembly for Wales (English and Welsh), the Scottish Parliament (English and Gaelic) and a joint project for the Irish Parliament and the Northern Ireland Assembly (English and Irish).

For the record, the others are specialist dictionaries in Basque, Catalan, Danish, Dutch, French, German, Greek, Irish, Italian, Portuguese, Russian, Scottish Gaelic, Spanish and Welsh.

Since 2015 he has devoted his time entirely to writing fiction.

He lives with his wife, cookery writer Cassandra McNeir, and their delinquent cat, Marmalade, in a three hundred year-old cottage in a Northamptonshire village. Delightful as it is, it bears no resemblance to Knightly St John.

Books by Leo McNeir
published by enigma publishing

Marnie Walker series
Book 1 - Getaway with Murder
Book 2 - Death in Little Venice
Book 3 - Kiss and Tell
Book 4 - Sally Ann's Summer
Book 5 - Devil in the Detail
Book 6 - No Secrets
Book 7 - Smoke and Mirrors
Book 8 - Gifthorse
Book 9 - Stick in the Mud
Book 10 - Smoke without Fire
Book 11 - Witching Hour
Book 12 - To Have and to Hold
Book 13 - Beyond the Grave

The Apostle series
Gospel Truth
Pilgrims

Collection of novellas
Angels

Author's website **www.leomcneir.com**

Printed in Great Britain
by Amazon

32703004R00178